BROTHERS

BROTHERS

ANGELA ELWELL HUNT

BETHANY HOUSE PUBLISHERS
MINNEAPOLIS, MINNESOTA 55438

Published by Bethany House Publishers
A Ministry of Bethany Fellowship, Inc.
11300 Hampshire Avenue South
Minneapolis, Minnesota 55438

Printed in the United States of America.

Library of Congress Cataloging-in-Publication Data

Hunt, Angela Elwell, 1957–
    Brothers / Angela Elwell Hunt.
      p. m . —(Legacies of the ancient river)
    ISBN 1–55661–608–2
    I. Title. II. Series. III. Series: Hunt, Angela Elwell, 1957–
Legacies of the ancient river.
PS3558.U46747B76   1996
813'.54—dc21   96–45838
                                                    CIP

Which of us has known his brother?
Which of us has looked into his father's heart?
Which of us has not remained forever prison-pent?
Which of us is not forever a stranger and alone?

Thomas Wolfe
Look Homeward, Angel!

Contents

Author's Note

I must begin by giving credit to the works of Thomas Mann, specifically the novels comprising the *Joseph and His Brothers* series (Knopf, 1948). Though my books are nothing like his, Mann opened my eyes to several ideas and possibilities that would not otherwise have occurred to me. For this novel, I am also indebted to Donald W. McCullough and his book *The Trivialization of God* (NavPress, 1995). I would never have believed that idol worship was still as rampant as it is without McCullough's insights.

Reginald Heber, author of the moving hymn "Holy, Holy, Holy," once wrote, "The heathen in his blindness bows down to wood and stone."

In Romans 1:20–23, 25, the Bible amplifies his comment:

> For since the creation of the world God's invisible qualities—his eternal power and divine nature—have been clearly seen, being understood from what has been made, so that men are without excuse.
>
> For although they knew God, they neither glorified him as God nor gave thanks to him, but their thinking became futile and their foolish hearts were darkened. Although they claimed to be wise, they became fools and exchanged the glory of the immortal God for images made to look like mortal man and birds and animals and reptiles.
>
> They exchanged the truth of God for a lie, and worshiped and served created things rather than the Creator—who is forever praised. Amen (NIV).

As I researched the ancient Egyptian religion, I was struck by the similarities between their beliefs and Christian theology. In the earliest dynasties, the Egyptians were monotheistic, believing in an all-powerful and invisible God who created the world out of water. (Egypt was settled, after all, by descendants of Ham, one of Noah's sons.) They were devout believers in an afterlife. They believed that their Pharaoh, a physical incarnation of a god, could give his life in intercession for his people and resurrect in the afterlife to take his throne forever.

Though in the beginning they must have understood the truth, in a relatively short time they forgot about the invisible eternal God and began to worship gods they fashioned for themselves. They exchanged the infinite truth for a devious perversion.

But we must not feel superior to them. Men still replace God with idols of their own making, many of which appear at one time or another even in the lives of the most devout believers. To the human eye, the idols of our generation have little in common with the wood and stone figures of ancient Egypt, but to a discerning heart they represent the same substitutes for our devotion.

At various times during my years of following God Almighty, whom I know through the fellowship of His Son, I have allowed His image to be usurped in my heart by idols of my own making: my search for knowledge, my desire for personal comfort and happiness, a quest for the earthly definition of success, even the beloved faces of my husband and much-longed-for children. It is far too human a tendency to take our eyes off Christ and fasten our gaze upon substitutes, which, though they may be lovely and precious, were never intended to satisfy the soul's deep yearning for God.

But God Shaddai is faithful and forgiving beyond my capacity to understand. His mercy, a patient waterfall upon my stony heart, has hollowed out a place that can be filled with nothing but Him.

Prologue

Thebes, Egypt

ZAPHENATH-PANEAH, FATHER TO PHARAOH AND acting ruler of all Egypt, caught his breath as Queen Tuya lifted his hand and pressed it to her cheek. The hot dry wind of the famine's second year blew over the palace garden as the lovely woman seemed to struggle to frame an answer to his proposal of marriage.

"Asenath is a lovely woman, and you have two fine sons," she finally whispered, her eyes glinting with affection and warmth. "You will not be happy loving one wife and offering kindness to the other."

He listened with rising dismay, then a wave of relief flooded his soul. She was wise, his Tuya. But she had always been perceptive beyond her years. More than once in Potiphar's house she had guided him away from foolish headstrong mistakes, helping him remember that he could no longer think of himself as Joseph, the pampered son of Jacob, but as *Paneah*, a slave to an Egyptian. And even though he now ruled all Egypt at the young Pharaoh's side, Tuya's insight and love still sought what was best for all.

Curving his hand around her cheek, he pressed his lips together, not allowing himself to protest. While the queen lowered her thick black lashes, from the corner of his eye Joseph saw a servant enter the garden. Dropping his hand, he turned from the queen and composed his face into dignified lines as the dark-haired slave hurried past the reflecting pools where blue lotus blossoms bloomed in abundance.

Slapping the tile, the attendant fell at Joseph's feet.

"Life, health, and prosperity to you, most noble and excellent vizier!"

"Yes?" Joseph stopped before the prostrate servant.

The man lifted his head a few inches from the pathway. "The steward of your house begs your indulgence and your pardon for this interruption. He waits outside Pharaoh's gate to give you a message."

"A message?" Joseph asked, aware that Tuya had moved away. He frowned. "What is of such importance that I must be interrupted at the palace?"

The servant ducked his head. "Ten men from Canaan wait at your house to buy food," he said, a note of apology in his voice. "Your steward says you would wish to be told of them at once."

Joseph took a quick sharp breath. "Ten Canaanites?"

"From Hebron, my lord."

A thrill of frightened anticipation touched Joseph's spine. "Yes," he murmured, "you were right to disturb me. Tell my steward that I will join him in a moment."

As the servant leapt up and retreated, Joseph turned to say farewell to Tuya. But like in the earlier part of his life, she had vanished amid the breathless beauty of the royal Egyptian garden.

MANDISA

*And the patriarchs became jealous of Joseph
and sold him into Egypt. And yet God was with
him, and rescued him from all his afflictions,
and granted him favor and wisdom in the sight
of Pharaoh, king of Egypt; and he made him
governor over Egypt and all his household.*

*Now a famine came over all Egypt and Canaan,
and great affliction with it; and our fathers
could find no food. But when Jacob heard that
there was grain in Egypt, he sent our fathers
there the first time.*

Acts 7:9–12

One

"YOU TWO! COME AWAY FROM THERE!"

Mandisa snapped her fingers at the two giggling slave girls who lingered in the doorway of the north loggia. With less manners than ignorant children, they had partially hidden themselves behind a pair of painted columns to gape at the dusty travelers milling about in the vestibule. At Mandisa's whispered rebuke, the two young ones bowed their heads in shame.

"Ani will be far less gentle than I if he finds you away from the kitchen," Mandisa said, stepping forward to urge the girls away from the open doorway.

"But, my lady," the first girl said, a glint of wonder in her eyes, "they are so strange a group! So much hair covers their faces!"

"We were wondering," the second slave added, lifting her fingers to her lips to suppress another giggle, "if they are as hairy all over. Look, Mandisa. Hair sprouts even from the throats of their garments!"

Intrigued despite her best intentions, Mandisa cast a quick glance through the doorway. She was accustomed to seeing foreign dignitaries in the vizier's vestibule, for since the advent of the famine, representatives from all the world's kingdoms had journeyed far to buy Egypt's grain. But the men who stood in the house wore neither the richly patterned garments of the Assyrians nor the carefully pointed beards of the Mitannis. They were clothed in the common woven garments and animal skins of herdsmen. Compared to the shaven Egyptians, they were hirsute, with hair to their shoulders and long full beards. What madness had possessed Tarik when he allowed this common rabble to pass through the gates of the vizier's villa?

She dismissed the question. The steward undoubtedly had his reasons. "Not everyone lives as the Egyptians do," she said, turning back to the ill-mannered slaves. She placed a firm hand on the shoulder of each girl. "Now away with you. Get back to your work in the kitchen. If the vizier has agreed to meet these men, he may want to feed them, and you may be sure that hairy men are hungry men. So hurry back to your grinding, lest Ani or Tarik finds you out here."

The two girls disappeared quickly at the mention of the steward and the captain of the vizier's guard, and Mandisa smiled, grateful that her stern words carried weight with *someone* in the house. Lately her son, Adom, had balked at both her requests and her suggestions, reminding her again how stubborn a twelve-year-old can be.

She sighed and folded her hands, ready to seek her mistress, but paused a moment, curiosity overcoming her finely tuned instincts. The band of men in the vestibule were like thousands of others who had come to Egypt in this second year of famine, so why had this particular group of Canaanites been invited to meet Egypt's royal vizier?

The men beyond did not appear wealthy or highborn. Theirs were the faces of sunburned herders. They gripped their staves with broad and callused hands. Generous strands of gray ran through several of their heavy beards and hair. Only one or two still possessed youthful and unlined faces. Their hands and eyes shifted restlessly, as if at any moment they might have to reach for a knife or spear to defend themselves. With one look, anyone could see these unruly shepherds had probably run as wild as the wind since infancy.

Mandisa bit her lip. She had seen men like these before. Her father and brothers were herdsmen. Like dogs, they had aggressively marked their boundaries and charged any lion, bear, or stranger who dared violate their territory. They, too, had habitually worn an uneasy look.

Memories came crowding back like unwelcome guests, and Mandisa closed her eyes, refusing to entertain them. Whoever these men were, they had nothing to do with her past or present. They would probably not be allowed to waste more than five minutes of the vizier's valuable time.

A snatch of their conversation caught her ear, and Mandisa tensed, recognizing the Canaanite tongue. The sound stirred up other nostalgic memories of her home and childhood, before Idogbe the Egyptian carried her away from her clan. She reached out to one of the pillars, steadying herself against the tide of strong emotions she could not stanch, then realized that the room beyond had grown unusually silent.

"This Egyptian prince has pretty slaves. I will not deny that." A sharp voice cut the silence, and the room came into focus. The man who had spoken stood apart from the others, his hands on his hips, a confident smile upon his face. Even in a crowd, his presence was compelling. An air of command exuded from him, and at the sound of his voice the entire group turned toward Mandisa.

She ducked behind the column, her cheeks burning. She had not meant to be seen! They must think her as ill-mannered as the two slave girls! And she was not a slave. She was a free woman, the personal maid to Lady Asenath!

"Ah, you startled her," another man said, a slight thread of reproach in his voice. "You should not be so brash, Simeon. You will frighten her away. She will run and tell her master that we are brutes, and then we shall never get what we have come for."

"We will, Levi. Never fear," the commanding man answered. "We will buy our grain and get out of Egypt as soon as we can. But what is the harm in admiring a pretty face while we are here?"

Mandisa flew out of the hallway and flattened herself against the wall separating the vestibule from the north loggia. She knew her cheeks were stained scarlet; she could feel blood pounding in her temples. How foolish she had been, allowing these rough men to gawk at her! They had talked about her as if she were a common kitchen slave, one of the vizier's many possessions! If they had not been ignorant foreigners, they would have known by her dress that she was no slave.

She shuddered in humiliation. And the powerful one who had spoken—how probing were his eyes! He had appraised her like a stockyard animal, then allowed his gaze to cling to her face as she burned in embarrassment.

By all that was holy, she hoped these herders were guilty of robbery or treason. She'd love to see them squirm before her master, the vizier. Especially the bold one who had propelled her into such an undignified and hasty retreat.

Wrapping the rags of her fragile dignity about her, Mandisa pulled herself from the wall and went in search of her mistress.

Two

SIMEON GROWLED UNDER HIS BREATH WHEN another pair of stone-faced Egyptian guards entered the great hall into which he and his brothers had been escorted. Did they think the sons of Israel planned to steal the vizier's treasures in broad daylight? They had come to buy grain, nothing more, nothing less, nothing else, and yet they had been yanked from the long line outside the royal granary as if they were ten of the kingdom's worst criminals. But criminals, he reflected, looking around, would not have been ushered into a villa fit for a king.

A king, it seemed, was determined to have an audience with them. The ruling Pharaoh, twelve-year-old Amenhotep III, had not yet attained maturity, and everyone who entered the Black Land known to Canaanites as *Mizraim* learned that the acting regent was one called Zaphenath-paneah, a man so wise and competent that the common people believed him to be a gift from the gods. Apparently this Zaphenath-paneah had either an extreme liking or great distrust for men from Hebron, for as soon as the brothers told the royal scribe their father's name and place of origin, they were ripped from their place in line and herded to the vizier's palace.

"Why do they stare at us?" Simeon muttered, fastening his eyes on the cool painted faces of the smooth-skinned guards. "Do they think we are beasts?"

"Who can tell what they are thinking?" Levi answered, his busy fists flexing behind his back. "They don't speak our language, and they hide their feelings behind those painted eyes." He whirled to face Reuben, the eldest. "Why did they bring us here? I tell you, Reuben, we should not have gone to the granary together. We attracted too much attention arriving in a group that way."

"Be silent, Simeon and Levi, and wait patiently," Reuben said, planted as solidly as an oak on the colored tile floor. He stood like a submissive servant, his hands folded, his eyes fixed on an elegant gilded chair upon a raised dais.

"How can you be so accommodating?" Simeon asked, lifting a fist. "We have done these people no harm. We have never even entered this cursed country before, and yet we are plucked from the mob and dragged away to face their almighty vizier. For what reason?"

"Perhaps God is testing us," Judah said, intervening. He had been walking around the room, studying a detailed and elaborate mural on the wall.

The painting made no sense to Simeon, for it depicted seven fat cows on the banks of the Nile. Simeon hadn't seen a fat cow in two years.

Now Judah stopped before Reuben and offered a smile. "You forget, brother. Though *we* have never made the journey to Mizraim, our great-grandfather Abraham once brought extreme sorrow upon Pharaoh's head. I have often heard Father tell the story."

"But this vizier would know nothing of our forefathers!" Levi protested, joining the circle. "And we cannot be held accountable for a sin Abraham committed years ago."

"But God knows all," Judah said, nodding toward Levi. "As He knows the hearts of all men. And if the people are right, and the Spirit of God rests upon this vizier, perhaps he knows more than we think. Perhaps he even knows what happened . . . at Dothan."

A visible chill seemed to fall over the group. Simeon felt it and resisted. "We did nothing wrong at Dothan," he said, his mood veering sharply from irritation to anger.

"Have you forgotten that we sold our brother years ago to a caravan bound for the Black Land?" Judah went on, his voice hardening ruthlessly. "To *Egypt*, my brothers. Our brother, if God wills that he still lives, is a slave in this land. Perhaps in this very house."

"Our *brother*," Levi spat the word, "is certainly dead. Joseph was too proud, too arrogant, to survive as a slave. Can one who imagines that the moon and stars must one day bow to him survive long under the whip? You cannot seriously believe that a man as great as this vizier"—he waved at the ornate columns covered with ornamental inscriptions and decorated with green lotus capitals—"would endure the insolence of our favored brother."

"Levi is right," Simeon snapped. His voice, like his nerves, was in tatters. The unendurable monotony of waiting had destroyed what little satisfaction he felt when they finally reached their destination. "Joseph is gone. Instead of worrying about the past, we should discuss how we shall answer this vizier." A heavy dose of sarcasm laced his voice as he turned to Judah. "And I would not worry, brother, about the power of the vizier's god. The Spirit of God Almighty is far from this heathen land. Did you see their temples filled with their stone idols?"

"The Almighty does not dwell in houses made with human hands," Judah answered, looking at Simeon with a wry but indulgent glint in his eyes, "but in the hearts of men. How do you know, Simeon, that this vizier does not hear God's voice?"

"Because El Shaddai chose *us*!" Levi said, thumping his chest. "We are the people of the Almighty. We, the sons of Israel, are the chosen ones. Simeon is right. We have nothing to fear from this Egyptian. He has no supernatural power."

"His natural power concerns me most," Reuben said, nodding for emphasis. "He commands Pharaoh's army. At this moment a host of guards waits outside this house to answer his bidding. He has the power to put all of us in prison, and without the grain he controls, our little ones will starve. Think, brothers, before you speak rashly in this room."

Stepping forward, Dan held up his hands in a gesture of peace. "Let us answer favorably whatever questions he might ask. If we please him, we will soon be on our way from these loathsome painted people."

"We will answer all his questions truthfully," Judah said, crossing his arms as his eyes fastened upon Simeon's. "Look around you at the wealth of this place, of this man. See the guards at the doors and remember the strong company of men who brought us here. Strength and power are on the side of this vizier, and we will not risk his anger."

"I've looked around," Simeon snapped. "I've seen. I've heard. And it should all be cursed. The people here clothe themselves like their forefather Ham, who spied upon his father's nakedness without remorse. They wear garments as thin as a spider's web, covering their bodies without hiding them. Their women are clothed indecently, yet they walk with their heads held high as if they are proud of their shame. One merchant offered to sell me a kilt and bragged that it was as light as woven air."

"Their habits are not our concern," Levi inserted. "Let us satisfy this man and be gone from here."

Simeon opened his mouth to argue again but stopped when a trumpet blast ripped through the hall like the alarm of war. A dozen hulking lance-bearers, each clothed in a snowy white linen kilt and a leopard skin belt, marched in double columns toward the front of the large room. Only when they had parted and stepped aside could Simeon see the trim imposing figure that marched in the midst of them: the Egyptian, the vizier of the Two Kingdoms, the Father to Pharaoh, and the acting ruler of the Black Land. Zaphenath-paneah.

———————

A whirling rush of emotions ripped through Joseph's soul as he stood and stared into the faces of the Canaanites.

His network of spies had been alerted to watch for men from Hebron, and this time they had actually snagged his brothers. Ani reported that there were ten. Who was missing? Benjamin, without a doubt. The others had either thrust him out, killed him, or left him at home with Jacob, his father. Why? Did they still hate the sons of Rachel, the true and beloved wife? Or had all their hate been reserved for him alone?

Ceaseless inward questions hammered at Joseph, but he could not speak. He stared at the men before him, his eyes narrowing. *Joy, be still! Dread, contain yourself! Laughter, tears, be gone! This is not the time to give words to emotion. It is a time to be wary, to carefully take the measure of men capable and guilty of murder, malice, and monumental jealousy.*

Twenty-two years had passed since he had last seen these who were his own flesh and blood—more than half his lifetime—and yet the stinging memory of their treachery rose before him as fresh as the morning breeze off the Nile. He would never forget a single detail of that day and night at Dothan: the pit, the pain of his broken arm, his brothers' taunting jests, and their expressions, which ranged from indifference to smirks of delight. His gaze darted to Levi's hand, which had clutched Joseph's many-colored robe, then shifted to Simeon's fist, which had gripped a hungry dagger. As the images focused in his memory, the old anguish of knowing that his father had mourned pierced Joseph's heart again.

Though his mind burned with painful memories, he fixed his face into stern lines, determined that his brothers should not see beyond the painted shadows of his eyes or the thick texture of his wig. Remembering the multicolored garment they had torn from his back, he fingered the fine pleated linen of his spotless vizier's robe. A flicker of irrational fear licked at his heart, then resolve overrode all things.

What could they do to him now, these sons of Israel?

They had stared at him for a full five minutes, and not one had recognized him as their long lost half brother. Apprehension glimmered on their faces. Drops of sweat glistened above Reuben's lined lip. Judah kept his eyes to the ground as if shame held him on a leash. Issachar, Zebulun, and Dan leaned heavily upon their staves, their eyes cautious and bright. Simeon and Levi stood with defiant fists clenched. Gad, Asher, and Naphtali gaped like anxious children about to be punished.

Almighty God, how am I to address them?

A dim ripple ran across his mind; a long-forgotten dream materialized and focused. He and his brothers had been binding sheaves of wheat in the field, and their sheaves had animated themselves and bowed down to his.

Without hesitation, Joseph uttered an abrupt order to the captain of his guard. "Tell them to bow."

———

Tarik heard the undercurrent of emotion in his master's voice and barked out the command. "Bow before the royal majesty of Zaphenath-paneah, Father to the divine Pharaoh, Sustainer of Breath, the Bread of Life!"

He was not certain how much the Canaanites understood, but they could not mistake the tone of his voice. Carefully, quietly, they fell to their knees on the tiled floor, one or two moving more slowly than the others. Tarik thought he spied an expression of resentment upon the face of the largest, most muscular man, but it vanished when one of the guards lifted his lance and took a step forward.

"We will need a skilled interpreter," the vizier said, keeping his voice low so that only Tarik could hear. "These men speak the Canaanite tongue. Though you have managed very well thus far, Tarik, I would not miss a single shade of meaning in their words."

"The woman who serves your wife speaks Canaanite," Tarik volunteered.

"Very good. Send someone to fetch Mandisa." As Tarik

gave the order and jerked his head toward one of the guards at the door, his master completed his measurement of the men bowed before him with a cool appraising look, then turned with regal grace toward the gilded chair in the center of the great hall.

The guard flew away with the speed of a gazelle and returned a moment later with Lady Asenath's handmaid. Tarik noticed that Mandisa flushed as she entered the room, her gaze darting nervously from her master to the prostrate men on the floor.

Keeping a careful distance from the Canaanites, Mandisa bowed before the vizier. "May I serve you, my lord?" she murmured.

"Stand, Mandisa, and interpret whatever these men say," Zaphenath-paneah answered, sinking into his chair as his dark eyes moved slowly over the group. "Do not spare a word for their sakes or your own, but speak truthfully and honestly."

"Yes, my lord." Mandisa stood and turned slightly so that she faced both the Canaanites and her master.

After a moment's hesitation, the vizier spoke again, strengthening his voice in a deep tone Tarik had never heard before.

"Where have you come from?" he demanded in the Egyptian tongue.

Not lifting her eyes, Mandisa interpreted and waited for a response.

For a moment no one answered, then a gray-haired man in the midst of them lifted his head from the floor. He did not speak as rapidly as Mandisa, and Tarik had no trouble understanding the Canaanite's halting words.

"Tell your master that we are from Hebron, in the land of Canaan. Like so many others presently in your city, we have come to buy grain."

After hearing the interpretation, Zaphenath-paneah shifted his weight slightly as if to establish perspective, then folded his arms and shook his head in disapproval.

"No. You lie. You are spies. You have come to look at the undefended parts of our land."

"No!" another man cried after hearing Mandisa's reply. He lifted his shaggy head but remained on the floor, cringing like a scolded puppy. "Assure him, we have come only to buy food for our families. We are honest brothers, all the sons of one man. We are not spies."

Mandisa turned to Zaphenath-paneah and repeated their assurances. The master's eyes flashed with an indefinable response, then he wrapped his hands around the arms of his gilded chair. "Tell them," he said, his body tensing, "that I am certain they have come to spy out the nakedness of the land. We are in the midst of famine. They want to take advantage of our weakness."

Tarik put his hand to his sword as Mandisa spoke the interpretation.

"This is crazy!" The muscled man with angry eyes lifted his head and shoulders from the floor as if he would rise to challenge the master. Tarik was about to step forward and answer him with a blow, but another brother silenced the loud one with a reproachful glance.

"Tell your master," the more reasonable man continued, "that we are his servants. We are twelve brothers in all, the sons of one man who lives in Hebron."

The vizier shifted in his chair as if he would speak, then he pressed his lips together and stared resolutely at the paintings on the back wall of the chamber. Tarik could see a deep well of emotion stirring beneath the smooth surface of Zaphenath-paneah's face.

The captain caught his breath. Already they had lied. They were not twelve, but ten.

"You are ten!" he shouted, stepping forward.

"Tell your master," the careful man went on, bowing his head in respect, "that we are not twelve today because our youngest brother is with his wife and children at home with our father in Hebron. And our other brother . . . is no more."

Mandisa bowed her head and began to interpret the

man's words, but something in Zaphenath-paneah's expression worried Tarik further. A suspicious line had etched itself into the corners of the master's mouth, and the vizier's eyes gleamed strangely. Were they wet or was the sunlight from the high windows playing tricks upon Tarik's mind?

"They are not twelve today," Mandisa said softly, as Tarik observed an unusual ripple of passion beneath the polished exterior of the master's handsome countenance, "because their younger brother is home with their father—"

"You say your father lives, but you are old men," the vizier interrupted in a harsh raw voice. "How can I know you speak the truth?"

Mandisa interpreted, and the silver-haired one lifted his head.

"As I live, my father was alive when we left him," he said. "I am Reuben, my lord, the firstborn. If I am lying, you may take my life."

"I will hear no more," Zaphenath-paneah said, interrupting the translation. As the Canaanite men lay with their foreheads pressed to the ground, the vizier closed his eyes. His jaw clenched for a moment, as though he struggled against a strong sentiment. For an instant his eyelids fluttered like the heartbeats of baby birds.

Something tightened in Tarik's chest. There was more to this encounter than he knew, something awesome and mysterious and hidden. A warning voice whispered in the captain's head, then Zaphenath-paneah's chiseled face suddenly distorted with anger.

"No!" he shouted, his voice ringing in the empty spaces of the great hall as he leapt to his feet. "It is as I said. You are spies, and by your own speech you will be tested. As Pharaoh lives, you shall not leave this place unless your youngest brother comes here to prove your words!"

Zaphenath-paneah slapped his hands together in an explosive sound, and the unexpected gesture startled an aproned page who waved an ostrich-feathered fan at the vizier's side. "I will send one of you that he may bring your brother to me, but the rest of you will remain confined," the vizier pronounced, arteries throbbing in his neck as he surveyed the men before him. "We will see whether there is truth in you. If you are lying, even in this, then by the life of Pharaoh, *you are spies.*"

The vizier did not wait for the interpretation but swept out of the reception hall toward his private chambers. Baffled, Tarik hesitated, then hurried after his master. Behind him, he could hear Mandisa quavering through the translation of the master's last words.

Zaphenath-paneah stopped suddenly in the hallway. "Tarik?" he asked, not turning around.

"My lord, I am here."

The vizier squared his shoulders as if an invisible enemy stood before him. "Take them to Pharaoh's prison in the house of the captain of the royal guard. They shall spend this night in the prison pits."

"Yes, my lord." Tarik nodded in a quick bow, then hurried back to the hall. Immediately upon entering, he motioned for the lance-bearers to make their spears ready.

"By command of the Lord High Zaphenath-paneah, Vizier of the Double Kingdoms," he called, his voice crisp and clear in his elementary use of the Canaanite language, "you shall be confined in Pharaoh's prison." To reinforce his meaning, he pulled his own sword from its sheath.

"Confined?" One of the brothers rose to his knees, his face clouded with fear. "How long must we remain here? Our families are starving. Our father will worry."

A half-smile tugged at Tarik's lips. "You will remain in Pharaoh's prison until Zaphenath-paneah is inclined to show mercy."

~⊃ Three ⊂~

"TELL ME, MANDISA," ASENATH URGED, HER lovely eyes filled with dark trepidation, "what is it about these Canaanites that disturbs my husband so? He came into my chamber after seeing them, and his countenance was . . . much troubled."

Mandisa turned away to lift her mistress's full wig from its stand, hoping the younger woman wouldn't see the anxiety in her own eyes. The afternoon had been totally unnerving. First she had embarrassed herself by spying on the visiting herdsmen, then the master had asked her to interpret their words. Standing before them, feeling their eyes upon her, she had relived her humiliation all over again.

"I'm not certain why these men are troublesome, but they are," Mandisa answered, taking pains to speak slowly so her voice remained steady. "Perhaps the master has heard rumors of Canaanites who plan to attack Egypt. But these are things we need not concern ourselves with, my lady."

"My husband has dealt with rumors of war before," Asenath answered, studying her reflection in a bronze mirror as Mandisa pulled the wig snugly over her lady's close-cropped hair. "And he has never held such worries close to his heart. Something happened today, Mandisa, that shook my dear one to the depths of his heart. Though he pretended nothing was amiss, his hands trembled when he came to see me, and his eyes were as remote as the stars." She pressed her lips together as she lowered the looking brass. "Tarik would know what troubles my beloved."

"I daresay the captain of the guard does not know more

of my lord's heart than you," Mandisa replied lightly. "My master shares with Tarik all things concerning the governance of Pharaoh's house, city, and country, but matters of the heart he reserves for you alone."

Asenath turned and lifted a questioning brow. "Were these men so unusual? Were they disfigured or sick? Did they display some sorcery that upset my husband?"

"They were common herdsmen, my lady," Mandisa answered, lowering her hand to her mistress's soft shoulder. "When I lived in Canaan, I saw hundreds of men just like them, rough as the wind and as steady as the sun. No, there was nothing in their appearance or manner to disturb my master."

At the sound of fine leather slapping against tile, Mandisa pulled away, prostrating herself on the floor as Zaphenath-paneah entered the room. Startled, Asenath bowed her head, but when Mandisa looked up, she saw that her mistress was peeking through the fringe of her bangs, keeping a wary gaze on her pacing husband.

"I said I would keep nine and send one back to Canaan," the master muttered, thrusting his hands behind his back. He spoke rapidly in the Canaanite tongue, amazing Mandisa with his fluency. If he spoke it so well, why had he needed her to interpret? And whom was he addressing now?

"Something in me demands that they suffer the darkness of the prison pits for as long as I did," he went on, speaking to the air. "I wonder if they are now tasting the fear that filled my mouth, even my heart, when they turned their backs on me. But they are grown men, and I was only a boy—"

"My husband?" Asenath interrupted, her voice a mere squeak in the room.

The vizier stopped pacing and looked at the women as if seeing them for the first time. "I am sorry, my dear," he said, again speaking in careful Egyptian. "And, Mandisa, you may rise. I forgot to thank you for your help this morning."

"It is an honor to serve you, my lord," Mandisa said, rising slowly to her feet. Her heart yearned to ask for an explanation, but though the vizier ran a remarkably easygoing household, a well-trained servant did not inquire after her master's business.

Asenath rose from the low stool by her dressing table and crossed to her husband's side. "My lord, your skin is cold," she said, pulling his hands into hers. "And you are trembling! Shall you not tell me what has upset you?"

He looked at her, and for a moment Mandisa thought he would speak, but suddenly he sighed and gave his wife a slow sad smile. "You are so young," he whispered, brushing the back of his hand across her lovely cheek. "Why should I burden you with the sorrows of the past? Bring my boys to me, Asenath. Let me play an hour with Ephraim and Manasseh. They always lighten my heart. They always help me to forget."

Asenath smiled and pulled away to fetch her sons from their schoolroom. Mandisa was about to follow her from the chamber, thinking that the master wished to be alone, when he suddenly stopped her with a question. "Mandisa, know you of El Shaddai?"

A terrible tenseness seized her body. The master was speaking again in the Canaanite language! And he spoke the name of a God she had never expected to hear in this Black Land.

"My lord?" she stammered, her tongue suddenly thick and unwilling.

"I know you were not born here in Mizraim," Zaphenath-paneah answered, using the Canaanite word for Egypt. He lowered himself to his wife's stool, and his voice took on an absent, almost melancholy, quality. "But like me, you have adopted this land as your own."

"My husband was Egyptian," she stammered in bewilderment. "And my son is thus an Egyptian, so I never thought to go anywhere else."

"There will come a time," the master went on, still speaking the foreign tongue, "when my sons will not think of themselves as Egyptian, for they are like me, and I am not of this place. Like you, I was brought into this country as a stranger. I was born Joseph, the son of Jacob, who is the son of Isaac. When last I saw my father, he had settled in Hebron."

"Jacob!" Mandisa's breath caught in her lungs. "I have heard of this Jacob. He was a mighty prince in the land of Canaan. My father said Jacob was rich in possessions, servants, cattle, and flocks. The elders of my village called him a great prophet, a wise man filled with the knowledge of God."

The beginning of a smile tipped the corners of the vizier's mouth. "So you knew Jacob as a prince?"

"And as a distant kinsman, my lord. My father's uncle was Uz of Aram, and his father Laban, the father of Leah and Rachel."

"My father's wives." To her surprise, the vizier showed little reaction to her announcement that they shared a common heritage. Though he smiled, the weight of apprehension did not lift from his strong face, and his deep eyes darkened. "And so the Almighty works again in ways I cannot fathom," he remarked, shaking his head. "But you have not yet answered my question, Mandisa. What do you know of El Shaddai, the God worshiped by Jacob of Canaan?"

She shook her head. "My family knew of Him, my lord, but my father and my father's father worshiped other gods," she replied, lowering her eyes to the floor. "I often heard stories of how Jacob's Almighty God increased his flocks and blessed his wives with many sons, but my family did not make sacrifices to El Shaddai."

The vizier tipped his face to a stream of sunlight that poured in through one of the high windows. "I have not ceased to pray to God Shaddai since I came to the Black

Land," he said, a spark of some indefinable emotion flickering in his eyes. "He lifted me out of prison and slavery and made me sit at Pharaoh's right hand. More than that, He saved Egypt, perhaps even the entire world, from this famine that shall continue for another full five years. Until today, I thought God's plans for me had been fulfilled. But an hour ago I looked out upon the faces of Jacob's sons— my treacherous brothers."

His *brothers*? Mandisa was too surprised to even nod.

"I wanted to run forward and embrace them," he went on, his voice dropping in volume, "but on at least one face I saw anger and hatred as strong as it was the day they cast me into a pit." He lowered his head and stiffened as if momentarily ashamed. "I was almost afraid."

Mandisa quickly defended him. "You are not a coward, my lord."

The vizier studied his hands. "I no longer fear for myself but for my father and my other brother. I fear they might hate Benjamin and hurt him, and so bring my father to his grave with even greater sorrow."

"And so you cast them into prison." Mandisa whispered the words in a neutral tone, not knowing whether he hoped for approval or condemnation.

"Benjamin is the only other son of my mother, Rachel," he said, lifting his eyes to meet hers. "How can I know the sons of Leah do not hate him as they hated me? How can I be certain they will not do him harm?"

"They said he is alive and well with your father." Mandisa lowered her eyes, uncomfortable with the frankness of the conversation. Masters did not usually ask their servants' opinions about such personal matters.

"My father, if they speak truly, has lived one hundred twenty-nine years," he went on in a hushed whisper. "Benjamin is a grown man of thirty, with children of his own. For his sake and the sake of his children, I must test the hearts of the other ten."

Mandisa bowed her head. "I will do anything I can to help, my lord."

The laughter of children danced into the room, and the vizier's mouth curved into an unconscious smile as he recognized the sounds of his sons. But before they entered, he spoke a final word to Mandisa. "Do not speak to anyone of this, not even your mistress. Do not reveal my past or my link to the men in Pharaoh's prison. I must seek the face of Almighty God before I know how to proceed."

She bowed again as the boys spilled into the room. "I will do my best to serve you, my lord."

Four

AS HIS BROTHERS SNORED UNEVENLY AROUND him, Simeon lay upon his back and studied the dark circle of sky above the prison pit. Glorious Thebes had held them in awe as they entered the royal city, but no signs of its marble-washed opulence existed in this forsaken place. No colorful ornate pictures or grand pillars adorned the mud-walled pit into which they had been thrust after leaving the vizier's villa. They were not even allowed the luxury of a view. With scorched black earth around them and an ebony sky above, Simeon felt as if they had sunk into the abyss. How could they have fallen so far in such a short time?

There had been nothing to indicate trouble was afoot when they approached the royal city. Though a severe drought had scorched the fields outside the walls of Thebes, reports from passing travelers indicated that the city's granaries and storage houses overflowed with barley and emmer wheat, onions and leeks, lettuce, pomegranates, apples, olives, figs, and the smooth wine of Ka-en-keme, better and sweeter than honey. Thebes was a luxury-loving lioness that rejoiced to feed her young, passersby had told the ten brothers. Because of her generous bounty, the life-giving river at her breast teemed with boats large and small, for joy inhabited her gates.

The city lay like a glittering jewel in the merciless Egyptian sun with her crowded streets laid out in straight lines that crossed at neat right angles. Even in the grip of famine, fishes glittered in her ponds, and nesting birds squawked beside her pools.

The Egyptians in the merchant stalls seemed simple,

cheerful, and likable. Slighter than the robust men of Canaan and better adapted to the stifling weather, the simple people wore their brown hair short or shaved their heads. The intense dry heat dictated the apparel of the day. Men wore eggshell-colored kilts of pleated linen. Occasionally a richer man appeared in a voluminous cloak edged with colorful weavings and embroideries.

Naked children scampered among the crowd at the marketplace by the river. Regal young women in gossamer gowns kept a careful eye on the youngsters while they bartered for household goods and exotic trophies from foreign lands. The women of Egypt dressed themselves in linen sheaths—long shirtlike garments exquisitely cut and sewn and tied at the neck with delicate tassels. They seemed industrious happy creatures, but Simeon found it difficult to consider anything but their immodest attire.

After inquiring among several merchants for direction, the brothers followed a sea of visitors to the royal granaries of Thebes. An official explained that all first-time foreign visitors were required to register directly with the vizier's representative. After this initial contact they would be spared the journey upriver and would be permitted to buy grain from one of the more remote outposts.

After waiting for hours in the hot sun, the brothers had finally reached the head of the line. An Egyptian official sat on the ground, a papyrus reed in his hand, his lips pursed with boredom.

Simeon closed his eyes, struggling to remember every detail of the morning. Surely they had said something or committed some careless small act that aroused suspicion. He could think of nothing he had done, but there were ten of them, and any one of his brothers could have lost custody of his thoughts or words for a moment. Perhaps Levi had frowned at one of the naked slaves, or Judah had unconsciously snubbed one of the bald priests.

"What is your name, and from where do you come?" the scribe had asked in a bored tone, not even looking up.

Reuben, as eldest, stood at the head of the line, with Simeon immediately behind him.

"I am Reuben, son of Jacob of Hebron," he answered, folding his hands calmly. "We have brought silver to buy a ration of grain from Pharaoh. There are ten of us, and each man will need four hundredweight of grain, emmer, and barley—"

Even from where he stood, Simeon could see the sudden tremor that shook the scribe's hand. "Reuben, son of Jacob?" he interrupted, looking fully into Reuben's face for the first time. "From Hebron of Canaan?"

"Yes," Reuben answered, strengthening his voice as if the scribe had suddenly gone deaf. He lifted a hand to indicate the others. "These are my brothers."

The scribe's face drained of color. "Hold your place, but you must excuse me," the man muttered. Without hesitation, he rose and ran doubled over into the brick building near the beehive-shaped granaries.

"What did you say to him, Reuben?" Gad called, joking. "Or perhaps I should ask what you have eaten of late. Did your breath make him ill?"

"No more than yours would," Reuben answered lightly, but Simeon could see that a lightning bolt of worry had darted into his eyes.

They waited thirty eternal minutes. The foreigners behind them, cursing and sweating, lost all patience. First they called upon their gods to deliver them from the oppressive heat that covered the city like a blanket, then they demanded that their gods curse the man responsible for the delay. Finally another official appeared and addressed Reuben. "By the order of the Lord High Vizier, Father to Pharaoh, Acting Ruler, and Commander of Pharaoh's Royal Army, you and your company are to come with me."

"Come with you?" Reuben asked, his heavy eyebrows arching in surprise. "Where are we going?"

"Are we not allowed to buy grain?" Simeon asked, stepping forward. "Are we and our families to starve? For what reason?"

From out of nowhere, three dozen armed men appeared, instantly silencing the noisy rabble behind the brothers. Lance-bearers, the sharp blades of their spears gleaming like razor-sharp talons, surrounded Jacob's sons.

"You will come with me," the Egyptian commander repeated, eyeing the brothers with a critical squint.

"We will come without argument if we may know where we are going," Judah said, moving toward Reuben.

But the commander did not answer, and in the face of such an armed force, the brothers did not protest further. They stumbled in a frightened bewildered huddle to the gates of the largest villa Simeon had ever seen. Then they were escorted into the front hall of the house itself.

And for what? Though he had struggled with his questions all night, Simeon still had no idea why they had been selected from the thousands in line at the royal granaries. Had they offended one of the Egyptians' stone gods? Or one of the naval commanders at the river? Had their father or grandfather conducted some secret dealings with the Egyptians that now bode ill for his descendants?

Simeon could find no answers in the night sky. Groaning, he turned onto his side and closed his eyes against the depressing veil of blackness. For a shepherd accustomed to sleeping with the unfettered breath of the open land upon his brow, the prison pit was cramped, suffocating, and cruel. He did not know who deserved the blame for thrusting them into this situation, but when he discovered the truth, that one would be made to pay dearly.

⟶ Five ⟵

THREE DAYS AFTER THE CANAANITES HAD BEEN taken to Pharaoh's prison, Mandisa received a summons from her master. She hurried to Lady Asenath's chamber, where Zaphenath-paneah was breakfasting with his family.

"My master and mistress, may you live long and happy," she murmured, entering her lady's chamber and prostrating herself on the floor.

Zaphenath-paneah nodded in greeting and wiped his hands on a small square of linen on his breakfast tray. "Mandisa, would you ask your son to take my boys into the garden to play? But please return here after you have spoken to him."

Mandisa rose to her feet and held out her hands to Ephraim and Manasseh, the vizier's young sons. "Come, boys," she said, smiling. "Adom is in the courtyard with Tarik, learning how to throw a lance. Would you like to join him?"

The two boys, ages five and seven, reached out to her with trusting hands and let her lead them from the room. She found her own son, Adom, standing at the edge of the front portico, his gaze wistfully fastened to the courtyard where the captain was busy inspecting his guards.

"I thought Tarik was going to teach you this morning," she whispered, slipping up behind the slender boy.

Adom cast her a quick glance over his shoulder, then returned his gaze to the men in the courtyard. "I don't think he has time, Mother," he whispered, his voice heavy with disappointment. "He has to conduct the inspections, and then the vizier wants him to bring some captives from Pharaoh's prison."

"There will be another time, then," Mandisa whispered, giving what she hoped was the proper dose of encouragement. Stepping to his side, she took the small boys' hands. "But I've brought you something to do. The vizier has asked if you would take his boys to the garden."

Adom's gloomy expression brightened at the suggestion. "Of course," he said, grinning at Ephraim and Manasseh. "I don't mind."

"I know you don't. You're a good son."

Adom shrugged off the compliment and took the younger boys' hands and led them toward the garden. Mandisa paused a moment, watching the trio depart. Ephraim and Manasseh were blessed to have a loving father and a myriad of caretakers to teach them all that boys ought to know. Adom was less fortunate, for he had only her, and a woman alone could do only so much with a son.

She tucked her thoughts away and urged her feet back toward her mistress's chamber.

———

Slaves were removing the breakfast trays when Mandisa returned. Zaphenath-paneah listened to his wife's pleasant chatter while the room was cleared, but when the slaves had gone, he folded his arms and regarded Asenath with a grave expression.

"What?" Asenath asked, her hand at her throat. A flicker of a smile rose at the edge of her mouth, then died out. "Have I done something to displease you, my husband?"

"No, beloved." The vizier's eyes flickered toward Mandisa, then he motioned to an empty stool near his wife. "You may sit, Mandisa. I want you both to hear what I am about to say."

Without speaking, Mandisa slid into her place.

"My love," the vizier of all Egypt began, his eyes tenderly melting into his wife's, "days ago you asked why the arrival of a group of men from Hebron upset me so. I could not tell you then, being unsure in my own mind what I should do, but I have prayed to the Almighty God and have an answer for you today."

"Go on, my husband," Asenath said when he paused. Her hands fidgeted in her lap.

The vizier gave her a forced smile and a tense nod of assent. "I have told you, Asenath, of my past and the treachery that brought me to Egypt. And now I must tell you that the men in Pharaoh's prison are my brothers, the sons of the maids and the sons of Leah."

Mandisa heard her mistress's quick intake of breath, but the lady said nothing. She sat motionless at her husband's side, looking blank, amazed, and very pale.

The vizier's gaze shifted from his wife to her handmaid. "I have decided to remove the men of Canaan from prison today and will need an interpreter when I speak with them."

"But if they are your brothers . . ." Asenath began, shaking her head.

"I must know the intentions of their hearts before I reveal myself. I had thought to keep nine of them in Egypt and return the one who wields the most influence with my father, but in these hungry times it is too dangerous for one man to attempt the desert journey alone. I had also thought to punish them," his voice softened, "but God has shown me that revenge is not the answer."

Mandisa pressed her lips together and nodded, signaling that she understood. Her master had obviously thought much about what to do with his recalcitrant guests. "So you will allow them all to leave?" she whispered.

"No." Zaphenath-paneah gave her a slow smile. "I will keep the one most likely to cause trouble among the others. There are five years of famine yet to come, so they must eventually return to Egypt for more food rations. As long as I am holding one brother, they will return to Thebes. My father is an honorable man. He will demand that they re-deem whomever is left behind.''

"Are you certain?" Asenath's hand flew out to rest upon his muscled arm. "My husband, what if they never come back? Won't you regret sending them away without telling them the truth?"

The vizier leaned forward in a casual posture, his el-bows on his knees. "Mandisa, you are a Canaanite. You know their ways. Tell your mistress—if these men were of your clan, wouldn't they return to secure your freedom?"

Mandisa shriveled a little at his words. Her father had married her to Idogbe, a man she did not love, and allowed him to carry her to Egypt against her will. In thirteen years, no one from her family had visited or sent word. If not for the goodness of Zaphenath-paneah and Lady Asenath, both she and her son would be enslaved or dead, for none of her father's people cared that Idogbe had vanished and left her pregnant and alone. But if she had been born a son instead of a daughter, the situation would have undoubtedly been different.

"Yes, my lord," she whispered in a strangled voice, denying her own bitter reality. "I am certain you are right."

He sat back, reassured. "God knows what is in my broth-ers' hearts, but He intends that I discern their hearts myself. Mandisa, be ready to face them within the hour. I am send-ing Tarik to Pharaoh's prison immediately."

"My husband?" Asenath whispered, her voice shat-tered. "Should I be with you . . . to face them?"

"Not now, beloved," the vizier answered, taking her hands in his. "Be patient. If God is willing, you shall be at my side on a far happier day."

Irritated, dirty, and uncomfortable, Simeon shifted un-easily as he followed his brothers into the vizier's great re-ception hall. In the vestibule, slaves had removed their san-dals and washed the black dirt of Egypt from their feet, and as the brothers entered the spotless and elaborate hall, another army of servants lined the walls, each waving an ostrich-feathered fan to circulate the ambrosial odors of incense that wafted from ornately carved stands along the sides of the room. From someplace out of sight, gentle hands plucked soothing melodic music from a harp.

Simeon steeled himself for whatever was to come. These gestures of sweet softness were obviously meant to emphasize the difference between the vizier's luxurious presence and the barren prison pit into which they had been thrown. *Why?* he wondered.

After a few moments of nervous silence, a pair of trumpets sounded. The double columns of lance-bearers again marched into the room, and the handsome, most elegant vizier ascended his gilded throne. His full linen garment, falling like chiseled marble from his throat to the floor, did little to disguise the strength of his frame. A heavy chain of gold hung about his neck, and the finest leather adorned his feet. His heavy wig had been shaped and oiled to perfectly frame his regal face.

For a moment woven of eternity, no one dared break the silence. As much as Simeon wanted to look away, he found himself staring at the king's regent. Zaphenath-paneah's ruggedly handsome features nudged some distant experience in Simeon's memory, but he pushed the feeling aside. The vizier *should* look familiar, for his likeness had been painted on half the statues and frescoed buildings in Thebes. Though Simeon guessed the man was less than forty years old, his sharp profile spoke of power and ageless strength. Yet his mouth wore an expression of familiar softness, the way Jacob, his father, looked just before he smiled.

From lowered lids, Simeon shot a hostile look at the man. *Is he gloating because of his harsh treatment of us? Does he think we will confess to spying just because we endured two days and two nights in his pitiful prison pit? Or is he enjoying the thought of what he will do to us tomorrow if we do not confess today?*

"Grace and peace to you, Most High Vizier," Reuben said, falling to his knees. The other brothers followed Reuben's cue and lowered themselves until every man lay prostrate on the gleaming floor. From another entrance to the room, the female servant who had previously acted as interpreter came forward and spoke for Reuben again.

"Rise. You may kneel before me," Zaphenath-paneah responded, holding out a golden rod. "I have consulted my God and have brought you out of prison to speak what is on my heart."

"My brothers and I are listening," Reuben answered, rising to a kneeling position.

The vizier waited for the interpretation, then seemed to fix his gaze squarely on Simeon, who had lifted his head as high as he dared.

"I have asked my God for wisdom," the vizier said, derision and sympathy mingling in his expression, "and He has provided an answer. If you do what I will tell you, you shall live, for I fear God."

Simeon automatically shifted his gaze to the woman as she provided the interpretation, and he lost all control of his eyes as the vizier's words flowed from her tongue. He had noticed her on their arrival, for what man would not? But today her loveliness seemed to fill the room with light.

Slender, poised, and fiery, the woman looked ethereal in the slanting sunbeams falling from the high windows. The dark curls of her wig twisted and crinkled across her wide forehead. Her shadowed eyes glowed, piercing the subdued light of the room. A leather belt around her waist defined its smallness, and the milky apricot color of her skin blended into the sheer material of a gown that did little to disguise her womanly curves. She paused, and her eyes flitted around the room, then locked with Simeon's. He caught his breath, but she dropped her eyes before his steady gaze.

"What shall we do, my lord?" Reuben's voice jerked Simeon back to reality.

The vizier stiffened in his chair, and his voice rose in a commanding tone. "If you are honest men, let one of your brothers remain here confined in prison. But as for the rest of you, go, carry grain to your households lest the famine destroy you. And when your food rations are depleted, bring your youngest brother to me, so your words may be verified. If you are willing to do this, and you have not lied, you shall live."

"Bring Benjamin?" Zebulun gasped in horror. "It is impossible. Our father will never agree to let his youngest son leave his side to come here."

The vizier listened to the translation, then managed a short laugh and a reply.

"The vizier Zaphenath-paneah says your brother is a grown man and married. He is no longer a child," the woman interpreted. "You must bring your youngest brother before Zaphenath-paneah."

A flicker of apprehension coursed through Simeon at the words *your youngest brother*. Once the sons of Israel had known two younger brothers, but though Joseph still haunted Simeon's dreams, he was gone forever. There remained only Benjamin.

Reuben responded to the interpreter's words. "My lord, let me speak to my brothers."

His request needed no interpretation. Apparently understanding, the stony-faced vizier nodded in assent.

Reuben stood. Turning his back to the vizier, he looked at the others. "We must do as he says," he whispered, his voice low. "We have no choice."

"Bring Benjamin?" Judah's brow creased with worry. "Father will never allow it. He would die himself before he would let us take Benjamin from Hebron."

"Would you rather our father lose ten sons?" Levi snapped, flinging a hand upward in frustration. "If we agree to this, we will have time to prepare Father for what must be done to appease this Egyptian."

"Levi is right," Dan added. "And the man has made a

reasonable request. If we do not consent, we are practically admitting that we have lied. The vizier will be convinced we are spies, and he may kill us all—now." He lowered his eyes to the floor. "Perhaps we deserve death. After what happened at Dothan with Jo—"

"Don't say it," Simeon snapped, stiffening as though Dan had struck him. Though their absent brother's name singed every conscience, if they did not speak of him, they would not have to remember. "Dothan was more than twenty years ago!" Simeon went on. "Our father has put the past behind him."

"Our father has not ceased to mourn for Joseph," Reuben interrupted, his mouth set in annoyance. His voice, cold and exact, echoed in the cavernous hall. "You know I speak the truth. Answer me truly, Simeon. Did I not warn you that we should not sin against the boy? But you would not listen, and now comes the reckoning for his blood. Now we will pay for what we have done."

A sudden choking sound disturbed the silence behind them, and Simeon turned in time to see the vizier, his hands over his face, rise from his chair and flee the room. Like a pursuing shadow, the captain of the guard followed.

"Now we will be meat for the vizier's dogs," Levi said, his mouth grim as he turned back to the others. "Whatever the Egyptian ate for breakfast does not agree with him, and we shall pay the penalty for his ailing stomach when he returns. We must agree to his plan, and we must agree quickly."

"But which one of us?" Asher asked, looking around the circle. "Which one of us will remain here in prison while his family suffers alone?"

No one spoke for a long moment, then Reuben lifted his eyes. "We all have children," he said simply, giving Simeon a look that was compassionate, troubled, and still. "But we do not all have wives. You, Simeon, have no wife waiting at home. You should volunteer to remain behind."

"I'll not stay here," Simeon answered, glaring at his

brother. "I may not have a wife, but I am the only one who remembers to provide for our sister. With no husband to provide for her, Dinah depends upon me."

"I'll look after Dinah," Judah volunteered.

"And my sons?" Simeon asked, frowning. "Who will see to them? Someone else must stay here. I came here to get my grain and get out, and I would sooner die tomorrow than remain here one day longer than necessary."

"But we have wives!"

"I have six sons!" Simeon answered, seething with mounting rage. "You, Reuben, are the oldest. Why don't you volunteer for prison? You're always quick to speak up when it is to your advantage. Or Judah! With all your talk of God and holiness, why don't you offer to stay here?"

"Father listens to Judah," Dan inserted, "while you howl like the desert winds and our father pays no mind. You are the Destroyer. You bring nothing but trouble."

"Enough!" Judah cried, lifting his hands as he stepped into the center of the circle. The bickering gradually stopped. Judah ran his fingers through his strong gray hair in a distracted motion, then looked up to the ceiling as if the answer would be found there. "El Shaddai will make the choice," he said simply, his shoulders drooping. "We will listen and accept His will."

Six

MANDISA TRIED TO FOLLOW THE RISING BABBLE of the brothers' conversation, but then she felt the light touch of a hand upon her arm. "The master seeks you," Tarik whispered, lingering behind a column as the prisoners bickered in the center of the chamber.

Mandisa turned silently and followed Tarik into a small room off the great hall. The noble and mighty Zaphenath-paneah sat motionless on a bed as if his mind and body were benumbed. His eyes were red with weeping, and dark stains of kohl blackened his cheeks.

"Please, Mandisa, freshen my toilette," he said, offering her a tremulous smile. "I must not appear weak before them."

He offered no reason for his behavior, and Mandisa knew from Tarik's mystified expression that the master had not explained his connection to the troublesome men in the hall. Quickly she reached into a cosmetics box she carried for just such emergencies and reapplied the master's face paint in swift sure strokes. Within a moment he had assumed his former regal appearance, but his voice was unsteady when he thanked her.

"Here," she said, pulling a scrap of linen from a basket on the floor. "Let them think, if necessary, that the desert winds have given you a cough."

He took the square of cloth and crumpled it in his hand, then leaned forward as if to stand up. "What are they arguing about?" he asked, pausing. "Were you able to hear?"

"They are quarreling over who should remain behind," she said, folding her hands. "The spokesman, Reuben, says the one called Simeon should remain in Egypt, for he has no wife waiting in Canaan. But this Simeon"—she felt her cheeks color as she said the bold one's name—"says he has a sister and six sons who need him."

"Six sons."

A wistful note echoed in Zaphenath-paneah's voice, and Mandisa felt her heart contract in sympathy for him. The single sorrow that lay over the vizier's household resulted from the fact that Lady Asenath had been warned by the royal physicians that another child would certainly hasten her death. She had borne two healthy sons during the days of plenty, then had suffered three miscarriages, the most recent of which had occurred during the time of the Nile's last flooding. That unborn child nearly dragged Lady Asenath with it into the otherworld.

Now the mistress's womb lay as barren and shallow as the starving Nile itself. Zaphenath-paneah had consoled his wife with great tenderness and compassion, assuring her that he loved her, even though he would no longer visit her chambers when she might conceive a child. He was content with her and their two sons, he often assured her, especially since his responsibilities to the kingdom and Pharaoh often drained him of strength.

"But you renew me," Mandisa had heard him whisper to his whimpering wife one afternoon, "you and Ephraim and Manasseh. I am blessed beyond measure, for your smile alone is enough to strengthen my heart, soul, and body."

The master looked as though he needed one of his wife's smiles now. He stood, remained absolutely motionless for a moment, then moved toward the hall with long purposeful strides.

Drawn by curiosity and duty, Mandisa and Tarik followed.

————

Feeling the full intensity of their eyes upon him, Joseph

mounted the dais and turned slowly, regally, toward his brothers. "Tarik will take the one I choose to prison," he said, speaking in Egyptian. And then, as Mandisa translated in a breathy frantic voice, Joseph lifted his hand and pointed squarely at Simeon.

The man was a thorn. Twenty years ago, he had been one of the first to call for Joseph's death after they dropped him into the pit. And at every family gathering, whether around a meal or a well to water the flocks, Simeon had managed to find a reason to needle the others. As strong as an iron chain and as unyielding as a rock, his opinions inevitably divided the brothers. In Joseph's day, even the women had learned to avoid him.

Without Simeon, the others would have a far happier journey home—seventeen or eighteen days of relative peace. Jacob would not have to hear Simeon's negative, slanted version of their encounter with the Egyptian vizier, and Benjamin would not have to make the long journey to Egypt in the company of a murderous madman. For a moment, Joseph wished he'd had enough forethought to order Levi's detention, too, for he and Simeon usually united to cause trouble. But of the two, Simeon was by far the most likely to erupt.

Tarik snapped a command, and a column of guards moved into the knot of Canaanites and effectively separated Simeon from the others. As a pair of guards advanced to bind the captive's wrists, the burly shepherd lunged like an animal, grabbing and then neatly breaking one guard's arm over his knee. A melee broke out. The dignity of the chamber vanished as crazy full-throated shrieks echoed from the high ceiling and bounced among the pillars. Most of the cries came from Simeon, a few from the injured guards. The other brothers cowered against the wall, their faces conveying emotions ranging from embarrassment to sheer horror. Mandisa, the vizier noticed, had covered her eyes, afraid to look at the vicious spectacle before her.

Two guards grabbed for Simeon's right hand, then were

launched across the room. Another had the misfortune of connecting face first with Simeon's fist. From where Joseph stood, he saw Simeon's punch crush the man's jawbone. A shoulder throw sent another pair of guards crashing to the floor. One foolish young fan-bearer, who thought to enter the fray with only the pole of his fan for a weapon, found himself lying on the floor at Simeon's feet, the breath knocked out of him.

The lance-bearers moved forward, tightening their circle, and though the captive still crouched menacingly, the fight was over. Tarik waded through the injured guards to catch and bind Simeon's flailing fists. Another guard shackled and hobbled the shepherd's feet with a length of rope. He could still run, of course, but he would not get far.

Joseph pressed his lips together, smothering a grim smile. He should have warned Tarik. A man did not grow up with eleven brothers without learning how to fight. And it was not on a mere whim that the others had named Simeon the "Destroyer."

"The rest of you may go," Joseph said, looking out at them with a dispassionate stare as if nothing out of the ordinary had happened. "But if you return, you will not see this one again unless you bring your youngest brother and thus prove your own words. Then you may come and trade for food in peace." He paused, concern and contempt warring in his soul, as Mandisa translated in a trembling voice.

"I give you one warning—use the grain of Egypt for bread, not for seed. Nothing will grow for five more years. Now go," he rushed on, feeling a disturbing quake in his control, "and may all be well with you and your father."

The trumpets blared as he stood. Amid a storm of mingled shouts from the brothers, the guards led Simeon out of the room. Ignoring their farewells, Joseph left the hall through another exit.

Safe from prying eyes in the small adjoining chamber, Joseph turned to Tarik, who had followed for instructions. "Listen carefully," he said, keeping his voice low. "Do not return the man to Pharaoh's prison, but prepare a secure room here in my house. Do not withhold from him any luxury save that of his freedom."

"Is that wise, noble vizier?"

Joseph nodded. "I do not believe he will hurt anyone here. He is a shepherd, Tarik. He knows the law of fight or flee, and since he could not flee, he fought. I expected it, and I should have warned you."

"My men should have been better prepared," Tarik answered, coloring fiercely. "Their performance was shameful."

"They actually did very well," Joseph answered, resting a hand on his hip. "Simeon is strong. He has always been dangerous."

If Tarik was relieved by his master's assurances, he didn't show it. "And what of the others, my lord?"

"Allow them to purchase grain rations from my own granaries, but instruct the scribes to return each man's silver to the mouth of his sack." This, Joseph noticed, elicited an uplifted eyebrow. He clapped his hand on the captain's bronzed shoulder. "I can't take silver from my own brothers, Tarik."

Surprise blossomed on the guard's handsome face, and Joseph held up a warning hand. "Not a word to anyone. My wife knows the truth, and Mandisa. But no one else."

"Should Ani be told?"

"No." Joseph gave Tarik a conspiratorial wink. "Ani is a very wise man, but his wisdom is forever flowing forth from his tongue. He will not be harmed by not knowing."

Regaining his composure, Tarik bowed. "Is that all, my lord?"

Joseph paused. "They will need fresh donkeys and provisions for their journey to Hebron. Have Ani make preparation for these things, then send the brothers away as quickly as possible." He grimaced in good humor. "The sooner they are home, the sooner they will return and take their troublesome brother with them."

Tarik's usually stern mouth spread in a toothy grin. "It shall be done as you say, my lord."

———

Simeon stared around the room in wonder. After his outburst, he had expected to be thrust into another prison pit, possibly one more barbaric than the first, but instead he had been marched through the villa's courtyard and given a clean private room within the walls of the vizier's palace.

The low bed of polished wood was generously covered with skins, cushions, and fresh linens. The neck rest had been padded with the softest down. A pitcher and basin stood on a stand near a high window that brought in fresh light and air. Next to the bed, half a dozen blue lotus blossoms floated in a bowl of water and sweetly scented the chamber.

Amazed, Simeon sank onto the seat of an elaborately carved chair and fingered his beard. He could imagine several explanations for this unusual treatment, but the most obvious answer was that the vizier of Egypt was demented. Alternately hostile and forgiving, this vizier had already demonstrated capricious whims of fancy. Simeon had heard that the Egyptians were a cheerful and superstitious lot. This Zaphenath-paneah probably hoped to pacify some god by allowing Simeon to enjoy a few days of luxury before relegating him to a dungeon of torture.

But though the chamber was pleasant and probably better furnished than half the houses of Thebes, Simeon was no city dweller! He wanted the open spaces of the earth around him, the spiraling stars above. The sweet scent of lotus blossoms and the delicate taste of dainty shat cakes were not for him. He longed for the earthy smells of goat and cattle dung, the robust flavors of desert-toughened meat, and rough breads sweetened with wild honey.

Yes, Simeon reflected, lifting his eyes to the rectangular window higher than his reach, for a man of the wilderness, even a king's palace could become a prison in time. Perhaps

Zaphenath-paneah was not deranged after all.

————

Hours later, Tarik summoned Mandisa and the steward, Ani, to the foyer off the vizier's bedchamber. "Our master is with Pharaoh for the rest of the day," the captain said, lifting his head in unconscious pride, "and he has instructed me to tell you what we shall do with this captive in our house. We three shall deal with him. None of the others shall have anything to do with him."

And two of us, Mandisa thought, watching Tarik with a keenly observant eye, *know who and what he is. But though he is the vizier's own brother, he is dangerous, too powerful to be held here.*

The steward bowed his bald head as a sign of respect, an unnecessary gesture because Ani was at least as important as Tarik in the villa's social system. The Egyptian steward ran the house, overseeing and orchestrating every action from simple housekeeping and meal preparation to the fields, granaries, and livestock. And though Ani looked like a little wet bird, behind his self-deprecating facade was an encyclopedic mind, a dynamic force born of wisdom and certainty gleaned from years of loyal service. Of no steward in all of Thebes was more expected, and none of the others came close to duplicating the elegance and prosperity of Zaphenath-paneah's large estate.

"I was curious about the man," Ani admitted, his lined mouth cracking in a smile. "I thought the circumstances of this morning were quite . . . *unusual*."

"We are not to talk of this man with the children or the other servants," Tarik went on. "His needs are to be met daily."

The captain's eyes turned toward Mandisa. "If you are willing, lady, the master asks if you will consent to take the prisoner his food and tarry if he feels the need for conversation. There are few here who speak the Canaanite tongue as fluently as you do."

Mandisa paused, considering. She knew her master well enough to know he would not command her to obey his wish, for she carried a full work load attending to the vizier's wife and sons as well as Adom. She had every right to decline the job of caring for a captive with the temperament of an underfed lion, especially since the smoldering flame in his eyes half frightened her.

But no one else spoke his language. And she had come to Egypt as a foreigner. She knew all too well the pain of not understanding and not being understood.

"Do not worry, I will get one of my guards to tend to him," the captain said, waving his hand as if he understood her hesitation.

"There is no need. I will do it," she said, avoiding Tarik's eyes.

"So be it," the captain answered slowly, tilting his head as if he weighed her motives. "If at any time you wish to surrender this responsibility, you may."

"I understand."

"I see." Tarik pressed his lips together. "The master will periodically ask you for news of this captive. You are to speak freely with Zaphenath-paneah, apprising him of anything that happens with the prisoner while he is with us. Such information may be useful in the future."

"Of course." Mandisa lifted a brow and turned toward Ani. "I am not accustomed to working in the kitchens. May I have the kitchen slave Halima to help prepare the captive's meals?" She looked back to the captain of the guard. "And is it permissible for me to take Halima with me when I visit this herdsman? I would fear for my safety if I ventured into his room alone."

Tarik and Ani studied each other for a moment. "If it is to fulfill the master's wish, you may use any slaves you please," Ani said, folding his arms.

"I see no harm taking the girl with you," Tarik answered. "But no one else is to visit him. Only we three and the slave Halima, if you need her. Of course, if you feel threatened at any time, you may call one of the guards to stand outside the door."

"Thank you." Mandisa nodded.

"Is there anything else?" Ani asked, pressing his hands together.

"No." Tarik thrust his hands into his sword belt. "Let us hope the uncouth beast remains silent and does not disturb the household. I will beg the gods of Egypt to swiftly return his brothers so we may be rid of him."

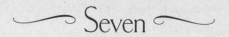

Seven

JOSEPH DISMISSED HIS GUARDS AT THE GATE OF the villa and walked alone up the winding pathway through his courtyard. He felt hollow, lifeless, totally spent by the affairs of the day. The meeting with his brothers and Simeon's outburst had drained him completely, and his afternoon with the young and energetic Pharaoh had left him feeling like a man twice his age. His back ached between his shoulder blades. He knew his face was pale and pinched. More than once Amenhotep had asked what troubled his most trusted friend and counselor. Joseph had only smiled and said that Pharaoh would understand once he had established a family of his own.

The night was sultry and still, so quiet that Joseph thought he could hear even the lapping of wavelets on the shore of the Nile outside the walls of his estate. The sun had dropped behind the western Theban cliffs an hour before, joining the dead in the valley of the kings. Torches burned along the pathway, pushing at the gloom, and the noise of laughter suddenly echoed from the slaves' chambers, warming the courtyard with sounds of life.

Joseph's heart lifted a little. His brothers had come and gone, expanding and emptying his heart in the space of twenty-four hours. But Simeon was still here, breathing the same darkness, hearing the same heartwarming sounds. What was he thinking, the one they called Simeon the Destroyer?

Joseph turned, following a branch of the courtyard path to the small temple of his estate. Like the temples of other Theban villas, the elegant and simple structure had been designed to hold images of the household's gods, but his temple stood empty, without idols or trays of burning incense. Joseph had only allowed Ani to install two torches, which burned through the night in case a visitor wanted to enter the temple and pray.

Joseph knew his servants thought it odd that their obviously devout master and vizier did not worship a visible god, for it was commonly repeated that Egypt grew gods as abundantly as the black flood-watered land grew grain. When Tuthmosis IV elevated Joseph from prison to the palace, he proclaimed that the Spirit of God rested upon the man who would henceforth be known as Zaphenath-paneah. After Pharoah's divine proclamation, no one in Thebes, or in all of Egypt for that matter, dared to doubt the significance of the vizier's beliefs. Those who knew him understood that he worshiped the invisible and almighty God known in the Canaanite tongue as El Shaddai. The Egyptians had another name for this most ancient deity: *Neter*, the almighty God who was One.

The torches cast a dim light in the small temple, and Joseph leaned against the doorpost, studying the small chamber. In deference to the master's chosen God, Ani had painted the wall above the empty altar with the picture sign for Neter, an axhead fastened into a long wooden handle by thongs of leather.

A smile ruffled Joseph's mouth as he studied the drawing. "The mightiest man in ancient days was he who had the best weapon and could wield it with the greatest effect," he murmured, crossing his arms. "If your power, El Shaddai, were an ax, how well did I display it today?"

The still small voice he had heard a hundred times before did not answer, and Joseph lowered his eyes. "I do not know if my brothers will come again. And I do not know what I shall do with Simeon if they do not."

Wait.

A thrill shivered through his senses. His heart recognized the Voice, more a certainty than an audible sound, and Joseph closed his eyes in contentment. God had brought him to this place. God would keep him. And obviously God had not yet finished His work.

Humming quietly, he turned and walked toward the house.

"My husband?"

Joseph stirred on his bed, struggling to find wakefulness through the embracing folds of sleep.

"My husband, Ani is here with his morning report. Shall I send him away?"

"No," Joseph said, forcing his eyes to open. He sat up, throwing off the linen sheet that covered him, and ran his hand through his close-cropped hair. Age had not lessened his strength, but it had increased his requirement for rest and recovery. But the pressing needs of a pharaoh, a kingdom, and an estate could not wait.

"Tell Ani to come in," he said, focusing on Asenath for the first time. She hung shyly about the doorway, a vision of loveliness even at this hour of the morning. Youth and freshness still radiated from her delicate oval face. She had grown from an attractive girl into a vividly beautiful woman. She smiled at him, and he held out a hand, beckoning her closer. "Why do you linger in the doorway like a child?" he said, his voice still gruff with sleep. "Come here and kiss me, wife."

She flew to him like a bird, wrapping her arms about his neck and covering his face with happy kisses. "I've missed you, beloved," she said, the scent of her perfume warming his senses. "You were busy from sunrise to sundown yesterday, and your sons and I have missed you sorely."

"As I have missed you," Joseph murmured. He smiled against her mouth and drew her into his arms, returning her kiss.

"My lord and master, live forever."

Ani's voice, brimming with suppressed humor, interrupted their embrace. Joseph lifted his lips from Asenath's long enough to command the steward away. "For the space of a few moments, at least," Joseph called, nuzzling his wife's neck, "I would like to spend some time with the lady of the house."

"As you wish, my lord," came the reply as the old man chuckled and moved into the hall.

"A few moments?" Asenath asked, a teasing note in her voice. She buried her face against his throat. "Why not longer?"

"Why not?" Joseph laughed softly as he stroked her cheek. "Because Pharaoh will demand to see me this morning. And before I go to him I must check on the captive here in our house."

"Pharaoh does not sneeze without asking you whether or not he should," Asenath answered, playfully tweaking his ear. "And the prisoner is in Tarik's custody. He will not escape or do harm."

She kissed him with her eyes, and he met her lips with his own, tempted by the idea of a sweet rendezvous with his beloved wife. A nagging thought intruded, however, and he pulled his face away and regarded her with a gently reproachful gaze.

"How long has it been since your red moon flowed?"

She pouted prettily. "I don't know, my husband. Mandisa keeps account of these things."

"Asenath, tell me. Don't be coy."

Her lower lip edged forward. "I'm certain it's all right, beloved."

"How many days?"

She closed her eyes in a gesture of defeat. "One week. Ten days."

He sighed, amazed at her careless attitude. Though the physicians had warned her that another pregnancy might take her life, Asenath seemed not to care.

He brushed a gentle kiss across her forehead. "Not today, my love. It is too dangerous. I would not risk losing you for an hour of pleasure."

Her hands tightened around his neck. Even now, her painted eyes teased and caressed him. If he could not escape the tumultuous feelings she aroused . . .

"Ani!" he called over her shoulder, pulling her hands from his neck. "I am ready to hear from you."

The pout was genuine this time. Asenath stood to her feet and brushed imaginary wrinkles from her gown, unspoken pain glowing in her eyes.

"I'm sorry, my love. When the time of conception is past—"

"Of course," Asenath said, moving away. She threw a falsely bright smile toward him as she moved through the doorway. "Your steward is here, my lord."

"Send him in."

Joseph lowered his feet to the floor and buried his face in his hands, grateful that at least Ani would demand nothing of him so early in the morning.

Asenath kept her composure until she reentered her chamber, then she sank to her bed and covered her face as the salty tears of despair splashed her fingertips. Life was not fair! Of all the women in Thebes, she should have been the most blessed, for everything Zaphenath-paneah touched thrived and blossomed under his care. His God had blessed him with beauty, wealth, power, wisdom, and the adoration of the Egyptian nation, yet tongues throughout the royal court were wagging because his wife apparently could no longer bear him children.

She loved Ephraim and Manasseh dearly, but their lives had been won without a struggle. They fell from her womb as easily as she had learned to love her husband. A powerful man needed many sons, and Zaphenath-paneah should have had more than a dozen, yet she could offer only two. Three times she had conceived children and failed to bring them into the world, and now, at twenty-four, the bloom of her youth was fading. Once she had even asked if her husband would be willing to sleep with her maid, Mandisa, in order to gain more sons, but he only shook his head and smiled at her in tender refusal. He kept insisting he was happy, and he was careful that she should not conceive again, yet Asenath did not believe that a man who had everything could be satisfied with only two sons.

Rumors from the palace did not help her anxious state of mind. Tattling tongues and jealous palace rivals had often gossiped that Asenath's beloved was secretly in love with Queen Tuya, Pharaoh's royal mother. Within the last week, Asenath heard rumors that Zaphenath-paneah had even asked Queen Tuya to marry him. And only a few months ago, a rival to the throne had accused the vizier of fathering Pharaoh Amenhotep. Her beloved was found innocent of the charge, and his accusers were sent into exile, but a shadow of doubt lingered in Asenath's mind. Queen Tuya was breathtakingly lovely, even for a mature woman, and she and Zaphenath-paneah shared a past of which Asenath could never be a part.

Her husband loved her, of that she had no doubt. But they were fifteen years apart in age, and she often felt that he thought of her as someone to please and pet, a child to guide and spoil. She had been a mere girl of fifteen when Pharaoh Tuthmosis IV presented her to the newly proclaimed vizier as a prize and reward, and Zaphenath-paneah had guided her to womanhood and thrilled her with the power of his unseen and almighty God. And she *had* been like a child, easily impressed, devoutly in love with her husband's strength and character, overwhelmed by his integrity and complete kindness.

During the years of plenty she had loved him with the ardent hero worship of an adolescent. Now that she had reached mature womanhood, she yearned to love him as an equal, a *partner*. But what could she do to foster this kind of love? He did not need her to manage the estate. Ani ably handled the house, the fields, the entire government of the vizier's villa and saw that Ephraim and Manasseh received instruction from the most capable tutors in the kingdom. Tarik controlled the guards and the force of men necessary to safeguard the vizier's family. Mandisa saw to every personal need Asenath or her sons might ever anticipate. There was little left for her to do.

If she were to become more than her husband's child-bride, she would have to prove herself worthy of him. She would have to provide something no one else could: sons.

She wiped her tears from her eyes, gathering her courage. Until now she had been willing to wait and hope that her husband's desire for more children would override his insistence that she was not strong enough to endure another pregnancy. But her patient waiting had come to an end. She had stolen a look at his ten brothers, and she had inwardly trembled after seeing his reaction to their reunion. Though he had tried to hide his feelings, his meeting with them had left him sorely shaken. His eyes had glinted with hope and fear and something else . . . a sense of *completeness*, an overriding joy at being reunited with his family.

She herself had been overwhelmed by the realization that a single man could have twelve powerful sons, any one of whom would stand out in a crowd. And her husband, the brightest of them all, had just two.

She clenched her jaw to kill the sob in her throat. She would have to do something. If Zaphenath-paneah would not sleep with her handmaid or take another wife, Asenath would bear him sons herself. And since her husband's invisible God had been unable to give life to the children within her womb, she would return to the gods of her childhood.

Her father served as a high priest at On, known more familiarly as Heliopolis. Tomorrow she would arrange for a caravan. She would go home and consult her father about her situation. And while she sojourned at Heliopolis, the primeval birthplace of the earth, she would beg her father's gods for another son.

Zaphenath-paneah would not like the idea of her journeying so far to worship another god, but what her husband did not know could not disturb him.

～ Eight ～

SIMEON STIRRED ON HIS BED AS SOUNDS OF activity reached his ears. Cattle lowed in the stockyard. Egyptian slaves laughed and chattered together outside his chamber as they went about their morning chores. Occasionally he heard the squeak of saddles and the shudder of horses—the magnificent animals he had glimpsed only from a distance. On this morning the scent of hot dry earth mingled with the lusty odors of dust and livestock, and the mouth-watering aroma of baking bread wafted into his room from the kitchens.

How clever was this vizier, how fiendishly evil! While pretending to attend to Simeon's comfort, this brilliant madman had instead arranged for even sounds and smells to torture his prisoner. Of what comfort was a spacious well-furnished room, when the man inside yearned to be outdoors in the discipline of the sun? To hear horses and not examine them was agony. To smell baking bread and not taste it was an exquisite torment. He had been given a soft bed; he was used to sleeping in the sand with his head pillowed upon a rock. Four stout walls isolated him from the activity of the household; Simeon was accustomed to the constant company of his brothers, his sons, and his servants. Someone had left a breakfast of fruit and milk on a tray inside the door; he wanted goat meat and honey over rough brown bread.

How long could he endure this unbearable torture? He could have borne the claustrophobia of the prison pit better than the soft succor of this brightly painted room.

Frustrated beyond endurance, he closed his eyes and screamed in fury.

⌒⌒ Nine ⌒⌒

"USE THE GREEN EYE COLOR TODAY, MANDISA," Asenath said the next morning, peering into her looking brass with a perturbed expression. "We are going to visit my father at Heliopolis. He mustn't think that I look tired or aged."

"You? Aged?" Mandisa managed a diplomatic laugh as she picked up the delicate alabaster kohl pot containing her mistress's favorite color. "You are five years younger than I, my lady. If you are aged, then I am as old as Pharaoh's beard."

Asenath stared into the mirror for a moment, then burst out laughing. Though only twelve and unable to grow a beard himself, the Pharaoh Amenhotep wore the royal beard of state on all official occasions. The long narrow-braided hairpiece, attached to the king's chin by straps that hung over his ears, had been worn by a succession of pharaohs, including Hatshepsut, a woman who ruled in her young son's place for twenty-one years.

Mandisa smiled at the light of joy in her mistress's eyes. After the death of her last baby, Asenath had been troubled and depressed for many months. She had done nothing but lie on her bed and moan that she had nothing to offer her husband. But on this morning, at least, Asenath seemed happy to put the dark past behind her.

"What will you wear, my lady?" Mandisa asked. She pulled the polished stone applicator from the narrow tube and gently stirred the iridescent mixture that would sparkle like the green waters of the sunlit Nile on her mistress's eyelids.

"I think," Asenath answered, closing her eyes while Mandisa applied her cosmetics, "that I shall wear the new beaded gown created for me last week. And the fringed wig with many layers. My father has an appreciative eye for new fashions."

"A good choice, my lady," Mandisa answered. She put down the alabaster container and picked up the black kohl pot to outline her lady's eyes. As she stirred the applicator in the narrow tube, she wondered if she dared ask what had suddenly brought on this desire to visit the priest of Heliopolis. Mandisa could not remember Asenath ever venturing out to visit her father. The venerable priest had only come to Thebes three times: once to pay his respects upon Pharaoh's coronation, and twice to congratulate his daughter after the birth of her sons.

"I know what you are thinking," Asenath said, looking up at Mandisa with a faint gleam of reproach in her eyes. "You may as well ask, Mandisa. You'll worm the answers out of me sooner or later."

Mandisa felt an unwelcome blush creep into her cheeks. "It does not matter why you want to visit your father, my lady. My only wish is to serve you."

An easy smile played at the corners of her mistress's mouth. "Then serve me well in this: whatever I may do in Heliopolis, you need not mention it to my husband."

Mandisa bowed her head. "As you wish. But if you have need of anything, I am certain my lord the vizier would move heaven and earth to procure it for you."

"What I need the vizier cannot procure for me," Asenath said, picking up the looking brass again. "And I have tried to move heaven, but my prayers to the invisible God have availed nothing. I will speak to my father and sacrifice in his sacred temple. Then we shall see if my petitions are successful."

———

Mandisa hurried through the hall of the villa toward the

spacious kitchen. She had less than a quarter of an hour to say farewell to Adom, take the vizier's captive his daily ration, and meet her mistress in the courtyard to join the caravan to Heliopolis. For a moment she regretted her decision to help the vizier with the rugged Canaanite. She was a ladies' maid, after all, and unaccustomed to the ways of a brutish goatherder, even if he was the vizier's half brother. But Zaphenath-paneah had asked. And since the day he had found her abandoned, impoverished, and desperate enough to sell herself and her son into slavery, Mandisa had not been able to refuse her gracious master anything.

She found Halima in the kitchen, her round face flushed by the heat from the fiery ovens. "Hurry, help me prepare the tray and let us be on our way to him," Mandisa said, taking a moment to wipe a trickle of perspiration from her forehead. Her braided wig seemed unusually hot and heavy, and she found herself wishing she could go bareheaded like Halima.

"Must I go with you again into *that* room?" Halima asked, pressing her hands to her ample chest. She cast Mandisa a frightened glance. "He is so loud! You did not hear him, for his room lies far away from the family quarters, but yesterday he screamed for more than an hour. Though I couldn't understand a word of what he said, I'm sure he cursed us, our master, and even Pharaoh himself."

"Then he shall answer to us, our master, and Pharaoh," Mandisa said, placing a tray in Halima's outstretched hands. Rummaging through baskets, bowls, and jars, she selected foods she thought the man might like—a hearty helping of ox meat basted with sweet-scented honey and a bowl of brown beans and chick-peas mixed with lotus seeds and flavored with marjoram, coriander, and dill. She grabbed a slice of bread that had already been properly softened with water, and a jug of beer flavored with pomegranates and figs.

"That platter is fit for Pharaoh's table," Halima said, eyeing the food with a covetous glance, "but the loathsome toad to whom it is going will not appreciate one bite."

"He's not a loathsome toad," Mandisa said, moving through the doorway ahead of Halima. "A loud one, perhaps, but not loathsome."

———

Simeon stiffened on his bed as he heard the wooden bolt slide away from the door. The treble murmur of voices told him that the two women stood outside—the pretty one who spoke his language and the hefty one with eyes as wide and nervous as a rabbit's.

He bit back an oath, annoyed that they did not send someone more important or daunting to deal with him. Did no one know, or care, that a son of Jacob was imprisoned in this Egyptian idolater's house? Jacob was Israel, the keeper of God Almighty's covenant promise to bless the entire world! Jacob was a leader among the people of Canaan, both a wealthy man and a respected one. And Simeon was his second-born son!

The door opened and the timid woman held it while the pretty one walked in and placed the tray on a stand near the bed. She had courage, he had to admit, especially since he had recently decided to do whatever he could to make the Egyptian vizier regret his decision to imprison a son of Israel.

"Well?" she asked in his language. She swallowed hard, lifted her chin, and boldly met his gaze. "Have you need of anything today? Have you any news for my master the vizier?"

"I want proper food," he said, making a face as he reached out and poked a finger into the soggy bread. "Real meat cooked directly over the fire, not boiled to mush in a pot."

She sighed and turned away, ignoring him. How dare she! His mouth tightening with mutiny, he scooped up the hunk of meat and flung it across the room. True to his aim, the congealed glob missed her head by inches and struck the wall. Like a stubborn living creature, it clung to the painted plaster for a moment, then slid down, marking the wall with a sticky brown trail.

The timorous woman squeaked and covered her mouth with her hands, but the slender one turned and came toward him, her hands on her hips. "If you continue to waste your food in that way," she said in the tight tone she might have used to scold a child, "you will starve. The vizier's cooks do not feed men who do not appreciate their efforts."

"I would rather starve with my brothers than eat this rot," Simeon snapped, glaring up at her.

"Your brothers," she said, throwing the words at him like carefully aimed stones, "are neither starving nor complaining. The vizier sent them away with bags of Egypt's best grain and their treasure as well. They have their silver they brought from Canaan; their bellies are full, and because you are gone, they are enjoying peaceful quiet—probably for the first time in their lives!"

"Careful, woman," Simeon said, rancor sharpening his voice. "She who uses a sharp tongue will cut her own throat."

"You'd do well to heed your own advice," she answered, picking up the tray. Without another word, she turned to leave.

"Wait," he called, reaching out a hand to stop her. She jerked away in surprise at his touch, and he frowned at the revulsion on her face.

"What sort of game is your master playing?" he asked, choosing to overlook her expression. "Why does he accuse my brothers of spying and then fulfill their request to buy grain? And why would he return their silver?" He lowered his voice a fraction. "Is he truly mad?"

She paused, a flutter of apprehension shadowing her face as if she had said too much. "I do not question my master," she answered finally, moving resolutely toward the door. "And you should not, either. His way is not always my way, but he holds my life in his hands, as he holds yours.''

"He holds nothing of mine," Simeon retorted, his temper flaring. He lay back upon the bed and crossed his hands under his head. "And yes, I have a message for your master. Tell him I defy him. Tell him that I intend to make his life miserable. Indeed, I will make you all miserable until he releases me. Or let him kill me, I care not. But if my brothers return and find that I am no longer here, your master will have to deal with Jacob of Hebron."

Inexplicably, she handed the tray to the fearful slave, then turned and faced Simeon again, every curve of her body speaking defiance. "You will not order me around," the woman answered, lifting her chin in a fiercely proud gesture. "I am not a slave but a free woman and handmaid to Lady Asenath. I am here because my master cares whether or not you are comfortable. If I were you, I would try to show a bit of gratitude."

"Your master may rot in Sheol!" Simeon retorted, rolling to his feet. He clenched a fist, ready to strike something, but she saw the gesture and quickly stepped through the doorway.

"If anger is your meat, you may eat it for dinner," she said, throwing him a bright smile. "We will be out of your way."

He picked up a vase and flung it to the wall with all his might, but the woman slammed the door. Amid the shattering of pottery, Simeon heard the bolt slide into place.

SIMEON

His heart is as hard as a stone;
Even as hard as a lower millstone.

Job 41:24

~∽ Ten ∾~

LIKE A CAGED ANIMAL, SIMEON PACED BACK AND forth in the darkness of his chamber. The sun had not yet risen. Soft gray shadows still decorated the bed, the chair, the chest against the wall. He hated the gilded luxury. The room was nothing but a pleasure palace for soft Egyptians. And the endless solitary confinement, without the company of his brothers or anyone who could speak his language, tortured Simeon worse than physical pain.

Within the first two hours of his imprisonment he had considered and abandoned every means of escape. Only one door led into the room, and he knew it was securely barred and bolted. He would not be able to dig through the polished marble floor with his bare hands, and he had no tools. Even if he could chisel a passage through the thick walls, shiny with painted plaster, they only led to other hallways in the vizier's villa. Two high windows brought in air and light from the outside, but though they were as wide as Simeon was tall, they were no more than a hand's length in height. A child might have been able to slip through the opening and drop to the ground below, but Simeon would never fit.

He had never been so alone in his forty-five years, and Simeon was horrified to realize that solitude frightened him. With no human companionship, ghosts from the past rose in his memory, and he spent his daylight hours pacing as if he could outrun them. In moments of unendurable frustration, he pounded the walls, cracking the plaster, then fell upon his bed, slumped in morose musings. When tides of weariness and despair completely engulfed his body, merciful darkness and sleep would press down upon him.

But he could not find rest or peace, even in sleep. Often he dreamed that he stood in the center of a burning lake, unable to escape the heat that split his lips and parched his tongue. Other nights he would awaken in a cold sweat, convinced that an arm or a leg was missing, torn away. Awake and shivering in the dark, Simeon tasted thoughts as bitter as gall until the endless night finally grayed into dawn. Instead of relief, however, the sun brought him new resolve to thwart his captors and a fresh hatred for Zaphenath-paneah and all things Egyptian.

At his moments of greatest loneliness he almost hoped to see the dark-eyed interpreter, reasoning that hostile discourse with an acid-tongued wench was better than no conversation at all. But she had not appeared since the day she warned him that anger would be his dinner. Now only the pale plump servant brought his food, and she was always accompanied by the small tightly muscled man in charge of the vizier's guard.

Their morning routine did not vary. The guard would slide the bolt and open the door, a strong light of disapproval in his eyes as he stared at Simeon. As quick as a rat down a rope, the slave would rush in, leave the tray on its stand, empty the sand-filled drawer under the wooden toilet seat into a refuse container, then hurry out of the room. The guard never spoke but watched Simeon with speculative, cautious eyes until the slave girl had safely left the chamber. Then the door would close, and the bolt once again rumble into place.

Simeon stopped his frantic pacing and slammed his fist against the wall, his breath burning in his throat. Oh, if only Levi were here with him! Levi was cunning and clever. He would think of a ruse, some way to get the guard into the chamber. While one of them held that sloe-eyed Egyptian in a rear hug hold, the other would grab the guard's sword and cut the tendon at the man's ankle. After a front snap kick to the Egyptian's groin, they'd leave him gasping on the floor while they stole horses from the courtyard. The Egyptians would try to catch them, but Simeon and Levi would be halfway back to their tents in Hebron before the vizier and his men gathered their wits enough to pursue them.

A cynical inner voice cut through his reckless thoughts. *You are alone, fool, without Levi, without Reuben, without even the younger ones, Issachar and Zebulun. They are at home with their wives and children and do not even think of you.*

Did they think of him? Had any of his brothers made plans to rescue him? If Reuben or Levi had been taken prisoner, Simeon knew he would have rallied the others to storm the vizier's house. Israel possessed great wealth, and though the cursed vizier was undeniably clever, he was obviously not well-informed enough to know who Jacob of Hebron was. If Zaphenath-paneah had known, he would have asked for compensation and arranged for Simeon's return. Jacob's second-born son was certainly worth his weight in silver, unless . . .

Would Father care enough to send a ransom for the Destroyer? His father did not like him, Simeon knew, for many reasons, but chiefly because he sprang from Leah, not the lovely Rachel. Benjamin was the only fruit remaining from that beloved wife.

Leaning against the wall, Simeon slid into a crouch, then hugged his knees to his chest. With every morning that passed, he wondered if his father might not be more willing to let Simeon languish in prison and let the rest of the family starve than to send Benjamin, his nearest and best-beloved son, to Egypt.

He bit his lip until it throbbed like his pulse. He had never thought that he could miss the babble of his brothers' bickering or the sound of their women complaining. Even the laughter of the children, which had always grated on Simeon's nerves, would be welcome in this silent heathen house. Except for a busy hour in the morning and the meal-time at noon, this Egyptian palace was altogether too quiet for him. Though he occasionally heard the lowing of cattle and the distant thunder of drumming horses' hooves, the sounds of running water from the garden muted the ordinary noises of community.

Simeon let his head fall back to the wall. A faint light glowing low from the opposite window indicated that the sun had crossed her threshold. Unconsciously, his entire being concentrated in his right ear for the sound of approaching footsteps. Today he would insult the guard again. He might even threaten the plump slave girl. He'd do anything he could to rouse the guard to anger, for if the captain lost his temper, perhaps he would remove Simeon from this cell and drag him before the exalted vizier. Simeon would yet show the great Zaphenath-paneah how fierce a son of Israel could be.

His heart thumped against his rib cage at the soft sound of voices and the patter of sandaled feet. The woman and the captain were near, doubtless eager to get this despised chore out of the way before they began their day. He heard a whisper at the door, then the dull grumble of the beam as it slid from its place.

The door opened and the guard's blank eyes met his. Simeon stood, anxious to face his jailers.

"Speak to me, you whose breath is fouler than a lizard's," he growled, moving forward. But the stalwart Egyptian did not respond. The woman paused and glanced at the guard; he nodded and placed his hand upon his sword. The unspoken message was clear: *make a move and I will strike.*

Simeon tensed, debating his options. Every fiber of his being screamed for action. The Egyptian captain came only to Simeon's shoulder, so he was not a great threat, but he was quick. He would draw his blade if Simeon lunged, and the woman would panic and might be hurt in the struggle.

Simeon could not, would not, be responsible for hurting a woman. Not after what had happened to Dinah.

Reluctantly he stepped back.

Taking a deep unsteady breath, the woman advanced into the room, lowered the tray to its stand, then scurried to clean the toilet area. Simeon crossed his arms and would have moved to sit on the bed, but a muscle flicked angrily at the guard's jaw, and Simeon understood the silent warning. The mighty vizier had probably told the guards that this Canaanite was no great prize and would not be missed if his death proved necessary.

As the woman went about her work, the guard stood frozen in the doorway, his painted eyes narrowing into a bemused thoughtful expression. *Why does he look at me that way? Does this idolatrous dog dare to mock a son of Jacob?* In a silent fury that spoke louder than words, Simeon reached out and slammed his arm down on the fragile table next to him, shattering the delicate wood. The slave screamed in fright, nearly dropping the burden in her arms, but the guard only lifted an inquisitive eyebrow.

"You will not jeer at me, you pompous jackal," Simeon roared, fury nearly choking him. "You think I am your captive, but I am only waiting until my brothers return. Then you shall know the full fury of Jacob's wrath. You shall see the power of Israel's God unleashed upon this land!"

Though the outburst left Simeon seething with anger and contempt, the captain only motioned for the slave girl to hurry about her duties. As she finished her work, the guard folded his arms and stared at Simeon. His brows flickered a little as he spoke slowly in the Canaanite language. "My master commands me to wish you peace." After making that simple declaration, he stepped back and motioned for the slave girl to leave.

Simeon watched in wordless amazement as the woman hurried past. Like a child who gazes at an animal in mingled wonder and fear, she lifted her eyes and stole a terrified glance at his face.

Simeon sank onto his bed, his eyes clouded with visions of the past. His wife had worn just such an expression when he had carried her to his tent.

~~ Eleven ~~

SIMEON'S FIRST WIFE HAD LIVED IN THE CITY OF Shechem, the prosperous walled town situated in the green valley between Mount Ebal and Mount Gerizim. As the children of Israel prepared to move their flocks and tents into the region, Jacob, who had been strong and confident in those days, reminded his sons that when Abraham set out from Ur of the Chaldeans, he and his people passed through the country as far as Shechem.

"There the Lord appeared to my father's father and said, 'To your descendants I will give this land,' " Jacob announced one night at dinner, his hand falling upon young Joseph's shoulder as he spoke. "And so to you and your descendants, my sons, this land will one day belong."

Simeon had not fully understood why Jacob chose to reenter Canaan after so long an absence. He had been only twenty-two at the time and ignorant of the situation that led to the dispute between his father and his uncle, Esau. He only knew that Jacob woke up one morning determined to take his people and possessions from the region of Haran where he had married Rachel and Leah to the land God had promised them.

Simeon left his youth and idealism behind forever on the day Esau marched with four hundred men to meet his brother, Jacob. There, in a visible display for the entire world to see, Jacob defined the depths and limits of his love, and Simeon's eyes opened to see his father for the first time.

Jacob had ordered that gifts for Esau be sent in the forefront of the procession: she-goats, two hundred, and kids, twenty; ewes, two hundred, and rams, twenty; nursing camels and their young, thirty; cows, forty, and bulls, ten; she-asses, twenty, and colts, ten.

After the generous gifts, Jacob's own herds of cattle, sheep, and goats followed.

Finally, Jacob advanced his family. The two female slaves, handmaids to Jacob's wives, mounted donkeys. With their four sons, they fell into line behind the flocks and herds. Simeon remembered the gritty taste of desert sand between his teeth as he stood beside his mother, waiting for his father to lead them to meet the brother he feared. But Jacob had not even glanced their way. "Leah, you and your children will proceed next," he called over his shoulder, his dark eyes squinting toward the distant horizon.

"My lord?" Leah cried, stunned to the point of tears. But Jacob had been too engrossed in what might happen to hear her.

"Go now, and your sons with you," he said, impatiently gesturing toward them as if they were little more than stray cattle. "Have the older boys take care of Dinah. Do not fear, for I will go ahead of all of you. But take care that Rachel and Joseph remain at the back of the procession, in case trouble lies ahead."

In that instant, Simeon understood with fearful clarity a lifetime of his mother's tears, his aunt's victorious smile, and his father's haggard expression. His father did not love his mother! He loved beautiful Rachel, Joseph's mother, the wife who now struggled with the nausea of another pregnancy.

It stood in front of the morning, that truth, killing all joy. In that moment, the larger-than-life enthusiasm with which Simeon had confronted the world compressed into a shrinking space between the weight of his mother's despair and his own welling anger. How could his father treat his first wife with such blatant indifference?

Reluctantly, his movements stiff and awkward, Simeon had followed his mother and brothers in the processional line. The harder he tried to deny the truth, the more it persisted. He had always accepted his father's aloofness as a natural part of the way things were, yet Jacob had now cut through the veil of assumption and laid bare his true feelings.

"If Esau comes with an approaching army to kill us all," Jacob's actions proclaimed, "let him kill me, the maids and their children, Leah and her sons, but Rachel and Joseph must remain alive to inherit God's blessing."

The bitterness of gall rose in Simeon's throat as the desert wind slashed and drove against him and his brothers. Beside him, his mother's face was pale, her eyes red-rimmed, her chin aquiver with unspoken hurt. For the first time Simeon understood why.

Esau had not come to kill but to forgive. With joy and praise, Jacob, now known as Israel, reentered the land of his father with all his family and all his belongings. After a few weeks, they came to the town of Shechem and Jacob bought a piece of land from Hamor. There he erected an altar and called it El-Elohe-Israel, *God, the God of Israel.* Simeon watched his father worship the almighty God called El Shaddai, but his heart, filled with bitterness for his mother's pitiable plight, was not stirred by his father's fervent reverence.

In the camp, Simeon now looked upon the usual comings and goings of his family with enlightened and wary eyes. Rachel, her maid, and her children lived in a spacious, well-appointed tent, while Leah dwelt with her handmaid and her younger children in another tent not nearly as large or luxurious.

Jacob's older sons, Reuben, Simeon, Levi, Judah, Dan, and Naphtali, had long since left the women's tents to sleep under the stars with the flocks they guarded. Reuben and Levi had already begun to talk about taking wives for themselves, but Simeon could not bring himself to discuss marriage, especially not in his mother's presence. Couldn't the others see the pain in her pale eyes? Were they, too, going to abandon her?

Of all Leah's children, Simeon supposed that Dinah might have a special empathy for their mother's sorrow. After all, Dinah was a woman, too, albeit a young one of fourteen. But he soon discovered that his sister's sympathy turned in only one direction: inward.

One afternoon not long after their arrival at Shechem, he found Dinah sitting outside Leah's tent, her long and lanky form bent into an ungraceful crouch, her face covered by her hands.

"What ails you, sister?" Simeon asked, kneeling beside her. His voice sounded more abrupt than he'd intended, and he made an effort to soften his tone. "This wind is biting, you should go inside."

"Not with her," Dinah whispered brokenly, lifting tear-filled eyes to his face. "I'll not stay inside with Mother one more minute. Rachel isn't feeling well, and Mother is upset. She has taken to her bed with a headache and blames me for everything."

"Rachel carries a baby—she can't help her sickness. But what have you done to upset Mother?" Simeon asked, pushing a tangle of curls away from her wide forehead. "You ought to be more help to her. She does not have an easy time of it here."

"*She* does not have an easy time?" Dinah shrieked, an edge of desperation in her voice. "She is a wife of Jacob, the wealthiest and most respected man in all of Canaan. She has a maid, servants, and the costliest clothing a woman could want. Her husband is respected in the city yonder. By her our father has eight sons."

"But has she his love?" Simeon asked softly. His eyes wandered toward Rachel's tent. Even above the dull roar of the constant wind, he could hear Joseph's carefree laughter spilling from that habitation. "Think, Dinah, of the pain our mother endures constantly. Think of what she must face every night when Father finishes his dinner and then goes"—he inclined his head—"to the *other* tent."

"I don't care!" Dinah screwed up her face like a petulant child. "Mother doesn't have to live with eleven brothers! Mother isn't the only girl. She has a sister! She has never known what is like to be alone, to be the only daughter."

For a moment Simeon was tempted to slap sense into the overgrown girl's head, but he only grunted in disapproval and looked away. "You talk like a spoiled child."

"No." Her voice grew still, and through the dark arch made by her falling hair, he saw a tear run down her cheek. "Look at me, Simeon," she whispered, her tone light and bitter. "I am a grown woman. I am ready to take a husband, but my father and my mother care more for their sons' plans than their only daughter's. They have not given one thought toward finding me a husband. There has been more discussion about finding wives for you and Reuben and Levi."

"I do not want a wife," Simeon said, suddenly bored with the conversation. He slapped sand from his legs and stood. "And if you are wise, little sister, you will go about your business and rejoice that you are a daughter of Israel. Even if you never marry, your life will still be richer and fuller than any Canaanite girl's."

He reached out to pat her on the head the way he always did whenever they had a fight, but Dinah ducked, retreating from his reach. She closed her eyes and shook her head, her signal that he had transgressed the bounds of human understanding.

"You are a fool, Simeon," she whispered, staring past him as the wind blew the mane of tangled curls across her oval face. "You will never understand."

"No. You are the one who does not understand," he said, listening to the sound of his mother's weeping from inside her tent.

———

Dinah wandered away, alone, from the family compound that day, and the next, and the next after that, but

Simeon paid her no mind. She was probably sulking in the desert, he imagined, or trying to incite them to worry about her. She would probably hide if he went out to search for her, so he would not give her the satisfaction of knowing that he'd missed her. But since the Canaanites considered unmarried women legitimate prey, Simeon slipped away from his flocks and his brothers each night and hiked back to the family tents just long enough to make certain that Dinah slept in her usual place beside Leah.

One afternoon he and his brothers had been moving the herds from one field outside Shechem to another, and at the well he saw a group of gaily painted girls. The Canaanite women were godless idolaters, Jacob had warned his sons, and the children of Israel were neither to speak to nor look at them. But forbidden fruit cast a sweet spell, and Simeon found his eyes drifting toward the chattering group of women as he and his brothers approached.

The painted courtesans said nothing but coyly continued their giggling conversation until the sons of Israel were nearly upon them. Suddenly one of the girls shrieked and ran toward the wide gate of the walled city.

"Simeon!" Reuben cried, disbelief echoing in his voice. "That was our sister!"

Simeon started to object but glanced toward the girls again. The remaining circle of women had stopped their chattering and stared at the sons of Jacob with hard stone-cold eyes. Why would they do such a thing? . . . unless Dinah had poisoned them with lies.

"Dinah!" Simeon dropped his shepherd's staff and ran toward the city, his sandaled feet skimming the sandy ground. "Dinah, daughter of Jacob, come out! I must take you home!"

The gray stone of the city's protecting wall flew by his side, but he halted in the wide gateway. A knot of men had gathered there, and they blocked his path, staring at him in undisguised curiosity. The people of Israel had not had many dealings with the men of Shechem, and Simeon instinctively knew he would not be welcomed in the city.

Craning his neck, he peered past the men. Beyond the gate, the city hummed with busy women and romping children, people going about their daily affairs. But nowhere could Simeon see any sign of Dinah.

Faltering before the sharp eyes of the men, Simeon stepped back. "Excuse me," he said, dipping his head in respect. "I thought I saw my sister enter here. But I must have been mistaken."

One of the men snickered and whispered to his companion, and Simeon felt a blush burn the back of his neck. He, one of the chosen people, had no obligation to deal with these uncircumcised barbarians. Before any one of them could speak to him, he whirled and left the gate of Shechem.

Distraught and confused, he and his brothers returned to the fields. A few hours later a messenger arrived from Leah. "Your sister Dinah arrived home a short while ago, her face watered with tears," the servant said. "Your mother asks you to come home at once. Hamor the Hivite is at the compound to speak to your father."

"Hamor the Hivite?" Reuben asked, a frown settling on his brow.

"I have heard of him," Simeon answered. "He lives in the city of Shechem and has a son by the same name." He glared at the messenger. "What was our mother's mood when she bade you come and fetch us?"

The servant's face went grim. "She has not ceased to water her couch with tears. Jacob entertains his guests in a gracious manner, but your mother Leah will not come out of her tent. She remains inside with Dinah, and both women do nothing but weep."

"Why do they weep?" Simeon snapped.

"It is said," the servant whispered, his expression growing hard and resentful, "that Shechem, young son of the prince Hamor, has defiled your sister. By force he has humbled her."

"I knew it!" Simeon slammed his fist upon his palm. "Nothing but evil could come of Dinah's sporting with the women of Shechem. I warned her. I tried to convince her to remain at home!"

"This is not good," Levi said, his fist tightening around his staff. "But we will not cast blame until we have heard the tale." He nodded toward the messenger. "We will come at once."

They hurried home, borne on wings of righteous indignation and morbid curiosity. When they arrived at Israel's camp, they found Hamor the Hivite, a tall slender man with a carefully shaped beard, seated beside Jacob's fire. Hamor rose to his feet in a measure of respect as Jacob acknowledged his sons, then the Hivite extended his hand to introduce a young man who sat beside him.

"This is my son, Shechem," he said, nodding gravely. He paused and drew his richly colored robe closer about his shoulders. "He is a fine youth and stands to inherit all I possess." Respectfully, the older man turned his attention back to Jacob. "The soul of my son longs for your daughter, Dinah. Please give her to him in marriage, then, as I have told you, our communities shall be joined. You shall dwell with us. Your daughters will marry our sons, and your sons may take wives from among our daughters. The land will be open before you to live and travel in it, to acquire property in it. The land is rich, my friend Israel, and we can prosper in this place together."

Simeon felt his anger begin to boil at the older man's words. Hamor offered riches and prosperity as if the land were his to give, but he was an ignorant fool! Why should they share Canaan with this man when God had already promised all of it to Israel and his descendants?

Not to be outdone by his father, the younger man stood. "May I only find favor in your sight," he said, his dark-eyed gaze passing easily from Jacob to his sons. "However much you say to me, I will give in payment. To whatever extreme you multiply the bride-price and the marriage gift, I will give it. Only please, I beg you, give me the girl to be my wife!"

"Hasn't he already taken her?" Reuben growled in Simeon's ear.

"This man has done a disgraceful thing," Dan murmured, his voice pitched for his brothers' ears alone. "Such a thing ought not to be done."

"Careful, brothers," Levi whispered, a considerate smile slipping over his face. "We will not arouse the anger of these people. Hamor is a prince in the land. He commands a large force within the city. Would you have them come and take Dinah by force? We must stall them. We must think of something to bring a respite of time."

Simeon looked to his father. Jacob was watching them, his expression an unreadable mask of stone. Why didn't he rise to Dinah's defense? Why didn't he say something?

As if he had read Simeon's thoughts, Jacob turned to the Hivite. "My sons," he said to Hamor, tilting his head casually toward the brothers, "confer among themselves, my esteemed friends. They are close to their sister, closer even than I am. Since what you propose concerns their future, let them decide what we shall do. I will abide by their wishes."

Hamor frowned slightly at Jacob's words, but Simeon turned to face his brothers with a new sense of purpose. He shouldn't have been surprised that Father wished to cast Dinah off. He had practically washed his hands of all Leah's children since the day of their births. Now Jacob sat dumb by the fire, without remorse for his daughter's defilement, without regrets, without concern for any of them. Very well. Since he didn't care what happened to Dinah, he shouldn't care if his sons chose to avenge their sister. If Jacob would not defend Leah's children, Leah's children would defend one another.

"What shall we do?" Simeon asked, looking up at Reuben.

While Reuben faltered for words, Dan spoke. "We

should give her to this youth. He is a comely lad, and he seems to genuinely care for Dinah. I have heard nothing but good spoken of Hamor's son since we have come to this place."

"We can't give her to uncircumcised idol worshipers!" Judah said, aghast. "And what Hamor suggests is impossible! We should remain a separate and distinct people. We are not to intermarry with those who serve strange gods!"

"Hamor would never accept our refusal," Reuben spoke up at last. "He would see it as a sign of hostility. He and his men would come for her when we least expect it. Can we leave our mother and father unprotected while we are away with the herds? Are we prepared to fight off Hamor's men if they should begin to harass us in the wilderness? We will die if we refuse this man. I am certain of it."

"Then we shall not refuse him," Levi said, a slow smile spreading across his face. "We will give him what he wants, for now. And then we will defeat him before he can defeat us. And we will redeem our sister and bring her back."

"We will give her to them?" Simeon could not believe he had heard correctly.

"Yes," Levi answered, his strong hand gripping the back of Simeon's neck. His eyes smoldered with fire. "We will tell this Hamor and his son that we would be pleased to intermarry with them. But we will say we cannot give our sister to one who is uncircumcised, for that would be a disgrace to us. Only if every man in the city becomes circumcised can we give our daughters to them. We will tell them that if they agree, we will settle among them and become a single people."

"He will never agree," Judah said, shaking his head. "It is too much to ask of a man."

"Did you not see the light of love burning in that young man's eyes?" Levi asked, gesturing toward Hamor's handsome son. "He will agree. I would take an oath on it. And when they have fulfilled their part of the bargain, we will take our sister and make young Shechem pay for his lustful folly."

As much as he wanted to believe Levi, Simeon was honestly surprised when Hamor and Shechem did agree to the proposal. And when Zilpah, Leah's maid, brought Dinah forth from her mother's tent, Simeon gaped in astonishment as his sister walked forward with a smile of genuine joy on her face. He had expected to see pain, humiliation, and shame, but love shone from her gray eyes, lighting her narrow face with a beauty he had never seen in her before.

"I will not delay to do the thing you have requested," Shechem said as he took Dinah's hand. Though he spoke to Jacob and the brothers, his eyes never left his bride's face. "And I accept your daughter as my wife. I will live with her nobly and bring her nothing but honor all the days of her life."

"I will speak to the men of our city tomorrow," Hamor promised, turning to Jacob. "When the men meet at the gate of the city, I will tell them that this union will benefit both of us. We shall live as one—your children and mine—and together we shall become a great nation."

Simeon heard Hamor's words as if from a great distance, so amazed was he by the aura of loveliness that emanated from his sister. Her slim young figure, now enveloped in a gauzy cloak of iridescent colors, moved with the sure grace of a dancer. Loose tendrils of shining dark hair softened her face, and her eyes shone bright in the pale light of the transforming moon. She stepped toward Shechem and reached out, lacing his fingers with her own.

"Can it be?" Simeon whispered to himself. "Can she truly love this son of a goatish barbarian?"

He shook his head, disallowing the thought, and stood aside with his brothers as the wedding couple walked out of the camp toward the dull glow on the horizon that marked the city of Shechem.

———

Three days later, well before sunrise, Levi and Simeon slipped away from the herds and hurried toward the walled city. They had sharpened their daggers, and each brother sprinted with a deadly lance in his right hand. On the previous night, a spying servant had confirmed their hopes. Hamor, prince of the city, had spoken to the other men at the gate. The greedy fools, eager to share wealth with Jacob and his people, had consented to circumcision. And today, twenty-four hours after the mass ritual, every man in the city was bound to be incapacitated and in great pain.

As soon as the first tangerine tints of the rising sun touched the city walls, Simeon and Levi attacked. The brothers dispatched the guards at the gate without a scuffle, and from there they separated, each to go his own murderous way. Revenge was easy, for most of the city's men still lay deep within drug-induced sleep. In each house, Simeon slew every male without remorse while one thought repeated itself in his brain: "For Dinah. For Leah. For those Jacob has cast aside."

The screams of waking women and crying children alerted the settlement's remaining terror-stricken and helpless inhabitants, but Simeon and Levi moved through the city like a stormy sea, overcoming anyone who rose up against them. Simeon felt his pulse quicken when he entered a large house and recognized Hamor in his bed. He struck before the old man even had a chance to protest. A stumbling noise from an adjacent room led Simeon to a slow-moving Shechem, and Simeon paused a moment, his dagger in one hand, his lance in the other. His brother-in-law stared at him with eyes like clear black glass, impossible to read.

As Dinah screamed and threw herself in front of her husband, Simeon dropped his lance and used his free hand to pull her away from the young man crouching on the marriage bed. "Get dressed and rejoice that you are going home," he said, yanking her from the bed by force.

"Simeon!" She shouted his name in a shriek he would

never forget. "What are you doing?"

"I am taking revenge upon the stranger who defiled you. He is not a fit husband for a daughter of Israel."

"But you promised! You and the others—you gave your word!"

"A word spoken to a liar is not a lie."

He crouched and shifted his position, never taking his eyes from the man on the bed. Shechem's eyes seemed to dim, then leaked little strings of tears as he tore his gaze from Simeon to look at Dinah.

Simeon saw his chance and lunged forward, but Dinah grabbed his hand, pulling the dagger from his grasp. Shechem sprang forward, his weight toppling Simeon to the ground. The younger man gasped as he kicked and threw halfhearted punches, but Simeon knew the youth's body had not recovered from the painful events of the day before. He brought his knee up in a forceful thrust, centering on his adversary's vulnerability.

With an agonized cry, Shechem reeled away and coiled into the shadows of the doorway, releasing a tiny whine of mounting dread. Regaining his feet, Simeon looked around for his weapons but saw only a stone in the doorway, a solid doorstop. Using both hands to lift the rock overhead, Simeon brought the stone down, silencing Shechem's cries.

"Sim-e-on!" Dinah tore her clothing and keened the dreadful ululation of mourning. "Why? Why have you done this?"

Simeon rocked back on his heels and stood. Then he brought the palm of his hand across his mouth, wiping a trail of blood from his face. He saw his dagger and lance on the floor and bent to retrieve them. "Get dressed, Dinah. And hurry."

"But, Simeon! I loved him! You killed him! I shall hate you forever!"

Suddenly she was upon him, scratching his arm, struggling for his blade. A scream clawed in her throat as she grappled with him, and for a moment he could do nothing but stare at her, baffled. But then he saw blood from her own hands upon the silver of his dagger and realized that she intended to harm herself with the knife, to die with the idolaters.

"May God forgive you!" Without thinking, he drew back his hand and slapped her hard. Sobbing, she retreated and huddled in a corner, pressing her hand to the red mark on her face.

"You don't know what you are doing," Simeon said, anger and pity twisting his heart as he stared at her. "You are a child. You know nothing of love. And I am taking you from this cursed place, so put on your shoes."

She did not answer but reached for a pair of delicate leather sandals, turning her head as she tied the laces. He heard her whisper in a trembling and broken voice, "You are the one who knows nothing of love. Perhaps you never shall."

Ignoring her words, he pulled her from the floor and led her from Hamor's house. They had just stepped outside when a babble of familiar voices greeted them. "Simeon!" Reuben hailed him, his sword in hand and a smile on his face. "We have come to join you!"

"You are all too late," Levi answered, grinning as he walked up. He reached for Dinah's limp hand and lifted it like a trophy. "We have her back! And every man in the city is dead!"

"It seems the city is ours, then," Judah said, looking around. "Rejoice, brothers, for whatever you see belongs to you. We have conquered this place today in the name of our sister, daughter of Israel!"

His statement brought fresh weeping from Dinah. Sighing in resignation, Simeon caught Asher's eye and told the younger man to take his sister home.

"Are you really taking everything?" Asher asked, his eyes sweeping over the rich settlement as he took Dinah's hand.

"Whatever we can carry or drive out," Levi answered.

"Flocks and herds, donkeys, women, children, and what-ever wealth we find in the houses. The spoils of war, little brother, may be hard won, but they are ours!"

While Asher led Dinah away, Simeon moved through the buildings, helping his brothers herd weeping women and wailing children into the street. One small dismal-looking structure stood in an isolated corner of the city. Simeon approached the sprained door carefully, unable to recall if he'd visited this house earlier on his killing spree.

The single room inside lay wreathed in shadows. One small table near the door bore a handful of treasures, as if the owners of the place had been about to gather their be-longings and flee. Simeon lifted his shepherd's sling from his shoulder and tossed the golden idols, earrings, and sil-ver trinkets inside. A richly colored embroidered garment hung from a peg in the wall, and he took that, too, tossing it over his shoulder. When he felt confident the house had nothing else to offer, he lifted his sling and turned toward the door. A soft gasp broke the stillness, and he froze.

A warning spasm of alarm erupted within him. *Some-one hides under the table. Did one of the men escape us?*

His hand darted to the dagger in his belt. Slowly, care-fully, he pulled it free, then turned in a quick move and knolt. All his fear and anxiety came tumbling out in a flood of curses when he saw a young woman crouching beneath the table, bright copper ringlets curled on her forehead and the nape of her neck. Her frail knees trembled beneath the hem of her tunic, and her dirty bare feet were delicate, com-pletely unlike Dinah's.

Something about her fragile innocence sapped the kill-ing strength of his arm. "Come out," he commanded, his hand dropping harmlessly to his side. He gentled his voice and gestured to her. "Come out or die, for we will burn what is left of this city."

She crawled out then, a girl of about Dinah's age with tangled curls, delicate wrists, and eyes as wild as a spooked horse's. And when Simeon lay with her under the stars that night and claimed her as his wife, he told himself the wrongs committed at Shechem had finally been put right.

————

In one morning Jacob had gone from being one of the wealthiest men in the land to *the* wealthiest from horizon to horizon, but his face purpled in fury when his sons rode victoriously into camp, bringing the treasures of Shechem with them. Without a word he took Joseph's hand and stalked to Rachel's tent, steadfastly refusing to look upon his other sons.

Simeon silently watched him go, feeling the distance between them like a widening space within him. What had he expected? Congratulations? A display of fatherly pride?

Jacob confronted them later as they gathered to eat. "How could you do this?" he cried, his features contorted with shock and anger. "Without thinking, you have rushed in a violent flight toward destruction, both ours and Shechem's!"

Shifting awkwardly from foot to foot, Simeon looked down at his hands. Dried blood still darkened the crescents of his nails, deep smears covered his arms and even his legs. Levi and the others looked just as gruesome.

"Look at you. You are all a shame to me!" Jacob cried, pathos in his voice. "Adorned in jewels yet dripping with blood!"

"We had to do something, Father," Reuben spoke up. "Simeon and Levi were right to take vengeance for our sister's cause. And you gave us permission. You told Hamor that we would decide what happened to our sister."

"So we did," Levi said, thrusting his jaw forward. "And you should be proud. We have avenged our sister. We have brought you slaves and great riches."

"What did it matter if Dinah married Shechem?" Jacob asked, lifting his hands in despair. "The girl was happy. And I would not have allowed you to take women from that city! I wanted you to journey to your eastern kinsmen for brides, just as I traveled to Haran to find my Rachel."

Simeon's rebellious emotions erupted. "And your Leah," he said, a sudden thin chill on the edge of his words. His eyes glared hotly into his father's.

Jacob stared at him a moment before answering. "Yes, and Leah," he answered, nodding slowly. "But now you have taken the women of Shechem by force, a worse crime than what Shechem did, for Dinah has confessed to me that she encouraged the young man's attentions. You have brought trouble on me. You have made me repugnant among the inhabitants of the land. In fear for their cities, the Canaanites and the Perizzites will attack us. And we are few in number, while they are strong. Prepare yourselves, my foolish sons, for they will gather against us. If God Shaddai does not protect us, we will be destroyed."

"Should he have treated our sister like a harlot?" Reuben growled, stepping forward.

But Jacob waved him away and turned toward the tent where Rachel and his beloved Joseph waited.

———

The next day Jacob commanded the entire household to gather up the tents, animals, tools, and shelters. "God has told me to go to Bethel," he told his sons. "I am to construct a slaughter site there to God-El, who appeared to me when I fled from my brother, Esau."

A vigor that had not been apparent the day before emanated from his body, and an odd vitality rang in his voice. His eyes seemed to probe his sons' souls as he looked at them. "You must put away the foreign gods you took from the houses of Shechem. You must bathe and purify yourselves and change out of the colored garments you took from the men of Shechem. Take the rings from your fingers and ears and bring all the spoil from that place to me."

Spurred by their father's command and their own guilty consciences, Simeon and his brothers gathered all the goods they had plundered from the walled city. They released the slaves and piled the pilfered goods into baskets. The girl Simeon had taken, however, refused to leave with her own people. "Nothing remains for me in that place," she said simply, her eyes as clear as the wide sky above. "You called me your wife, and so you shall be my husband from this day forward."

After all the goods had been accumulated, Jacob himself led the train of treasure-laden donkeys to the huge oak that stood outside Shechem. There he and his sons buried all the spoils. Shortly after returning to camp, the entire company set out for Bethel.

The journey was tedious, the weather hot and dry. Whirlwinds spun and swayed across the plains; the distant cliffs shimmered in the rising heat mirage. Dinah and Leah rode in woven baskets that hung on opposite sides of a single camel's hump, and Simeon noticed that Dinah spent much of the time with her head hanging out of the swaying basket, her face as pale as death. On a camel at the end of the caravan, the very pregnant Rachel curled into a similar basket opposite eight-year-old Joseph, who was too spoiled to dirty his feet on the trek.

After reaching Bethel, where Jacob built an altar and spoke with his God, the company moved on. They were nearing Ephrath, or Bethlehem, when a shrill cry halted the caravan. Jacob's face paled when Zilpah announced that Rachel's travail had begun. The uncomfortable journey and the heat had apparently sapped her fragile strength, for shortly after giving life to another son, Jacob's beloved Rachel died.

Simeon, his brothers, and the servants sat silently outside the hastily constructed tent, their ears tuned to the mingled cries of a newborn infant and his grief-stricken father. After three hours of weeping in protracted grief, a strangely quiet Jacob stepped out of Rachel's tent and held the baby aloft for all to see.

"His name is Benjamin, son of my right hand," he said, his voice breaking. "And she who bore him is lost."

Jacob's face had the withered look of a thirsty rose. The life had completely gone out of it. He sat in the shade of the tent, holding the baby on his knees as tears rolled silently down his craggy face. Mumbling excuses about tending the herds or erecting shelters, Jacob's other sons slipped away one by one. As an act of mercy, Judah pulled Joseph from the tent where Leah and the maids prepared Rachel's body for burial.

Simeon remained outside near Jacob, wondering if he should feel guilty for the relief that filled his soul. He had liked Rachel and was sorry for her death, but for his mother's sake he could not honestly mourn. And so he sat across from his father, grappling with his thoughts and silently rejoicing that after years of suffering Leah would finally enjoy her husband's undivided attention.

The thick air around them seemed oppressive, the desert light melancholy and filled with shadows. The baby mewled softly, seeking a life-giving breast, but Jacob did not rise to surrender it to a nurse. He quietly examined the child, an expression of mingled fascination and revulsion on his face, much as one would regard a beautifully jeweled dagger. Then the baby cried in earnest, flailing its tiny fist. Lifting the infant, Jacob pressed his lips to the child's wrinkled forehead.

Simeon sighed, grateful for at least one small tear in the tent of grimness enclosing his father. Jacob's soul was still heavy with grief, but in time he would surely come to cherish the child.

"He is a handsome baby," Simeon offered, hoping to encourage.

"Simeon," his father spoke without lifting his eyes from the baby in his arms, "I want you to know something."

"Yes, Father?"

Jacob's face hardened into a marble effigy of contempt. "If you and Levi had not attacked the city of Shechem, we would not be here in the wilderness. And Rachel, who could not withstand the journey, would not be dead."

He said no more, but his meaning and intention were clear: he held Simeon and Levi responsible for Rachel's death, and he would not soon forgive them.

Simeon bowed his head in respect and said nothing as he stood to his feet and walked away. But he felt ice spreading through his stomach, frigid fingers seeping into every pore of his skin. The coldness, like fire, twisted and turned inside him, upending every belief, every dream, every hope, until Simeon knew he would never be the same again.

~⌐ Twelve ⌐~

A PAIR OF OBELISKS, CALLED *TEKHENU* BY THE Egyptians, rose up from the sacred city of Heliopolis at the site where the annual inundation of the Nile first began to recede. The city's soil, fertilized by rich layers of silt and nurtured by the life-giving sun, received a full measure of all the gods had to offer. To the Egyptians the hallowed ground represented rebirth and creation, and Mandisa knew her mistress hoped the holy city would bless her body and enable her to bring forth another son for Zaphenath-paneah.

They had enjoyed a week's visit with Asenath's parents, but now Asenath wanted Mandisa to rise before dawn each morning and accompany her to the sacred temple of Khnum. Her mistress wished to greet the god as he awoke in hopes of impressing him with the earnestness of her desire.

"Perhaps," she whispered one morning as Mandisa carefully applied kohl to her lady's sleep-heavy eyelids, "the god will think I have remained in his temple all night, attending to him without even stopping to sleep."

Mandisa lifted a brow but did not answer. If a god could be so easily fooled, how could he be a god? For many months she had watched Zaphenath-paneah, and she had to admit that his great and invisible God seemed more powerful and more logical than any Egypt had to offer. She had heard the master tell his sons that his God was all-seeing and all-knowing, so nothing a man did could trick or sway the Almighty One. God Shaddai knew every individual's name. He even knew and understood a man's inner heart and its secrets. Apparently Asenath had never placed much faith in her husband's lessons.

"Khnum is the divine potter. He fashioned the other gods, the divine kings, and all mortals on his potter's plate," Asenath murmured sleepily as Mandisa completed her toilette. "He will not fail me."

"Why is this god special, my lady?" Mandisa asked, trying to be polite.

Asenath let her bare head drop forward onto her folded arms. "He knows the secrets of creation. His priests taught the ancient pharaohs how to mix water and clay to create the living stone of the pyramids. His breath turned a handful of reddish brown clay into the first mortal man."

"And you think this god of clay and pottery can create new life in you?" Mandisa whispered, slipping her mistress's wig from its stand. She waited a moment until Asenath opened one eye, then groggily lifted her head.

"He will," the young woman answered, "for I have my father's prayers to support me. He has dedicated himself anew to the worship of Khnum, and he is a powerful priest. We are to join him today, Mandisa, and pray that the god will think favorably of us."

Mandisa slipped the wig over her mistress's shorn head, then pulled it downward for a tight fit. For Asenath's sake, she hoped that some good would be accomplished soon. She missed her son. She missed Thebes. She missed Halima. *May the gods help me*, she thought, patting Asenath's shoulders in approval of the lady's looks. *Though I was happy to leave the responsibility of his care behind, I think I might even miss the noise of the obnoxious captive in my lord's house.*

———

Potiphera, high priest of On, clapped his hands in booming approval when his lovely daughter stepped out of her litter at the temple. As shriveled as an old fig, he wore the white kilt of the priesthood and had shaved his entire body, including his eyebrows, lashes, and whatever sparse hairs might have grown on his chest. A small round paunch bulged over the waistband of his kilt, proclaiming his prosperity and his secure place in Pharaoh's favor.

Mandisa lowered her eyes from the priest as she followed her mistress out of the litter. The sight of Potiphera, glowing and bald in the torchlight, lifted the curtain on memories she had tried to forget. Her husband, Idogbe, had fancied himself a priest of Sebek, the crocodile god who represented the destructive power of the sun, and had shaved his massive body in a similar way. Once he had even tried to become a lay priest at the temple in Thebes, but because he kept insisting that Sebek desired human sacrifices, the chief priests dismissed him.

Mandisa shook her head as if she could dislodge the disturbing thoughts. Once, long after she had been safely installed in Zaphenath-paneah's house, she had asked Ani about the Egyptians' sacrificial rites. He told her that in the first dynasty women slaves were often sacrificed at the graves of their dead masters, but no one now would ever consider such a barbaric practice. In these enlightened days of the eighteenth dynasty, a few temples still practiced animal sacrifice on special occasions. But only the cult of Osiris, of whom Pharaoh was the principal figure, incorporated human sacrifice into worship. "The only human life worthy of sacrifice, you see," Ani had said, inclining his head, "is the divine king's, for because he is god and man, he alone has the power to bridge the gap between us."

Asenath tugged on Mandisa's cloak, abruptly bringing her back to present reality. Potiphera was leading them into the rectangular enclosure surrounding the innermost temple, so Mandisa lengthened her stride to keep up with her mistress. When they were safely inside, the old priest pressed his hand to his daughter's cheek, then took his leave of them. But Asenath knew what to do. Devoutly pressing her hands together in front of her bosom, she walked through the semidarkness toward the god's habitation, her eyes wide with expectation.

From the outer courtyard they moved into Per-Hair, the House of Rejoicing. In the stillness of this columned hall, Mandisa could hear the ghostly sounds of ritual chanting. She knew from Idogbe's tales that the priests rose in the darkness each morning to chant and purify themselves in the sacred pool before entering the temple.

Catching her breath in a quick gasp, Asenath stopped. Mandisa stepped forward to see what had distracted her mistress. Like a procession of spirits in the morning gloom, the line of shaven white-robed priests snaked out of a subterranean chamber. The priests' hairless chests gleamed with the sacred water. The white of their kilts dazzled even in the dim light of dawn.

"Look at my father," Asenath whispered, a note of pride in her voice, and motioned toward the venerable old priest who walked first in line, the place of highest honor. "He will personally speak to the god for me," Asenath murmured, her voice no more than a breath in the reverent stillness. "And the god will supply what I am seeking."

They waited, and Mandisa recalled what Idogbe had told her about a temple's morning ritual. At dawn's first ray, the clay seals to the god's inner sanctuary would be broken and the doors opened to disclose the idol that represented the divinity in all his power. The highest priest would enter and lie prostrate before the image, then upon rising, he would utter prayers while other priests perfumed the air with incense. The god's nightclothes would be removed, the figure bathed and anointed, then clothed in fresh apparel. Food and drink had to be offered to the image, and after the god's spirit had sufficient opportunity to feed itself, the priest would open the doors to any and all supplicants who wished to address the divinity.

While the priests ministered to Khnum, Mandisa waited with her mistress in silence for the space of an hour. Finally a priest beckoned, and Asenath moved forward through a pair of heavy double doors into the innermost sanctuary.

Mandisa had never been inside an Egyptian temple, and she felt herself staring upward and outward in wonderment. Gold covered every conceivable surface, sparkling in the gilded paints on the muraled walls, in the serving pieces, in vases and bowls that stood on trays before the stone statue. Rush torches in their brackets threw ruddy wavering lights that seemed to wake the bas-relief carvings on the walls and make them dance.

The god himself sat upon a platform behind a flower-strewn altar. Priests hovered nearby with the remnants of his breakfast.

Mandisa blinked in astonished silence as she stared upward at the idol. The statue of Khnum rose over fifteen feet into the air. She felt as small as a street sparrow before it. The body of the image was that of a well-formed man, but the head wore a ram's snout and face. Two horns curled to the right and left through a braided wig, upon which sat the traditional crown of reeds and ostrich feathers.

Mandisa stepped back in stunned revulsion, but Asenath fell to her knees and bent to touch her head to the floor three times. Though she had not visited a temple since her marriage to Zaphenath-paneah, apparently she now intended to atone for her past indifference.

"Speak, child, of your petition to our mighty Khnum," a voice called. Mandisa jerked her head up and looked around. The speaker was Potiphera himself, but his voice sounded strangely altered, as though it moved through thickened air.

"Divine Khnum, creator of all that lives and breathes and is," Asenath said, not lifting her eyes from the floor, "your daughter Asenath has a boon to ask of you."

"And what is it you seek?" the priest prodded gently.

"A child, most divine god. A child only you can provide. You have given me two sons, but a man as great and favored as my husband should have more."

Potiphera nodded, then turned to face the gruesome god standing dark and grim in the torchlight. The ebony eyes that stared out from the ram's head seemed fixed upon Asenath as Potiphera called upon the god.

> "Beautiful is your shining forth on the horizon, O
>   living Khnum, beginning of life!
> You who bring children into being in women, and
>   make fluid and clay into mankind,
> Who nourishes the son in the womb of his mother,
> Who soothes him so that he weeps not, O nurse in
>   the womb!
> Who gives breath in order to keep alive all that he
>   has made;
> When he comes forth from the womb on the day of
>   his birth,
> You open his mouth in speech, and give all that he
>   needs.
> You have created the earth according to your desire,
>   while you were alone.
> You are in my heart, and there is no one who knows
>   you but Potiphera, your son.
> Hear me now, O Lord of the Sacred Land, and grant
>   this woman's request.
> For you, O Divine Potter, Lord of the Kingdom, have
>   molded men upon your potter's wheel, and given
>   them strength to walk upon the earth. . . ."

On and on the priest droned, his voice rising and falling as he flattered, cajoled, and finally threatened the god into hearing and granting Asenath's request. After a while, the sense of awe which had surrounded Mandisa wore off, and she clenched her jaw to stifle a yawn.

Why did her lady want another son so desperately? She had two fine boys, as handsome as they were bright, and Zaphenath-paneah obviously adored them. As far as Mandisa knew, the master had never expressed a desire for more children, yet Asenath seemed willing even to risk her life for the simple pleasure of placing another child in Zaphenath-paneah's arms.

Could she not see how much the vizier loved her? Why couldn't she rest in his love?

I will never be blessed with love like that, Mandisa thought, smiling wryly. *And I find that one son is more than enough. Adom is a fine boy, but how he ties my hands! He is too full of himself, so grown up in many ways yet such a child in others. And I cannot teach him! The master's sons will be tutored in the scribe's schools, but Adom has no place there, for he is a servant's son. And yet*—her thoughts drifted wistfully—*a father could lead him, could explain the things a woman cannot know. Soon Adom will have questions I cannot answer, and even now he yearns for a man's attention. Tarik and Ani are friendly, but they have responsibilities and so little time. . . .*

Her son needed a father. Mandisa did not necessarily want a husband, for she'd been married once and had no wish to repeat the experience. But Adom needed a man's influence, someone to guide, teach, and train him. She was altogether too gentle. She knew he would have a difficult time outside the protective walls of the vizier's villa because he had never learned how to properly defend himself. And soon he would want to know about a man's way with a woman, and how could she explain what she did not completely understand herself?

Adom needed a father, but how was she to provide one? For a brief moment she considered joining her mistress on the floor, but she could not in good conscience make a request to a ram-headed idol who stared at food without eating and listened to hour-long prayers without hearing.

But Zaphenath-paneah's invisible God was present everywhere, or so the vizier had said. If her master spoke the truth, this El Shaddai would hear her prayer even if it sprang from Khnum's temple. And perhaps, if she found favor in his sight, He would answer. In any case, it would not hurt to attempt one small petition.

While Asenath pressed her forehead to the floor and her

father droned out more flattery to the granite god, Mandisa closed her eyes to block out the scene and quietly asked El Shaddai to send someone from whom her son might learn to be a man.

~ Thirteen ~

THE NEW TABLE, DELICATE IN DESIGN AND INLAID with gold, crashed against the door. "You foul Egyptians will learn this about me!" the prisoner roared, his words punctuated by the shattering of pottery. "I once killed a thousand men in a single morning! If God is willing, I will do it again!"

Outside the captive's chamber, Tarik folded his arms and smiled at Halima. "My grasp of the Canaanite tongue is improving," he said, nodding with satisfaction as he consoled the trembling slave girl. "I understood every word of that threat. The man thinks he will kill us all."

"Sometimes I think he *will*," Halima answered, the breakfast tray in her hand shaking so violently that the pottery bowls clattered against each other. "I have nightmares about him. In the dark, sometimes I feel an evil weight pressing on my chest, and I open my eyes, expecting to see him."

"Never fear, sweet Halima," Tarik said, glancing around. They were alone in the hallway, so he took the tray from the poor girl's hands. It wouldn't do for the captain of the vizier's guard to be seen helping a lowly kitchen slave, but the young woman had shown uncommon courage in facing the Canaanite barbarian.

Her eyes came up to study his face, and he smiled at her. "A runner has come from Heliopolis. The lady Asenath returns within a few days, so Mandisa will come back with her. Soon you will not have to deal with this sour Canaanite."

"I do not mind . . . so much," she whispered, her round

face softening in a wistful expression. "But I would not attempt it without you, Tarik."

He shrugged off the implied compliment. "I would not
have persevered if not for our master's command. A prisoner belongs in prison, not in a house," he said, moving
away from the wall. The captive's door shuddered again as
some object collided against it. A chair, from the wooden
sound of the crash. "But Zaphenath-paneah says the man
is not to be harmed, nor shall he be allowed to injure himself. Yesterday I discovered that he had shredded his garment into long strips, doubtless attempting to fashion a trap
of some sort for you or me, Halima. So I had the strips removed, as well as what remained of his garment. Today he
wears nothing but an Egyptian kilt, and if he attempts to
shred it, he shall have only his inflated dignity to clothe
him."

"Tarik, you are shameful!" Halima laughed softly.

The captain noticed that the resulting light in her eyes
tremendously improved her appearance. "I am only obey-
ing our master's orders," Tarik said, grinning at her. "And
though I would rather throw this Simeon to the dogs than
keep him here, I will obey the vizier. In the nine years I've
known the master, I've never seen him make an unwise decision."

"What about the Canaanite's food?" Halima whispered,
putting her hand to the tray. "I have prepared a delicious
choice of breads, and we ought not to waste it."

"It will not be wasted," Tarik answered, kneeling to
place the tray on the floor. "Let the ants eat it. At least they
know how to behave in a civil manner. If the man insists
upon raging like a wild animal, we will let him starve like
the lions of the parched plains. Keep his water jug filled,
but do not feed him unless he grows more appreciative."

"Very well," the woman answered. She paused and
looked down at her empty hands. "I suppose I should return to my work."

"Yes," Tarik said, standing. Halima took a few slow

steps toward the kitchen, then quickened her pace in a resolute stride. Frowning, Tarik watched her go and wondered why she had hesitated to leave him.

———

Bored and frustrated, Adom wandered slowly through the villa's wide halls. In his hand he clutched a spinning top of carved quartz and a length of papyrus twine, but Ephraim and Manasseh were involved with their tutor and too busy to let him entertain them.

Adom stuffed the twine and top into a pocket of his kilt and tried to think of something else to do. He missed his mother. She had been gone nearly three weeks, and once Adom had heard Manasseh say that his mother had gone to live with her father in a place called Heliopolis. Wherever Manasseh's mother went, Adom's mother followed, and for several nights he'd been terrified to think that the two women would not return to the vizier's villa. But he'd shyly caught Zaphenath-paneah in the hall, and his heart had warmed when the great and noble vizier looked him in the eye with gentle understanding. "Why, Adom, of course your mother is coming back," the vizier said, his hand warming the boy's head. "Very soon, in fact."

But soon wasn't soon enough. Adom had spent the morning wandering through the stables, but the master's groomsmen chased him away.

"Get out of here!" one of the slaves yelled. "The master's horses are spirited. One kick will crack that soft head of yours like a melon!"

From the stable yard he wandered into the area where the granaries held the villa's stores of grain and wheat, but his mother's warning voice echoed in his brain. "Countless children and drunken fools," she often told him, her eyes darkening in seriousness, "have climbed the stairs to peer into the open tops of the hive-shaped cones and fallen in, suffocating as they struggled to get out."

A line of donkeys and their attendants were standing be-

fore the granaries where Zaphenath-paneah's servants bus-
ily measured grain for an official who had not planned for
the famine. Overwhelmed by the sight of so many serious
faces, Adom sprinted through that yard, through the front
courtyard, and into the main hall of the house. Several visitors waited outside the central reception hall for an audience with the vizier, and Adom got as far as the vestibule
before a guard caught his arm.

"Where are you going, Adom?" the guard asked, bending down.

"I thought I might look for my mother."

"She is not inside. She and the Lady Asenath are still
away."

Adom felt himself fidgeting. "Then perhaps I can ask
the master when she will return."

The guard chuckled. "No, my young friend, you cannot.
The master is busy. We all have our jobs to do. The Double
of the King, the Good Shepherd of the People is meeting
with four kings of Megiddo, two princes of Shahuren, and
one king from Ascalon."

"I will wait for him, then. I will be quiet."

"No, Adom, you cannot. The Nourisher of Egypt, the
Prince of Mediation dines today with shepherds from Syria
and Lebanon, Bedouins from Edom, and the host of kings
who visit with him now. They have come a long way to seek
your master's face, and they have been waiting longer than
you. Run along, Adom, and play with your little friends."

"They are having their lessons."

"Then find them, and listen to Ani as he teaches. Even
the son of a servant should know the truth of the world."

The guard straightened, and Adom knew he was no
longer welcome in the house. Dejected, he walked through
the front portico and found the path that led to the garden.

Ephraim and Manasseh sat on papyrus mats before Ani,
steward of the estate and tutor of Zaphenath-paneah's children. Though next to the powerful vizier Ani seemed a thin
shrunken man, now his extraordinary eyes blazed and

glowed in the center of his face. Adom thought that Ephraim and Manasseh looked like two small dolls before a giant, so imposing was the wise man's manner as he swayed before them, spinning a tale.

Interested despite himself, Adom knelt on the stone pathway a few feet away, aware than Ani had seen him approach. The two boys, intent upon their teacher's story, did not stir from their mats.

"In the beginning," Ani said, drawing an imaginary line in the air, "nothing existed but one God, the invisible God who cannot be configured in stone."

"Neter?" Manasseh asked.

Ani frowned. "You are not to interrupt, young master. A wise student listens and learns, and questions only after his teacher is done with explanations."

Manasseh hung his head, and Ani placed his freckled hand upon the boy's shaved head. "Do not be discouraged, little prince. You may discern the answer to your own question before I am finished."

Manasseh looked up again, encouraged, and Ani went on. "This invisible God is not to be found in inscribed shrines. There exists no habitation that can contain him, and you cannot conceive his form in your heart. This God is one and alone, and no others exist with him. He is the One who made all things. God is from the beginning, and He has existed of old when nothing else had being. He is the father of Beginnings, the eternal One, the infinite One who endures forever and ever. He shall endure to all eternity. He is hidden from gods and men, and He is a mystery to his creatures. No man knows how to know him. His true name is a mystery even to his children. Though some call him Neter, his names are innumerable, manifold, and no one knows their number."

"If no one knows his name, then why do my father and Mandisa call him El Shaddai?" Manasseh interrupted again.

From his hiding place, Adom grinned. Manasseh was

always questioning, and no mere warning from a teacher would silence him.

Ani sighed in exasperation. "Listen, Manasseh, and you will understand. 'El Shaddai' is a Canaanite term for 'Almighty God,' a name which describes one of His attributes. God is almighty, just as He is truth. He lives by truth; He feeds on truth. He is the King of truth; He rests upon truth. He fashions truth, and He executes truth throughout all the world. God is life, and through Him alone man lives. He gives life to man. He breathes the breath of life into his nostrils.

"God is both father and mother—the father of fathers, the mother of mothers. He begets but was never begotten. He produces but was never produced. He begat himself and produced himself. He creates but was never created. He is the maker of his own form, the fashioner of his own body. He is the Creator of the heavens, the earth, the deep, the waters, the mountains. When He spoke his word, it came to pass, and his word shall endure forever."

"If there is only one God," Manasseh said, his handsome face twisting into a frown, "then why are there so many temples in Thebes?"

Ani held up a finger. "The invisible God is the father of the gods and the father of all deities. He formed mankind and the primeval potter Khnum, who turned men and gods out of his hands, forming them upon a potter's table.

"You see, my students," Ani said, sinking to the ground before them, "once neither heaven nor earth existed, nothing but the boundless primeval water shrouded with thick darkness. The water contained within it the seeds of things, and at length the spirit of the primeval water felt the desire to create the world. The spirit of the water uttered a word, and the world sprang into being, just as the spirit of the water had decided it should. The next act of creation was the formation of an egg. From that sprang Ra, the sun-god, in whose shining form we see the almighty power of the divine spirit."

"That's not what my mother says," Adom announced, forgetting himself.

Three pairs of eyes turned to him. "Adom," the tutor said, suddenly sounding tired, "why aren't you out helping someone?"

"There's no one to help," Adom answered, looking down at his hands.

"Then didn't you hear what I just told Manasseh? A wise student listens. He does not disagree with his teachers."

"But my mother says something different, Ani. She says that God created the world and then destroyed it with a flood, and Egypt came out of the flood, just like the whole world did. But this God never made other gods—He only made people. My mother calls him El Shaddai, and so does the master. I've heard Zaphenath-paneah talk about Him—"

"Enough!" Ani closed his eyes and held up a warning hand. "I think tomorrow we will talk of something else. We are finished today, boys. Run, go play, for I have work to do."

∽ Fourteen ∼

FROM HIS VANTAGE POINT ON THE RIDGE OF A hill at Hebron, Jacob stared into the distance toward Mizraim, the Black Land. Not far away a traveling party crawled northward into the teeth of the gusty breeze that blew up small whirlwinds of desert dust and grit, but he could not discern Simeon's broad shape among the men.

He sighed. So much for vain hopes and dreams. He had prayed that Simeon would find the courage and strength to escape the vizier who held him, but God had not seen fit to answer those prayers any more than He had answered Jacob's desperate pleas when Joseph disappeared.

"Do I ask too much?" he whispered, lifting his tired eyes to the sky. "Why, Almighty God, do you allow your chosen ones to suffer so? Famine grips our land. The cattle are thin and hungry. My sons' wives are as withered and worn as the stones of these mountains, and yet you do not offer respite or rain. You have taken Rachel, Joseph, and Simeon, and this foreigner of Mizraim demands my Benjamin, too. This I cannot do, Lord God. I cannot lose the son of my right hand."

In spite of his resolve never to revisit the past, his mind returned to the day when Benjamin had come into the world and Rachel had gone out of it. "He shall be called Ben-oni, son of my sorrow," she had whispered, struggling for breath, knowing she would die.

"No," Jacob had answered, resting his hand on her wet brow. "He is the son of my darling, my right hand. He shall be Benjamin, as dear to my heart as you are."

That parting remark was the first and only lie he ever

told her. For though he did love Benjamin more than life itself, Jacob could never look upon his youngest son without seeing the instrument God had used to take Rachel from him. And so, in the years after her death, Joseph received the fullest measure of Jacob's devotion and attention—brilliant, handsome, charming Joseph, Rachel's long-awaited firstborn, the delightful pride of her heart.

And then El Shaddai demonstrated His jealousy. To teach Jacob that He deserved and demanded first place in a man's heart, El Shaddai removed Joseph, just as He nearly took Isaac from Abraham. Jacob knew enough about his God to know that the Almighty would not tolerate an idol, be it a graven image or a flesh-and-blood creature. Anything given more love, more time, or more devotion than God could not be allowed to usurp God Shaddai's rightful place.

"You allowed Abraham to keep his beloved son," he whispered, subconsciously aware that he had reawakened both the memory of Joseph and the dull ache in his soul, "and yet you took mine. Was my sin so much worse than my forefather's?"

The sky glared hot and blue. The Almighty did not answer.

Coming out of his musings, Jacob saw that Reuben was climbing the hill. He closed his eyes, guarding his secrets.

"Greetings, Father," Reuben called, his voice unnaturally bright and careful. "I have just finished talking with the others."

Jacob shifted on his stiff hips and opened his eyes to study the horizon again. "And?"

"The famine still weighs heavy upon us, Father. The seed we planted has not sprouted, for there has been no rain. We have grain for now, but soon, when there is nothing to harvest, we will starve."

Reuben paused, and Jacob braced himself for what he knew would come next.

"Father, we can go back to Egypt if you'll only allow Benjamin to go with us. The Egyptian will give us grain, enough to see us through the coming year."

"No." Jacob ground the word out between his teeth. "No! No! A thousand times no! You shall not take Benjamin with you. I will not allow him to leave me."

"Father." Reuben dropped the conciliatory tone. "Benjamin is a grown man, with children of his own. Your continual insistence that he remain in your camp is an embarrassment to him. He wants to go with us. He is more than willing."

"No!" Jacob felt himself shaking with impotent rage and fear. "I let Joseph go, and he never returned! You, the sons of the others, came back with only his ornamented coat"—he gestured toward the ground as if the blood-stained garment still lay at his feet—"and I knew I was wrong."

For loving him too much. For loving him more than God Shaddai.

"Father, listen to me." Reuben's dark eyes narrowed and hardened. "That happened a long time ago. Would you have all of us starve because of one accident?"

"As long as there is breath in my body, I will guard Rachel's remaining son with my life. Benjamin will not go with you." Turning on his heel, Jacob flung the edge of his cloak over his shoulder and stomped away toward his tent.

⟿ Fifteen ⟿

DOCILE AND PATIENT, THE LITTER-BEARERS waited under a blistering sun. Asenath paused for a moment on the marble steps of her father's villa, then reached out to embrace him one final time. "I shall miss you, Father," she whispered, placing her cheek next to his. "But please continue to offer sacrifices and prayers to Khnum for me. I cannot tell you how earnestly I desire another son."

"Daughter." Potiphera pulled her from his embrace and held her at arm's length. "Do you love your husband?"

"Love him?" Asenath laughed gently, amazed that her father would dream of questioning her devotion to Zaphenath-paneah, the flower of all Egypt. "Of course, Father. How could I not love him? He is truly the wisest man in the land, except for you, of course, and Pharaoh could do nothing without my husband's guidance. He is kind and gentle and would do almost anything to please me."

"If you love him, Asenath, you should want to obey him. If he does not want another child, you are foolish to think you can make him happy this way."

"But he does not know what he wants! He loves Ephraim and Manasseh so much that I know he would adore another son—even a daughter! And so, no matter how much he protests on my account, I will pursue this." She lowered her voice, instinctively aware that Mandisa, who waited in the litter, did not completely approve of her plan. "And since my husband's god has not been strong enough to prevail in this, I beg you to seek help for me from Khnum."

"But the vizier's god is strong. His hand alone has preserved Egypt since Hapi's waters have failed to flood the land."

Fighting hard against tears of frustration she refused to let fall, she gave him a blazing confident smile. "Trust me, Father. I will win this time. My husband will come to me, the seed will be planted and bear fruit, and I shall be delivered of another son, perhaps even two. And when the famine is done, as my love says it will be, your grandsons shall grow strong and capable in Pharaoh's house."

Her subtle appeal to her father's ambition seemed to allay his fears, for he nodded and released his grip on her arms. "Be careful, daughter," he said, his eyes drinking her up as if he might never see her again. "Do not trifle with divinity, for a sleeping god may wake and take offense at your games. He may draw you out to a place where you can never return."

"Do not worry, Father. I have you to protect me." She gave him another quick kiss on the cheek, then turned and skipped lightly down the steps to her litter. Mandisa pulled the sheer curtain aside, and Asenath sat down and pulled her legs up out of the swirling dust at her feet.

Her father had not moved but stood with a worried expression on his face. *Foolish man, he is always worrying about something.* Giving him a final confident wave, Asenath let the curtain fall and settled back among the pillows in the conveyance. "Tell the litter-bearers to proceed," she said, giving Mandisa a weary smile. "Tell them to run. I would like to be home as soon as possible."

~ Sixteen ~

"LIFE AND HEALTH TO YOU, LADY ASENATH! WE are so glad you have returned!" After delivering a formal greeting and bow to his mistress, Tarik gave Mandisa an exaggerated wink as she wearily climbed from the litter. The perspiring litter-bearers, who had jogged in the merciless heat with only occasional breaks, looked as though they would expire on the spot. Lady Asenath did not even glance backward toward them as she skipped up the stairs of the villa's welcoming portico.

Mandisa turned to the commander of the company of guards who had escorted them from Heliopolis. "Refresh your men and these slaves in the garden," she murmured. "Take care not to disturb the family. I will send food from the kitchens and fresh water from the well."

The commander gave her a stiff salute, appreciation gleaming in his eyes. When Mandisa began to walk toward the house, Tarik fell into step beside her. "Is there something I can do for you, captain?" she asked in surprise, then she halted, her heart jumping in her chest. "Has something happened to Adom?"

"No," Tarik said, offering her a quick reassuring smile. He gestured toward the path that led to the kitchens and caught her by the elbow, leading her away from the villa. "Shall we walk together? Your son is fine, unless you consider that he continues to thoroughly vex Ani during the young masters' lessons. Apparently Ani's recounting of the primeval creation does not agree with what you have told your son."

"Oh," Mandisa said, lifting her brows. "I don't know

what is to be done about that. I have taught Adom what my father taught me, and I believe it is the truth. But Ani is a stubborn old man. He will not change his ideas."

"That is not why I sought you out." Stopping abruptly in the path, Tarik thrust his hands behind his back. "In your absence, the duty of looking after our lord's Canaanite prisoner has fallen to me and Halima."

She laughed at his somber expression. "And that chore has not been pleasant?"

"He grows more unruly and dangerous with each passing day. He has not eaten in nearly a week, for we cannot go near the door to bring him food. He throws things." The captain's brows drew downward in a frown. "If he were any other captive, I would have whipped him long ago. He would learn that such behavior will not be tolerated! But the vizier will not let us harm him. We are to leave him alone and let him rage."

"Is there nothing you can do?"

The guard's tight expression relaxed into a half-smile. "I have tried other ways to calm him. To thwart his devious plans, I removed all his clothing but a kilt, and we have not replaced the furniture, the vases, or bowls. As long as he rages, we do not even enter to clean his . . . uh . . . private area. He sits in a loathsome stinking shambles, and yet he still roars."

"A starving animal will bellow until it is nearly dead, Tarik," Mandisa said, moving along the path again. "You are a hunter. You should know that. And this beast is a particularly proud one, I daresay. He may not stop howling until he is too weak to be saved."

"That is why the gods have returned you," Tarik said, flashing a brilliant smile.

Oh no. She'd seen smiles like that before. They were nothing but bait for hungry fish. Well, this minnow would not bite.

"Did you think I could talk to him?" She grinned in amused wonder. "Ah, Tarik, you have been praying in vain.

All the gods in Egypt couldn't force me into that room."

"But the vizier asked you to help."

"And I did. For several days. And the man hated me as much as he hates you."

"But he was not as violent when you visited him. And you are the only one fluent in his language. Surely you can try to reason with him once more."

Annoyed, Mandisa looked beyond him and saw Halima just stepping out of the kitchen. Halima offered a shy wave of greeting. Her singularly sweet smile faded, though, when she saw Tarik, and Mandisa did not need to be told why the girl's cheeks suddenly flooded with color.

Mandisa had long suspected that the slave girl was hopelessly in love with the vizier's captain. How could the foolish man not notice?

Smiling in the calm strength of knowledge, Mandisa returned Halima's wave, then looked back at the desperate guard. "I don't know how I can help," she answered. "But if Halima will help me, and if you will stand guard when we must go in, perhaps the three of us can manage the brute."

Tarik looked over his shoulder, and Mandisa studied him as he nodded a greeting to Halima. Did he have any idea that love bloomed in the poor girl's heart? Apparently not, for he turned back to Mandisa and demanded to know if they could go immediately to face the Canaanite captive.

"His room stinks," the guard said, tossing his head in exasperation. "It is an affront to heaven itself, and if the vizier happens to wander in that part of the house—"

"I will go soon," Mandisa interrupted, moving past him to have a private word with Halima. "When I have refreshed myself. I am yet covered with dust from the journey."

———

After tending to her mistress and unpacking the baskets of belongings brought from Heliopolis, Mandisa went in search of her son. She found him in the garden with Ephraim and Manasseh. "Adom!" she called, her heart singing with delight at the sight of him.

"Mother!" He left his young playmates and threw his arms around her shoulders in a light embrace. "I am glad you are home!"

"I am happy, too." She held him for a moment and breathed in his sweet scent. "But I hear that you have been interrupting Ani's lessons."

"He tells the story wrong," Adom said, lifting his chin in a stubborn gesture as he pulled out of her arms. "He said that God Almighty created other gods."

"You should not contradict a teacher, especially an elder," she said, bending forward. She pressed her hand on the smooth skin of his shaved head and playfully tugged on the single long lock of hair that grew from his temple. Soon he would have to grow his hair out to a more manly length. Ephraim and Manasseh still wore the long forelocks of childhood, but Adom was nearly grown. At some point in the near future he would also have to find an occupation, something to fill his days, a way to earn a wage and make a life for himself.

"Adom," she said, drawing him to her in a sudden rush of emotion, "I have prayed that El Shaddai would send someone to us. Someone who can teach you."

"Ani has taught me many things. I can read and even write a little."

"No. Other things, my son."

"Will I have a tutor?" Adom asked, lifting his head to look into her eyes.

She cringed inwardly at his assumption. He was a servant's son, and yet he too often assumed that he was just like the vizier's children, born to the ruling dynasty. Had she made a mistake in allowing him to spend so much time among people born far outside his station in life?

"Not exactly a tutor," she said, sinking to a garden bench. She pulled him to her side and ran her hand over the olive skin of his bare back. "I have asked God to send someone who can teach you things I cannot—how to work in the fields, perhaps, or how to mind the animals."

He nodded slowly. "I like horses. I wouldn't mind working with them."

She wrinkled her nose. The stables would not have been her first choice, but as long as the boy had *something* to do . . . "I suppose you could be of use to the stablemen. But I'm not certain who will come, or what he will teach you. But when this teacher comes, Adom, you must treat him with respect, listen to him, and learn from him. Do you understand?"

He regarded her with a wide speculative gaze. "Is it the man in the locked room?"

Mandisa felt her mouth drop open. "The man—the prisoner? By heaven, child, why would you think such a thing? Do you think God would send us someone as brutish as that?"

Adom shrugged. "I heard the slaves say he was from Canaan, the same place you were born."

"Well," Mandisa answered, annoyed with the gossiping slaves, "just because we come from the same region doesn't mean we are connected in any way. No, son, I am praying that God would send us a *good* man, an honorable teacher." She brightened her smile. "And I don't think the captive is particularly good or honorable, do you?"

Adom's childish mouth twitched with amusement. "No, Mother. I've heard him curse. He doesn't know I can understand him, but he yells the same words I've heard the sheepherders use."

"Don't listen to him or the herders." Mandisa stood and gave him a playful nudge. "Now find the little ones and enjoy the time you have with them. But do not contradict Ani again."

Adom loped away, and Mandisa took a moment to adjust the edges of her heavy wig, then turned toward the slave quarters and the captive's chamber. She barely had time to bathe and reapply her makeup, but she had been determined to do so before facing the roaring lion of Canaan.

She frowned, remembering Adom's question. The prisoner as a suitable teacher—how had Adom come by such an outlandish idea? The captive was a savage monster, his hate a living visible thing. Mandisa had seen bitter men like him before.

But she had agreed to help him. Girding herself with resolve, she walked with brittle dignity toward the captive's chamber.

Not willing to deal with the heightened emotions of Halima or Tarik for this first meeting with the Canaanite, she pulled one of the gate guards from his post. "Remain in the hallway and do not let the prisoner see you," she told him in a low voice. "I am going into the chamber alone."

"Alone?" The young man's brow furrowed. "But he is violent, and Tarik says—"

"Tarik has asked me to see to him," she cut the guard off, nodding with more bravery than she felt. "But I do not want him to escape and harm anyone in the household. So watch from behind the wall, out of sight, and if he leaves the room without me, summon help immediately. But if my suspicions are correct, there will be no need for a general alarm."

The guard stepped into her path and shot her a half-frightened look. "The captain will not approve of this, lady. We are under orders that no one approaches that chamber without Tarik, and absolutely no one removes the bolt unless another guard stands near to offer assistance."

"The stain of disobedience will be on my head, then, not yours," Mandisa answered, abruptly waving aside his protests. She walked around him without a further word and moved relentlessly toward the door.

———

Simeon tensed as he heard the slow rumble of the bolt.

Had the guard come back with that pale-faced wench who squeaked like a weasel every time he looked at her?

His stomach growled in anticipation of food, yet his anger strangled the sound. He glanced around the room, but he could find nothing else to throw at his tormentors. Broken shards of pottery and timber littered the floor. No furnishings remained but a down-filled mattress. Every single piece of costly furniture and bric-a-brac had been shattered or ground to dust, a just penalty for the guard's foolish decision to take Simeon's clothes from him. A decent man did not walk around half-dressed, not even in sweltering Egypt!

Crouched with his back against the wall, his hands gripped the sturdy linen of the kilt wrapped around his waist. If the guard came in, he would lunge forward and kill the man with his own bare hands! Weak from hunger and numb from the monotony of confinement, Simeon's strength and patience had completely evaporated. He would not bear another day of this torture.

The bolt fell to the floor outside with a hollow thumping sound, and the latch clicked. Simeon frowned. The approach was different, the intruder's movements too carefree and confident. Could it be that the great vizier himself stood behind the door? If so, there were probably a hundred guards outside as well, each eager to aim a javelin at Simeon's throat.

Slowly he slid upward along the wall, not even feeling the rough plaster as it scraped his skin. Cold sweat ran from his pores, beading under his arms and on his upper lip. *God above, if this is the moment I must die . . .*

"Grace and peace be unto you." The words were Canaanite, the voice a woman's. Simeon slumped back to the floor, his knees suddenly weak as the adrenaline left his body. His head swam with dizziness as the door swung open. Then his eyes met the invader's, and he recognized her. The interpreter. The traitor.

"Grace and peace?" he snarled, wishing he had the energy and inclination to send her away. "What would you know of grace or peace? Only someone born in Canaan would speak as fluently as you, so you have sold your heart and soul to these idolatrous people."

"I have sold nothing and am not for sale," she remarked, calmly stepping into the room. She actually turned her back on him as she lowered a water jug from her hip and closed the door.

Surprise emptied the blood from Simeon's face and dragged the power of speech from his tongue. He could think of nothing to say as she entered, *alone*, and pulled a fresh loaf of bread from a bag slung over her shoulder.

She kicked a few pieces of broken debris out of the way, then knelt before him and extended the bread in a graceful gesture. "My family sold me to a passing Egyptian who thought to have me as his wife," she said simply, her paint-lengthened eyes intent upon his. "He brought me here and disappeared a year later. I am certain he is dead. He left me with a mountain of debts and a son."

Only half-listening, Simeon focused on the door and the hallway beyond. He could not hear movement of any kind outside the door, so this was not a trick . . . unless it was a very clever one. This foolish woman had apparently come to him unescorted, and though his strength had been depleted by hunger, he knew he could overpower her if he needed to. In this room, at least, he held the upper hand.

But he did not have to strike her now. Carefully, he reached out and took the bread. He sniffed it. The aroma was strong and hearty, without a trace of suspicious odors. And the loaf was rough and crusty, not soft and mushy like that the other woman brought.

"So tell me," he said, breaking the loaf, "how did you come to live in the house of the mighty vizier?"

The tiny beads in her braided hair clacked softly as she tilted her head slightly. "I was sixteen when my husband disappeared. For three years I did whatever tasks a woman alone could find, but even in the time of plenty, my son and I nearly starved. The man who owned the house I lived in threatened to throw me and my son into the streets because we owed him so much. Finally he brought his case before Zaphenath-paneah. Standing before the vizier, I had to admit that I had no silver to pay my debts. And Zaphenath-paneah ruled that the landlord was right to collect what I owed him."

Her delicate features softened as she smiled. "And just when I thought that we would be sold into slavery and I would never see my son again, I begged for mercy. And the one they call the King's Shadow Dispenser took pity on me and brought shade into my life. He paid my debts and restored my freedom, and then he asked if I possessed any skills. When I replied that I would learn any honorable trade in order to serve him, he said that his wife, Lady Asenath, needed a handmaid. And so Adom and I came to this house. We have been here nine years."

Simeon ate silently, absorbing her words as his stomach rumbled in appreciation of the bread. She spoke with complete transparency and without hesitation, so she either spoke the truth or was an accomplished liar. But why would she lie? And why was she here? She had probably been ordered to feed him, and she had, but still she remained. What sort of plot was this?

"How many are outside the door?" he growled, impatient with her games. "And why do I not hear them? They make me nervous, these plotting, prowling Egyptians—"

"No one is outside the door," she said, folding her hands. "One guard watches from down the hallway, but he is neither prowling nor plotting. I have been away with my mistress for many days and thought you might like to talk with someone who speaks your language. Ani tells me that speech is civilization itself, and if we are to keep you civilized, you must be engaged in conversation."

Converse? With a woman? Is *that* why she lingered? Simeon grinned and looked away, biting back the urge to laugh in her face. He might have missed the company of his brothers, his family, even his sons, but never in his life had he missed the conversation of women!

"Did I say something funny?"

Unable to stop himself, Simeon threw back his head and let out a great peal of laughter. "By all the gods of this Black Land, yes! Why would I want to talk to a woman? Especially a painted harlot with an adder's tongue, a creature who serves the demented madman who holds me captive!"

Mandisa stood to her feet in a regal powerful gesture. A crimson flood colored her face and belied her calm exterior.

"Ani says that isolation leads a man to depression, paranoia, even self-destruction," she said, moving toward the door. "But if it is only food you want, that is all you shall have." She paused and crinkled her nose in distaste as she looked around. "I had hoped we might clean this room."

"I am a herdsman. I like living like an animal," he snapped back. Then, as he exploded in bitter laughter, she slipped from the room and slid the bolt back into place.

Simeon knew she would not return that day, and something within him wondered if she would ever come again. By his harsh words he had probably sentenced himself to weeks of visitation from the captain and the squeaky slave girl, neither one of whom cared enough to offer Simeon a decent or interesting word. For the first time in his life, Simeon began to regret something he had done.

No one came the next morning, and Simeon spent an hour tossing broken pottery chips at the door, certain that the Egyptians had decided to starve him. After a week had passed, perhaps longer, they would haul his emaciated corpse from this ruined chamber and disembowel it in one of their bizarre mummification rituals. Then, when his brothers returned with Benjamin to prove that the vizier had imprisoned an innocent man, the deranged Zaphenathpaneah would summon servants, who would then bring in Simeon's desiccated mortal shell. "Take *this* back to your father, the old man," the vizier would shout. Judah would grow pale, unsophisticated Benjamin would faint, and Levi would throw himself at the guards, only to be killed by the steely eyed captain. . . .

Yes, Simeon decided, sitting on the dusty floor with his hand over his ever growling belly, he had definitely misspent his last chance for survival. He had almost been enjoying his conversation with the woman, until in one moment he insulted her beauty, her master, even her morality.

And women didn't forgive easily. He had only to remember his mother to understand *that* truth. After Rachel's death, his father had continued to spend his nights in Rachel's tent with Joseph and Benjamin, for he found little comfort in Leah's cold shoulder.

At sunset, when Simeon had almost given up hope, the woman returned. The bolt slid away as before, the door opened, and she stood before him, her slender white neck rising above a silken gown like silvery tissue. But this time she kept her eyes averted from his. Though she came into the room as bravely as she had the previous day, the bold and confident attitude had disappeared.

"If you are hungry, here is bread." Her sharp tone stabbed the air. She did not move to extend her hand.

"I am hungry," he admitted, slowly rising to his knees.

Almost reluctantly, she pulled the loaf and a bit of cheese from the pouch at her waist. Cautiously, she extended both, and as he stood to take them, her eyes lifted to meet his.

Ah, the pain there was like Leah's, dark and brooding. For a brief instant her eyes shimmered like pools of appeal, then she lowered her glance and turned toward the door.

"Don't go." The words slipped from his mouth before he had even willed himself to say them.

"Why should I stay?" Her back was to him, yet she stopped, hearing the plea in his voice. "You are hungry. I brought you food. Surely there is nothing else that you need. You *like* living like an animal, remember?"

"I was wrong." His voice grated harshly in his own ears. "You were right. I would like—I *need* to talk to someone."

Levi would faint if he could hear me now. "I would like to apologize. Please forgive me."

She turned slowly, and the heavy lashes that had shadowed her cheeks flew up in surprise. "*Forgive* you?"

By the sun and moon, would she make him repeat himself? But these were conditions of war, and a man was allowed to do anything necessary to remain alive. "Yes. I must beg your forgiveness."

She tilted her head regally, like a queen granting favors, and he thought he saw a faint look of amusement on her face. "Very well. I accept your apology."

He sank back onto the floor, attempting to put her more at ease, and unwrapped the square of cheese she'd given him. Cautiously, she knelt in a small cleared space by the door. "I suppose we could start with introductions," she said, modestly tucking her legs under her. She folded her hands primly in her lap. "I am Mandisa, handmaid to Lady Asenath."

Simeon nodded and swallowed a mouthful of cheese. "I am Simeon, second-born son of Jacob." He realized that his tone was as dry as his mouth. "And I suppose you remember why I am here."

"Of course."

A long silence followed, and Simeon cast quickly about for a topic of conversation. He was unaccustomed to the social company of women. He had married two, buried two, slept with them, eaten their food, and disciplined their children, but he couldn't recall ever *conversing* with a woman. Except Dinah.

"How old are you?" he asked abruptly. Caught off guard, she laughed, the most delightful sound he'd heard in weeks.

"Why do you ask?" she said, her hand creeping to her brightening cheek. "Do you think me a horse, that you could buy me? Would you like to count my teeth?"

His mouth trembled with the need to laugh with her. "No," he said, embarrassed. He looked down at the bread in his hand, again at a loss for words. "You said yesterday that you were not for sale. I believe you."

They sat in silence for a moment more, then Simeon bit off a huge hunk of bread. As long as he chewed, she wouldn't expect him to talk. And as long as he behaved civilly, she wouldn't leave.

He didn't know why it was suddenly so important that she stay. She was certainly unlike any other woman he'd ever met. She had walked boldly into his room when he was at his worst, not flinching at his stench, his words, or his threatening aspect. And while most women chattered among themselves like a mob of flighty sparrows, this woman weighed her words. Perhaps it came from working for a highborn lady, or perhaps her quiet spirit was innate, like his own quick temper. . . .

She leaned forward and lifted a brow. "Tell me about your family."

And so he did. As he ate he told her of his mother, Leah, and his father, Jacob. He laughed, describing the comical exploits of his children, and sobered as he spoke of Reuben and Levi, Judah and Dan. And as he talked, he found that revisiting his memories somehow brought his loved ones near, held them close.

He might have talked for an hour or more. He only knew that he was disappointed when she finally stood to leave. "Must you go?" he asked, glad that the gathering darkness hid the blush upon his neck.

"My lady will need me to see her to bed," Mandisa answered, quietly moving toward the door. She paused for a last look at his room before leaving. "I will send a maid to clean this pigsty if you promise not to throw things at her."

Simeon flushed, helpless to halt his embarrassment. "I will not . . . throw anything."

She smiled, then said, "I will send fresh clothes and water to bathe with also. Tomorrow I will return, and you can tell me more, Simeon. Until then, sleep well."

Strangely enough, Simeon did sleep more soundly that night than he had since coming to the Black Land.

⟶ Seventeen ⟵

ANI WATCHED THE GROWING FRIENDSHIP between Mandisa and the Canaanite captive with growing approval. The entire household had benefitted from the relationship. Mandisa endured what she called her "daily trial" with good grace. The prisoner threw fewer tantrums, and his rages of temper were generally less violent than before. Tarik, visibly relieved that he would not be forced to take extreme measures to control Zaphenath-paneah's pampered prisoner, never ceased to praise Mandisa's gentle work with the captive. And Halima actually sang in simple gladness because she no longer had to venture near the room where the caged animal roared.

The proper duty of a steward was to act as the eyes and ears of the house, so Ani habitually crept along the hallways, listening at windows and eavesdropping with an ear to the walls. Zaphenath-paneah seemed strangely distant these days, and Ani assumed that the vizier was preoccupied with the famine and the distribution of grain to the far-flung cities of the kingdom. But though the vizier rarely followed up on a prisoner after a sentence had been rendered, Ani noticed that Zaphenath-paneah made a point of being in his wife's chamber every night as Mandisa readied her mistress for bed. During his nocturnal rounds, he discovered that the master never failed to question Mandisa about the Canaanite captive, and Zaphenath-paneah seemed pleased that Simeon seemed happier in recent days.

One night Ani pressed his ear against the outer wall of his mistress's chamber and strained to hear the low murmur of Mandisa's voice. "I was wondering, my lord, whether or not it might be good for my son, Adom, to spend time with this Canaanite," he heard her ask. "Adom is half Canaanite, and I have asked your Almighty God to bring a strong man into his life. The captive is not as gruff as he would have us think. I believe that under that rough exterior beats a vulnerable heart."

Ani clung to the wall in a paralysis of astonishment. Mandisa would trust her son to the caged beast?

Zaphenath-paneah must have read Ani's thoughts. "You trust him?" he asked. "I know he has calmed considerably, but he is unpredictable—"

"It if please you, my lord, I have heard him speak tenderly of his sister and his children," Mandisa answered. "I do not believe he would hurt Adom. But of course, I will be nearby."

"If you trust Simeon, far be it from me to interfere," the vizier answered, a trace of humor in his voice. "But proceed carefully, Mandisa. The man has a vicious temper."

"By the horns of Khnum, don't we all know it," Ani murmured, leaning away from the wall. He rubbed his chin with his wrist and stared thoughtfully at the empty hall ahead. Zaphenath-paneah would never have agreed to allow Adom, of whom he was genuinely fond, to spend time with a spy. So if the vizier believed this Simeon was innocent of the charges against him, why did he still hold him?

Ani walked away, carefully lifting his feet so that his papyrus sandals made no sound across the marble floor. Something unusual bubbled beneath the surface of life in the vizier's house, but Ani had never encountered a mystery he had not been able to fully unearth.

TIZARA

For you shall not worship any other god,
for the Lord, whose name is Jealous,
is a jealous God—
lest you make a covenant with the
inhabitants of the land
and they play the harlot with their gods, and
sacrifice to their gods,
and someone invite you to eat of his sacrifice;
and you take some of his daughters
for your sons,
and his daughters play the harlot
with their gods,
and cause your sons also to play the harlot
with their gods.

Exodus 34:14–16

⟶ Eighteen ⟵

MANDISA LICKED THE TIP OF HER FINGER AND dabbed at a smudge on her son's cheek.

"Mother!" Adom complained, ducking.

"There. At least you look presentable." She turned back to the table in her small chamber and idly fingered her comb, wondering why Simeon's opinion of the boy should matter to her. Adom was her son and she loved him. Simeon was a captive who would soon leave the vizier's house and return to his home in Canaan. But in recent days she had entertained the niggling idea that God Shaddai might intend for the Canaanite prisoner to teach her son. She had spoken to the vizier, and she had prepared Adom. But she had not dared to ask Simeon if he would be willing to spend time with the boy.

Better to urge him gently, to let him volunteer. In her short time of marriage, she had learned that men responded better to diplomatic hints than to forthright suggestions.

"Do you understand that you must not make him angry?" Mandisa asked, turning to her son.

"You've asked me that ten times already."

"Well, if you are to visit the captive with me, you must be on your best behavior."

"I understand, Mother," Adom answered, self-consciously tugging on his kilt.

With a flash of understanding, she realized he was nervous. He had heard the screams and curses from Simeon's chamber during those early weeks.

"Adom," she said, gently running her fingers through

his silken lock of hair, "you need not fear Simeon. He has a sharp tongue, but the best way to take the wind out of an angry man's sails is to stay calm."

"I know, Mother," Adom said, squirming under her touch. "Can we go? Ephraim and Manasseh want me to tell them what he looks like and how he talks. Manasseh says he has heard that the captive growls even in his sleep."

Her smile faded a little. "Surely you don't believe that?"

"No," Adom admitted sheepishly. "I told them that my mother wouldn't go near a man who growled."

"You are right. I wouldn't," Mandisa answered. She gave his cheek a playful pinch. "But our friend Simeon is tired of being confined. He likes open spaces, and he misses his freedom."

"Then why doesn't the vizier let him out?"

Mandisa tilted her head. "I don't know, son. If Simeon can be trusted to control himself, perhaps Tarik will allow him to walk in the gardens or the courtyard. We shall have to ask our master."

"All right, let's go!" Adom reached out and tugged on her hand so hard that he nearly pulled her off balance.

"I'm coming," she said, following him. "But first we find Halima and prepare Simeon's tray, then we visit the prisoner. He will be hungry."

As Adom raced ahead of her toward the kitchen, Mandisa's thoughts filtered back to recent conversations in which Simeon had spoken of his own children. He had six sons by two different wives, he had told her, unaware that her smile dimmed when he spoke of other women. His oldest son was twenty-one, the youngest, fifteen, and they blended seamlessly into the family compound, no more Simeon's children than Levi's, no less Simeon's sons than Reuben's. "Since my wives died, and they have had no mothers to spoil them," he said, his eyes darkening with an emotion she couldn't read, "they have made themselves at home wherever they could. Judah's wife is good to the younger two, and Reuben's wife is partial to the older ones, I think. In any case, I have never worried about them. They are in the good care of their uncles."

Mandisa couldn't understand why he seemed willing to allow his sons to remain separate from him, for he seemed a natural and patient teacher. Once he had put aside his resentment toward the vizier and his captivity, his tongue loosened and he had talked to her of many things, mostly of his brothers, the land of Canaan, and the simple beauty of an agrarian existence. Lately she had found herself recalling the life she had known before coming to Thebes, but she hastily closed the door on those memories. Nothing remained for her in Canaan, so there was no use thinking about the past.

Simeon seemed to fill her thoughts a great deal. It was only to be expected, she told herself, that she should think of him when she spent at least two hours a day doing what Ani called "keeping the beast at bay." Without someone to talk to, Simeon grew restless and was apt to storm about his chamber and disrupt the household.

Even with her attention, he was often irritable and gloomy, but she had learned how to lift his spirits by asking for his advice. On one occasion she brought him news of a sickness affecting the vizier's cattle, and he had prescribed powdered root bark of the *avionah*, or caperbush, the perfect poultice to draw out the infection and cure the animals. Another time she told him about a goat that no longer gave milk, and Simeon prescribed a mash of falcon's eye, or chick-peas. The concoction spurred the nanny goat's milk to flow within two days.

He had flushed in pleasure when she reported the success of his efforts, but his good nature could change as swiftly as a chameleon changes colors. Extremely stubborn, he refused to alter a position or opinion even if she pointed out its falseness. Yet he was unfailingly loyal to the few people he held in affection: namely, his sister and his brothers. He could be caring and even gentle. Once she was several hours late bringing his meal, and instead of the rage she feared, he greeted her with tenderness, concerned that some evil or illness had befallen her.

Halima warned Mandisa that Simeon might be using her. "He is a savage," she announced every afternoon as she helped prepare his dinner tray. "He will take advantage of your kind sympathy, my friend. One day when you least expect it, he will strike you and flee from this place. He hates us all. I've even heard him call down curses upon our master's god."

Mandisa did not believe Simeon's newfound stillness rested upon ulterior motives, but often she wondered if he could be trusted completely. Though he obviously hated his confinement, he behaved as though it hadn't occurred to him that she might ask the master for permission for him to wander freely around the house and grounds. Yet he had to know such permission was within her grasp. A few of her words in the master's ear would certainly win approval, and yet Simeon did not suggest or even hint that she press for his liberty.

So what was she to him—an ally, a necessary evil, a benevolent captor? She did not know but hoped that he was friend enough to agree to spend time with Adom. Simeon was rugged, rough, and wise in the ways of men—everything she was not—and Adom would need those qualities if he were to survive in the world beyond Zaphenath-paneah's house.

El Shaddai, she reasoned, worked in unexpected ways, but she could not doubt that He was working.

———

Simeon lifted his head in anticipation when he heard Mandisa's familiar rap. An idea had occurred to him in the night, and he had many things to ask her. He wanted to know more about the Egyptian festivals, for if the vizier celebrated a feast day, perhaps he would be inclined to release his captives for at least a few hours of liberty.

The bolt thumped onto the floor outside and the door opened, but instead of the woman he expected, a slender bright-eyed boy stepped into the room.

"What variety of desert dung are you?" Simeon snapped in annoyance. The boy stepped back, his eyes widening, and Mandisa swept in behind him, anger lighting her eyes. "In the name of decency, Simeon, can't you bridle your tongue for an instant? This is my son, Adom. He had thought he would like to meet you."

Her reprimand tore away the few remaining shreds of his good humor. "Am I a monkey in a cage that the children of this cursed house come to gape at me?" Simeon asked, clenching his jaw tighter. "It is bad enough that I must talk to you or go mad. I never said I would perform for your son."

"Adom, go outside and wait in the hall for me," Mandisa answered, her eyes darkening as she held Simeon's gaze. When the boy had left the room and closed the door, she advanced toward him with the fury of a determined tigress. "You have six sons, and you ought to miss them," she said, her lower lip trembling as she glared up at him. "I thought it might do you good to spend time with a boy who needs a father."

"A father?" He nearly choked on the word. "By heaven, woman, what makes you think I want to be around children? I don't spend time with my own boys. I certainly don't want to entertain yours."

She stepped back, her eyes bordered with sudden tears, and Simeon gritted his teeth, irritated beyond all reason. "I don't know what you want from me," he said, absently scrubbing his hair with his knuckles. "A father brings children into the world. That's what I've done. That's all I know how to do."

"A father," Mandisa said, crossing her arms across her heaving chest, "loves his children. He spends time with them. He teaches them what they need to know in order to survive in the world."

"Well," Simeon said, drawling in distinct mockery, "perhaps that is what *your* father did, but my father did nothing for us. Jacob, son of Isaac, begat twelve sons and divided his love between two. The rest of us were left to tend to our mothers and learn from each other."

She flinched slightly and did not answer, but some of the fire went out of her eyes. Simeon put his hand on his hip and looked down at the floor, strangely disappointed at the unexpected turn of events. He had hoped to pass the afternoon with Mandisa, but now she was upset. And, like a woman, she wouldn't be able to walk away and forget this conversation. She'd want to talk more about it, but Simeon decided years ago not to waste his energy or breath talking about Jacob.

"I'm sorry that your father did not give you what you needed," she finally said, her voice fragile and shaking. She kept her eyes averted from his face. "But you must understand—I fear for my son, who has no father at all."

His mind rumbled with sour thoughts. "Perhaps he is better off."

"I think not." She looked at him then, and her eyes narrowed in pain. "Simeon, my son needs someone to teach him, to talk to him. Ephraim and Manasseh are too young. Tarik and Ani and Zaphenath-paneah are too busy."

"And I have nothing to do. Is that it?"

"No." She uncrossed her arms and lowered her head. "I have prayed that God Almighty would send someone to me. In the last few weeks I have realized that the someone God has sent might be you."

Incredulous laughter floated up from his throat. "You think God put me in prison for *your* sake?"

"No." She shook her head, but the beginnings of a shy smile tipped the corners of her mouth. "I think God Almighty can transform ill into good. You are from Canaan, as am I, and Adom speaks the Canaanite language. My son would be honored—he would be *blessed*—to learn from a Canaanite man like you."

Simeon stiffened, making an effort to conquer his involuntary reaction to that gentle loving look of hers. No one had ever looked at him that way . . . as if he might be *admirable*. His anger evaporated, leaving only confusion.

A mocking voice inside insisted that she lied, that she was not to be trusted, that she spied for the cursed vizier.

Simeon stepped forward until he stood only inches away from her. "Tell me, Mandisa," he said, his tone commanding her to look up at him, "why would you trust your son to a man you consider dangerous? I am hated and feared in this house. I hear the servants whisper as they run by my door."

"You may be feared," she whispered, her eyes growing large and liquid as they lifted to meet his, "but it is your strength that frightens them. You have a temper, Simeon, no doubt, but you also have great courage and persistence. There is much in you that is good."

He looked away, unable to think under her steady scrutiny. What if she was using him, trying to coerce a confession of some sort? Did the vizier hope to disarm and dupe his captive through the charms of a lovely woman? If so, he would fail.

Simeon stood there in the hush, thinking, until he had an answer. If the vizier was using Mandisa, then Simeon could use her, too. "I will talk with your son," he said, suddenly aware that the scent of lilies rose from her skin, "if you speak to the vizier about allowing me out of this chamber." Drawing a deep breath, he managed a ragged smile. "I have been a model prisoner of late; the guards will support your request. I want to be released for half a day every day."

"An hour or two only, and Tarik will not want you to leave the villa," Mandisa answered quickly, looking away.

Simeon smiled. Her reply had come too easily; she had obviously anticipated his request. Either the captain or the vizier had coached her.

"Perhaps your son and I can walk around the villa together," he said, breathing in the scent of her. "But you must take my request to your master before I will allow your boy to come into my sight again."

She did not look up but nodded and moved toward the door.

"And, Mandisa," he called, dropping his voice, "I don't know what good I will be for Adom. I don't know how to be a father. I'm not sure I knew how to be a son."

Her eyes lifted toward him with a tenderness he'd never seen in them before.

"Thank you, Simeon," she whispered, her voice a velvet murmur in the room. "Thank you very much."

He was not surprised when Mandisa rapped early the next day. The captain of the vizier's guard stood outside with her when she opened the door, then Adom stepped around the corner, his young face bright with eagerness. A quick glance left and right assured Simeon that the captain had taken no chances. Guards stood in the hallways, blocking all possible means of escape.

"The garden," Mandisa said simply, pointing the way.

Ignoring the boy for a moment, Simeon walked through the hall. A roofed portico bridged the gap between the house and the garden's open expanse, and Simeon moved through it quickly, eager to feel the sun on his face. Once inside the walled garden, he closed his eyes in simple relief. Sunlight burnished the late morning air. He could almost feel his skin toasting under the warm rays. The wind smelled sweet, and the air vibrated to a long drop of birdsong from the nearby Nile.

Opening his eyes, he thought he had never seen a garden so spectacular. A fishpond dotted with blue lotus blossoms dominated the large rectangular area, and the fertile black mud on its banks had been planted with a mixed border of red poppies, blue cornflowers, and yellow-fruited mandrakes. Several varieties of flowering and fruit-bearing trees, each sitting in its own well of water, surrounded the fishpond: Carica figs and sycamore figs; date palms and dom palms, carob trees, willows, tamarisks, myrtles, and brightly petaled acacias. A host of gardeners, each working with a shaduf, poured water from the pond into runnels that crisscrossed through the garden plots. Standing amid the flowering beauty of the vizier's garden, Simeon found it hard to believe that famine and drought raged just outside the villa's pink-washed walls.

"Come, boy," he said after a few moments of basking in the sun. "Come sit beside me and I'll teach you how to get water from the desert grass."

"Truly?" The boy's countenance lifted, and the long-legged youth fell into step beside Simeon.

"It will be difficult, seeing that this is not the desert," Simeon said, shrugging as he moved toward a stone bench beside the pathway. "But once you know a thing that can save your life, you don't forget it."

"I can learn," the boy answered, his eyes shining with enthusiasm. "Teach me something that Ephraim and Manasseh do not know."

"And who are Ephraim and Manasseh?" Simeon asked, sinking to the bench. He propped his elbows on his knees and glanced around. Mandisa and Tarik had retreated to the portico beside the house, giving him at least the illusion of freedom.

"Ephraim and Manasseh are the master's boys," Adom answered.

Simeon lifted a brow. The names were remarkably similar to words he knew, but surely the Lord High Vizier of all Egypt would not give his sons Canaanite names.

"All right." Simeon bent to the boy's level. "The most important thing to remember in the desert is that all trails lead to water. And death comes quickly, my boy, to a man or an animal without water."

"All trails?" Adom asked, a skeptical look on his face. "Is a trail like a path?"

"By heaven above, woman," Simeon called, looking over at Mandisa. "Has the boy never been out of this house?"

"Of course," Mandisa answered, indignation on her face. "But he does not roam about in the wilderness as you seem to expect he should."

He would have answered that the wilderness brought up better boys than the opulent atmosphere of an Egyptian villa, but he held his tongue. He had to be careful. He had worked too hard to earn this woman's trust. In her, he knew, lay the keys to greater freedom. If he had to play nursemaid to her son for a few hours of escape, he would do it. But nurturing did not come naturally, for the sons of Israel had never tolerated softness. Of all his brothers, only Joseph had ever played nursemaid to a younger sibling. From the first, Joseph had delighted in baby Benjamin, coddling him as if he could make up for the baby's missing mother. . . .

Joseph again. Abruptly, Simeon returned his thoughts to the matter at hand. "All trails—yes, paths—lead to water, and if you are thirsty, you should follow the direction in which all trails converge. Trails will be marked by signs of camps—campfire ashes, animal droppings, trampled terrain. Also, birds tend to circle over water. Most flocks fly to watering places at dawn and sunset. Just as the earth points to the Creator God, so birds will point you to water."

"Which Creator god do you speak of?" Adom asked, a strangely adult gleam in his eye. "Neter or El Shaddai?"

Simeon lifted a brow. "Neter?" he asked, not familiar with the name. "Is this some Egyptian idol?"

"Neter is the unseen God of the Egyptians," Mandisa answered, unable to resist meddling in the conversation. She stepped forward from the portico, apparently no longer willing to pretend that she could leave them alone. "But most people in Thebes pay Neter no attention. They prefer the gods who live in temples, gods they can see and placate."

"I understand," Simeon said, nodding. He looked back to the boy, approving of the intelligence he saw in the lad's face. "Each man worships his own god, boy. You will have to make your own choice."

"Which god do you worship, Simeon?" Adom asked.

Simeon cast a quick look at Mandisa. "None, at the moment," he answered, shooting her a withering glance. "For I am not at *liberty* to worship any. But my father worships God Almighty and clings to the belief that he and his people are part of a chosen race. He says that the Almighty made a covenant with our grandfather Abraham."

"What covenant is this?" Mandisa asked, her eyes burning with eager curiosity.

Simeon looked away and stared into the memory of his past. "God Shaddai called Abraham out of his country and promised to make him a great nation, to magnify his name. In return for Abraham's obedience, God promised to bless those who blessed Abraham and his seed and to curse those who offered curses instead of blessing. He promised to give us the land of Canaan as an eternal dwelling place and to bless all families of the earth through our family lineage."

"A great honor," Mandisa whispered. Her voice trembled, as though some emotion had touched her.

"A great fantasy," Simeon answered, meeting her eyes. "The land of Canaan is not ours and never has been. We own only a pitifully small burial plot there. And our family has not been blessed but cursed. One of my brothers died at seventeen; two nephews were struck down in their youth; my sister has been forever disgraced. That bloody business at Shechem hangs over our heads. Then Reuben slept with one of my father's concubines and angered the old man beyond belief—"

He stopped and bit his lip when Mandisa jerked Adom to his feet. "Your lesson is done for today," she said, pushing her son toward the house. "Go find Ani and ask where you might be of help."

Simeon waited until the boy had left the garden, then he stroked his beard in what he hoped was a properly reproachful posture. "I'm sorry," he said, sighing. "But I warned you. I don't know how to behave around children."

"You might learn how to speak of more pleasant things," she said, wrapping her arms about herself as if to defend her honor from the wickedness he had described.

"My family is not pleasant," he responded sharply, abandoning all pretense. "Murder, rape, incest, disloyalty, betrayal—all these I have known within my own kin. If my clan is not unsullied enough for your tastes—"

"Mine is no better," she answered, meeting his icy gaze straight on. "But I do not discuss such things around children. And I would not dare call the promises of Almighty God a mere fantasy."

"Your faith is stronger than mine, then," Simeon answered lazily. He stretched out one leg and crossed his arms. "Don't tell me you would choose the invisible El Shaddai over the Egyptian gods. I hear the idols take cruises up and down the Nile, visit harems of beautiful women, and bestow gifts to the crowds who follow them."

"I prefer a god who does not make me yawn with familiarity," she answered, moving toward the portico. She turned and cast her parting words over her shoulder. "A god who fills me with awe. A god I cannot control, but who can control me."

"Good luck in your search, then," Simeon said, smiling at her naiveté. "When you find this awe-inspiring God, be sure to let me know. I may want to worship Him, too."

"Perhaps He will find you," she retorted. She nodded to Tarik, a signal that Simeon's liberty had come to an end.

The captain approached, grinning, and Simeon reluctantly stood. He had managed to remain outside for nearly half an hour, far less time than he had hoped for, but probably far longer than he deserved.

⌒ Nineteen ⌒

MANDISA HAD NOT WALKED MORE THAN TEN paces from the garden when she sensed that something was amiss in the villa. The usual noises of the house had abruptly ceased. Waves of silence seemed to reverberate through the hallways.

"Adom!" she gasped, fearing the worst. He could have run from the garden and dashed under the hooves of a chariot horse, or run in front of Tarik's archers as they practiced their marksmanship. . . .

She hurried through the halls, and the hard fist of fear tightened in her stomach when she saw a crowd gathered on the portico at the front courtyard. The house slaves and servants were clustered in a knot on the front steps; herdsmen, stableboys, and guards ringed the periphery. Every eye was fixed upon something in the distance. Every mouth remained silent as the members of Zaphenath-paneah's household strained to hear whatever was happening near the gatekeeper's lodge.

"What is it?" Mandisa cried, struggling to push her way through the crowd. "Is anyone hurt?"

One of the women on the portico turned, and Mandisa nearly melted in relief when she recognized Halima. "Halima, what has happened?" Her hand flew to her throat as a new thought struck her. "Have the brothers from Canaan returned?"

"We could not be so fortunate." The slave girl shook her head and lifted an eyebrow in amused contempt. "I don't know why the men are behaving like such fools. The master buys new slaves at least once a month."

"New slaves?" Mandisa's mind whirled at the girl's dry response. "All of this—the guards have gathered—just to look at new slaves?"

"One slave," Halima corrected, envy twisting in her voice. "They've come from their duties to look at *her*."

Mandisa stared in confusion, and Halima pointed over the heads of the men in front of her. "Ani and Zaphenath-paneah visited the slave market this morning. I've already heard the story from one of the guards who accompanied them. It seems that *she* was up for auction and creating quite a disturbance, and one of the onlookers challenged Ani to buy her. He refused, knowing full well that such a woman only causes trouble."

"Trouble?" Mandisa asked, not understanding.

"In fact," Halima said, lowering her voice as she pulled Mandisa from the crowd, "one of the bodyguards told me that the master had already turned to go, but the auctioneer called out the wench's name. And then, without explanation, the master ordered Ani to buy the woman and bring her here."

A shadow of distress crossed Halima's face as she thrust her hands on her wide hips. "I was thanking the gods because the Canaanite had calmed. But now our master has brought us another troublemaker, and this one will create a different kind of difficulty."

Muttering under her breath, Halima walked away. Driven by curiosity, Mandisa wormed her way through the group of onlookers until she looked out toward the gatekeeper's lodge. A woman in a gauzy garment stood there, her wrists and ankles shackled. Ani, who seemed unusually agitated, stood behind her, urging the gatekeeper to hurry and remove the woman's bonds.

Mandisa would have recognized her as a harlot even without the earrings, the nose ring, the bracelets and bangles. The woman's curled hair flowed down onto her shoulders in a soft dark tide that shone in the sunlight as though with an inner fire. Her bearing was about as subtle as a parade, her shape as sensuous as her ripe mouth. She stared out at her audience like a black panther, darkly beautiful but deadly. For some inexplicable reason, Mandisa felt her stomach contract in an odd little spasm.

"Who is she?" she whispered, not expecting an answer.

"Her name is Tizara," a guard next to her replied, his eyes as fixed as a stone idol's. "She is our master's new slave."

Amid a scattering of nervous laughter, one of the kitchen slaves joked, "I don't think the mistress will be letting the master anywhere near her."

Obviously uncomfortable, Ani lifted his eyes to the congregated slaves and clapped his hands in disapproval. As the slaves, guards, and servants reluctantly returned to their duties, a guard gingerly took Tizara's arm and escorted her to the slave quarters.

Mandisa had nearly reached her own small chamber when Ani appeared at her side. "You must help me," he said, anxiously shifting his weight from foot to foot. "I don't know what I am to do with the creature, but I could not dissuade the master. I tried to convince him she would be a problem, but he insisted that I bring her here."

"Why did he buy her?" Mandisa asked, lifting a brow. "Can he not see what she is?"

Ani shrugged. "He said something about no soul being beyond redemption. How could I argue with that? You know he has a softness in his heart. He is continually buying slaves in order to free them."

"But what does she know how to do?" Mandisa interrupted, frowning. "I mean, of what *practical* use is she?"

"I don't know." Ani wrung his hands. "If I put her in the kitchens, the men will fight over the opportunity to grind corn next to her. And if I send her to the fields—oh, by the gods, I could never do that. Nothing would ever get done, and she'd be too far away for me to watch her. I could never assign her to the master or mistress, and *I* have no use for her."

"I still can't see why he bought her," Mandisa said, shaking her head. "He is not the type to be moved by a woman like that."

"Our master did not even look at her," Ani answered, color rising on his cheeks. "He had walked away, but then the auctioneer called the woman's name and said she was from Shechem."

Shechem. That bloody slaughter at Shechem.

"She is a Canaanite, then," Mandisa said, not daring to look Ani in the eye. He would not understand, but she grasped at least a little of the reason for the master's compassion. This woman was from his country, from Mandisa's and Simeon's.

"Ani, why don't you assign her to the children?" Mandisa suggested, giving the steward a bright smile. "She can keep an eye on Ephraim and Manasseh when they are not having lessons. Since the Canaanite captive has come, I do not have as much time for them as I used to. The slaves who have been watching the boys would rather be back to their former work."

A cry of relief broke from the older man's lips. "Ah, Mandisa. You are a jewel! For now, at least, you have solved the problem. And since this is your idea, you must help me with the girl. You must make certain that she never goes directly into the Lady Asenath's presence. That would never do. And since you are a lady of noble bearing, perhaps you can teach her how to be modest and carry herself like a proper lady."

Mandisa put up her hands in defense. "Wait, Ani. I don't want to care for your little scarlet bird. The master told *you* to buy her."

"But what can I do with her?" The old man clapped his hand to his balding head. "You, my dear Mandisa, are the one to oversee her. Promise me that you will."

"I won't."

"But it is your master's wish."

"He has said nothing to me about it."

"But he will. All I have to do is put a word in his ear."

Mandisa paused, knowing that Ani spoke the truth. The same compassion that had inspired Zaphenath-paneah to ask if Mandisa would be willing to comfort Simeon would soon ask her to guide this shocking and offensive harlot. Because she loved her master and his wife, she could refuse them nothing . . . and it would be more noble and gracious to volunteer before being asked.

"All right," she said, throwing her hands up in resignation. "I'll look after her. Send her to me in the morning after our mistress is dressed, and I'll take her on a tour of the villa and tell her how to care for the children."

"Mandisa, I could kiss you," Ani said, clapping his hands together. And then, while she gasped in surprise, he pulled her forehead to his lips and did just that.

Two weeks later, as Thebes was ariot with the celebration of the new year, Tarik was more concerned about keeping peace within the walls of Zaphenath-paneah's villa than controlling the boisterous drunks in the streets. Standing by the gatekeeper's lodge, he stiffened as the new woman walked across the courtyard, two mystified little boys in her wake. A man would have to be made of stone not to notice her as she passed by. Her slow and swaying carriage summoned lustful thoughts from their hiding places, and when her eyes turned toward a man, his face and blood grew hot. . . .

"Tarik." A soft voice wrested his attention from the scene in the courtyard, and he jerked in surprise. Halima stood next to him, undisguised hurt in her eyes.

"What is it, Halima?"

"There is trouble in the kitchen. The baker says he is to serve Tizara and the children at the midday meal. The vintner insists it is his duty. An hour ago they came to blows, and though they have ceased striving for the moment, I am afraid one will kill the other."

"They are fools," Tarik muttered under his breath, willing himself not to take one last look toward the temptress in the courtyard. Placing his hand upon the knife in his belt, he strode toward the kitchen, dimly aware that Halima followed.

———

"Will you little monkeys be quiet?" Tizara forced the words with studied calmness, afraid that one more boyish outburst would force her to scream and tear her hair.

Ephraim, the most naturally quiet of the pair, looked up. He lay under his brother in the sand of the courtyard, the loser in a lopsided wrestling match.

"Tizara?"

"What, Ephraim?"

"Can we splash in the garden pool? If we promise not to make much noise?"

She sighed. If they got wet, she'd have to march them into their chambers for fresh kilts and a hair-washing, past a hundred scorn-filled disapproving sets of eyes, but at least they'd be entertained for a while.

"Yes, but walk, don't run, to the garden. I will join you there."

The boys took off like jackrabbits, and Tizara bent to gather their tops, toys, and sandals. *What am I doing here?* she asked herself again as she bent to retrieve Manasseh's paddle doll. Try as she might, she could not put all the pieces together.

She had not been surprised when she brought a high price at the slave auction, nor was she shocked to learn that she had been purchased by the Grand Vizier of Egypt, regent to the young Pharaoh. She knew her special skills were in great demand. She felt her power every time she walked before a crowd and adopted the role men seemed to expect of her. The act was second nature to her now—a certain way of walking, a manner of half-closing the eyes, a bold smile that promised a moment of immortality, a sensuous note in the voice . . .

But a nursemaid needed none of those skills. So why had the vizier paid a top price for her and then assigned her to his children?

Tizara had gaped in disbelief when the disapproving steward told her of the vizier's wishes. "Two children?" she had asked, practically stammering in confusion. "The vizier does not want me for himself?"

"The vizier contents himself with the charms of his wife," the steward answered, his expression taut and derisive.

"Then perhaps he intends to give me to Pharaoh." She smiled and studied her henna-tinted fingertips. "Perhaps you should check with the vizier before you send me to care for children."

"Believe me, young woman, if given my choice, I'd send you onto the street," Ani answered, eyeing her like a haughty rooster. "But the vizier expressly asked me to find you a job, and I'm assigning you to his children. It is my wish; therefore it is your command."

Throughout Tizara's twenty-two years, men had vied for her and lied for her. She had seen them make fools of themselves to spend a week, even a night, with her. She had been used and abused, petted and praised, bartered and sold. She thought she had seen everything, that nothing would ever surprise her again. . . .

But Zaphenath-paneah had. She had caught a glimpse of the handsome vizier in the slave market and sighed in relief when she learned he had bought her. Most of the men she had encountered in her brief lifetime had been hardened by desire and made ugly by defiant determination. Whether they were soldiers, priests, husbands, fathers, farmers, or kings, they all wore the same twisted lecherous look when they came into her tent. At the slave market she had suspected that Zaphenath-paneah might be unusual, but she had no idea how different he would prove to be.

As the weeks passed, Mandisa rejoiced that at least one male in the household remained free of Tizara's influence. Since Simeon's last visit with Adom had not gone as she expected, he had remained confined to his chamber and so had neither seen nor heard of Tizara. Mandisa was determined that he would not. The man was difficult to manage even in his calmer resigned state of mind. His boiling blood did not need to be stirred by the sight of a harlot from his own country.

Grudgingly keeping her promise to Ani, Mandisa met with Tizara each morning to outline the slave's daily duties with the children. After watching a blush run like a shadow over Adom's cheeks the first time he met Tizara, Mandisa decided that he did not need a nursemaid. Ephraim and Manasseh, on the other hand, needed constant supervision. And though they were old enough to realize that Tizara was very pretty, they were still young enough not to care.

Each morning Mandisa listened to Tizara's complaints with a vague sense of unreality. Though the slave understood very well her effect upon men, she could not understand why the women of the vizier's household seemed to regard her with open disdain. "Women just don't like me," she told Mandisa one morning, lifting a slender bare shoulder in a gesture that captivated the attention of the guards twenty paces away. "I have no idea why."

Mandisa wanted to scream that perhaps it was because Tizara was shallow, flighty, egotistical, and lazy, but she had promised to help, not hinder. So she bit her tongue and walked toward the garden, reluctantly resigned to the fact that Tizara would follow.

Mandisa was willing to admit that Tizara provoked them all to jealousy, but her willowy beauty, while exceptional, sprang more from attitude than physical perfection. What was it, Mandisa wondered, that made her seem more sensuous than other women? Tizara's eyes were wide, her nose straight, and her lips full. But occasionally Mandisa caught the slave in an unguarded moment of deep thought, and the hard bitter look on the woman's narrow face was anything but beautiful.

The slave had but one duty—to watch over and attend to the master's sons—but while the boys studied with Ani, Tizara flitted around Mandisa like an annoying mosquito. The former harlot had both a low tolerance for routine and a wild imagination, and Mandisa found it difficult to keep her temper when the girl buzzed around with complaints and wild stories.

Through a stream of constant babble, Mandisa did learn the slave's history. Tizara had been raised in Shechem, sold into slavery at a young age, and trained in the "art of pleasing" before she had even reached maturity. A group of camel traders had owned her first, carting her from settlement to settlement, offering her services for silver. She had known both pleasant and brutal masters, she told Mandisa, but never thought to enter as boring an existence as the one she had come to know in the vizier's house.

"I am caring for children!" she exclaimed, following Mandisa into the garden. "I don't know why. I will never have them, and I don't really know what to do with them."

"You'll never have them?" Mandisa interrupted, stopping. Despite her irritation at the woman's ceaseless and shallow chatter, she was curious. "Why won't you ever have children?"

"One of my masters paid an eastern physician to do something to me." For a moment, Tizara's eyes seemed as empty as a blind man's, then she shrugged. "But I never wanted children. What are they, but helpless little people?"

"Some would say they are the most precious treasures on earth," Mandisa answered, bending to snip a few lotus blossoms for Lady Asenath's afternoon bouquet. "Our master and mistress adore their boys. And your duties are not difficult. Some would say you are fortunate to care for the children."

"Fortunate." Tizara shook her head at the word. "I'll admit that life here is pleasant. There is enough food, and the steward does not beat his slaves. But I am not happy. I yearn for something . . . more."

"More?" Mandisa asked, her lips thinning with irritation. She placed the flowers in her basket and shot Tizara a penetrating look as she straightened. "You live in the finest house in Thebes. Only the king's palace is greater. You have a kind master. You care for two charming and delightful little boys—"

"Have you never wanted more, Mandisa?" Tizara interrupted.

The question caught Mandisa off guard, and she felt herself stammering. "Of course not. I am happy to serve my master and mistress. I have a wonderful son. What more could I want?"

"Perhaps you have everything, then," Tizara answered, disbelief in the tone of her voice. "But I don't. I want to do something that matters. I want to know someone who cares. I want to *feel* again. . . ."

A dim flush raced like a fever across her pale and beautiful face, and for a brief moment her countenance seemed to open. Behind the mask Mandisa saw bewilderment, fear, and indescribable pain, but then Tizara drew back inside herself.

She pouted prettily when she felt Mandisa watching her. "Don't take me seriously, Mandisa. No one else does. And tell me again why I shouldn't take the boys to the temple of Min. She is a fertility goddess, and her priests and priestesses perform the best dances."

"Our master's sons must learn to read and write, not dance," Mandisa answered, sighing as she moved away from the lotus plants in the garden pool. "Please, Tizara, just make sure they practice their lessons. That is all you have to do."

Later that afternoon, exhausted from debating with Tizara, Mandisa gathered Simeon's tray from the kitchen and took it to his room. She found him in a more sullen mood than usual.

"What, no greeting?" she asked, setting the tray on a stand. "No 'Thank you, Mandisa, and how are things in the world today?' "

"Why should I care?" he growled. He was sitting on the floor in a darkened corner of the room, ignoring the fine furnishings Ani had supplied to replace the things Simeon had broken. Mandisa had assured Ani that the prisoner would not break anything else, but now, seeing the gleam of fire in his eye, she wondered if she had been too hasty in her promise.

"What is wrong?" she asked, breathing an exasperated sigh. She folded her arms and leaned against the wall in a pose of weary dignity. She would have to speak to Zaphenath-paneah. Because of her master's good nature and compassion, she did nothing these days but endure and debate stubborn Canaanites.

"What month is it?" he snapped, not looking at her. "The house rings with the noise of celebration, and I've picked up enough of the Egyptian language to know that the people look forward to the coming of a new year."

"Of course," Mandisa answered, her voice heavy with sarcasm. "Are you upset because Pharaoh did not invite you to the palace? Or perhaps the star of the new year should not have risen without your permission."

"What month is it?" he repeated, giving her a black look. "How long have I been here? It has not been a full year."

"The vizier's house, as much as you would like to disbelieve me, does not revolve around your coming and going, Simeon. Our year begins with the rising of the star Sirius and the inundation of the river in the season of Akhet. You and your brothers came here during the season of Shemu, the drought. So you have been here five months."

"If the river is rising now, the flood will come and the famine will end," Simeon remarked with a helpless wave of his hands. "My brothers will not come for me."

"Of course they will! Your father will send them."

"No. He cares more for the son at home than for me. Rachel bore Benjamin, you see. My mother was Leah. My father bears little love for anyone not born of Rachel."

Mandisa regarded him with somber curiosity, not knowing how to answer. She had sensed that Simeon harbored deep feelings of animosity toward his father, but she had never heard the true state of affairs so baldly stated. Was this the unhappiness that fueled Simeon's deep-seated anger?

"I am certain your father cares for you," she said finally. "All fathers love their sons. You need only to ask him, Simeon. Confront him with your feelings so he can tell you how much he loves you."

"It doesn't matter. I stopped caring long ago," Simeon interrupted, his lids slipping down over his eyes.

"Of course you care," she whispered, moving toward him. Her senses reached out into his loneliness, struggling to understand the forces that had hardened his heart. Suddenly, in a breathless flash of insight, she thought that God Shaddai might have placed her beside Simeon not to serve Zaphenath-paneah or win a father's influence for her son, but to bring light to a tormented and dark soul.

She knelt to look into his face. "Your brothers *will* come for you. God has told Zaphenath-paneah that the river will not flood this year, nor the next, not until five more years of famine have passed."

Her words seemed to amuse him. "You are an intelligent woman, Mandisa. Yet you would believe the prophet of an Egyptian god."

Lowering her voice, Mandisa pressed her hand upon the fist he clenched at his knees. "Zaphenath-paneah listens to the Almighty God, El Shaddai. You will find no idols in his temple, no other god in his heart."

For a moment his eyes held hers, seeming to clutch at the hope her words offered like a drowning man reaches for the shore. But then the light in his eyes dimmed, and he drew his lips into a tight smile. "El Shaddai is the God of Abraham, Isaac, and Jacob, not of the Egyptians," he said, his voice final and flat. "The Almighty would not speak to your vizier. Your master has tricked you, Mandisa. He has lied."

She closed her eyes, resisting the impulse to tell Simeon that Zaphenath-paneah was his own long lost brother. Surely then he would understand and have faith in the future! But the master had charged her to keep his secret, and she would not disobey, not even for this desperate and lonely man.

"You must believe me," she finally answered, moving her hand to his forearm. "Your brothers will return, and you will be freed."

"They must. I cannot live long like this, Mandisa," he whispered, his hand catching hers. His voice quavered with long-suppressed emotion. "I feel like a bear in a pit. Sometimes I think my heart will burst."

"This time of waiting will be over soon," she said, calming him. Gently, tentatively, with her free hand she reached out and nudged an unruly lock of dark hair from his forehead. Underneath his angry bluster he was as much a boy as Adom, and Mandisa had always known how to soothe her son.

But Simeon was not her son. Abruptly he dropped her hand and pulled his head away from her ministering fingertips. "If they do not come, I will escape this room and flee, even if it costs me my life," he said, crossing his arms. His eyes caught and held hers. "If you hear that I have escaped, Mandisa, lock yourself in your chamber, for I will kill anyone who crosses my path or tries to stop me."

"Simeon, you don't mean a word you're saying." She reached out, trying to recapture the tender emotion they had shared a moment before, but he leapt to his feet and retreated across the room. Standing against the wall, tall, rawboned, and bearded, he looked like a giant, and she knew his strength of will matched the power of his arms and back. He meant every word of his warning and intended for her to heed it. Did he also intend for her to pass it on to the vizier as a threat?

He could threaten all day, and she could carry a million messages to the vizier, but not one of them would affect his situation. Simeon might think the vizier controlled his destiny, but Mandisa knew Zaphenath-paneah waited upon God Shaddai.

How could Simeon have grown up in the vizier's family, under the same father, without coming to know and serve the same God?

"I wonder," she said, rising slowly to her feet, "do your strong arms never tire of resisting the Almighty God of your fathers? How blind are your eyes, Simeon, that you cannot see Him?"

Stiffening in response, he closed his eyes and clenched his fists. And as she slipped from the room, she heard him scream in despair.

— Twenty —

SIMEON'S HEAD ACHED WHEN HE AWOKE THE next morning and sat up in bed. He had passed a nearly sleepless night, bothered by dreams and images of people long dead and not quite forgotten. His wives, young Joseph, and the thousand men of Shechem had all filed past his bed, pointing at him with glowing fingertips while blame and accusation burned in their eyes. "You, Simeon, stole our lives while we were young and entitled to many more days," they all whispered, their gentle voices mocking his fear. "For as long as you live, we will steal your nights."

Clapping his hand to his head, he groaned and wished for Mandisa. But she would not come until later, especially after the scene last night. She had been an angel, kneeling at his feet as if to comfort him, but no one could comfort away the hurts of forty-five years.

How like a child she was! She talked as if she had endured much in her past, but what could she have experienced in twenty-odd years of life? She lived in a magnificent estate, worked for a woman who adored and trusted her, and had been blessed with an intelligent, beautiful son.

Simeon could even admit that she was charming. In a way she was more desirable than the vizier's coolly beautiful wife, whom Simeon had glimpsed when he and his brothers first entered the vizier's palace. Like the esteemed Lady Asenath, Mandisa was small of form and features, but unlike the vizier's wife, she moved with the graceful air of a woman who is at home in many worlds. He could imagine her drawing water from the wells outside his father's tents, and he had already seen that she was completely at home in the throne room of a king's regent.

Stop this, you fool. Do not torture yourself with what can never be! Mandisa had already made her home in a prince's villa. She had established a wholesome and prosperous life in Thebes. She no longer belonged to Canaan, and he could not imagine her agreeing to return to a world of sandstorms and camels, of dung fires, tents, and work-worn women.

Grunting, he turned and rested his elbow on the ridiculous padded support the Egyptians used to pillow their heads. A stentorian voice rumbled through the hall—the voice of the esteemed Zaphenath-paneah—and a slight chill passed over Simeon as he listened.

How hauntingly familiar the vizier's voice was! Even though Simeon understood only a few of the words, the man's tone rankled something in Simeon's memory, jarred some fragment of recollection from its proper lodging place. But everyone in this house, from Ani the steward to the lowliest kitchen maid, revered and respected the great vizier. Unconsciously they copied his manners and morals, their voices quietly imitating his. It was not surprising that the vizier's voice now seemed as familiar as the sun and the moon.

Simeon lifted his head, wondering if the great and mighty vizier would open the door to this room. *Come on,* he thought, not moving on his bed. *I won't stand up for you. I won't adjust my kilt. I won't even push the hair out of my eyes. You will take me as you find me, great vizier, and I won't care if you don't like what you see.*

But the door did not open. Strangely disappointed, Simeon lowered his head and listened to the soft tramping of passing footsteps, undoubtedly the vizier's entourage of guards, scribes, and servants.

He turned flat on his back and wearily considered the ceiling. Time, which he had once thought precious and fleeting, now stretched before him like an endless barren plateau, more desolate than the deserts surrounding Egypt. The day would offer nothing new. Mandisa would come at some point to bring his meal and clean his room. Perhaps, if Simeon was very lucky, that little preening captain of the guard would enter, scowl, and exchange a threat or two.

In the meantime, he had nothing to do but plot his escape. Despite what Mandisa had said, Simeon knew his brothers would not come back. Jacob would sooner die than allow Benjamin to leave the family compound with the same brothers who had lost Joseph. And if the famine ended, there would be no need for any of Israel's clan to journey to the Black Land. And the famine would end soon, no matter what the vizier had told Mandisa. Never had the earth known famine for seven years. The world could not survive such a disaster.

Zaphenath-paneah listens to the Almighty God, El Shaddai. You will find no idols in his temple, no other god in his heart. The memory of Mandisa's words brought a twisted smile to Simeon's face. The woman was indeed gullible. How had the vizier convinced her that El Shaddai spoke to him? Mandisa was from Canaan, so the name of Jacob's God was probably familiar to her. She had undoubtedly heard Zaphenath-paneah speak of the invisible Egyptian god and assumed that he spoke of El Shaddai. Or perhaps the vizier had the brazen boldness to claim that he spoke for the God of Israel! But Jacob's God wouldn't— *couldn't*—speak to an Egyptian. He had adopted the children of Israel for His own. He had no use or plans for the other peoples of the earth. The Almighty certainly would have no reason to speak to the cursed Egyptian who had imprisoned Jacob's second-born son.

"When I escape," Simeon murmured, locking his hands together behind his head, "I will find Zaphenath-paneah and kill him for his bold effrontery. Then no one will say that this vizier speaks for the Almighty God of Israel."

———

"Mandisa?"

The Simeon who greeted her at midday seemed relaxed

and amiable, and Mandisa found it difficult not to return his disarming smile.

"Yes?" She lifted a brow as she entered with his meal tray, pleased that the captive seemed to be on his best behavior. He sat on the floor, his back supported by the frame of his bed, his bare legs stretched out across the cool marble.

"I am ready to venture out again and willing to teach your son. But first, in fairness, there are things I should tell you. Can you take some time to talk today?"

Mandisa thought of Tizara, who'd soon be lingering in the hallways, waiting to hector her. "I have all the time in the world this afternoon," she answered, grateful for Simeon's conversational mood. "My mistress has gone to the palace with Zaphenath-paneah, and there is nothing else for me to do." She lowered his tray to a stand. "What did you want to talk about?"

His lips twisted into a cynical smile, and the mask of good humor fell away. "I suppose I could begin by asking a question. What is the worst thing you have ever done?"

He spoke in his casual way, and she assumed he was teasing.

"Oh, I don't know," she said, moving toward the chair against the wall. "Once I ate one of the cook's shat cakes when he wasn't looking. Halima was about to be blamed for it, but then I confessed."

His laughter contained a sharp edge. "Is that all?"

"I don't know." She sank into the chair, then settled back to search his face. "Why do you ask?"

His dark eyes narrowed speculatively. "You have asked me to spend time with your son. I want to do it. I want a few hours of liberty, but I'm not sure you know what sort of man I truly am. I have done many things, Mandisa, of which you would not approve."

"I think I know what sort of man you are, Simeon, son of Jacob," she answered, pretending to pick an imaginary piece of lint from her gown as she fought to control her swirling emotions. "You are strong and loyal. You have often been misunderstood."

"Would you like to know the worst thing I have ever done?"

She looked away. "Not really."

"But I should tell you. I once killed nearly a thousand men."

She raised her eyes to find him watching her. Lines of concentration had deepened along his brows and under his eyes.

"Of course, my brother Levi helped me. We did it to avenge our sister, Dinah, who was taken by force and treated like a harlot."

"You don't have to tell me this." Icy fear twisted around her heart. Could he be telling the truth?

"That wasn't the worst, Mandisa. My sister, Dinah, gave birth to a child. My father would have nothing to do with the baby, for when the child came, he was still mourning Rachel's death. My brothers knew Dinah would never be married if she kept another man's child, and so—"

"Simeon, stop." She cut him off, her heart in her throat.

"At the time I didn't think it was so terribly evil to rid ourselves of it. Many of the other clans in the area would not have hesitated. So, while my sister slept, I took the infant away and left it in the wilderness."

"Abandoned!" Mandisa shuddered as the word slipped from her lips.

A cold congested expression settled on his face. "I have nightmares. The men I have killed march by my bed and promise to terrorize my sleep for the rest of my life. They do not frighten me with their threats, but if I hear a baby's cry in the night"—his eyes widened, and Mandisa could tell his thoughts had wandered far away—"it is as if I have suddenly found myself at the edge of a precipice."

His face darkened with unreadable emotions. As she studied him, a cold lump grew in her stomach, spreading tendrils of uneasiness through her limbs. She was sitting alone with a murderer of men, and even worse—a baby killer. But she had known from the first that he was capable of such things, for Zaphenath-paneah had warned her. And what was past was past, lost in the well of yesterday, and should not be dredged up again.

"Would you do it now?" she asked, dismayed to hear a faint thread of hysteria in her voice.

"What?" His mouth dipped into an even deeper frown.

"If Dinah had a baby tomorrow, would you kill it?"

He stared at her with deadly concentration for a long moment. "I don't know," he said finally, tenting his fingers in front of his face. "No, I don't think I would. But I don't know, Mandisa."

Pressing her lips together, she rose from her chair. "Your anger has led you to commit grievous acts in the past, Simeon," she said, lifting a brow. "And just as a reasonable man is seldom angry, an angry man is seldom reasonable. But I think you are becoming a reasonable man."

Mandisa's hands trembled as she slid the bolt across Simeon's door. She was more shaken than she cared to admit. Did the loneliness of his solitary confinement lead him to such introspection? She knew that dark deeds and even darker thoughts lay in every man's heart, but she was not accustomed to being invited to hear such secret confessions, especially from a man she had come to admire.

She had changed the subject as rapidly as she dared, hastening to assure Simeon that the river had not risen to its normal level, therefore the famine would continue, and his brothers would eventually be forced to return to Egypt. But he hadn't responded to her forced good cheer. He had only asked whether she would still allow Adom to visit, and if such a visit might be arranged for the afternoon.

She had looked at him with surprise, remembering his initial hostility toward the idea and his reluctant confession. "I don't know. I suppose so," she said, nearly dropping his dinner tray in her anxious confusion. "I will find him and ask whether he wants to talk with you again."

She had forced a smile to her lips and lightened her tone. "He actually enjoyed learning from you last time, Simeon. He has begun to watch the birds fly home at sunset, knowing that they are flying to water holes."

"Call out your guards, then," he had murmured satirically, reminding her of the other half of their bargain. "I will want to walk in the garden. And I promise that your son will be safe with me."

She had nodded and promised to return before long with Adom. And now Simeon was waiting behind the door, listening for her footsteps, wondering if she still trusted him enough to fetch her son.

She did. But she would feel better knowing there were guards around. She turned and drew up in surprise when she nearly bumped into Tizara in the hall outside Simeon's room.

"Are you all right, Mandisa?" the slave girl asked, a coy smile on her face. "You are quite flushed." She peered past Mandisa toward the bolted door. "And what, may I ask, is kept in that room? No one will tell me."

"Nothing," Mandisa answered, instantly on guard. She fixed her features in a stern expression and took two quick steps toward the kitchens. "Nothing that concerns you, Tizara."

"Since the door is bolted on the outside," the slave answered, moving forward and placing her hand upon the door's rough wood as if she would caress whatever lay inside, "you are trying to keep someone in." She quirked her brow in a question. "Does Zaphenath-paneah have an idiot son who must be shielded from the light of day?"

"Our master has only two sons—those in your care," Mandisa answered, fighting the impulse to physically pull the girl from the doorway. "And if you must know, a captive resides in that room. Tarik supervises him."

"Tarik . . . and you."

"I do not supervise. I am needed because I speak Canaanite, and so does the captive."

"I speak Canaanite," Tizara whispered. She leaned against the door, closing her eyes. "Is he a very wild man, Mandisa? I've yet to meet a man I cannot tame. I have reduced many to sniveling idiocy. If our master needs this Canaanite brought to submission . . ."

"The master needs nothing," Mandisa answered, her voice hoarse with frustration. She gritted her teeth, irritated with this girl and herself. Ani expected her to *help* this harlot? A leopard could not change its spots.

"Wherever the children are, I'm sure they need you," Mandisa said, firmly taking Tizara's arm and pulling her away from Simeon's door. "Find them, or I shall have to tell Ani that you need more work to fill your hours. Perhaps kitchen duty would suit you."

"Perhaps it wouldn't," Tizara answered, laughing softly. She walked slowly away, her glance cutting from Simeon's door to Mandisa with a look that said she understood completely.

When the girl had disappeared, Mandisa knotted her hands into fists and blinked back tears of frustration. *Why, El Shaddai, have you brought her to this place?*

Twenty-one

ASENATH FELT HER SMILE FADE AS THE LAST OF her guests left her private sitting room. She had entertained twenty ladies of the royal court, young Pharaoh's cousins, concubines, and a host of other relatives. Though the extravagant party had been a rousing success by Theban standards, it left Asenath feeling dull and drained.

Four months had passed since her visit to her father's temple, and she had not seen a single sign that Khnum intended to answer her prayers. Zaphenath-paneah was loving and dutiful, pleasant and considerate as always, and he often took her into his arms to express his love in the intimate mystery reserved for husbands and wives. But never did he enter her chamber during the week when Asenath knew she might conceive. Even though the pressures of Pharaoh's kingdom, a host of duties, and the crisis of famine bore down upon him, her husband remembered to count the days on the calendar and abstain from marital pleasures during the ten-day week when a chance visit to his wife's bed might result in a child.

And Khnum had made no difference. Over the past weeks she had written almost daily letters to her father, begging him to offer whatever Khnum required, be it incense, fruit, or even blood offerings. And just as regularly her father replied that the god did things in his own time, that she should be careful and not rash, that she should not unduly pester a cautious god.

"My lady."

Mandisa's gentle voice broke the stillness of the empty chamber, and Asenath tapped her fingers over her lips in a dainty yawn. "Come in, dear. I was just thinking how relieved I am that they are all gone."

"Another letter has arrived, my lady. From Heliopolis."

More useless words of wisdom, more patronizing drivel. With an air of unutterable boredom, Asenath accepted the papyrus scroll in Mandisa's hand, then studied the seal imprinted on the wax. The unusual design was not her father's mark.

"Thank you," she murmured, dismissing her maid with the wave of her hand. Mandisa did not leave the room but moved toward the pottery lamps burning on low stands, snuffing the flames and trimming the wicks for their next use.

Intrigued, Asenath broke open the seal and began to read:

> The priest Pe-uhem informs the Lady Asenath:
>
> In life, prosperity, health, and in favor of Amenhotep III, King of the gods, and Zaphenath-paneah, Nourisher of the King's Soul!
>
> This is to let my lady know that I have heard of your frequent discourse with your father. He has sent me to offer gifts to Khnum in your name. But if you will forgive my boldness, I have a more direct piece of advice for you, my lady.
>
> If the gods do not bend themselves to our wills, sometimes it is because we pray to the wrong gods. If fertility and children are what you desire, why do you send gifts to Khnum, the divine potter? Offer your gifts instead to Min, the rain goddess who brings life to the barren earth and strengthens fields of wheat. Just as Min strengthens the weak limbs of men, my lady, she will bestow her powers of life and fertility upon you if you are willing to offer yourself. And I would be honored to be your ally in this your fervent desire.
>
> Send word to me on the day of your choosing, when Min will most richly bless you. Together we will meet in the temple at Thebes and offer ourselves to the god-

dess who ripens the fertile plains of our land, who wa-
ters the earth with life-giving water. Do not let my brash
desire to serve offend your gentle ears, but know that I
am, in truth, wholly devoted in service to you,
Zaphenath-paneah, and Pharaoh—may he live for-
ever!

A blush burned her cheek as she lowered the letter. Part
of her soul recoiled from what was nothing less than a brazen attempt at seduction, but her brief embarrassment
quickly faded to humiliation when she realized that someone else knew her most intimate secrets. What had her father told the other priests? How many wagging tongues
knew of the vizier's unwillingness to bear a child with his
wife?

Smarting in fresh resentment, she rolled the parchment
and gripped it while her thoughts scampered frantically. As
she weighed the structure and probability of events, she
gradually relaxed. If anyone of the royal court knew of
Asenath's distress, some well-meaning tattler would have
already alerted her. Some secrets were too delicious to be
contained. Since she had heard nothing, it was likely that
her father had confided only in this young assistant.

Pe-uhem. His name echoed in the black stillness of her
mind. She thought she remembered meeting him at her
father's villa in Heliopolis. If she was associating the right
face with the name, he seemed a pleasing sort, younger
than her husband, but with a commanding manner and polished veneer.

But—to commit adultery! For that is how Zaphenath-
paneah would see it. He would be wounded, perhaps angry.
He would have every right to cast her away and put another
woman in her place.

But perhaps the goddess Min would not see the act as
adultery, and who but the gods could judge what was right
and what was wrong? Asenath would surrender herself
once, in an act of worship intended only to honor her hus-

band. If by some remote chance the priest later attempted to accuse her of untoward conduct, she could simply deny the charge, for everyone in Thebes knew her as a faithful and chaste wife. No one would believe such an outlandish accusation, even if it came from a priest.

"Can I bring you anything, my lady?"

Mandisa's gentle question startled Asenath. She had forgotten her maid lingered in the room. "No. Go now," she answered, clenching the scroll tighter in her hands. "I shall not need you again tonight."

When Mandisa had gone, Asenath padded to the table where she kept a sheaf of papyrus parchments, a reed stylus, and a bottle of ink. Thanks be to the gods who urged her father to teach his daughter the sacred hieroglyphics! With a trembling hand she began to pen a reply:

> The Lady Asenath inquires after the success of her father's friend, Pe-uhem.
>
> In life, prosperity, health, and in favor of my husband Zaphenath-paneah and Amenhotep III, King of the gods! I say to Khnum and to Min every day: may you be in health.
>
> Furthermore, your words contained wisdom I have not found elsewhere. I will send word to you at the temple of Min in Thebes when the time is right to petition the goddess according to my heart's request. If there is any offering I should bring, I pray you to send word of it before the appointed occasion.
>
> Have no anxiety about me. I am committed to my desire.

———

Two weeks later, as the winter moon lit the high walls of the vizier's villa with a cold white radiance, Ani wandered in the black shadows of the courtyard below. Two sleepless nights were bearing down on him with an irresistible and delicious weight, but he would not allow himself to sleep. Some nameless, formless trouble stirred in the house of Zaphenath-paneah, some impending disaster not even the master had sensed. But Ani, whose duty required him to foresee these things, remained ever alert, waiting for the bough to break.

Trials enough moved openly through the household. The simple presence of the harlot Tizara had sown discord among the men of the house, soldiers and servants alike. And Mandisa, who had promised to help him manage the girl, had proved to be no practical help at all. Whenever Ani asked her to teach Tizara a more ladylike way to conduct her affairs, Mandisa always found an excuse, an errand to run, or some reason why she couldn't be bothered. Most of the time her excuses centered around the prisoner, Simeon.

And Simeon. That Canaanite had lately proved himself altogether too adaptable. Something ailed a lion that did not roar, and Ani wasn't sure if the captive was sick or simply saving his strength for his next attack. But if he was saving his rage to vent it later, the house might not be able to contain his next outburst.

Even Lady Asenath, that most gracious and predictable kitten, had been short, irritable, and bothered of late. Last week she had offhandedly mentioned that she would soon require a litter to visit a temple of Thebes during the Feast of Opet, but she had specifically remarked that Mandisa would not be accompanying her.

"The master will be with you then," Ani answered, bowing.

"No, the master will be with Pharaoh," Asenath replied, dropping her eyes. "I will take the litter alone."

"But it is not fitting! You must have a guard with you, at least. A lady of your position should not go about in the streets during a festival! The men will be drunk and the women senseless. There are apt to be sights unfit for your eyes."

"You may send a guard, but he must remain outside the temple with the litter-bearers," Asenath answered, running her fingers over the alabaster tray holding the remains of her breakfast. "I am a priest's daughter. I can worship alone. How can I commune privately with the gods if I am watched like a hawk?"

For that he had no answer. But his dear lady's voice had been flat, absolutely emotionless, and the sound of it chilled him worse than the night breeze that now blew off the river and over the villa.

"Oh, Thoth," he babbled, turning his chattering teeth into the wind, "god of learning and wisdom who has blessed me with insight and power, show me what to do! For I am at a loss. My senses and insight tell me that doom hangs over us like a black cloud, and I am powerless to banish it!"

Asenath waited until the first full week after her red moon had flowed, then she summoned Ani and told him that she would visit the temple of Min that night.

"Min!" The name slipped from the steward's tongue like a curse.

She knew his birdlike brain bulged with questions about why she wanted to visit the goddess of fertility, but he had no right to interrogate her.

"This parched land is in need of rain, which Min can provide," she said, avoiding his bright speculative eyes. "I will need Mandisa to help me prepare, but only one guard to run beside the litter-bearers."

"Tonight the moon will be full and very bright," Ani said, folding his hands in a form of entreaty. "Bright enough to embolden any robbers or strangers. Please, my lady, put this journey off until my lord your husband can accompany you."

"My husband has no use for the temples of Thebes, nor for Min," Asenath answered, the steward's unusual persistence gnawing at her confidence. "Now I will not brook another word of opposition, Ani, so leave me!"

A warning cloud settled on his features, but he bowed

and turned to leave. A small voice inside Asenath's head wondered why she had been so short with him. Ani was a capable steward and a harmless busybody. She and her husband owed much of their well-being to the careful way he regulated the household. Well, tomorrow she would make it up to him. And when the vizier held a new son in his arms, Ani would be as thrilled and happy as the drunken fools who would celebrate a noble birth in the streets of Thebes.

In one fluid motion she rose and made her way to her innermost chamber. Without waiting for Mandisa, she dressed in a simple but elegant linen sheath that fell from her armpits to her ankles without wrinkle or ornamentation. Thin straps held the garment over her bare shoulders. Slowly, she oiled her skin, perfumed her neck, and carefully outlined her dark eyes—black kohl underneath, green malachite on the lids.

Her eyes, without a doubt, were her best feature. Zaphenath-paneah had often told her they shone like "stars of twilight fair." Well, tonight he would be with Pharaoh at the palace, and her eyes would be shining elsewhere. The thought tore at her insides, but she drew a deep breath and forbade herself to tremble. If Zaphenath-paneah wanted to please her, he would give her what she desired. If he truly loved her, she wouldn't have to do this.

Mandisa came into the room, breathless, and blushed when she saw that Asenath had already dressed. "I'm sorry, my lady. I had no idea you wanted to go out," she said, wiping her hands on her skirt. "But Adom was with Simeon, and I had to oversee them—"

"Just help me with my cloak," Asenath interrupted, replacing her looking brass on the tray top. She had seen her reflection and was satisfied. Her wig was heavy and lush. Her makeup all but disguised her features. Anyone who saw her enter the temple in the concealing cloak and wig would never guess her identity.

"Going to one of the festivals, my lady?" Mandisa

asked, slipping the full cloak over Asenath's shoulders.

"One of them," the lady answered. And before Mandisa could ask anything else, Asenath moved confidently out of the chamber.

Twenty-two

"I MUST WEAR THIS?"

Tarik nodded, imposing an iron control on himself as he slipped a wrist cuff onto the Canaanite captive. Zaphenath-paneah had told Mandisa that the prisoner might be allowed to walk freely about the courtyard, not just in the walled garden, and Tarik knew he had no right to question his master's judgment. Still, such a move seemed ill-advised, particularly with *this* captive, a man as ill-tempered as a wasp in a bottle.

The shackles were Tarik's idea. "While in the courtyard, you must remain tethered to Mandisa at all times," he said, slipping the other iron bracelet around the woman's slender wrist. "That way, at least I know you will not get far if you decide to run out the gate."

"Why would I want to run with this woman chained to me?" Simeon growled. "No man in his right mind would take a nagging tongue with him."

Tarik looked up, expecting to see hurt in Mandisa's eyes, but one corner of her mouth twisted upward in a wry smile. Apparently she had grown accustomed to the Canaanite's surly manners.

"As you can see, Tarik, the emptier the pot, the quicker the boil," she quipped, lifting a delicate brow. "I suggest, Simeon, that you calm yourself and try to be pleasant. If the servants hear your continual carping, they are likely to bribe me to keep you out of sight. If you want a change of scenery as much as you say you do, you should adopt a more peaceable demeanor."

Tarik smothered a smile as he turned to open the cham-

ber door. The savage man from Canaan may have been a
brute when he arrived in Thebes, but already Mandisa had
gained the upper hand. How long would it take the captive
to realize he had been tamed?

Tarik stepped aside as Mandisa led Simeon out like a
puppy on a rope. Tarik knew every fiber of Simeon's stiff
body rebelled at the thought of being pulled about by a
woman, but when he stepped from the hallway into the
open air of the courtyard, his posture changed dramatically.

Even from a distance Tarik could see the man relax. His
broad shoulders flexed as he stopped to breathe deeply. Ignoring the hustle and bustle of the courtyard, he placed his
hands on his hips and lifted his shaggy head and face to the
sun.

Mandisa stood by his side, silent and approving. With
a gasp of astonishment, Tarik realized that love radiated
from her dark eyes.

Why are you surprised? he wondered, rubbing his jaw.
He should have known that she would not spend hours
with the captive unless she loved him, for she could have
fed him and cleaned his chamber in the space of five minutes or had one of the kitchen slaves tend to the odious barbarian. But she had invested her time, herself, even her son.
Perhaps unwittingly, Tarik thought, she had invested her
heart.

How can a servant find love in the vizier's house? Tarik
wondered, leaning against the wall as he watched the two-
some in the distance. His only thought, his highest aim,
was to please his master. He had been born the youngest
son of a simple farmer, probably the lowest position in the
Egyptian social system, and yet he had systematically risen
through the ranks of society by striving hard and doing his
best in every undertaking. Though the others around him
seemed consumed by the desire to eat, drink, and make
merry, Tarik realized at an early age that success did not lie
in the overwhelmingly approved national philosophy.

No. The way to achievement lay in planning one's work, placating the gods of prosperity, and pleasing one's master. His chosen god was Wepwawet, the jackal-headed god known as the Opener of the Ways. Wepwawet, who piloted the sun boat as it traveled through the chambers of the night, had guided Tarik toward success. And as long as he persisted in ardent worship and sacrifice, Tarik was certain Wepwawet would continue to lead him. For of what use was a god who allowed his petitioners to suffer pain? A man's god should lead him to prosperity, not failure.

And so Tarik had joined the local guards, and then accepted a promotion to Pharaoh's cavalry. In time he had earned a place keeping watch over the villa of a governor. There he caught Zaphenath-paneah's eye. Sometimes Tarik toyed with the idea of lifting his sights to serve in Pharaoh's palace, but as long as the king was under the age of majority, the real power lay in *this* house. As captain of the vizier's guard, Tarik held one of the loftiest positions in the land, and yet sometimes—his eyes fell again upon Mandisa and her beloved captive—sometimes he wondered if life could offer more than success.

Twenty-three

"*THIS* IS WHAT YOU'VE BEEN HIDING? NOW I understand your reasons for secrecy, Mandisa."

The voice was soft, sensual, and faintly mocking, and Simeon jerked his head toward the source of the sound. From out of the courtyard dust, it seemed, a woman had appeared. She stood before him now in the sheerest Egyptian gown he had ever seen, revealing a slender but alluring body. She did not wear an Egyptian wig but allowed her mass of wild hair to creep down her back in raveled locks. Her dark eyes shimmered with dazzling light, and her appearance was so unearthly, so unexpected, that Simeon took a hasty half-step back, struck speechless.

He must have worn his surprise on his face, for the woman laughed softly and put out a delicate finger to touch his bare chest. "You are pale, friend," she whispered in his own beloved tongue. "You should have made these heartless Egyptians bring you out sooner."

Her words implied that he could make his captors do anything, and his chest heaved in exultation at the reassuring sight and sound of her. Something about her reminded him of the wind-blown wilderness, and for a moment he forgot that he wore a chain about his wrist. His awareness of Mandisa vanished like a desert mirage.

"My name is Tizara," she whispered, a purring sound in her voice as the sweetly intoxicating musk of her body overwhelmed him. "I will see you later . . . I promise."

She turned and walked away toward the gardens, emphasizing the sway of her hips because she knew he watched. Simeon felt his blood rush to her fingerprint on his skin, and his heart thumped uncomfortably as a quiver surged through his veins.

"I think this heat has been too much for you," Mandisa said, yanking at his chain. Her voice was abrupt, clipped. "Your face is crimson, Simeon. You should not have stood so long in the sun."

He scarcely felt her fragile strength upon the chain that held his wrist, but after a moment he followed her back into the cool hallway that led to his room. She was right. His eyes did burn with the afterimage of a white-hot heavenly body. He had been blinded. But not by the sun.

———

From his observation post on the vizier's balcony overlooking the courtyard, Ani shook his head. Foolish Mandisa, why had she led her newly tamed cub into the panther's den? He clicked his tongue against his teeth in silent sympathy. She should have known better, but she was young and still inexperienced in many things.

After a few moments, Mandisa reentered the courtyard alone, her hand shading her eyes from the sun and prying glances.

"Mandisa!" Ani called, looking down over the stone railing.

She looked up, her chin quivering. "Yes?"

"Come up here at once. I would have a word with you."

Appearing reluctant, she turned toward the house, and Ani paced along the walkway, debating his approach. Should he be honest and tell her that this Canaanite would soon leave and join his own family? That she had no business risking her heart when her loyalties belonged to the family and household of Zaphenath-paneah?

Women in love rarely wanted to hear truth.

"Yes, my lord Ani?"

She had been crying, the wetness of tears still clung to her lower lashes.

"Sit, my child," he said, indicating a stone bench

carved into the railing. He paused, pressing his lips together. "I saw what just happened in the courtyard."

Her pretense vanished, tears again welled within her eyes. "I don't understand him, Ani!" she said in an aching, husky voice. "I have willingly cared for him these many months. I, a free woman, have cleaned up after him like the lowliest slave. I have borne his jests, his cruelty, his anger. I have listened to his stories about his home and family. I know secrets the clan of Jacob would kill to keep silent!" She paused as a hot tear rolled down her cheek. "I know he is a murderer and a hot-headed rogue, and yet my heart breaks just to look at him. I shared my precious son to help ease his loneliness! But for all my efforts, he forgot I existed when that harlot walked by!"

Ani clapped in satisfaction. "So he is unredeemable. You now hate him. This is good."

"But there is such strength in him, Ani! When he is not thinking about the past, he is loyal, devoted, and concerned about people. And he is wonderfully wise about the desert and all sorts of animals! He has taught Adom so many things—truths about life that I would never understand! And he knows many stories about the invisible and Almighty God. He is proud of being one of God Shaddai's chosen race. He respects his brothers and is quick to defend his mother's memory."

"Our master knows the stories of the almighty God, too," Ani said, stiffening. "And yet he is quite a different man from this Simeon."

"Our master," Mandisa said, making an obvious effort to chose her words carefully, "worships the Almighty God. Zaphenath-paneah trusts in Him. But though Simeon speaks of this God, I do not think he trusts anything but his own strength—the strength of his anger."

As she paused to wipe tears from her face, Ani sank beside her on the bench. Whether Mandisa knew it or not, she had revealed her heart. "So you love him."

"Against my better judgment," she said, a slight tinge of

wonder in her voice, "I suppose I do."

"Are you certain? If it is marriage you seek, let me remind you that you were married once before. And that husband did not bring you happiness."

"Idogbe bought me from my father and paraded me around Egypt like a possession, not as a wife," she answered, her words as cool and clear as ice water. She paused to wipe a fresh tear from her eye. "He was proud of me until he heard I was with child. Then he left without a word of warning."

"Perhaps," Ani said, casting about for the right words, "you should thank the gods he stopped loving you. If the man made you so unhappy, his disappearance saved you much distress."

"He never loved me," she said, turning to him. "And only after I saw true love did I fully understand that. When Zaphenath-paneah gave me a place in this household, I saw what love truly is." She smiled to herself as she spoke. "As I watched him love Lady Asenath through the birth of two sons and the deaths of three others, I realized that honest love is gentle. It is persistent but not demanding. It protects and trusts and does not use its loved one for display. If you love someone, Ani, you will not abandon them."

"And they say I am the one who is wise," Ani answered, taking her hand. He squeezed it gently, another question on his reluctant tongue. "Daughter, you have answered your own questions, and you say you love this Canaanite. But does he love you?"

She closed her eyes and pressed her free hand over her heart. "That," she whispered, "is what I must discover."

Simeon turned on his bed, agitated and unable to sleep. He had enough sense to realize that Mandisa was furious when she left him, and he didn't suppose he could blame her. After years of trying to block the bitter glances between his mother and his aunt Rachel, Simeon knew about female jealousy. But he also knew that women somehow managed to deal with their grief and anger. His mother had, and life had continued despite the differences between Jacob's wives.

But that woman in the courtyard today—her touch, her words had evoked feelings he had thought long dead. In her eyes he was strong and free, a Canaanite warrior, a giant among men. In one glance she had restored the confidence and courage this captivity had inexorably drained from his heart.

He, Simeon the Destroyer, had begun to adjust to confinement. The realization stunned him. But which of his brothers would not have grown soft in such a place? The months had crawled by with agonizing slowness, the moments frozen in place like the granite statues lining the streets of Thebes. He had asked Mandisa to bring him a shadow clock for telling time, and though she laughed at what must have seemed a foolish request, she had brought the clock and set it on a stand before his window. Every day he watched the shadow of the upright beam move as slowly as a worm over the calibrated horizontal arm. The only hours that passed with any swiftness were those he spent in Adom's or Mandisa's company.

Until today. How long had he stood before the woman who touched him? It might have been five minutes, but the span passed like a heartbeat, so quickly did she come and go. The experience was an instant of pleasure he would have to stretch into a week-long memory if he were to endure this enslavement much longer.

He turned again on his bed, unable to find a comfortable position. Sometimes he felt as if evil hands clenched his heart, slowly twisting the life from it. He had felt this guilty pressure many times before—at the slaughter of Shechem, at Dothan when he would have killed Joseph—but lately the tension had intensified. He had to escape, to flee this misery, but he had no weapons and no tools with which to form them, unless . . .

His eyes fell upon the shadow clock, useless in the night. The upright pole had been crafted of polished copper, a sliver as long as a man's hand. A dagger, in the right fist.

He rolled out of bed and gripped it. The horizontal piece broke off with one abrupt snap, leaving a jagged edge along the base of his new blade. The implement was not sharp, but if thrust with enough force, it would bite deep.

His mind curled lovingly around the thought of freedom, of his triumphant return to the camp of Israel. Already he could hear his brothers' cries of rejoicing, feel Dinah's proud arms around his neck. And he would finally win his father's approval, for Simeon's escape would cancel Benjamin's obligation to journey to Egypt. They would find grain somewhere else. If necessary, they would bribe their neighbors to buy food rations for them.

Then, from out of nowhere, came the realization that he could escape only if he used this tool against Mandisa or Tarik, the only people who ever unbolted his door. One of them would have to be held hostage if Simeon's plan was to succeed. Killing the captain would not be problematic, even though Simeon had come to respect him, for a soldier expected such risks every day of his life. But he did not think he could hurt Mandisa or even pretend that he might. She knew him too well. She would call his bluff.

The copper blade slipped from his hand and rang on the tile floor. Better to remain forgotten and alone than to risk failure and face humiliation again.

A scratching sound at the door interrupted his thoughts.

———

"Simeon." Tizara paused, waiting for the sounds of movement. Was he asleep? She dared not speak louder for fear of waking others in the house.

"Who is there?"

She smiled, hearing the sounds of urgent breathing through the heavy wood. He was just on the other side, awake and alert, as she had suspected he would be once he heard her voice.

"I am Tizara. Who else would come to you like this?" She couldn't restrain a ripple of laughter. "Would you like me to come in?"

She heard frantic scrambling sounds. In a moment he would be pounding on the door. "Hush, be still," she whispered, pressing her hands against the wood. "I have not come to pleasure you but to help you return to freedom." She paused, listening. "You and I together will escape from Mizraim. Would you like that?"

She felt a solid thud against the wood and knew that he leaned against the door.

"Why should I trust you?" he growled.

"Because I am a Canaanite like you. Because I hate slavery as much as you hate captivity. And," she lightened her voice, "because I like your looks." Flattery always worked.

"Open the door."

"Shhh. Not now, my friend. Not tonight. We must first make plans. We will need provisions to survive the desert journey. I will procure a supply of food, cloaks, water pouches—"

"Why do *you* want to leave?"

His question caught her by surprise, and for a moment her facile tongue stilled. "Because . . ." she said, stammering. "Because doing anything as a free woman is better than doing nothing as a slave. I am not a nursemaid! I am tired of men telling me what to do."

She sank to the floor and leaned her shoulder against the door. "When we return to Canaan, I will build my own house within the strong walls of Shechem. I will own my own herds. I will do as I please and never call anyone master again."

He did not answer, and for a moment she wondered if she should open the door so she could face him as she explained herself. No. This man was strong, resolute in purpose and desire. She dared not trust him until she absolutely had no other choice.

"All right," he said, a bitter edge of cynicism in his voice. "While you are stealing, then, make sure you take enough of the vizier's silver to outfit this new house. Do not count on a marriage price from me."

She laughed softly. "Marriage? Did I say I would marry you?"

"It matters not," came the slow and steady answer. "I will not marry again."

———

Tizara's visit seemed dreamlike in the reality of morning until Simeon saw the broken shadow clock on the floor. So the harlot wanted out, too! Why not let her help him? She had access to tools and provisions, and with her aid he could slip away without involving Mandisa. He would leave in the middle of a night, and Mandisa and Adom would know nothing of it until the next morning.

How long would it take Tizara to prepare? The question buzzed in his brain all morning, unasked and unanswered, distracting him even when Mandisa brought him breakfast. She moved efficiently about the room, making casual and pleasant conversation, but she did not mention the possibility of his going into the courtyard or the garden. Neither did she refer to the events of the day before, but Simeon knew her well enough to know the encounter with Tizara rested heavily on her mind.

When she turned to leave, he put out a hand to stop her. "Mandisa," he said, regarding her with a careful smile, "I suppose you are angry with me for what happened yesterday."

"Angry women make themselves beds of nettles," she replied, averting her eyes from his face. "And I slept well last night, Simeon."

"So you are not upset with me?" His index finger rose to her trembling chin. "I think you are lying. About your anger and about how you slept."

"I must go." She turned, hiding her face, and fumbled with the latch on the door.

"Don't." He reached out and caught her arm, and her muscles tensed suddenly under his hand. Her back was to him, but if he would soon be gone, he wanted her to know that he appreciated all she had done for him.

"Mandisa, I—"

"Stop, Simeon," she interrupted, her head falling forward.

He realized with sudden horror that she was weeping.

"All right. I will confess," she said, the words broken between her sobs. "I was angry. I am trying to help you, but I cannot . . . love you . . . until I know how you feel."

A new and unexpected warmth surged through him. By earth and heaven above, did she say *love*? Did something stronger than mere possessiveness lie behind her jealousy of Tizara? His heart swelled with the knowledge that she *had* been jealous, that she did desire him. She probably felt she couldn't compete with Tizara's bold seductiveness, but she could easily find a place in his arms. He owed her so much! If not for her soft presence, he would have lost his sanity here in the Black Land.

Firmly he turned her and pulled her to him, cradling her head against his chest. "Mandisa, little bird," he whispered, caressing her wet cheek with the knuckle of his forehand as he bent and pressed his lips to hers. The kiss sent the pit of his stomach into a wild swirl, and he crushed her to him, enjoying the sensation of her warm willingness in his arms. He would demonstrate his gratitude in the best way he knew. Perhaps, if her gods smiled on her, she would bear a son to remember him in the days to come.

She trembled in his arms, and he raised his mouth from hers and met her eyes.

"Simeon," she whispered, placing her hands on his chest, "I don't think you understand."

A fleeting doubt took shape in her eyes, but before she

could utter it he shushed her softly. "If you want my love, let me give it here, now," he murmured, moving his lips toward the base of her throat. "I owe you my life, Mandisa. Let me share my strength with you."

He lifted his lips to take hers again, but instead of a kiss he found himself moving toward empty air.

"Simeon! No! Let me go!" she cried, twisting in his arms.

"What?" A frustrated scream rattled at the back of his throat.

"This is wrong! Release me. Now!"

"But it is love! If you want love—"

"*This* is not love! And I can't do this!"

"But you *can*!"

"No! You don't understand! You don't understand *anything*!"

In dazed exasperation he released her. Spinning out of his arms, she bolted like a frightened animal for the door, then slammed it shut. He heard sobbing as she slid the bolt back into place.

"Mandisa," he said, his pulses pounding as he walked to the door and pressed upon it, "you don't have be so skittish. You are neither a virgin nor a child."

"You don't understand," she whispered again through her tears. But at least she lingered outside.

"What's wrong with you? I was *gentle*!" He gritted his teeth against the rising anger in his voice. "Woman, if I wanted to hurt you, I could have taken you at any time!"

He heard a renewed cry, then the sound of her footsteps running away.

~ Twenty-four ~

HE CURSED UNTIL HE COULD THINK OF NO MORE vile words to say, then he paced from wall to wall until he thought he would go mad with frustration. The sun set. The sounds and activities of the vizier's house faded into the quiet lull of nighttime. Simeon kept an eye toward the door, thinking that Mandisa might send Tarik to rebuke or punish him, but no one came to his chamber, no one moved in the hallway beyond.

Finally, when night had completely covered the villa, he stretched out on the too short bed and closed his eyes. He slid into a light doze, but the sound of the bolt sliding from its brackets brought him instantly awake.

His eyes flew open as anger and anxiety knotted inside him. Had Mandisa changed her mind? He wouldn't have her now, not for all the silver and gold in Pharaoh's treasure tomb. But Mandisa wouldn't come to him in the night. It had to be Tarik outside the door, ready and eager to punish Simeon for affronting one of the vizier's servants.

His hand closed around the dagger, and in one swift agile move, he rolled from the bed and leapt to his feet. Despite his fears, he felt a hot and awful joy that *finally* he might have a chance to prove himself, to confront the enemy on fair and equal terms.

His chest felt as if it would burst as the door swung open. He held his breath, expecting to see the captain's compact muscled figure in the torchlight. But a woman stood in the doorway, draped in concealing veils.

The voice was unmistakable. "Did you think I would not come so soon?" Tizara purred.

"No." Simeon cleared his throat as a flash of sanity and calm returned to his fevered brain. "I did not expect you tonight."

"After the madness of your afternoon, I expect you did not," she answered, her dark eyes shining from beneath a veil. She lifted it with two hands and gave him a frankly admiring glance. "And I thought, Simeon, that you burned for me alone."

"Did the entire house hear?" he asked, suddenly unnerved.

Even the smile in her eyes contained a sensuous flame. "None heard but me. I was lingering beneath your window in hope of forewarning you that I would come tonight. I heard everything, but Mandisa has said nothing to the others."

Simeon nodded, mollified. At least he would not be leaving Mandisa to face the humiliation of public shame—not that he cared. But for Adom's sake, it would be better if the household did not hear what had happened between Simeon and his mother.

Tizara tilted her head, and her smile took on a mischievous aspect. "That gossipy old steward tells me you have been married twice, Simeon, so I marvel that you know so little of the softer sex. Did neither of your wives tell you that the joining of a man and woman has little to do with love?" One dark eyebrow slanted upward as she finished in a dry voice. "Trust me. I know about these things."

"Women," Simeon said, clenching his jaw, "are foolish, and there is no pleasing them."

Her soft laughter warmed the room. "I would say the same thing about men," she answered, "but we can argue on the journey. We should go while the house is quiet. All but a few guards are asleep. Are you ready?"

He looked around the room. He had no possessions, nothing to take but the makeshift dagger. He thrust it into the belt of his kilt, then caught the heavy cloak Tizara tossed him.

"The guards will change their watch soon," she whispered, leading him out into the hallway. "We will slip by them now while their eyes are heavy and they dream of finding their couches to sleep."

Simeon nodded, his courage and determination like a rock inside him. "Then let us go."

Tarik sat up, breathless and cold on his bed as the real world slowly made its way back into his consciousness. He pressed his lips together, listening to the house around him and hearing nothing but the pounding of his heart. With his knuckle he wiped small sparkles of sweat off his upper lip. The nightmare had fled, leaving behind only a phantom of terror, a premonition of disaster.

A shadow stirred in the darkness, and Tarik fumbled for the dagger beside his bed.

"Stop! It is Ani!"

The old steward stepped into a small rectangle of moonlight near the center of the room. The pulsing knot within Tarik relaxed. He lowered his shining blade and swung his legs to the floor. "Ani, what are you doing here?"

"Do you not sense it?" The old man looked around and sniffed the air like a dog parsing the scent of his quarry. "This afternoon when I poured oil into the master's divining bowl, the shape of Anubis came to me, then vanished. The raging fiend stalks our house tonight, Tarik. I thought you might sense it, too."

"I had a nightmare," Tarik said simply, but he didn't refute Ani's word. Rising from his bed, he slipped his dagger into his kilt and strapped on his sword belt. Within a moment he had lit a lamp and led the way into the hall.

"Silently now, awake the master but not the other family members," he told the steward. "I will summon extra guards from their beds and surround the outer walls of the villa. We will double the guard and keep watch all night if we must."

Ani nodded in agreement, a watchful fixity in his face.

————

Tizara's preparation impressed Simeon, but her lack of strategy distressed him. As they slipped through the quiet hallways, she told him she had assembled food, extra garments, thick leather sandals, and several gourds for water. She had even managed to pull a donkey from the herd and tether him to the gate of the stable yard. She gave Simeon a confident smile. "As soon as we gather the supplies I have hidden by the well—"

"But the stables and the well are on opposite sides of the villa!" Simeon protested, halting in midstride to glare down at her.

Like all Egyptian villas, the innermost house was surrounded by a series of open courtyards that separated it from the noise, sights, and smells of the servants' quarters, granary, stable, kitchens, and garden. The stables and cattle yard were on the southwestern side of the villa so the prevailing winds could carry away the odors, but the well was located on the eastern side of the estate. In fact, Simeon thought, recalling what he knew of the house, the well was located near the vizier's quarters so his servants would not have to walk far to draw their master a bath. Simeon and Tizara would have to walk beneath the ears of the sleeping vizier!

"Foolishness, thy name is woman," he muttered, leaving the harlot in the shadows as he stomped toward the well.

————

Mandisa woke to screams and shouting. Awareness hit her like a punch in the stomach, and one thought pierced through the fog of sleep. *They've killed him!* Then she heard Simeon's angry bellow and knew that Tarik had mercifully stayed his hand.

She dressed quickly, bent to check on her sleeping son,

then, as duty demanded, stepped into her mistress's chamber. Asenath had awakened and dressed, too, and seemed remarkably clearheaded as she picked up a burning lamp and inclined her head toward the hallway leading to the master's chamber. "They will bring him to my husband, and we shall hear a full accounting of it," she said simply, leading the way.

Mandisa followed, grateful that Asenath had not remarked upon Simeon's foolishness or stupidity. How had he managed to escape? And why had he risked his life? She had assured him time and again that his brothers would return before the famine's end. Zaphenath-paneah had promised it, and he had never been mistaken about a revelation from God.

The master was awake and dressed when the women entered, his bed covers unrumpled. If he had slept at all, he gave no indication of it as he stood and greeted his wife with a kiss on the cheek. Asenath murmured a word in exchange, then took her seat at the carved chair by his bed.

Mandisa retreated to a corner of the room, but Zaphenath-paneah caught her eye. "Come, Mandisa, and stand closer," he said, friendliness and concern in his tone. "Do not assume that I do not know what feelings you hold for the man who has been in your care." A half-smile crossed his face. "You love him, even as I do, and yet he continues to try our patience."

"Yes, my lord," she whispered, relief flooding her soul. She moved to Lady Asenath's side and had just managed to compose her face into stiff stern lines when the double doors of the master's chamber burst open. A dozen erect guards, led by Tarik and followed by Ani, brought in two captives. Mandisa had expected to see Simeon, but anguish almost overcame her control when she saw Tizara by his side.

Simeon planted himself before the vizier with his feet spread apart, his head defiantly thrust back. His bold black eyes raked the gathering, then trained in upon Zaphenath-paneah. Mandisa could feel the strength of his hatred from where she stood.

Tizara, on the other hand, smiled shamelessly at the master, apparently not caring that his wife sat only a few feet away. She returned the master's scrutiny gaze for gaze, then a sudden tremor touched her smooth marblelike lips. A blush colored her cheek as she lifted her eyes to the ceiling and stared at nothing.

Zaphenath-paneah sat in his carved chair and took his wife's hand. "Why did you run from my house?" he asked, intending the question for both prisoners. He spoke in Egyptian and Mandisa translated rapidly, nearly forgetting that Simeon still did not know the truth about her master.

When neither captive answered, the vizier turned to Tarik. "Were any of your men hurt?"

"One stableboy was cut with this," Tarik said, holding forth the broken arm of a shadow clock. Mandisa recognized it and closed her eyes in despair. Simeon had used her gift as a weapon. Against a youth.

"Will he live?"

"Yes." Tarik nodded. "The royal physicians are attending to him now."

"For harming this boy," the vizier said, his eyes flickering over his captives, "I could have both of you confined to Pharaoh's prison. But I am curious, and you have not yet answered me. Why did you run?"

Mandisa translated again, and this time Simeon spoke. "If you knew what captivity does to a man," he snarled, spitting the words in contempt, "you would not ask such a foolish question."

Mandisa wrung her hands and managed a quick translation. Though the vizier had thus far shown mercy, his patience would not last forever. Every servant in this house and most of the shrewd citizens of Thebes knew that her master had been both a slave and a captive. Would Simeon *ever* learn to restrain his temper? His anger was a wind that blew out the lamp of his mind.

"If I had been a captive, it is not likely I would have known the gracious treatment you have enjoyed," Zaphen-ath-paneah went on, not raising his voice. "Have you been whipped? Have you been chained so that your wrists bled? Have you been forced to lie in the filth of your own body until maggots attacked your flesh? Aside from the consequences of acts of your own choosing, have you been deprived of human companionship or kept from a kind word or a soft voice?

"I know what captivity does to a man," the vizier went on, pausing often for Mandisa's translation. "Imprisonment, even slavery, can be the stone God uses to crush an impossible person who must rise to accomplish an impossible task. Will you be crushed, Simeon, son of Israel? Or will you resist the work of God and harden your heart still further?"

The vizier turned his attention to Tizara. "And you, young woman, have you been mistreated in this house? Has any man forced himself upon you? Has any woman cruelly mocked you? You stood in sore need of love and mercy when you first came to us. We have been generous with both, but have you accepted them?"

Mandisa felt the bitter gall of guilt burn the back of her throat as she listened to her master's words. How many times had she avoided, scorned, and railed against Tizara? She had never said anything rude in the girl's presence, but she had made her thoughts known among the other women as they gossiped in the kitchen and worked at the well. Tizara was no fool. Though the master had been loving and merciful, his servants had not fulfilled his expectations. And Mandisa had specifically promised to help the young woman feel at home.

Tizara did not answer the master but lowered her gaze to the ground as he continued questioning her. When he had finished, she lifted her eyes. Dark glimmers of pain were reflected there.

"I am sorry, my lord," she whispered in a voice fainter

than air. "You are right. You have treated me far better than I deserve."

Zaphenath-paneah offered a forgiving smile, then stood. "Tarik, take his man back to his room and secure the door again. Do not whip or punish him. Tomorrow we shall continue waiting for his brothers."

"They will not come!" Simeon roared, struggling against the cords that held his arms.

"They will come," Zaphenath-paneah answered, and for an instant Mandisa wondered if her master spoke out of conviction or desperate hope. Then the vizier lifted a hand and pointed toward the doorway. "Take him now."

Tarik and the guards pulled Simeon away, and the brightness of a dozen torches left the chamber. When the men had gone, Zaphenath-paneah turned again to Tizara. "You may go back to your room," he said simply. "You sleep in the chamber next to my sons, do you not?"

She nodded woodenly. Tears had tangled in her lashes and smeared the paint around her eyes.

"Resume your place, then," the master said. "On the morrow, we shall not mention this again." His voice was oddly comforting in the stillness, and Mandisa took hope from its gentle tone. If Tizara could be forgiven for running away, Mandisa would be forgiven for her less-than-loving attitude.

Turning with stiff dignity, Tizara walked through the doorway. When she had gone, the master gave his wife a bright smile.

"That was not so bad, was it?" he said, his manner suddenly light and carefree. "I was afraid one of them would be hurt."

Asenath looked at him in surprise. "Did you know they would try to escape?"

"I would have been surprised if they had not," Zaphenath-paneah answered, sinking back into his chair. He relaxed, stretching his legs out in front of him, and gestured to Ani. "My wise steward anticipated their moves, too, and made their provisions readily accessible. I wanted them to prepare without trouble and be stopped without bloodshed."

"Both you and your steward are wise, my lord," Mandisa said, finding it impossible not to return the vizier's bemused smile. She stepped out from behind Asenath's chair, ready to join in the mood of good cheer.

"Thank you, Mandisa. Ani, I must thank you for your attentiveness. Now that the excitement is finished, we should sleep well tonight."

Smiling out of an overflow of well-being, Mandisa looked to her mistress. But Lady Asenath was not happy. Her face had emptied of expression and locked. "My lady," Mandisa whispered, "is something wrong?"

Zaphenath-paneah's smile quickly faded.

"My dear Asenath," the vizier repeated, "is something troubling you?"

"I am not troubled, my love," she said, speaking in a suffocated whisper. "We are going to have a baby."

~ Twenty-five ~

PACING IN HER CHAMBER, MANDISA PRESSED HER hands over her mouth, stifling the cry that threatened to burst forth and wake Adom. In a thousand years, she could never have imagined a moment as dreadful as the one in which Asenath told Zaphenath-paneah that they would have another baby. Even Ani had been stunned by the news. The four of them, connected by the intimate ties of matrimony and servanthood, knew that the vizier cared too much for his wife's life to have fathered the child. Unless the gods had assumed human form and visited Lady Asenath as they reportedly did during the conception of the pharaohs, the lady had been unfaithful to her husband— and he knew it.

Zaphenath-paneah's handsome face had not altered at the news, but he flinched as hurt and longing filled his gaze. Mandisa closed her eyes against the memory, unable to recall the pitiful sight of her sorrowing master without aching in regret. Her teeth chattered, her body trembled as she paced. What tremors must her master be enduring?

Zaphenath-paneah had said nothing immediately after his wife's announcement. He sat back and closed his eyes, his face utterly blank. Awkwardness hung in the room like a mist, so thick that the foursome could scarcely see each other through it. Asenath murmured something about how the gods had finally answered her prayers to give the mighty Zaphenath-paneah another son, but no one listened to her. Mandisa had gripped the back of Asenath's chair, her own emotions bobbing and spinning like a piece of flotsam caught in the Nile.

The master had foreseen and planned for Tizara's and Simeon's escape, but how could he have prepared for treachery coming from one so close to his heart?

After a long brutal interval of silence, the vizier had stood and extended his hand to his wife. Trembling, Asenath placed her hand on his, then closed her eyes as he bent to kiss her forehead. Without another word, he lifted his wife's hand to his cheek, then gave it to Mandisa. Through an icy chill that engulfed the group, the handmaid led her lady from the vizier's chamber.

Mandisa tried to frame words of congratulation, but Asenath stopped them with an upraised hand. "I will talk no more tonight," she whispered, her face suddenly looking much older than her twenty-four years. She would not even allow Mandisa to see her to bed, but dismissed her with a rapid shake of her hand.

The same hand the master had caressed.

Mandisa quivered at the memory, pressing her palms to her forehead. Only two days before she had told Ani that the master and mistress demonstrated love in a way she had never seen before, but apparently the master's love had not been enough for his lady.

So Zaphenath-paneah would cast her off.

And love was as insubstantial as mist on the water.

JACOB

But the famine was heavy in the land.
And so it was,
when they had finished eating the rations that
they had brought from Egypt,
that their father said to them: Return,
buy us some food rations.
But [Judah] said to him, saying:
The man warned, yes, warned us, saying:
You shall not see my face unless your
brother is with you.
If you wish to send our brother with us,
we will go down and buy you some food-rations.
But if you do not wish to send him,
we will not go down. . . .

Genesis 43: 1–5

The Five Books of Moses[1]

---

[1]*The Five Books of Moses*, translated by Everett Fox (New York: Schocken, 1995), p. 204–205.

Twenty-six

THE SKY ABOVE HEBRON STRETCHED PURE BLUE from north to south, with no more than a little violet duskiness lingering in the west. Leaning heavily on his staff, Jacob moved stiffly toward the oak tree outside his family's settlement. The yellow day had opened peacefully enough, but within a few moments the sky would begin to smoke with heat haze. Torridity would beat down upon the camp like the strokes of a coppersmith's hammer, and the gaunt hills flanking Hebron would tremble.

Safe in the shade of the stalwart oak, Jacob gently eased himself to the ground and tried to swallow the despair in his throat. He knew the inevitable confrontation would come today. They thought him old and blind, but last night when Dinah remarked that the women had opened the last bag of grain, he had seen the looks of concern that passed between Reuben, Judah, and Levi.

Their food was nearly gone. If Israel and his children were to survive the months ahead, another trip to Egypt would be necessary.

A tight pain squeezed his heart. For months he had dreaded this day. He had filled his prayers with petitions for Simeon's escape, for rain, for a brilliant plan to find food from some source other than the formidable Black Land whose vizier now held Simeon. *Surely the kings of the east have managed to store surplus grain*, he had reminded God Shaddai. *Or the kings of the Mitanni Empire . . .*

When God did not openly respond to Jacob's hints, he took action for himself. For months he had been quietly sending servants to Togarmah in the north, Shinar in the

of the south, but the famine had struck
ciously as it had Canaan. The people of
ught grain in Egypt, too.

head, amazed that only one empire had
visdom to prepare for disaster. Egypt's
further complicated the matter, for an intricate
network of unimpeachable governors, captains, and scribes
connected Egyptian cities and nomarchies to its capital at
Thebes. Only the most skilled spies would be able to slip
into a frontier outpost and buy grain without approval from
the powerful vizier of all Egypt, and Jacob's sons were not
skilled spies. They had trouble enough playing the role of
brothers.

A pair of vultures circled over a carcass in the distance,
but Jacob stared past the brown hills of Hebron into his own
thoughts. How could God Shaddai allow universal famine?
Never in the history of the world had every kingdom on
earth been driven to another one for its survival. And despite Simeon's detention in Egypt, Jacob had to admit that
the vizier behaved generously. He graciously fed those who
came to him with outstretched hands, though he could
have forced the hungry nations into slavery and submission. Pharaoh would profit nicely for his vizier's largess,
Jacob knew, but the king's representative had not attempted
to take unfair advantage of nations weakened by starvation
and destitution.

So why had this wise and discerning vizier doubted his
sons? Why had he insisted upon testing the truth of their
words?

A familiar nagging suspicion reared its ugly head. Perhaps the man was astute enough to sense duplicity, even as
Jacob had once smelled treachery on his sons as strong as
cheap perfume. But that had happened more than twenty
years ago. Since Joseph's disappearance he had negotiated
an uneasy truce with suspicion, just as he had learned to
share his empty tent with grief and loneliness.

He rubbed his chest, protecting the heart only Rachel

and Joseph had been able to fully enter. They had slipped from his grasp like steam from a boiling pot, taking the better part of his life with them. Now dashed dreams and disillusionment raked at his soul. What remained of the covenant promise? Only a parched land and an assortment of bickering sons. El Shaddai had promised Canaan to Abraham. He had renewed his covenant with Isaac. He had wrestled with Jacob and spoken his promise yet again. At Bethel, the House of God, the voice of God Shaddai had promised that all families of the earth would find blessing through Jacob and his seed. *Here, I am with you*, God had said, *I will watch over you wherever you go. . . .*

"Father."

Jacob looked up, disturbed from his thoughts. Levi, Judah, Reuben, and Dan stood before him, a delegation of the eldest sons. "We have no food, Father," Reuben began. "We must return to Mizraim."

"Then go." Jacob nodded slowly, stilling the last voices of resistance within him. "Go back. Buy us a little food."

Reuben lifted a brow and looked at Judah. He obviously hadn't expected that answer.

"But," Judah said, spreading his hands in a gesture of helplessness, "the vizier solemnly warned us that we would not see him again unless our brother Benjamin is with us. If you will send Benjamin, we will go and buy whatever we need. But if you will not—"

Exasperated, Jacob slapped his hands over his ears. "Why did you treat me so badly? Why did you tell this man that you had another brother? If he had not known, he could not ask for Benjamin!"

"The vizier asked specific and particular questions," Levi answered, frowning. "He asked if our father still lived, and if we had another brother. We answered truthfully, never dreaming that he would command us to bring our brother to him."

Jacob lowered his hands and looked away, resisting.

"Father," Judah said, lowering himself to one knee,

"send Benjamin in my care, and we will arise and go so that we all may live. If we do not eat, you and the little ones will die. I myself will guarantee Benjamin's safety. If I do not bring him back and set him safe before you, then let me bear the blame forever."

"If you had allowed us to go when we first asked your blessing," Reuben said, pressing Judah's point, "we could have gone and returned twice by now."

Unwillingly, Jacob turned and held Judah with a long silent scrutiny. "I am an old man," he finally whispered, his voice breaking as he gazed past his sons toward distant memories of Joseph and Rachel. "In my youth I loved a woman and lost her. I loved a son and lost him, too. One son of Rachel's remains. If I lose Benjamin, all I shall have left are the raw wounds of an aching heart."

He lifted his eyes to Reuben's and strengthened his voice. "If you must go, take some of the best things we have as a present for the man: a little balm and honey, aromatic gum and myrrh, pistachio nuts and almonds. And take double the silver you did last time, so you can return the treasure you found in the mouths of your sacks. Someone certainly made a mistake by returning it to you."

His gaze lifted to the dun-colored lifeless hills. Death was bearing down on them with a slow and stately deliberation, and he could do nothing to stop it. He had no more choices, no way out . . . save one.

"Take your brother also," he whispered, a suffocating sensation tightening his throat, "and return to the vizier. And may El Shaddai grant you compassion in the sight of this man, that he may release to you Simeon and Benjamin. And as for me"—he closed his eyes—"if I am bereaved of my children, I am bereaved."

~~~ Twenty-seven ~~~

MANDISA SIGHED AS SHE LIFTED THE BREAKFAST tray her mistress had not touched. The morning sky was a faultless wide curve of blue from one edge of the garden wall to the other. The air shimmered in honey-thick sunshine. Ordinarily Asenath would have rejoiced in a day like this, but today she lay silent and still on her couch, one hand over her stomach, her pale face contorted by nausea.

"Dear wife," Zaphenath-paneah was saying, reaching to pat his wife's free hand, "I must know if you want to attend the party for Queen Tiy. Since Pharaoh's new bride is a commoner, he wants to invite as many of the nobility as possible. The guest list will be enormously complicated. . . ."

His voice drifted away when Asenath did not respond. Two deep lines of worry cut into his forehead, then his gaze caught Mandisa's. She shook her head, silently warning him off, and the hopeful glint in his eyes faded.

Mandisa clicked her tongue in quiet pity. In the months since Asenath's shocking announcement, the master had behaved more nobly than she expected. Indeed, he had done the complete opposite of what any other betrayed husband would do. Instead of casting his wife aside, he had said nothing of her obvious infidelity. With inconceivable patience, he looked on her with tender pity, even when Asenath battled the nausea and exhaustion of pregnancy.

The vizier was an endless surprise. His continued attention and affection toward his wife simultaneously baffled and thrilled Mandisa. Zaphenath-paneah remained at Asenath's side for longer periods of time than usual. He took care that luxurious bouquets of blue lotus blossoms, her favorite flowers, filled her chambers and asked Tizara to keep the boys quiet whenever Asenath was ill or resting.

The slaves, servants, and visitors who were not privy to the truth soon surmised that Asenath expected another child. Mandisa felt a curious tingling shock the first time she saw Zaphenath-paneah accept a round of congratulations with his customary polished charm. Immediately afterward, however, she caught sight of her master in an unguarded moment, and her heart broke at the flash of wild grief that ripped through his eyes. The heartbreak she had experienced over Simeon paled in comparison to the torrent of anguish she knew her master endured.

Mandisa removed the tray from the stand near her lady's chair. She was about to murmur some foolish pleasantry to lighten the dismal atmosphere when Ani burst into the garden. Startled, Zaphenath-paneah looked up, and even Asenath managed to turn her head and lift a brow in the steward's direction.

"Life, health, and prosperity to my lord and mistress," Ani babbled. He bent forward at the waist, a token effort to lower himself to the ground, but obviously had no time for formalities.

"Remain upright, Ani, and tell me what brings your aged legs here in such a hurry," Zaphenath-paneah answered, breaking into an open friendly smile.

"The Canaanites from Hebron," the old man gasped, an expression of wonder creeping over his face. "They are back. Even now they stand outside the gates of your villa."

The master stared at his steward, tongue-tied and shaken, while Mandisa took a wincing little breath. Ani still had no idea of the brothers' connection to the vizier. "Simeon's brothers?" she asked, finding her voice.

Ani's head bobbed like a cork on the river. "Yes, the loud one's bearded kin. Ten of them, my lord!"

"Ten?" All color drained from the vizier's face. "You say there are ten?"

"Yes." Ani grinned like a well-fed fox. "Ten. The nine who came before and another one, a younger man."

A muscle quivered in Zaphenath-paneah's jaw. "Tell the gatekeeper to hold them outside the villa. And send Tarik to my chambers at once. I will meet him there."

The vizier pressed his hand over Asenath's for a brief moment, then rose and left the women in the garden.

————

After inspecting the positions of his guards, Tarik turned with a quick snap of his shoulders and nodded toward the vizier's gatekeeper. The double gates swung open, and the ten Canaanites, wide-eyed and wary, progressed through the courtyard toward the portico of the vizier's home.

Watching them, Tarik marveled at the sense of wonder he felt. These humble shepherds, so indignant and insistent when they last stood before his master, had returned to submit to the vizier's demands. The strong-willed brothers who had rejected Zaphenath-paneah a lifetime before and argued with him but a few months ago were here to humble themselves.

Moments earlier, Zaphenath-paneah had given Tarik clear and concise directions: "Hold them at the portico that I may spy upon them from the balcony of my chamber," he said, his deep voice simmering with barely checked agitation. "If they are desperate, or if our father is truly unwilling to release my younger brother, they may try to slip an impostor by us. But if the younger man truly is Benjamin . . ."

The master's voice had trailed off, and Tarik had bowed and left, understanding his orders. Looking up as the dusty group now approached, Tarik openly stared, knowing that his master also studied them from behind a screen of palms on his balcony.

"Halt!" Tarik commanded, hoping his limited knowledge of the Canaanite tongue would prove adequate. "Line up, so we may be certain you have not dared to bring a sword into the vizier's house."

Obediently, the brothers stretched out in a line, shoulder to shoulder. Tarik's guards moved among them, patting their heavy garments with the flat edges of their swords in a calculated demonstration of diligence. While his guards searched for hidden weapons, Tarik found his eyes drawn to the younger man who stood awkwardly in the center of the group, his hands hanging limply at his side. A blush burned the man's cheek. His black hair gleamed in the bright morning sun, growing upward and outward in great masses of curls. His clothing was simple but rich. His head hung slightly forward in the attitude of one who lives in a perpetual state of embarrassment. A handsome square face framed dark eyes.

"By Seth's foul breath, those eyes!" Tarik muttered. "They are exactly like my master's!"

After a moment, Ani's thin tremulous voice spiraled down from the balcony. "The master says to bring them in," the steward called to Tarik. "I am to slay a lamb, and the men will dine with Zaphenath-paneah at noon."

———

Levi's head throbbed as he climbed the chiseled steps before the vizier's portico. He had slept little on the journey. Like the others, he worried that the Egyptian might wish to detain Benjamin as he had Simeon. He also worried because Simeon had not yet been brought out to them.

"What if this vizier has sold our Simeon to slave traders?" Asher whispered, hugging his arms as he walked. "Suppose the vizier realized he was not paid for our grain? What if he has sold Simeon to make up the difference?"

"What if he chooses to sell Benjamin, too?" Naphtali asked, his jaw thrust forward. "Or all of us? It is not good that he has summoned us inside, I tell you. If nothing were amiss, he would have taken our silver, given us Simeon and our grain, and sent us on our way."

"The Egyptian is odd. There is no predicting him," Reuben answered, running his hands through his hair as he looked around the reception area. "But whatever happens, we shall deserve it." Deadly calm filled his eyes when he looked at Levi. "In the past few months I have thought many times of Joseph, whom we sold into slavery. Can any of us say we do not deserve to suffer the fate we decreed for him?"

"Hush, Benjamin will hear you!" Judah hissed. Their collective gaze turned toward their youngest brother. Aloof and distant as always, Benjamin moved through the magnificent assembly hall, his hands behind his back, his eyes lifted to the wonderfully unusual paintings on the walls.

"Look, now, what is this?" Dan asked, nodding toward the other side of the room. A host of Egyptians, richly dressed in golden collars and white kilts, entered the room from another doorway. The latecomers recoiled somewhat when their painted eyes caught sight of the brothers. Levi cast them a withering stare in return.

"They look at us as if we are a bad smell," he muttered in a low voice, taut with anger. "I would like to wrestle that tall one with the earring. I'd show that self-important snob that we are not the stinking herders he thinks we are."

"Hush, Levi," Judah whispered, turning toward the entryway. "Someone approaches."

A pair of sandaled feet shuffled through the doorway, then the bald wiry man who had spoken from the balcony stood before them. "Greetings from my lord Zaphenath-paneah, Nourisher of Egypt and the World, Guardian of Pharaoh's Shadow," he said, speaking Canaanite in a clipped, careful accent. "You have been invited to eat the midday meal with my master."

"Eat with him?" Judah lifted a brow. "We have some news for him, but we do not require much of his time."

"You shall eat with him," the little man answered. "My name is Ani. I am Zaphenath-paneah's steward. If my master wishes to take time with you, it shall be taken." He glanced past them toward the portico and the courtyard beyond, then rested his hands upon his scrawny birdlike chest. "My master has instructed me to see that your donkeys are provided with fodder and that your feet are washed." He lifted his hands and clapped. Immediately half a dozen servants appeared behind him with basins, towels, and pitchers in their hands.

The steward's lined face arranged itself into a careful smile. "Is there anything else that you need?"

"Our brother," Levi said, stepping out of the circle. "What has become of Simeon?"

The steward bowed his head. "He is preparing for you even now. He will be restored to you soon."

"There is one other matter," Judah said, stepping closer. "When we arrived home after our last journey to Thebes, we found that our silver had been returned to our sacks. We didn't take it, and we want to pay for what we bought. So today we have returned the silver we owe, and we have brought more to buy what our families need."

"We have also brought gifts," Reuben interrupted, nodding gravely, "for your master."

The old man smiled again, an odd mingling of wariness and amusement in his eyes. "Be at ease. Do not be afraid," he said, nodding slightly. "Your God and the God of your father has given you treasure in your sacks. I had your silver. Now, if you will excuse me, here is your brother."

The steward turned and moved aside. A quartet of guards stepped smartly together through the passageway and separated when they reached the reception hall. Levi half expected to see the mighty vizier step out from behind them, but Simeon stood there, as massive and self-confident as ever.

"Simeon!" Levi cast his worries aside with sudden good humor.

The Destroyer's eyes flashed with approval. "Brother! How well you look!"

Ignoring the servants and the assembled Egyptians, the

brothers surrounded Simeon with much embracing and slapping on the back. He accepted their welcomes with unusually good nature, then slipped his burly arm around Benjamin. "My little brother," he said, his bushy brows rising in obvious pleasure, "I have never been so pleased to see anyone in my entire life!"

"Did they treat you well?"

"Were you in the prison pits?"

"You look well-fed, Simeon!"

"Not only well-fed, but someone has been pampering our brother!"

They laughed, poked, jabbed at one another in merry glee, and after a moment Levi pulled himself from the fray and stepped back to study his brother. He and Simeon had been closer than the others. Their mother had always said they were two of a kind, cut from the same cloth. He and Simeon had always understood each other without a word of explanation.

But this was not the same Destroyer they left here months ago. Some elusive quality in him had changed. An edge had softened. The warp and woof that comprised the fabric of the man had subtly altered. The old Simeon would have come charging out, threatening revenge and retribution, daring them to take up arms.

"Levi, why do you look at me like that?" Simeon asked, laughter in his voice.

The others grew still and parted, their faces alight with surprise.

"I thought you'd be glad to see me, Levi," Simeon went on, a faint glint of humor in his eyes, "but you're looking at me as if I had suddenly sprouted horns."

Levi felt the yawning chasm between them like an open wound. Perhaps Simeon had been tortured. Extreme pain could account for the way his voice had softened, for his carefree humor, and for the solicitous way he inclined his head toward Benjamin. Though physically he bore no marks or scars, the Egyptians might have bewitched him or forced him to participate in their vile idol worship. Simeon would have fought them, of course, but even the Destroyer's strength had limits.

But he would never admit them. As he would never confess that he'd been broken. But when they returned to the tents of Hebron, Simeon would heal and become his old self again.

"It is nothing," Levi murmured, his mind drifting away from the unsolvable mystery. He attempted to smile, then waved Simeon's concerns away. "You look different, that's all," he said, shrugging. "You're wearing a kilt instead of a robe. And someone has cut your hair."

"Bah. It couldn't be helped. The Egyptians have foolish ideas about such things," Simeon said, making a face as the others laughed. "At least I managed to keep my beard! But those things are done, my brother. I am ready to go home."

"Good," Levi answered, smiling thoughtfully.

———

Mandisa found her place beside Tarik in the master's entourage and resisted the urge to cast a questioning glance at the captain. The vizier had already given them strict instructions. "My brothers must be tested," he had explained, his arms behind his back as he prowled his chamber. "They have brought Benjamin, which is good, but how can I know that they will not cast him aside as they once did me? If their hearts are not loyal, I must be there to catch my younger brother when they cast him away. I would know the extent of their devotion. I must be sure their stony hearts have softened."

The master did not say exactly how he planned to prove his brothers, but Mandisa knew the elaborate stratagem would begin at dinner. She and Tarik were to enter the chamber ahead of the vizier's bodyguard, then she would take her place at Zaphenath-paneah's right hand as interpreter, while Tarik stood on his left, ever ready to defend.

One of the young fan-bearers coughed softly as he

BROTHERS

moved into line behind her, and Mandisa glanced back. Zaphenath-paneah stood behind the fan-bearers, a stiff and regal expression on his face.

Mandisa's heart stirred with compassion as she looked at him. For an instant, wistfulness stole into the vizier's expression as he met her eyes. Then he smiled.

"He is ready," she whispered to Tarik.

A trumpet sounded. Like actors in a play they swept down the passageway and into the hall. The servants had already done their work, providing each guest with a chair, a footstool, and an empty dining tray on a stand. Behind each chair a servant waited with an amphora of scented water, a copper wash basin, and fresh linen for drying the hands.

Zaphenath-paneah had been quite explicit in his directions regarding the Canaanites. They were to be positioned far away from his Egyptian guests and in a particular order. Reuben, the oldest, was to be seated farthest from the vizier, and Benjamin, the youngest, at the vizier's right hand.

The guests, both Egyptian and Canaanite, rose from their chairs and prostrated themselves upon the polished floor as the retinue entered. As Mandisa moved to her position between the vizier and the younger brother, Tarik barked the order giving permission for the guests to rise from the floor.

Shock ran through Mandisa when her eyes met those of the young man next to her. This Benjamin looked remarkably like her master without his wig and makeup. Surely the others could see the resemblance if they would only take the time to look!

Stepping away from his guards, Zaphenath-paneah took his seat in the gilded chair high upon the dais. Before the meal could begin, the oldest brother came forward from his place and dropped a heavy pouch onto the floor before the vizier. "If it please you, my lord," he said, pulling several smaller sacks from the pouch, "our father bids you accept these gifts from the land of Canaan. We have brought you balm and honey, aromatic gum, pistachio nuts, almonds, and myrrh.''

Mandisa hurried the translation, for tears were already rising in her master's eyes. He would have to be careful, or these men would know that he understood them. She rushed through the list of gifts, stumbling over the elder brother's words, then folded her hands as her master indifferently summoned a servant to take the generous tribute away. Bounty from Canaan! She dropped her lashes quickly to hide her disappointment, though she suspected Zaphenath-paneah's heart yearned to touch and smell and taste the things of home as strongly as she did.

The vizier sat forward and looked intently at the brother before him. ''You spoke of your old father when you first stood before me. Is he well?''

Mandisa translated the question and answer: ''Yes, my lord.''

''And this—'' The master pointed toward the man next to Mandisa. ''Is this the youngest brother, of whom you spoke to me?''

''It is, my lord.''

Scarcely waiting for the translation, the master leaned forward to peer directly into the younger man's face. Benjamin turned a vivid scarlet. Mandisa lowered her eyes, her heart aching with empathy, and her master swallowed hard and bit back tears. ''May God be gracious to you, my son,'' Zaphenath-paneah whispered in a choked voice. Then the vizier of all Egypt leapt from his gilded chair and ran from the room.

Tarik followed without hesitation, and after a moment of uncertainty in which the assembly stiffened in shock, Mandisa left, too. She found the master and his captain in the vizier's chambers, where Zaphenath-paneah had once again fallen prey to his feelings. Deep sobs racked him for the space of a quarter hour. Then he lifted his head, wiped his stained and streaked face with a square of linen, and asked Mandisa to reapply the painted lines of his eyes. He did not speak as she ministered to him, and Mandisa found herself silently asking the vizier's Almighty God to provide her master with the strength to confront yet another crisis in his life.

When she assured him that he looked as dignified and stately as before, he led the way as she and Tarik followed him back to the banquet hall.

Without a word of explanation, the vizier took his seat and commanded that the meal be served. The hungry Canaanites shifted in their chairs, unused to the Egyptian custom that often expanded dinner into a two- or three-hour ritual. Each tray or bowl had to be presented first to the master, who either kept it by his side or sampled it and sent it on its way to his other guests. Thus the hand of the vizier literally provided every dish.

While Zaphenath-paneah pretended to sample the feast of roasted duck, braised lamb, softened sweet breads, beans flavored with sweet oils, and honey-basted gazelle, Mandisa listened to snatches of the Canaanite conversation around her. The brothers, who still rejoiced at Simeon's reunion with them, remarked upon the bounty of the vizier's table and the striking fact that the Egyptian had unwittingly arranged them in birth order.

Afraid that her eyes might reveal too much of her heart, Mandisa kept her eyes from Simeon, forcing herself to concentrate upon her master and his concerns. But Simeon's booming voice, his wide gestures, and his resounding laugh seemed to fill the room, reinforcing her inexplicable feeling of emptiness.

She had not visited his chamber in weeks, not since the night of his escape. Lady Asenath had needed her in the aftermath of that bizarre episode, and the master had requested that Mandisa stay with his wife. Tizara had been elected to feed Simeon and listen to his complaints, so Mandisa was certain that the former harlot's image now filled his heart.

Amid the music of harpists and the twirling of dancing

girls, the guests accepted food from the vizier's generous hand and filled their hungry stomachs. Mandisa shot Tarik a wry smile when she realized this was no ordinary banquet. Halima and the other kitchen slaves must have worked themselves into a frenzy to prepare so much for so many on such short notice! And yet bowls continued to arrive from the kitchens: lumps of fat served with cumin and radish oil, bowls of brown beans, bright chick-peas sprinkled with soft lotus seeds and flavored with marjoram. Slaves bore pitchers containing fresh grape juice flavored with pomegranates, figs, mint, and honey. After the round of meats and vegetables came the sweets: bowls of shining pomegranates, grapes, jujubes, honey cakes, heads of garlic, and delicately flavored sycamore figs.

Though tradition demanded that he at least pretend to sample every dish, the master ate little but feasted instead on the sight of his brothers, particularly the youngest one. Every other dish went to Benjamin, until an obvious crowd of serving women clustered around the young man's chair. The Egyptian guests whispered among themselves at this peculiar demonstration of favor, but Zaphenath-paneah seemed oblivious to everything but the shy handsome man seated at his right hand.

Was he, Mandisa wondered, *trying* to incite the others to jealousy? Or was his heart overcome with longing for this brother who was a long lost shade of himself?

As she studied the faces of those eating and drinking in the reception hall, she realized that the twelve sons of Jacob had been reunited for the first time in over twenty years.

But only one of them knew it.

Twenty-eight

BENJAMIN HELD UP A WARNING HAND AS YET
another dark-eyed slave approached with a platter from the
vizier. "No, I couldn't eat another mouthful," he said, hoping the Egyptian girl would understand. He patted his
stomach and smiled. "It is delicious, but I cannot eat any
more."

The vizier's kind attention was embarrassing. Of course,
Benjamin thought, he had probably been awarded such
bounty because he sat closest to the vizier. The other Egyptians, stretching out to the vizier's left, had received com-
paratively little, but the vizier was obviously more interested in the men from Canaan. Did he still think they were
spies? Or did he simply consider them unusual because
they were eleven sons from one father? Reuben had warned
him of the great man's peculiarity, but Benjamin had seen
nothing unpleasant in the man's aspect or behavior.

His eyes caught the vizier's dark gaze, and Benjamin
turned his head away quickly, a blush burning his cheeks.
A moment later, the interpreter's soft voice cut into his
thoughts. "My master, Zaphenath-paneah, says you have
not eaten enough. Would you like more?"

"No." Benjamin looked up and into the man's dark eyes.
No trace of hostility dwelled there, only compassion and a
certain overarching kindness. "Thank him, but I have eaten
my fill."

The woman translated, and a strange, faintly eager look
flashed in the Egyptian's eyes. He spoke again and the
woman repeated his words. "My master asks if you are

well? What do you think of Egypt? How many children have you?"

Benjamin laughed, amazed that the great man would care for such trivial opinions and facts. "I am well. I am astounded by all I see here, and I have nine sons," he said, feeling the man's sharp eyes upon him as he talked. "My wife is expecting another child soon."

"Nine sons." The vizier's answer came through the woman. "Are you trying to populate the earth with Abraham's descendants completely by yourself?"

The teasing question caught Benjamin off guard. What had his brothers told the Egyptian at their first meeting? How did he know of Abraham? Jacob's grandfather had sojourned in Mizraim for a time, but the people of the Black Land would not know of El Shaddai's promise to make Abraham's descendants as numerous as the sand of the sea.

"My lord," Benjamin asked, turning so that he faced the vizier directly. "How do you know so many things? You have seated us according to our birth order, you know much about our father and our people, and yet you are a stranger to us."

The vizier watched Benjamin with bemused and opaque eyes as the woman translated.

"Who but God can reveal truth?" the vizier answered through the woman, fingering a graceful silver bowl on his dinner tray as he spoke. The vessel was engraved with the images of Egyptian gods, and Benjamin had seen similar bowls in the tents of many nomadic peoples. He recognized it as a divining bowl, used to foretell the future. A supplicant would fill the bowl with water, then pour oil on top of the water. During the chanting of incantations, the gods supposedly revealed truth in the swirls and designs of the floating oil.

"God has revealed these things to me," the vizier answered, lifting his eyes from the bowl to Benjamin's face. "And more which you shall know in time."

Benjamin could not think of a suitable answer, and the

vizier smiled and turned away. After lifting his hand and pronouncing a blessing of some sort in Egyptian, Zaphenath-paneah stood and left the room, his entourage trailing behind him.

———

"Another child on the way? Benjamin, you spend too much time at home!" Simeon teased, punching the young man in the arm. The brothers had been welcomed as guests for the night and given bedding in a large chamber of the vizier's house.

"At least I am not yet a grandfather!" Benjamin answered, returning Simeon's playful jab. "Your oldest, Jemuel, is searching for a wife even now. You will have grandchildren piling on your knee before the next harvest."

"Jemuel is a fool," Simeon answered, rolling onto his stomach. "Marriage is for men who have no other options." He propped himself on his elbows, grateful that the servants had furnished them with blankets and furs instead of those effeminate Egyptian beds. His brothers would tease him unmercifully if they knew he had lived in a dainty Egyptian chamber during his time of captivity.

"Are you sorry you married?" Levi asked, lifting a brow.

"A man may marry if he needs sons, but I have six sons already," Simeon answered, propping his head on his hand. "That's five legal heirs too many. I will never marry again."

"But men need women," Benjamin protested, sitting up. "Father says God Shaddai decreed it was not good for men to be alone."

"What men need there are women aplenty to give," Simeon interrupted, snorting. He lifted a brow. "Right, Judah?"

A silence, thick as wool, wrapped itself around them. Simeon stared at Judah, daring him to contradict his opinion, for they all knew that pious Judah had once unknowingly hired his own daughter-in-law as a prostitute.

"Indeed there are," Judah answered after a moment, his voice gruff. "But there are snakes in the desert, too, and I would not recommend that a man sleep with one."

Several of the brothers laughed, and the mood lightened. Simeon glanced around the circle, grateful for each bearded and sunburned face. "So, tell me," he said, looking at Levi. "Father is well, but how is our sister?"

Judah groaned and buried his head in the furs beneath him.

Levi's handsome face twisted in a smirk. "Dinah is as Dinah is," he said, shrugging. "She has not changed, Simeon."

"Has she married?" Simeon tried to keep his voice light.

"No." Levi shook his head. "Nor will she. She sits alone in our mother's tent most of the time, except when the servants enter to help her. Sometimes she sews. Sometimes she makes baby clothes."

Simeon said nothing but stared down at his hands, the same hands that had locked Dinah into the past. These hands had taken her baby and lowered it to the desert sands. . . . The sudden remorse that pricked his soul was the mere tip of a long seam of guilt that snaked its way back through the years to Shechem.

"Forget Dinah," Levi said, reaching out. His broad hand fell upon Simeon's arm. "Tell me instead about the pretty woman who interprets for the vizier. When you were not aware of it, she studied you." His lips parted in a sly smile. "Or perhaps you were aware of it."

"I thought she was watching me," Reuben said, pretending to pout.

"No," Judah said, lifting his head in sudden eagerness. "She was definitely watching our Simeon. So explain the sudden color in your face, Destroyer. You have been in this house a long time. You must know the woman's name."

Know her name? I know much more than her name, but I forfeited everything the night I tried to escape. She will

never look at me as she once did. She will never think of
me in the same way.

"Her name," Simeon said, closing his hands, "is Mandisa. She is the Lady Asenath's handmaid."

"Oh," Levi said, cracking an irreverent grin. "And why would a lady's maid care so much about you?"

"She was also my . . . *attendant*," Simeon said, searching for a word to describe the relationship he had not completely analyzed himself. "She speaks Canaanite, so the guards asked her to tend me. We became . . ." he paused, shrugging, "friends."

"Friends?" While the others wailed in laughter, Levi pretended to choke in disbelief. "Simeon, you have never been a woman's friend," he protested when he had regained his composure. "A woman can be your mother, your sister, your wife, or your lover. And since we know this Egyptian is not mother or sister to you—"

"She is not wife or lover or Egyptian, either," Simeon interrupted, looking at his hands again. "She is a Canaanite, and she is a friend, brothers. You may leave it at that."

Something in his face and voice silenced them. Outside the chamber the wind whispered and a group of servants tumbled into laughter, but silence filled the room until Benjamin lifted his head.

"Will she be upset, then, when you leave tomorrow?" he asked, the light of concern in his dark eyes. "Perhaps you should say your farewells tonight, when you may have a private word with her."

"There is no need," Simeon answered. He flipped on his back and pillowed his head on his hands. "She is nothing but a friend, no more to me than the cook or the guard who watched my room. I am ready to go home, brothers, and I suggest we sleep."

The others mumbled in reply and settled down on their beds. From far away Simeon heard the familiar sounds of food being scraped from platters and the fountain splashing in the garden. Would he ever hear those sounds again? He knew he would never again enjoy the anticipation of Mandisa's gentle rap on his door. He might even miss the sharpness of her quick tongue.

He lay awake for a long time, thinking.

———

Something moved in the darkness and Mandisa sat up, trying to see what had slashed her sleep like a dagger. "Who's there?" she whispered, drawing the linen sheet to her chest. Then she remembered her son and reached out to wake Adom.

"Shh, don't wake the boy."

Simeon's voice spoke to her, but she could not see him in the darkness. A moment of sheer black fright swept through her—had he come to take revenge for his imprisonment?—then she stiffened at the challenge his presence presented.

"You should not be here," she whispered in a voice of authority. "Come out and show yourself, or I'll scream and wake the guards."

He stepped from the darkness at the rear of her room into a small square of light left by the waning moon. He looked colossal, tough, and sinewy in the darkness, more powerful and determined than any man she could ever recall seeing.

"I should probably scream anyway," she whispered, heat stealing into her face as she remembered their last private encounter.

"Mandisa, I'm not here to hurt you," he said, moving a step closer.

"You have made a mistake. Didn't you mean to seek Tizara's chamber?" She cringed inwardly at the bitter tone of her voice. "I know what you want of a woman, Simeon, and Tizara is more experienced and, I daresay, more willing to provide it than I."

His lips thinned in anger. "Woman, will you be quiet and listen?"

Adom suddenly stirred on his bed. They stared at each other across a sudden ringing silence, neither of them willing to wake the boy. When Adom turned and stretched out, still deep in sleep, Mandisa clenched her fist and lifted it toward Simeon's face. "You have no more sense than a stone, coming to a woman's chamber at this hour! If you were a servant or even a guard, Tarik would have you flogged for this!"

"I am a prisoner here no longer," Simeon answered, stiffening at her words. "And my intentions are honorable. I came to ask if you will leave with me tomorrow. Adom, too. There is room in my tent for both of you."

The tender concern in his expression amazed her even more than the proposal he had just made. "You want me to do what?" she asked, wholly taken aback. "To go with you? To Canaan?"

"Yes." His expression stilled and grew serious. "It would not be right for me to leave you behind. I am now free. You should be, too."

Too stunned to answer, Mandisa said nothing as Simeon knelt beside her bed, lifted her hand, and pressed it to his heart. With a look that made her breath leave her body, his eyes moved into hers. "Mandisa," he said, thick intensity in his lowered voice, "I owe you so much. I am sorry if I have behaved wrongly toward you, but you must understand that I was not at my best while I was held here. But now I am free, so journey with us tomorrow and leave this Black Land. Return to Canaan, the place of your birth."

"Simeon." She turned her hand to clasp his, not daring to trust her turbulent feelings. Was this a dream? No, his flesh was warm, his hand all too real. For a long moment, she looked at him. "Are you asking me to be your wife?"

"By heaven above, no." He dropped her hand as resolutely as he'd taken it. "I will never marry again, Mandisa. I've had two wives, and while they lived I made both of them miserable. Since I have a legal son, I have no further need of a wife."

Her mind reeled with confusion. "So you would have me live with you as what? A *concubine*?"

He lifted one shoulder in a shrug. "We will make whatever arrangement you like, but I won't marry you. You have told me about your first marriage and its misery, and I saw how my father tormented my mother. So you shall remain free and independent. I will protect and provide for you and Adom. That is the least I can do to show my gratitude. But since marriage makes men miserable, you will be free to go anytime you please."

"And so will you." She pressed her lips together, trying not to lose her crumbling control. He could walk away at any time, just as he had planned to escape and leave her behind forever. He would abandon her just as surely as Idogbe had.

"You are wrong, Simeon," she answered, her cheeks burning as she stared up at him. "Marriage doesn't make men miserable. Men make marriage miserable, and you, Simeon, son of Jacob, have already brought me more misery than a hundred husbands!"

"What?" His eyes gleamed with honest surprise, then a bemused smile crossed his face. "Consider my proposition carefully, Mandisa. I know you love me."

"Love you?" She pressed her hand to her forehead, unable to believe what she'd just heard. "How could I love a man so filled with anger and bitterness that he cannot see God's plain truth before him?"

"There is only one truth to consider here." His hand gripped her arm. "You love me, and you need someone to care for you and the boy."

"Adom and I were fine before you came here, and we will be fine after you leave."

"You are a *slave*, Mandisa. Can't you get that truth through your lovely head?"

"I'm not a slave! I am a free woman!"

"No, you are not! You are bound to Zaphenath-paneah, his wife, his children, and his house, as surely as if you wore chains of iron around your dainty ankles! Your master says 'do this' and you jump. Your lady says 'I want,' and you would fly to the moon to fetch whatever she desires. You weep over your master's sorrows and celebrate his joys when you ought to be creating your own!"

"His sorrows are my sorrows," she answered, gasping as if he had hit her in the stomach. "And my lady's joys are my joys because I love her, Simeon. If you knew how to love, you would understand!"

His eyes, black and dazzling with fury, seemed to impale her where she sat. "You are a fool, Mandisa," he said, lifting his chin and releasing her arm. "I offer you the freedom to go where you want and do as you please, and you reject it. I offer you my gratitude and you scorn me. Well, so be it. As you labor for your mighty vizier and work yourself into an early grave, think of me."

"I will think of you, Simeon," she answered, her flesh burning where he had touched her, "every time I hear one of the guards lose his temper and every time Tarik must discipline an unruly slave!" The words poured from her like a river, impossible to stop. "You are a difficult man, impossible to endure! First you insult me by asking me to be a concubine, then you flatter yourself by saying that I love you. How could I? No woman could love a man like you, because you have no idea what love is! You think love is only found within a woman's arms, but it is truly found by a woman's side, facing together the good and ill that life brings. But you and your kind would weather a storm by storming the weather! You stomp through life, trampling the hearts of those who *would* love you if only you would let them."

"Love." The word fell from his lips like a curse. "Jacob loved Rachel. That love condemned the rest of us."

"Even if your father did wrong, Simeon, you cannot continue this way! Learn from his mistake! Reach out to him. Care for him!"

He chuckled, a cold and bitter sound in the darkness.

"How can I care for someone who does not care for me?"

"I've been asking myself the same question," she answered, assaulted by a deep unspoken yearning. "And I have realized one thing—you cannot offer love with a clenched fist. It must be given freely. I have tried to offer love to you, Simeon. But you would not accept it."

"You don't know what you are talking about." He stood, defiance pouring from his dark eyes. "It is you, Mandisa, who will not be loved. You hide yourself behind these walls, behind the distinguished and noble Zaphenath-paneah. You refuse freedom in order to spend your life serving a man who will never consider you more than a slave."

"No." She shook her head. "You are wrong."

"I am right." He bent forward until his face hovered only inches from hers. "When you think of me in the lonely years to come, remember that I behaved nobly toward you. In gratitude, I offered you a way out of the Black Land, and you refused it."

"I will remember this night until my dying day," she whispered, turning her face away. "But I will not be lonely without you, Simeon."

She didn't know when he left, but suddenly a chill wind blew through the chamber, and she shivered, feeling more alone than she ever had in her life.

~ Twenty-nine ~

AN HOUR BEFORE THE BARK OF THE SUN GOD WAS
to begin its journey across the dark sky, Tarik steadied the
lamp in his hand and urged the flame to strengthen itself.
When the coiled papyrus wick burned steadily, he held the
lamp aloft and moved through the dark courtyard, checking
to see that his master's orders had been carried out.
Zaphenath-paneah had been quite explicit. Each Canaanite's bag was to be filled to the brim with grain, then each
man's silver was to be returned to the mouth of his sack.
Tarik was commanded to personally take the master's exquisite silver divining bowl and hide it inside the youngest
brother's sack.

Moving steadily in the darkness, Tarik patted the sides
of the restive donkeys and fumbled with each sack until he
had checked all eleven. Then he slipped the silver bowl
from a pouch under his cloak and buried it under the grain
of the last donkey's load.

All was in readiness.

Half an hour later by the water clock, Ani stood with
Tarik on the wide porch as the eleven sons of Jacob strode
out of the villa and into the courtyard. The palm trees along
the villa's walls stood black against the brightening sky as
the brothers took the reins of their donkeys. Ani cleared his
throat and stepped forward to bid the brothers a final farewell. Zaphenath-paneah, he told them, wished them a safe
and prosperous journey. Speaking for the others, Reuben
thanked Ani for his master's hospitality and promised to

give the vizier's greetings to their aged father.

The loud one, Simeon, lingered a moment in the court-yard, looking around as if to imprint the villa upon his memory, then waved carelessly toward the portico where Ani and Tarik stood. "Farewell, Egyptians," Simeon called, flashing a tight, grim smile. "Forgive me, but I hope we never meet again."

"I share your feelings," Tarik called, resting his hands atop his sword belt. Then, in a lower voice, the guard murmured puzzling words. "If only he knew."

Knew what? Ani lifted a questioning brow toward the captain of the guard, but Tarik kept his eyes fastened to the departing men and did not speak again.

As the last donkey disappeared through the gate, a soft sound broke the stillness of the early morning. Ani turned to see Mandisa weeping in the shadow of a papyrus-shaped pillar. Despite the Canaanite's brazen attempt to run away with Tizara, Mandisa apparently still harbored deep feelings for him.

"My dear child," he said, walking to the young woman's side. "If you loved him, why didn't you let him know?"

"I did," she whispered, running the back of her hand along her wet cheek. "But he did not understand."

———

The shaded finger of the shadow clock seemed to be mired in the space between one black slash on the horizontal rod and the next, but finally the shadow moved. An hour had passed since his brothers' departure. Joseph's nerves tensed, half in anticipation and half in dread, as he turned to Tarik.

"It is time," Joseph said, his heart thumping madly as his gaze crossed the captain's. "Go after them."

Tarik gave a whirling salute and sprinted to join his men in the courtyard. Moving to his balcony, Joseph saw over twenty battle chariots assembled, each manned with a driver and an expert archer. The horses pawed the dust in eagerness, their heads straining forward, their tails arching.

Would this show of force intimidate his brothers into surrendering Benjamin? For an instant Joseph wondered if his plan was elementally unfair. Perhaps part of him *wanted* them to give Benjamin up. Joseph would keep his brother in Egypt where they could enjoy sweet fellowship and make up for twenty-two stolen years.

But if they surrendered Benjamin, shame itself would prevent them from ever returning to face the vizier of Egypt. And Jacob and his children would starve in the famine. Joseph could not believe that God Shaddai would allow such a thing to happen.

From the corner of his eye, Joseph saw Tarik jog across the sandy courtyard. The captain yelled out the command to mount up and leapt onto the back of his chariot. As the other drivers watched, Tarik lifted the vizier's standard with one hand and gripped a side rail with the other. At this signal, the villa's gates opened wide and cracking whips snapped the air. Amid the swirling dust, noise, and confusion, Tarik's chariot peeled away, and the others followed in a parade of swift, efficient force.

Simeon felt a strange and tangible rumbling begin to move along the ground, like a storm coming out of the Sahara. Strong and unreasonable anxiety spurted through him. He stopped and held up a hand to quiet his brothers, but they had already fallen silent. Their faces clouded with uneasiness as they turned in the sand to look back. Toward Egypt.

The earth trembled slightly with the force of galloping horses, and the brothers' donkeys flapped their ears uneasily at the prospect of facing their regal cousins. Suddenly, rising from a valley of sand, the source of the sound appeared. The sun glinted off the bright opulence of a fleet of bejeweled chariots that stirred up the dust and pressed toward them in a V formation. The quiet morning echoed with the roaring shout of the approaching storm, and yet above the tumult Simeon could hear his heart battering against his ears.

What evil was this? Were they never to be free from the power of the Black Land?

Before he could consult his brothers, the swift Egyptian guard had surrounded them completely. As the other sons of Israel stood in astonished silence, Simeon widened his stance and put his hands on his hips, ready for a showdown. He had thrown aside the softness of Egypt like an uncomfortable garment. His blood now stirred with familiar energy and old passions. If the Egyptians wanted a fight, they had come to the right place. His home, the desert.

"Not now, brother!" Judah called a warning.

Simeon held his stance, waiting.

The circle of Egyptians broke, and Tarik rode forward in a chariot that gleamed with gold. The captain's mouth was thin with displeasure.

Reuben, Levi, and Judah looked to Simeon. *You know him*, their glances seemed to say. *You handle him*.

"Life and health to you, Tarik," Simeon called, dropping the reins of his donkey as he took a step forward. The two men exchanged careful, simultaneous smiles. "Why do we meet again so soon?"

Tarik leaned forward and grasped the frame of his chariot, shifting his weight to his arms. "My master Zaphenath-paneah has sent me to find you and bids me ask you one question."

"Which is?" Simeon asked, his voice edged with guarded exasperation.

Tarik's cold proud eyes raked over the gathered brothers. "Why have you repaid good with evil? My master fed you, sheltered you, and provided for you, yet one of you has taken the silver bowl he uses for divination. You have committed a shameful wrong."

"Why does your lord accuse us of such a thing?" Simeon asked, staring at the captain in utter disbelief. "We would never steal from him. We are not thieves. If we were, my brothers would not have returned the silver they found in their sacks when they reached Canaan. Why would we want to steal from the vizier's house?"

Simeon felt a hand upon his arm. Judah had come to stand beside him.

"You may search us," Judah said simply, his voice steady and calm. "And if you find your master's bowl among us, the guilty one shall die and the rest of us will be your master's slaves. For I tell you the truth, the bowl is not here."

"I *will* search you," Tarik answered, his mouth twisting into a wry smile. He gestured to his guards, who dismounted from their chariots and tightened the circle around the brothers. "And the guilty one shall pay for his crime. The man with the cup shall be my master's slave, but the rest of you shall be held innocent of this offense."

Knowing that his bag did not contain the missing bowl, Simeon stood motionless while his brothers scrambled to untie their sacks. The Egyptians watched the unloading with keen interest, and Tarik insisted upon personally searching each brother's load. He would begin with the eldest brother, the captain announced, and work his way through the line to the youngest, so no one would be overlooked.

In the first sack the Egyptian found the double amount of silver Reuben had brought to Egypt.

"So you are not thieves?" Tarik asked, looking squarely at Simeon. "Obviously, you are not the innocents you pretend to be."

At the sight of the silver, Simeon wondered if they would all be imprisoned, but Tarik said nothing else and moved on to Simeon's donkey. Apparently Zaphenath-paneah cared little for silver, and he had sent his captain only after the divining bowl.

Simeon had already reloaded his donkey by the time Tarik reached Benjamin. Confident that the vizier's captain had made an embarrassing blunder, Simeon urged the others to load their donkeys as well. He had just stepped forward to help Levi with a stubborn strap when he heard Reuben cry out.

Simeon whirled around. From the sack on Benjamin's donkey, Tarik lifted the unmistakable silver bowl and held it aloft. As the sun winked at its engraved surface, Simeon gazed at it in despair, the spark of hope in his breast completely extinguished.

Tarik lowered the bowl and casually tucked it under his arm. "Only this one needs to return with me," the captain said, studying the others with a curious intensity. "The rest of you are free to return to your father in Hebron."

"No," Judah answered, his stentorian voice rumbling through the murmurs of sorrow around him. "I would rather die in Egypt than face my father without my brother."

"Almighty God, why?" Reuben wailed, ripping his cloak in agony. "One was arrogant, the other a thief. Why are the sons of Rachel a curse to us?"

"It matters not," Simeon answered, resolutely swinging Levi's sack onto the donkey's back. He reached for the girth straps and secured the load. "We will go back to Thebes with Benjamin. I have spent a long time in the vizier's house. Perhaps he will listen to me and show mercy to our brother."

And if not, he thought, closing his eyes against the wicked rush of a sudden wind, *someone else there might be persuaded to plead on our behalf . . . if I have not offended her too severely.*

⌒ Thirty ⌒

MANDISA HAD JUST FINISHED THINNING LADY Asenath's brows with a new pair of bronze tweezers when the master entered the lady's chamber. She paused, ready to bow or receive his instructions, but he moved easily and impatiently through the room, his hands locked behind his back, his mind miles away. After waiting for a moment, Asenath signaled Mandisa to continue her work.

As the tiny bronze hands of the tweezers moved deftly over the line of the lady's brow, the women whispered their small talk and waited for the master to speak. Occasionally Asenath asked Zaphenath-paneah about Pharaoh's wife or the upcoming party in honor of the Queen's birthday, but the master answered in incomplete short sentences, clearly occupied with other thoughts.

Why doesn't he speak? Mandisa wondered as she lowered the tweezers to the table and handed her mistress a looking brass. *Does he no longer trust Asenath with the secrets of his heart? Or is he as sorrowful as I am to see his brothers go?*

Asenath must have been thinking similar thoughts, for Mandisa could see water rising in her eyes, like a slow fountain coming up.

Mandisa gave her mistress a smile. "Be at peace, my lady," she whispered, reaching for Asenath's favorite jeweled collar. "The master's mind is burdened with many thoughts."

She had just finished fastening the collar when the vizier halted his pacing in midstep and cocked his ear toward the window. Mandisa paused, straining to hear whatever had alerted him and felt a shiver pass down her spine when she recognized the sound of hoofbeats.

Zaphenath-paneah's brows drew together in an agonized expression. "Quickly, Mandisa, go to the window," he said, his voice edged with iron. "And tell me what you see there."

Was his expression of anxious hope mirrored in her own face? Not daring to question him, she grabbed a chair and dragged it to the high clerestory window. After hopping up onto the seat, she peered out. "I see riders, my lord," she called over her shoulder, barely able to keep the excitement from her voice.

"Tarik and his charioteers?"

"Yes." She exhaled a sigh of contentment. "And donkeys."

"How many men on donkeys? One—or eleven?"

A thoughtful smile curved her mouth as she turned, understanding. "There are eleven, my lord. All of your brothers have returned."

The arrested expression on his face broke into a look of pure relief and pleasure. He dropped his gaze, as if to whisper a prayer of thanks to his God, then lifted bright eyes to Asenath.

"They came back together!" he said, the sound of tears in his voice. Eagerly he approached his wife, then bent and lightly fingered a loose tendril of hair upon her forehead. "Rejoice with me, beloved," he whispered, pressing a finger to her trembling lips, "for my brothers' hearts are changing."

He lifted his eyes from Asenath's and looked up at Mandisa. "If Tarik finds you, have him meet me in the central hall at once," he said, his voice ringing with command. He bent to place a quick kiss on his wife's forehead, then hurried from the room, intent upon reaching the reception hall. In her excitement, Mandisa nearly followed him before she remembered that her duty lay in serving the wigless woman who still waited in her chair.

"I'm sorry, my lady," Mandisa said, moving toward Asenath's dressing table. "I'm sure you will want to join them as soon as possible."

"Take your time," Asenath answered, her voice as flat as her eyes. "There is no hurry. He wants me to rejoice with him, but I cannot."

Mandisa had been about to lift the heavy wig from its stand, but she paused, surprised by her mistress's words. "He has found his long lost brothers," Mandisa answered, speaking in as reasonable a voice as she could manage. "And since he is your husband, they are your brothers, too. Surely you can be happy for him."

"I cannot understand why anyone would be happy to find relatives in Canaan," Asenath grumbled, picking at her gown in dissatisfaction. "The captive we kept in the house caused altogether too much commotion. And herders stink. They smell like sheep when they fill a room. And yet my lord and husband wants me to rejoice with him. He wants me to welcome the same brothers who once wanted him dead. Well, I cannot see them with his eyes. I do not love them, and I don't think I can."

Hot bitter tears slipped down her mistress's cheeks, and Mandisa took a quick breath of utter astonishment. Asenath had not given any sign that she would not accept the master's brothers. Mandisa had assumed she would be thrilled and delighted for her husband's sake.

"You are a loving and kind woman," Mandisa whispered. She left the wig on its stand and sank to her mistress's feet. "You charm all who meet you, my lady, and you are very dear to my master's heart. But you have been ill. You are not yourself."

"You are right. I am not myself," Asenath repeated dully, closing her eyes. "And I have done something terrible." She took a breath as if she would speak again, then apparently thought the better of it. "My wig please, Mandisa," she said finally, a cold, pinched expression on her face.

Mandisa stood and lifted the wig, fluffed it, and fitted it onto her lady's head. Asenath's countenance remained immobile, but the atmosphere of the chamber cooled as dramatically as if a rainy wind had blown through the house.

"If that is all, my lady, I will see if the master needs me," Mandisa said, pressing her hands to her knees as she bowed.

"Wait." When Mandisa looked up, Asenath's eyes had clouded with hazy sadness. "Have you noticed, Mandisa, that the master is not . . . happy about the coming child?"

Torn by conflicting emotions, Mandisa hesitated. Did Lady Asenath really believe she could deceive those who knew her best? Against all human convention and reason, her husband had continued to support her. Was his love not enough? Did Asenath expect him to *exult* in the result of her infidelity?

But it was not Mandisa's place to rip away the veil. "The master adores you, my lady," she answered truthfully, taking her mistress's hand. "Because he loves you, he will love any child that comes from your womb. But I am certain he fears for your health."

"Oh." Asenath managed a weak laugh of relief. "I have made arrangements for continual offerings to be made to Taweret, the goddess of prospective mothers. I know both the baby and I will be safe . . . this time."

"I pray you are right, my lady," Mandisa said. She calmly bowed again, masking her inner turmoil. Asenath needed a comforting counselor, someone who would speak plainly and bluntly, but Mandisa did not think that her mistress would listen to a handmaid.

And Simeon and his brothers were waiting. Backing out of the room, Mandisa left her mistress alone in her chamber.

⟶ Thirty-one ⟵

ZAPHENATH-PANEAH, TARIK, AND A HOST OF guards and servants had already assembled in the reception hall by the time Mandisa arrived. Ani and the brothers were not in sight, and Mandisa realized that once again she was to play a part in an unfolding drama. Today, however, though the stage was set for business as usual, everyone in the room knew some momentous event was about to take place. She could *feel* the vizier's excitement. It was something palpable. He exuded it like a scent.

Zaphenath-paneah smiled at Mandisa in gratitude as she took her place at his left hand, then Ani entered and bowed nervously before the vizier. "They are in the vestibule, Master, and as anxious as hens with one chick," he said, lifting his bright eyes. "Shall I send the Canaanites in?"

The vizier crossed his legs at the ankle and gripped the arms of his chair. "Yes."

Ani scuttled away, and Mandisa turned to catch Tarik's eye. A gleam of merry mischief shone there, and she drew in her breath, curious about the drama they were about to enact. Who had devised the script? Tarik obviously knew, and perhaps Ani, but she had no idea what might happen in the next few moments. Might Simeon be forced to remain behind again?

She closed her eyes, silencing the thought. *Don't wish it. Don't wish for him. He cares nothing for your heart. He does not love you. He has no idea what love is.*

The doors to the vestibule opened, and the brothers rushed in, their former deference and awe swallowed up by frantic worry. The youngest man, Benjamin, walked in between two guards. His wrists were bound, albeit loosely, his legs hobbled by a sturdy papyrus rope. One of Tarik's lieutenants brought forward the vizier's silver bowl and placed it almost reverently on a stand by Zaphenath-paneah's chair. At the sight of the waiting vizier, whose face was arranged into unusually stern lines, all eleven of the brothers prostrated themselves on the floor.

"What is this deed that you have done?" Zaphenath-paneah said through Mandisa, addressing the youngest brother, Benjamin. "Do you not know that God speaks to me? You could not have hoped to escape."

Benjamin lifted his head to speak, but one of the older brothers shushed him and rose to his knees. "What can we say to you, my lord?" he asked, opening his hands wide in entreaty. "I am Judah, and I have no words to offer in explanation. What can we speak? How can we justify ourselves? God has discovered your servants' crime!" He hung his head, and the silver threads of his hair glowed in the diffused light of the chamber. "Here we are, servants to my lord, we and the one in whose hand the bowl was found."

Mandisa froze when Zaphenath-paneah did not wait for the translation. "Heaven forbid that I should do this to you," the vizier answered in fluent Canaanite. "The man in whose possession the cup has been found shall be my slave. But as for the rest of you, go in peace to your father."

Judah shook his bushy head and stood. "Please, my lord," he said, apparently too worried to notice that the vizier now spoke his language like a native, "may your servant please speak a word in your ears. And do not let your anger flare up against me, for you are equal to Pharaoh! We know this. We would not take advantage of you."

Mandisa looked at her master. Slowly, regally, he nodded in assent, and Judah advanced until he stood only two paces from the master's elevated chair. The two men stared at each other eye to eye.

"My lord asked his servants," Judah began, lowering his

voice, " 'Have you a father or another brother?' And we said to you, 'We have an old father and a young son of his old age, whose brother is dead, so that he alone is left of his mother, and his father loves him.' Then you said to us, 'Bring him down to me that I may set my eyes on him.' But we said to you, my lord, 'The lad cannot leave his father, for if he should leave, his father would die.' But you said to us, 'Unless your youngest brother comes down with you, you shall not see my face again.' "

"Why are you telling me what I already know?" Zaphenath-paneah interrupted, his dark eyebrows slanting in a frown. "I am not a forgetful old man that you need to remind me."

"I beg your pardon," Judah answered, hanging his head. "But there is more to the tale, an episode you have not heard."

"Tell it," Zaphenath-paneah answered, his jaw tensing.

Judah thrust his hands behind his back and stiffened his massive weight. "When we returned to your servant my father, we told him your words. And after a while our father said, 'Go back, buy us some food rations.' But we said, 'We cannot go down. If our youngest brother is with us, then we will go down, for we cannot see the Egyptian's face unless our youngest brother is with us.' "

Judah fell silent, visibly trembling with the intensity of his memories. "Then your servant my father said to us, 'You know that my true wife bore me two sons; and the one went away from me, and I said, "Surely he is torn, torn to pieces!" and I have not seen him since. And if you take this one also from me, and harm befalls him, you will bring my gray hair down to Sheol in sorrow.' "

The roar of absolute silence filled the chamber as Judah paused. Zaphenath-paneah sat very still, his eyes narrow, his posture militant. Mandisa knew that she watched a volcano on the verge of erupting.

"So now," Judah went on, taking a deep breath, "if I return to your servant my father, and the lad is not with us—

in whose life his own life is bound up—it will be that when he sees that the lad is no more, he will die. And we will bring the gray hair of our father down to the grave in sorrow. But since I pledged myself for the lad to my father, let me bear the blame for this deed before you and my father forever."

Judah spoke in a shaken hushed voice as he dropped to his knees. "Now, therefore, please, my lord, let me remain here instead of the lad. I will be a slave to you in whatever capacity you wish, but let the lad go with his brothers."

"You would give yourself in his place?" Zaphenath-paneah asked in a choked voice.

"Yes." Judah lifted his eyes and his hands in a heartfelt gesture of supplication. "For how shall I return to my father if the lad is not with me? I cannot bear to see the evil that will overtake him. I cannot watch him die from grief."

Silence loomed between them like a heavy mist. Judah seemed to melt in the tension, floundering before the brilliance of Zaphenath-paneah's gaze.

"Tarik," Zaphenath-paneah finally said, his granite eyes locked upon Judah's, "clear the room of everyone but these men."

Tarik's face folded in disappointment as he gave the terse command. The fan-bearers, guards, servants, and incense-bearers silently filed out of the chamber. Mandisa hesitated, not sure whether or not she should stay, but then heard a soft message from her master's lips. "Mandisa, your mistress will need you now."

She slipped silently from the chamber, following Tarik. The double doors had just closed behind her when the reception hall filled with the sound of the master's weeping.

"I told you he was demented," Simeon said, lifting his head as the vizier broke into loud wrenching sobs. Such a noise! And why? Zaphenath-paneah ought to be angry. He should have thrown them all into prison, but the grand vizier of all Egypt had just thrown his arms around Judah and wept now as though his world had come to an end.

"What should we do?" Levi asked, warily rising to his feet. "Is he truly mad? What if he attacks us?"

"Be quiet. He understands you," Dan cautioned. "Did you not hear him speak Canaanite just now? He has deceived us, brothers."

"We are eleven against one," Simeon said, standing. He rested his hands on his belt and gazed at the inexplicable sight before him. Locked in the vizier's embrace, Judah turned slightly and threw Simeon a bewildered glance as he patted the vizier on the back, soothing him the way a woman comforts a hurting child.

"Do nothing yet," Reuben cautioned, keeping his voice low. "He has done us no harm."

Pulling away from Judah, the vizier turned to face them. "Ah, my brothers, I do not blame you for thinking me deranged," he said, palming tears from his cheeks. He opened his hands at his side. "Do you not see?" he asked, gazing at them with a look of mad happiness. "Can you not hear that I speak Canaanite as well as you do? Do you not know me?"

Simeon looked at Levi, who frowned and wrinkled his brow.

"I suppose I cannot blame you, for I am much changed," the vizier went on, looking at them with no trace of his former animosity. "I am Joseph. Your brother."

Wave after wave of shock slapped at Simeon. *Joseph.* That voice. That familiarity. He should have known. He should have *seen.* Who but a son of Israel would tell his servants about El Shaddai? But it was impossible!

"It is a trick," Levi said, stumbling backward.

Simeon peered at the man who had held him captive.

"Look, Simeon, do you not recognize me?" the vizier asked, swiping at the makeup on his face. "Look." He tore the alien wig from his head to reveal a close-cropped haircut, then lowered his hands to his side in an almost humble posture. His voice, when he spoke again, was low and husky. "I am your brother Joseph, whom you sold into Egypt."

"It is! It is Joseph!" Benjamin shouted, running across the room. Laughing, the vizier threw his arms around the younger man and pressed him to his chest, one joyful heart pounding against another.

"I cannot believe it," Levi muttered, watching through narrowed eyes. "Joseph was half dead when we sold him to the slave traders. How can one rise from the grave to a throne?"

"By the power of God," Judah answered, his face lighting up like sunshine bursting out of the clouds. He, too, ran forward to slap the vizier on the back and join the embrace.

The murmurs of the others rose like a fog around Simeon.

"Can this be true?"

"Over twenty years ago."

"He was only a boy."

"And we nearly killed him." A thin thread of suspicion still laced Levi's voice.

Simeon stepped closer to hear what the vizier was saying to Benjamin. "Do you recall how you always wanted to go with the older brothers, but Father made you stay with me?" Zaphenath-paneah asked, his eyes darkening with emotion. "We would tease Bilhah and Zilpah until even Aunt Leah was ready to chase us out of the camp. And of the women, you must tell me—how is Dinah, our sister?"

"By heaven above," Simeon murmured, "he *is* Joseph." For though he had often mentioned the names of Jacob's wives to Mandisa, he had never thought to tell her the names of the maidservants who became Jacob's concubines. And how else could the vizier know that Jacob sent Leah's sons to work in the fields while Rachel's sons remained safe in the camp?

Simeon's blood suddenly ran thick with guilt. Had he, in his innermost heart of hearts, known the truth? He had

certainly hated Zaphenath-paneah with the same intensity
he once hated Joseph! But now the Egyptian vizier who had
held Simeon's life in his hands reached out to welcome the
brothers who had abandoned him to slavery, even to death.

"Do not be grieved or angry with yourselves because
you sold me here," the vizier said, his deep-timbered voice
so different and yet so like Joseph's in Simeon's memory,
"for God sent me before you to preserve life. For the famine
has been in the land these two years, and there are still five
years in which there will be neither plowing nor harvest-
ing. The Almighty God sent me before you to make you a
remnant on earth, to keep you alive as a great body of sur-
vivors."

"But—we sold you," Judah said, shaking his massive
head.

"It was not you who sent me here, but God," the vizier
answered gently, his eyes glowing. "God Shaddai has made
me Father to Pharaoh, lord of the royal household, and
ruler over all the land of Egypt." The man's tear-stained
face broke into a smile. "Hurry and return to my father and
tell him all that has happened to me. Tell him that God has
made me lord of all Egypt, and tell him that I wait for him
to come down here. You shall all live in the land of Goshen,
where there is good land for grazing. You shall be near me,
you and your children, your children's children, and your
flocks and herds and all that you have. There I will also provide for you through the five years of famine to come, lest
all of you be impoverished."

"Can it be?" Levi whispered, his voice still heavy with
doubt.

"Yes," Joseph answered, his paint-lengthened eyes
meeting Levi's gray ones. He extended his hands. "Your
eyes see, and the eyes of my brother Benjamin see that it is
Joseph speaking to you. Now you must tell my father of all
the weight I carry in Egypt, and all that you have seen; and
you must hurry and bring my father down here."

And while Simeon watched, still wondering how such

a thing could be true, Zaphenath-paneah—no, *Joseph*—
flung himself upon Benjamin's neck and wept anew, and
Benjamin wept upon his neck. And then Judah and Reuben, Issachar, Zebulun, Gad, Asher, Dan, Naphtali, and
Levi went to Joseph, one by one.

Simeon was the last to greet his brother. Like the others,
he kissed Joseph on both cheeks, mingling his tears with
the vizier's.

～ Thirty-two ～

ANI SQUINTED AT THE SHARD OF CLAY IN HIS hand. He had scribbled several items of concern upon the pottery, things to do before the master's brothers departed for Canaan.

Such a to-do. Such a surprise! He never would have guessed that the noble Zaphenath-paneah had sprung from the same stock as the Canaanite herdsmen, but when the vizier mingled among them, Ani could see a faint family resemblance. There could be no doubt that the vizier was a bright star whose glory far outshone the others, but the youngest man, Benjamin, possessed a similar glow and good nature. . . .

Ani clicked his teeth, urging himself back to the duties he had yet to fulfill. Two days of feasting and rejoicing had been hurriedly planned to welcome the vizier's brothers to Thebes. Even Pharaoh and his house had been informed, so they, too, could celebrate this important event. The young Pharaoh had been most gracious, offering the vizier's family a place in the best land of Egypt as shelter against the famine. Pharaoh had also offered a fleet of wagons for the brothers to take with them to Canaan in order to bring their wives, children, and little ones to enjoy the Black Land's bounty.

The vizier had also been more than gracious. To each of his brothers he gave a luxurious set of garments, but to Benjamin he gave three hundred pieces of silver—far more rare and valuable than gold—and *five* sets of garments. To his father, Jacob, he planned to send ten male donkeys loaded with frankincense, scented oils, and medicinal herbs, the best products of Egypt, and ten female donkeys bearing grain and bread, sustenance for the coming journey.

The vizier's household had been completely shaken by the incredible news. Ani had been a little offended to learn that Tarik and Mandisa knew of the vizier's relationship to the Canaanites long before the weighty revelation, but his hurt had been assuaged when Zaphenath-paneah clapped him on the shoulder and told him he knew a man of Ani's wisdom would enjoy the challenge of seeking the truth far more than being told outright.

"You are right, as always, my lord," Ani had answered. "And I *had* discerned something special about these men. My gods were not far from revealing your secret, I am certain."

In the glow of Zaphenath-paneah's happiness and Pharaoh's blessing, the entire house rejoiced. But Ani noticed with some anxiety that there had been no signs of rejoicing from the mistress's chambers. After formally meeting and greeting her husband's brothers, Lady Asenath had withdrawn to her rooms, ostensibly to give her husband more time alone with his family.

Asenath was not the only woman to avoid the brothers' reunion. Tizara and Mandisa also took pains to remain out of sight. Tizara hid herself, Ani reasoned, because she wanted to remain on good terms with the master who had shown her mercy. Mandisa, on the other hand, probably wanted to avoid meeting Simeon.

Ani worried about Mandisa with fatherly concern. Under less hectic circumstances he would have sought her out and inquired after her feelings, but now he had no time for affairs of the heart. Donkeys waited to be packed, wagons needed to be oiled and inspected, a populace yearned for information about the vizier's great news. The women, Ani decided, would have to work through their own problems.

———

Just before sunrise on the day the brothers were scheduled to depart, Mandisa paused in the darkened passage-way that led to the garden and the kitchens beyond. Insects whirred in the tall grasses at the far edge of the garden pool, the leaves of acacia trees fluttered in light applause. Apart from the sounds of nature, this part of the house lay still and silent. After two days of nearly continual feasting and celebration, the vizier and his boisterous brothers slept.

She had come through the courtyard where a host of wagons and donkeys stood ready for the journey, freshly watered and harnessed. She had heard that the brothers had gone to sleep just after sundown so they might rise early and depart from Egypt in the cool of morning. A sense of precognition rose to mock her, and she shuddered. The household had experienced this scene of departure before, but Simeon had not come to her chamber last night to ask her to travel with him. He had not, in fact, sought her at all in the last two days. Now that he had been proclaimed brother to the vizier, he probably intended to find a more attractive, more extravagant-looking concubine.

The stars had begun to fade behind a sky of dark blue velvet as she slipped through the garden, and she knew she should hurry if she wanted to fetch food for herself and Adom before the brothers woke and demanded the ser-vants' attention.

She had just left the garden and entered the passageway leading to the kitchens when a massive Canaanite form stepped in front of her, blocking her path. "Excuse me," she said, not looking up. "I did not mean to intrude."

"Mandisa." Simeon's voice was cool and faintly re-proachful. "I wondered if I would see you before we left."

She steeled her heart and lifted her chin. "And so you have."

Despite her intention to remain aloof, he captured her eyes with his and gave her a smile that sent her heart racing. Her emotions whirled and skidded at the sight of *something* in those eyes, and for a moment she hoped he would ask her to leave with him again.

His fingers curved under her chin. "My gentle jailer," he whispered, his thumb tenderly tracing the line of her cheekbone and jaw. "I have been thinking in the last two days."

She nodded curtly. "That is good, Simeon. And a change for you, is it not?"

"Hush, woman." The glitter in his half-closed eyes was both possessive and gently accusing. "I was never in any real danger here, was I? You must have known who I was, and you would not have let the vizier's brother starve. And Tarik would not have hurt me, not even in an escape attempt."

She shrugged, irritated at the thrilling current moving through her. "No, I would not have let you starve," she repeated dully, wanting to be away.

"So you *did* know the truth. You knew the vizier was my brother, and yet you said nothing."

"What does it matter?" she asked, her brows lifting the question. Standing this close to him, knowing that he was about to leave, both pained and aggravated her. "I was commanded not to reveal what I knew."

"Again, like a slave, you obeyed. And yet you and I shared something special. I had the feeling you could tell me anything." From out in the courtyard, one of the horses whickered, the only sound in the morning stillness. She tried to relax, to look away, but he held her eyes. "We shared secrets, you and I. Why did you not tell me the vizier was my brother?"

"We did not share all our secrets, Simeon." She forced herself to think. It was difficult to remain clearheaded when he stood so close to her. "And my kindness to you had nothing to do with your relationship to my master. I cared for you because you needed help. And it was my master's wish."

"Is that the only reason? Halima took care of me, too, but she refused to come when my behavior became . . . intolerable."

"I can tolerate more than Halima."

"So you cared for me to test the mettle of your endurance?"

"I cared for you because I am a servant who chooses to obey her master. That is, was, and always will be my reason. It is why I take care of Lady Asenath, why I tend to the little boys."

"You're lying, Mandisa. You have told me yourself that you obey your master and mistress because you love them—just as you love me."

"You flatter yourself." Her blood pounded. Her face flamed with humiliation.

"You do love me. And yet you will not come with me. Why not?"

"I have told you. I will not be a concubine."

"What if I ask you to marry me?"

She bit her lip, caught off guard by the sudden vibrancy of his voice. Was he jesting? No, his dark earnest eyes were probing hers, seeking an answer. His hand caught her arm and slipped to her wrist. His fingers closed about her hand.

Had the last two days changed him? No. It was more likely that he fancied himself among the nobility and realized that a wife was more socially acceptable than a concubine. He wanted a legal wife by his side to share his glory as the vizier's brother, to oversee his home and his sons. . . .

Better to tell him the truth. "I cannot marry you, Simeon," she said, boldly meeting his gaze. "I cannot give myself to a man whose heart brims with anger and hate."

"But I was angry because I hated Zaphenath-paneah," he answered, shrugging almost casually. The steady, even tone of his voice gave her hope. "And now that I know he is my brother, I can no longer hate him. So all is forgiven. The past has been put behind us."

He stepped forward, penning her between his chest and the wall, radiating a vitality that drew her like the moon summons the sea. "Come with me, Mandisa," he said slowly, his hand tightening around hers. "The wagon is loaded, but there is room for you and Adom. Or say you'll wait for me, for we will return as soon as we have collected our father and our families.''

She closed her eyes as her heart swam through a haze of feelings and desires. As much as she wanted to deny it, she did care for Simeon, cared so deeply that life in the vizier's house would be as dull as a whetstone without his belligerent presence. And his hate of her master *had* dissipated since the vizier's startling revelation. But the hard layers of his heart could not be shed in two short days. The roots of his bitterness extended far deeper than his hatred and jealousy for one younger brother.

He was not yet the man who could love her the way she needed to be loved. At the first provocation, his temper would flare up, and he would strike out at whoever stood nearby. He had softened a little around the edges, but his stony heart had not changed.

And she knew just how to prove it to herself.

"No, Simeon, I'll not go with you," she whispered, opening her eyes. "You were right, you know, when you came to me in the night. Adom and I do need a man, but we are not possessions, and I will never settle for less than a man who loves me as his equal. Since Zaphenath-paneah paid my debts and redeemed me from slavery, I will never think of myself as less than a free and independent woman. I must have a man of strength, someone who will remain with me no matter what."

"Strength?" He dropped her hand and flexed, the muscles in his arms knotting. "Do you think I am not strong? I am twice the size of that Egyptian guard you're so fond of. And as for loyalty, Levi and I once killed the men of an entire city for our sister's sake!"

She shivered under the hot light in his eye. "A man who is quick to become angry with lesser men proves nothing but his weakness," she whispered, ready to duck if his temper lashed out in her direction. "And your anger strikes at everyone from the servants to the vizier himself." She leaned her head back and stared into his eyes. "Only a man of great strength can give the gentle kind of love Adom and I deserve. You might be capable of this love one day, Simeon, but I would rather serve here under Zaphenath-paneah's protection than go with you now. Until you change, I cannot give my heart to you."

"A woman does not ask a man to change," he said, crossing his arms as his curt voice snapped at her. His nostrils flared in fury. "Either she loves him as he is, or she does not love him at all."

She felt suddenly weak and vulnerable in the face of his anger. "Simeon, I didn't mean to—"

"Be silent." Cutting her off, he stepped backward, his eyes glinting with anger. "You have insulted my strength and my honor."

"Simeon, I am sorry," she whispered, her heart breaking. "You *are* physically powerful, but your weakness lies in the inner man. You must be strong enough to control your anger instead of letting it control you. Forgive me for hurting you, but I only did it to prove the truth of my words."

"Forgive you?" His bitter laugh raked her heart. "Never. A man can only bear so much."

Without another word he turned on his heel and strode away. She wavered, torn between remaining silent and running after him to assure him that she did love many of his fine qualities.

But if he had loved her once, he hated her now. Strength and loyalty were his two best attributes, and her biting tongue had just disparaged both.

Her experiment, however unwise, had proved her suspicions. Simeon the Destroyer remained the same roaring lion she had confronted nearly a year ago.

———

"Brothers, I bid you farewell," Joseph called, his eyes lingering fondly on each face as the caravan assembled in his courtyard. "Bid my father to hurry and come down, and do not argue on the journey. The strength of Israel is in your union. The only danger that can harm you is discord. Be at peace with one another from this time forth, and as brothers we can live together."

Benjamin left his donkey and ran forward for one last embrace, and Joseph clung to him for a moment, inhaling the scent of his strength.

"Hurry back," he said as Benjamin pulled away.

"I will." After one last look, Benjamin returned to his pack animal. Reuben gave the call, and the caravan started forward. Joseph left the portico and retreated into his chamber, his heart too full for words.

Thirty-three

"MANDISA, YOU ARE MOVING SLOWLY TODAY," Lady Asenath said, waving her hand lazily in the air. "I should think you'd be relieved that the rabble of relatives has gone."

"I am relieved, my lady," Mandisa said, forcing a smile. She turned toward the couch where Asenath lay. "Though they have only been gone a short time, the house seems quite empty without them, don't you think?"

"I think silence is sublime," Asenath answered, lifting her head so Mandisa could slip another pillow beneath it. "And I do wish my husband would hurry back from the palace. Pharaoh is demanding too much of his time these days."

"Pharaoh has much on his mind," Mandisa answered, sinking into a chair by Asenath's side. The lady's belly had grown rapidly in the last few weeks, and she was increasingly uncomfortable in social situations. Her gowns, designed to be worn like a second skin, did not forgive or allow the bulge of impending birth at her middle. Asenath preferred to sit at home in a loose-fitting robe rather than wear the pleated gowns that passed for maternity wear in upper Theban circles.

"When Zaphenath-paneah does come in, send a runner to fetch him to me," Asenath said, closing her eyes. She sighed and clasped her hands over her belly. "This is the seventh month, Mandisa, do you realize? The babies I lost early died in the fourth month. The gods will be good to me this time, I know it. Just as they performed the miracle at conception and allowed my husband's seed to grow within me out of season—"

"He knows, my lady." Mandisa bit her lip, horrified that the words had fallen from her lips before she could think. She was too tired—that was the problem. She had felt listless all week. Her eyes burned from sleeplessness, and an overwhelming numbness had weighed her down ever since the brothers departed.

"Who knows what?" Asenath asked, lifting her head. Her eyes were wide with false innocence, but her voice was thick and unsteady.

Mandisa sighed. She had spent every possible moment of the last month with her mistress, and she felt like a parent who has spent too much time with an unruly child. The lady's deception had drained her.

Gathering up her slippery courage, she leaned forward. "May I speak as an honest friend, Lady Asenath?"

Frowning, the woman on the couch nodded.

"Your husband, my master, knows the child you carry is not his."

"You lie!" The gentle lady's expression clouded in instant anger. "The child *is* his. The gods have worked a miracle! And my husband believes in miracles. He is always talking about the wonders of his God!"

"This is not a miracle of his God," Mandisa answered, sudden tears stinging her eyes. "And your husband knows it."

Asenath took a deep breath as if she would argue, but she stopped abruptly and let her head fall back to the couch. After a long moment, she pressed her hand to her forehead and began to weep. "Mandisa, I have done a terrible thing," she whispered as tears slowly found their way down her cheeks. "I went to visit a priest at the temple of Min."

Mandisa shook her head. "I do not know this god."

"She is the god of fertility, the bestower of potency. She is the god who brings rain to the parched earth, the one who quickens life within a woman's womb."

A sense of foreboding descended over Mandisa with a shiver. "You gave this god an offering?"

"An offering of silver . . . and . . . of myself. And the priest promised me that I would conceive, and he swore that only he, Min, and I would know of it." Raw hurt glittered in her dark eyes as she turned to her handmaid. "And now you tell me that my husband knows! How could he? And if he does, why does he treat me with such kindness?"

"Your husband," Mandisa answered, choosing her words carefully, "loves you as he loves his own flesh. When you turned from him to another, how could he not know it? But he treats you kindly because he loves you."

Asenath shot Mandisa a quick denying glance, then looked away. A host of emotions—denial, anger, fear, despair—flickered across her delicate face, then she looked at Mandisa with something very fragile in her eyes.

"Why?" she cried, her voice choked with sincerity. "Why does he—how could he still love me?"

"Because," Mandisa whispered, her words dredged from a place far beyond logic and common sense, "sometimes passion is unreasonable." Taking a deep breath, Mandisa strengthened her smile. "You need never fear, mistress. I know Zaphenath-paneah. At first I thought he would cast you aside, but I know now that he will never abandon you. You are very fortunate, my lady."

"Fortunate," Asenath echoed bitterly. The hand that had been stroking her belly stilled. "Will my husband feel *fortunate* to provide for another man's child?"

Mandisa squirmed beneath the touch of her mistress's gaze and the look of pain behind her question. "Zaphenath-paneah loves all children," she finally whispered. "Do not be anxious, my lady, about his heart. But have mercy on my master and do not ask him to pretend."

When Asenath finally slept, Mandisa left her guilt-ridden mistress in her chamber and walked to the garden to consider her own situation. In good weather, if all went well, the journey from Thebes to Hebron would take about two weeks. More than a month would pass before Simeon could return. But once they arrived in Hebron, the brothers would have stories to tell and plans to make, so perhaps they might tarry as long as two months, even three. But before the season of Shemu had passed, Simeon and his family would return to Egypt. Though the people of Israel were to abide in Goshen, Simeon might come to visit the house of Zaphenath-paneah. And he might press his case a third time. Perhaps he would even try to prove that he had changed. Or, because she had insulted him, he might visit with a Canaanite wife by his side.

In either case, she couldn't face him again, but what options did she have? Unless she could convince Lady Asenath to take an extended journey to Heliopolis, Mandisa had no place to go. But Lady Asenath had been complaining of pain for weeks and certainly was in no condition to travel.

A hoarse call from the balcony interrupted her musings. "Mandisa!" Tizara shrieked, her face ashen under the bright sunlight. "Come quickly! And bring Ani! The time of travail has begun!"

The baby would not come. Through hours of intense labor that wracked Asenath's frail body, the child refused to be born. Ani sent for priestesses of the goddess Taweret, but while they twirled through the room and whirled daggers at invisible spirits, Asenath grew pale and weak upon her couch. A pool of blood covered the bed linens like a crimson mantle, and though Mandisa had tried to change the soiled cloths, Asenath screamed and wept whenever anyone attempted to move her.

Zaphenath-paneah, who had been summoned from Pharaoh's house as soon as it became apparent that his wife was in danger, insisted upon remaining at her side. He sat at the head of the narrow birthing cot, his hand grasping Asenath's, his lips at her ear.

As night fell, amid the shrieking and wailing of the priestesses, Mandisa heard the midwife exclaim, "Thank your gods, my lady, you have a son!" Zaphenath-paneah's face went white at the words, and only then did Mandisa understand the full import of the midwife's statement. If the baby had not yet come forth and the midwife could see the male part of the child, the birth was breech.

"My mother," Zaphenath-paneah whispered to Mandisa, his eyes shining like black pools of fear, "she died when Benjamin was born this backward way."

"Do not be anxious, my lord," Mandisa murmured, giving him a smile more confident than she felt. "Asenath is in God's hands."

"Is she?" the master whispered back.

Asenath's hard labor continued into the night. By sunrise on the second day, the exhausted priestesses of Taweret abandoned the vizier's wife to her fate. The frustrated and tired midwife grew ruthless, attempting even to force her hand into the birth canal to turn the child. But the pressure and pain caused Asenath to faint, and the cord of life, visible through the birth opening, ceased to pulse with life.

When it became apparent that the baby had died, Zaphenath-paneah cradled his wife's head and shoulders in his arms and whispered words of comfort and encouragement.

By sunrise on the third day, everyone in the house knew the mistress stood on the threshold of the otherworld. Weeping and silent, Tizara brought Ephraim and Manasseh to say their farewells. They embraced their mother and kissed her on the cheek before Tizara led them away. Tarik, Halima, and a host of other servants paraded through the chamber and promised to do their best to prepare Asenath for her eternal life, but she had already closed her eyes and seemed not to hear their frantic assurances.

By midafternoon on the third day, both Mandisa and the

master were exhausted, drained of will and thought. "Why don't you go to your chamber and sleep for a while?" the master asked, stepping away from Asenath's bedside. He turned toward the high window and seemed to study the shaft of sun that angled down, trapping particles of dust.

"If it please you, my lord, I will remain until the—until she no longer needs me," Mandisa said, amending her original thought.

For another hour the two of them waited without speaking. They traded places: Mandisa stood beneath the window, lost in her own thoughts, while the master sat at the side of Asenath's bed, imprinting his memory with the image of his beloved wife, still carrying the unborn child.

Without warning the lady opened her eyes. "My husband?" Her words were jagged and sharp, like sounds torn by the blade of a knife.

"Here, beloved." Zaphenath-paneah lifted his head and tenderly took her pale hand in his.

"I have been very foolish, my lord. I thought another child would make you happy."

"All I ever wanted was you, Asenath. Children are an added blessing from God."

She spoke in a weak and tremulous whisper. "I have played the harlot with another god—"

"Shh, Asenath. Don't talk now." The husband lowered his face to his wife's, and Mandisa stepped back into the shadows of the room, unwilling to intrude upon the private moment.

———

The burning pain of her loins had faded to a distant memory, and Asenath's hands and legs were cold, as cold as an empty bed. She felt surprisingly light and carefree. The heaviness that had pressed upon her stomach, back, and legs had completely vanished. The only burden upon her now was guilt. But Zaphenath-paneah was by her side, his dark eyes inches from hers, his gaze probing her soul.

"I did something," she began, forcing the words from her stubborn tongue.

"I know all about you, beloved," Zaphenath-paneah said, his tone unfailingly patient and compassionate. "Your denial has kept us apart these last few months, but I was ready to listen any time you wanted to talk. Nothing you could ever do would make me turn you away."

"I was so selfish. When God Shaddai would not give me what I wanted, I left Him for another."

His fingers fell across her mouth. "You don't have to talk, Asenath."

She closed her eyes, too weak to resist him. "Please." His fingers lifted, and she ran her tongue over her parched lips, struggling to find the words. "I left your God, the Almighty One, because He seemed too distant, too slow, too unaccommodating. Because He said no."

Zaphenath-paneah did not answer, and with an effort she opened her eyes to look at him. His usually lively gaze sparkled now with weariness. She blinked in surprise when she saw that he held her hand to his cheek. She hadn't felt the pressure of his skin against hers.

"Beloved wife," he said, "God honors a repentant heart." His voice, without rising at all, had taken on a subtle urgency.

"I know." Tonight there were no shadows across her heart, only a feeling of glorious happiness within it. "When you did not cast me aside, my love, I knew your God would not abandon me, either."

He drew her into his arms, and Asenath closed her eyes, glorying in the shared moment.

———————

No! No! Asenath's ragged breathing stuttered and died, and then there was nothing but silence and the pounding of Joseph's own aching heart.

"Beloved?"

Her mouth was as pale as her cheeks, her eyes closed in

eternal sleep. Joseph sat up, still clutching her icy hands, his sense of loss beyond tears.

Why? Why could she not trust his love? He had spent the last years of his life protecting her, sheltering her, trying to convince her that she was the most precious person in his world, and yet she would not believe him. He had seen the pain in her eyes when he denied her requests, but he had only refused her out of love!

"Oh, Asenath," he whispered, cradling her against his chest as he tenderly traced her cheek with his fingers, "how like a child you were! Could you not know that I would give my own life rather than allow you to suffer like this?"

Somewhere outside the villa a pair of servants broke into a brawling argument, giving voice to the unuttered shouts and protests lodged in Joseph's own throat. He pressed Asenath to him, breathed in the scent of her skin and hair one last time, then released the keening wail of grief.

———

Mandisa couldn't hear the conversation between her master and mistress, but after a moment or two of shared whispers, Zaphenath-paneah bowed his head, then drew his wife into his arms, lifting her frail form from the bed. At that moment Mandisa knew Asenath was beyond pain.

For the second time in a month, the household shuddered at the sound of the master's weeping.

———

Tarik stood at attention by the gatekeeper's lodge, his eyes raking the face and figure of each guest. Hundreds had already filed through the villa to pay their respects to Zaphenath-paneah in the loss of his wife and unborn child.

The priests of Amun had come first to prepare Lady Asenath for mummification. Mandisa had helped them wash the body, excise the baby, and anoint the skin with oils and unguents. The tiny, perfectly formed child was also washed and wrapped in linen. The unnamed son would be placed in Asenath's arms, and together they would sleep in a coffin within a sarcophagus within a tomb.

Such great sadness after such great joy! Though Tarik stood like a warrior, stiff and proud, his spirit whirled in chaos. A war of emotions raged within him, a battle more vicious than any physical conflict he had ever experienced. Rumors within the household fueled his unrest. Some servants were saying that the mistress had tried to induce the labor of the child after discovering it would be the offspring of a Canaanite herdsman. Wiser, more practical voices proclaimed that the physicians had long said another pregnancy would result in Asenath's death. The incident had only proven the physicians right.

How could a man at the pinnacle of power be so vulnerable to pain? Tarik had never imagined that any earthly relationship could engender such feelings of loss and devastation, but he suffered with his master, and Zaphenath-paneah suffered greatly. The joy had gone out of the vizier's eyes, and despite the pleasure he found in making arrangements for his family's arrival in Goshen, sorrow had carved merciless lines on his strong face, muting his youth. Tarik wondered if the vizier would ever find a way to lift the shadows of pain from his countenance.

And yet Zaphenath-paneah persisted in his worship of the invisible and Almighty God. If Wepwawet had led Tarik through such a torturous experience, the captain knew he would have cursed that god and followed another. But the vizier did not condemn his God or cry out. He continued in his silent and steadfast devotion, preferring solitude to the noisy Egyptian ceremonies designed to speed Asenath to the otherworld.

There remained the traditional seventy days of mourning, the necessity of filling and preparing the lady's tomb, and the mummification of the body. It was a pity, Tarik decided, that Lady Asenath would not meet Jacob, Zaphenath-paneah's noble father. Perhaps in the afterlife the Egyptian noblewoman and the Canaanite prince would be friends.

Thirty-four

"THEY ARE HOME!"

One of the grandchildren released the cry, and Jacob lifted his head from his couch and pulled himself upright with an effort. His sons had been gone nearly forty days, more than enough time to make the trip to Mizraim and back, and with each day that passed, his heart had grown heavy with the nauseating sinking of despair.

Swallowing the grateful sob that rose in his throat, he stood up and hobbled to the opening of his tent. On the curve of the hilly horizon he could see a caravan of heavily loaded wagons and donkeys.

He frowned. The grandchildren were mistaken, for his sons had not left with the means to purchase such riches. This was another caravan, one bound for Aram or Uz. But perhaps they would have word of his sons and know if Benjamin was still among them.

Bracing himself for disappointment, he stepped out of his tent.

Simeon saw the old man before the others, recognizing his father's distinctive lumbering gait, the way he rocked on his hips as if they were stiff. Reuben had said they shouldn't expect to see him outside, but Simeon knew better. He'd been gone for nearly a year, so Jacob would be waiting with the children and the curious servants, eager for news of his second-born son.

Satisfaction pursed Simeon's mouth as he spied his father's white hair and flowing beard. Jacob had come forward to greet him. Perhaps Mandisa was right. Perhaps the old man did care.

His reserve and apprehension thawed in an instant. "Father!" he called, waving his arm as his confidence spiraled upward. He slipped from the wagon where he rode with Levi and thundered over the hard ground, ready to forget the past and embrace the man with whom he'd had so many misunderstandings.

Jacob's eyes lifted. He turned his head in search of the son who had called his name.

"Father!"

Another voice rang through the tumult of greetings, and Jacob's face brightened in a sudden look of jubilant eagerness. "Benjamin!" he cried, lifting trembling arms. "Blessed be God Almighty. He has brought you back to me!"

Simeon stopped abruptly and leaned forward, breathing hard. Benjamin raced to his father's arms and was enveloped in an embrace. The women, children, and servants surrounded the caravan, and after a moment Simeon heard Levi's voice in his ear. "Give him time with the lad, Simeon. He'll be glad enough to see you later. But now his attention is reserved for the young one."

Still catching his breath, Simeon nodded. Like an old wound that ached on a rainy day, he grudgingly welcomed the familiar pain he had nearly forgotten, then climbed back into the wagon.

———

Jacob did embrace him later, perfunctorily, when the brothers assembled to share their astonishing news. "Joseph is still alive," Judah repeated again as they sat in their father's tent. Jacob, his arm firmly entwined with Benjamin's, shook his head in disbelief.

"Indeed, he is ruler over all Egypt," Reuben added, leaning forward in eagerness.

"Why would the idol worshipers elevate a son of Abraham?'' Jacob said, patting Benjamin's arm as if to reassure himself that his youngest son had actually returned.

"How could we come to you with such fine wagons and the best goods of Egypt if they had not done so?'' Judah asked, gesturing outside where the children and wives were gleefully plundering the pack animals. "Joseph said to tell you that the hand of El Shaddai brought him to that place. God himself lifted Joseph from slavery and placed him on a throne equal to Pharaoh's so we might be preserved in this time of famine.''

Jacob shook his hoary head, still resisting the truth. Judah looked around the circle of brothers, his eyes pleading for help. He caught Simeon's eye, but Simeon only scratched his beard. *You are our spokesman, so speak for us*, he told Judah with a smile and a slight shake of his head.

They had been talking to Jacob for more than an hour. In that time they had confessed what happened at Dothan and quickly followed the news of their treachery with the glorious report of Joseph's current condition. And Jacob sat like a stone, with no reaction to either their shameful confession or to the stunning summary of their latest venture into Egypt.

"We are to leave this place and go there, Father,'' Judah said, frankly begging his father to believe him, "that we may prosper under Joseph's hand.''

"How can we leave the land God promised to us?'' Jacob said, waving toward the sullen fields outside his tent. "How can we leave the cave where our fathers and mothers are buried?''

"How can we remain here, knowing we will die?'' Levi demanded, his voice rising. "You talk of God, Father, and Joseph says God Shaddai has provided. If God can bring Joseph back to your life, can He not bring you back to Canaan when the earth is green again?''

Jacob lowered his eyelids, and Simeon couldn't tell whether the old man slept, prayed, or was simply considering their words.

"How like God Shaddai to do the opposite of what we expect," he finally murmured, lifting his gaze. His eyes had a burning faraway look in them, and when he spoke again, his voice was strong and fervent. "It is enough. My son Joseph is still alive. I will go and see him before I die."

———

Alive! The shock of realization hit Jacob again. Joseph was alive! Not dead, but living! And in Egypt!

He had waited until his sons left his tent, then he grabbed his walking stick and moved with as much speed as his old bones would allow toward the hill that looked toward the south. Now he stared toward Egypt, his heart stirring within his chest in a new and dangerous rhythm. A howling wind blew up from the desert, and through the roaring din, Jacob breathed one word: "Alive!"

A great exultation filled his chest and brought tears to his eyes. " 'If a man dies, will he live again?' " he murmured, recalling the words of Job, a wise man of Uz. " 'All the days of my struggle I will wait. For there is hope for a tree, when it is cut down, that it will sprout again, and its shoots will not fail. At the scent of water it will flourish and put forth sprigs like a plant.' "

Jacob closed his eyes, relishing the solitude of the hilltop. Because they had carried the guilty secret that Joseph lived, the other sons would never know the indescribable and unfathomable rapture that now rose from Jacob's spirit—the ecstasy of resurrection.

The son he thought dead now reigned at Pharaoh's right hand over all of Egypt.

A bottomless peace and satisfaction filled his soul. Joy bubbled from his lips in laughter. Jacob lifted his weak arms to the heavens, and his shuffling feet moved slowly over the sand. Through a blanket of clouds a single shaft of sun highlighted the hilltop where the happiness of Jacob's heart spun him around and around in a delirious dance of delight.

As the others gathered their wives and children and made preparation for the journey, Simeon wandered around the camp, refreshing the impressions and memories he had tucked into the dim recesses of his mind. The land of Canaan, once green with life, opened before him now like an arid dust bowl. The few leaves that still dangled from trees were yellow and brown and stained with death. Nothing could live in this place much longer. If Joseph spoke the truth, none of the people in the neighboring towns would be alive in five years.

He strolled slowly, blankly watching his sandals crunch into the dry and brittle sand. Before he ventured into Egypt, he had considered his father a leader among men, but today Jacob seemed a tired old man, one whose life revolved around a submissive son and a patch of dusty earth that yielded neither food nor water.

Jacob was the prince of a dead land. No wonder Mandisa had not wanted to return to Canaan. Who would want to live in this airless desolate region after enjoying the splendor and abundance of Egypt? But Jacob stayed because he believed he followed God's will. . . .

A hot wind blew by him and Simeon paused, remembering Joseph's words. *God sent me before you to preserve life.* Joseph was like Jacob. He believed El Shaddai took a personal interest in the sons of Abraham. Did He? Simeon knew that God Shaddai lived. He was more than the stone idols of Egypt. But could an Almighty God care about one man? Or was He concerned only with offerings and obedience?

Mandisa seemed to think her master's God could be known on a personal level. Abraham had experienced dreams and visions, and Jacob wrestled with God in the night. But Simeon had never heard His voice and never expected to.

Thirty-five

TIZARA'S CONSTANT WEEPING GRATED ON Mandisa's nerves. Zaphenath-paneah and the others had borne their grief stoically, knowing that they would weep and mourn with abandon when Lady Asenath was interred in her tomb, but Tizara could not stanch the flow of tears that began every time she looked at Ephraim or Manasseh. "Those little motherless boys!" she wailed, weeping into a square of linen. "I was a motherless child. I know what they are feeling."

In the days immediately after Asenath's death, Mandisa had gently replied that they still had a father and a maid to care for them. When that tactic failed to stop Tizara's tears, Mandisa tried adding extra work to the girl's assigned chores, hoping she'd be too busy to mourn. But Tizara merely went about the house with a scrap of cloth wadded in her hand and usually pressed to her nose.

Now, her patience completely evaporated, Mandisa was tempted to sharpen her tongue on the girl's grief. *Simeon would love that*, she thought, rising to her feet as Tizara paced in the women's reception hall, her eyes bleary and red. *I tell him that whatever is begun in anger ends in shame, and here I stand ready to begin my own shameful trouble. And it wasn't so long ago that I felt guilty avoiding the girl. Now I cannot avoid her.*

"Tizara," she said, making an effort to be pleasant, "I think I will take Ephraim and Manasseh to the garden to play with Adom. If you need me—"

She halted when Zaphenath-paneah entered the room. Duty forced her to stop and bow upon the floor.

The vizier told the women to rise, then took a moment to greet his sons. After listening to their chattering questions for a few moments, he sent the boys out to play. "I am glad to find both of you here," he said when the boys had gone. "I wanted to talk to you about the months ahead of us."

Tizara lifted her red-rimmed eyes toward the master. Mandisa sighed in exasperation, half-expecting to see some frenzied distress in the woman's expression, but only trust and compassion shone from Tizara's gaze. In fact, Mandisa suddenly realized, the girl wore a wholesome and appealing look, a complete transformation from the former manner in which she had carried and conducted herself.

When had this change occurred? And why had Mandisa not seen it before this?

"You may rise, Tizara," Zaphenath-paneah said, his expression softening into one of fond reminiscence. "Today I give you your freedom. After all you have learned, I think you will now be able to manage it."

"My freedom?" The girl's face suddenly locked with anxiety. "Must I leave here?"

"No," the vizier answered, sinking into a chair. "I hope you will stay and care for my sons. They are quite fond of you, and now they will need someone to watch over them more than ever."

A hint of tears glistened in the wells of Tizara's eyes, but this time she did not lose control. Instead she smiled in reverent gratitude and bent low to kiss the master's foot. "I can never thank you enough," she said simply, clinging to his sandal as if it were a life preserver. "I will serve you and your sons as long as I have breath in my body."

"I pray you will," the master answered, then he turned to Mandisa. A melancholy smile flitted across his features as he regarded her. "Your mistress is gone, and so is the man you tended," he said, seeming to weigh his words. "What, Mandisa, would you like to do now? You are a free woman. Perhaps you might like a position in Pharaoh's house."

"I have been thinking," she said, sitting back upon her ankles. She clasped her hands and bit her lip. How could she explain that she did not want to linger here for fear of seeing Simeon again? It would not be proper to announce that her heart had been broken by the vizier's brother. Though he had known of her affection for Simeon in the past, a reference to it now might be interpreted as a request for pity or even imply that Zaphenath-paneah owed her something. He did not. She owed him everything.

Better to leave the past behind completely.

"My lord," she asked, daring to look him directly in the eye, "may I ask what you believe about the afterlife? The otherworld?"

Zaphenath-paneah tilted his head in surprise. Obviously, he had not expected that question. "Why do you ask?"

"I want to know, my lord, what will become of Lady Asenath if I do not remain here for the full seventy days. I am her handmaid, and if I am not here to see her safely into her tomb, will she . . . suffer? I would not hurt her for the world, yet part of me wants to leave this place, very soon."

If he guessed at her reasons, he did not speak of them. Instead, the vizier closed his eyes. "I believe," he said, lowering his head into his hands and kneading his forehead, as though his head ached with memories, "that God Shaddai prepares a place for those who trust Him. I believe each individual is born with an immortal soul, similar to that part the Egyptians call the *ka*, that survives for eternity." He lowered his hands and looked directly into her eyes. "I do not believe that we need all the goods and foods the Egyptians place in their tombs, for they are forms that have nothing to do with life itself or with God."

He eased into a weary smile. "If it sets your mind at ease, Mandisa, know that Asenath is already in the otherworld. She has already passed from death to life. Before she died, she made her peace with God . . . and with me." He leaned forward and lowered his voice to a gentler tone. "If you wish to leave my house, your mistress will not suffer."

She nodded slowly and sighed in relief. "Then I will leave you, Zaphenath-paneah," she whispered. "With gratitude, honor, and respect, I and my son will bid you farewell."

———

"Halima, I wanted to speak to you before I left."

The slave girl's eyes rimmed with tears as Mandisa spoke, and she clasped her floury hands in front of her. "Mandisa, you can't really go!"

"I must," Mandisa answered, lifting her eyes to look one final time at the vizier's well-stocked kitchen. Jars of honey, dates, and raisins lined the walls; the day's catch of fresh fish lay neatly arranged on the table, ready for filleting. She and Adom would eat their fill today, for who could say when they would have another opportunity for a meal like this?

Halima forced a wavering smile to her face. "Let me at least prepare you a basket, Mandisa. You have been my best friend here. Sometimes I think you are the only friend who cares."

"Thank you. I would be grateful for a bread basket," Mandisa answered, sinking to a low stool away from the hot fire. "But I need to ask you to do something else for me, too."

"What?" The girl's eyes went round with curiosity.

"Be a friend to Tizara. Though at first I disliked her as much as anyone else, Zaphenath-paneah has shown me that I must serve her out of devotion to him, not for anything she has or hasn't done. I have tried to help her in the past few weeks, but I am sure I have not done all I should. But she is much changed since the night she attempted to escape."

"Me? Help *her*?" A certain thrill of alarm rang in

Halima's tone. "Mandisa, I can't do that!"

"She is no longer what she once was."

"I don't care what she was. She is still beautiful. And look at me! I'm plain. I'm a lowly kitchen slave, and"—her flush deepened to crimson—"I'm fat! How could I even speak to her, and why would she listen to me?"

"You are a gentle and compassionate spirit," Mandisa said, leaning toward her. "And you know something of heartbreak, for I have seen you look at Tarik when you think no one else sees."

Halima did not answer but pressed her hand over her mouth.

"Please, Halima. Succeed where I have failed. Serve our master by being a friend to Tizara, and God Shaddai will bless you for your efforts."

"God Shaddai?" Halima murmured, lifting a brow. "The vizier's invisible God? What could He possibly do for me?"

"More than you dream, Halima," Mandisa answered, rising from the stool. She paused to squeeze the girl's shoulders. "More than you can imagine."

IDOGBE

And I shall give them one heart, and shall put a new spirit within them.
And I shall take the heart of stone out of their flesh and give them a heart of flesh, that they may walk in My statutes and keep My ordinances . . .
then they will be My people, and I shall be their God.

Ezekiel 11:19–20

~ Thirty-six ~

AS A SCORCHING ARID WIND BLEW ACROSS THE drab valley of Hebron, Simeon turned into the current, seeking its hot breath upon his face. He needed to be alone with his thoughts. For the first time in his life, the close quarters of the family compound made him feel as crowded as a hen in a cluster of chickens.

He walked to a slope outside the camp, glad to be away from the tumult as his brothers and their families worked to disassemble nearly three decades of their lives. A myriad of scents and sounds reached him: a mewling wail from one of the children, the acrid odor of the donkeys' pen, voices raised in argument.

Joseph had told them not to bring possessions, for whatever they needed could be found in Egypt, but still the women clung to sentimental objects. Reuben's wife bickered with her husband, refusing to abandon the cradle in which she had laid her sons. At the edge of the clearing, Asher's and Dan's wives struggled to fit a bundle of sheepskins onto the back of an already overflowing wagon.

Simeon sighed and crossed his arms. He had no wife to argue with him and no sentimental attachments to this place or any other. His father felt fondness for Hebron because he grew up here and because Abraham had also sojourned in this fertile valley. It was here, Simeon reflected, Jacob had tricked Esau out of the eldest brother's rightful blessing, and from these pleasant pasturelands he had fled from Esau's fierce and angry hand.

How is my uncle faring now? Simeon wondered, studying the distant horizon. Esau and his people had moved south and westward beyond Mount Hor and had little contact with Jacob. Both brothers had departed from the land El Shaddai deeded to Isaac's descendants. Only Jacob had returned to claim it. But now, Simeon thought, his mouth tipping in a faint smile, Jacob prepared to leave his birthplace knowing full well that he might never return. Simeon supposed he understood why Jacob would leave his beloved homeland in order to be with a more beloved son, but when his eyes had filled with the glory of his long lost favorite, how could they ever turn with approval upon the less-than-glorious sons he merely tolerated?

Mandisa was wrong. Simeon lifted his eyes to the burning sun, welcoming its harsh heat on his face. *Mandisa said I should confront my father, that I would hear a reassurance that he loved me. But even as passionate as she is, she could never understand the depth of the love Jacob bore Rachel or comprehend the breadth of the indifference he exhibited toward Leah. Mandisa is a loving mother. She could never conceive the constancy of the hatred and blame my father holds toward me. For I caused Rachel's death, and he will never forget or forgive.*

A sensation of intense desolation swept over him and he rubbed his chest, massaging the stab of guilt that throbbed in his breast. A hunger for Mandisa's company gnawed at his heart, and he clenched his fist, fortifying himself against it. He was spending too much time alone. The solitude of his Egyptian captivity had affected him more than he realized.

He turned toward the camp, suddenly in need of companionship. Though joyous activity buzzed throughout the compound, one tent stood silent in the desert heat. It had been Leah's tent while she lived, and Dinah lived inside now, a ghostly image of her mother.

Simeon strode toward the tent, absorbing the sounds and smells of home: the aromas of dung fires and cooking food, the sharp clop of an ax, the tang of wood shavings. He was overdue for a visit with Dinah. He had not spent a moment alone with his sister since his return. Had she missed him at all during his time away?

Leah's tent was heavier and older than the others. Simeon lifted the flap and frowned. The air was heavy and thick, as if it had been breathed too many times. Squinting through the darkness, he saw Dinah standing by a pile of furs, tall and formidable, with a shiny smile that was the softest thing about her.

"Simeon," she whispered in a matter-of-fact voice.

She was a mature woman now, no longer a maiden. The dark hair that flew out from her head in silky tangles had begun to gray at the temples. Her face was square and solid with an aloof strength, but for the first time Simeon noticed a soft sag beneath the chin.

"Dinah," he answered, making an effort to keep his greeting light, "how is my favorite sister today?"

"Your only sister," she said, her smile as wry as ever. The gold in her eyes flickered with interest as he moved toward her. "You are heavier, Simeon. Did you eat too much at the Egyptian banquets?"

"I am not heavy. The others are too thin," Simeon answered, lowering himself to sit on a blanket. For a moment he said nothing as she sat down across from him, then he spoke again. "I suppose you have heard that Joseph is alive and the ruler of Egypt."

"Yes." Her face creased in a sudden smile. "I have always known he still lived."

Simeon stretched out on the blanket, casually amused and determined to humor her. "How could you know?" he asked, propping himself on one elbow. "None of us knew what happened to him."

"You knew," she answered, her voice flat and final. "Despite the story you told Father, I read the guilt in your eyes. And though for a moment I feared you had killed him, I knew God Shaddai would protect Joseph. He was too *special* to die so soon."

"Kill him?" Stroking his beard, he regarded her carefully. "Why did you think we would kill him?"

"You killed my Shechem," she replied, lifting one shoulder in a slight shrug. There was no rancor or blame in her voice, only the clear ring of truth. "And then you took my baby and left it in the wilderness. I knew a heart hard enough to kill my husband and abandon an innocent child to die in the desert would not hesitate to kill my brother."

Her words cut him, spreading an infection of remorse, but he gave her a narrowed glinting glance and refused to consider them further. "The stink of this tent has softened your senses," Simeon murmured, sitting up. "That man from Shechem treated you like a prostitute, Dinah! And the child was nothing, an illegitimate brat born of a cursed union."

"Shechem made me an honorable proposal of marriage," Dinah answered with quiet emphasis. "And the innocent child was as much a descendant of Abraham as *you* are, Simeon. You were wrong to take her from me."

"Father did not stop me."

"Father." She repeated the word in a faintly contemptuous tone and waved her hand in a dismissive gesture. "Far too many times Father has done nothing while his sons committed evil in the sight of God. But I have prayed, Simeon. I have agonized with the Spirit of God Shaddai. And for many years I have known that Joseph lives—just as I know my baby lives too!"

His shock yielded quickly to fury. "Sister, you are a fool!" Rising to his hands and knees, he crawled to her side and grasped her shoulders, resisting the urge to shake her into gasping denial. That child couldn't be alive. Nothing could survive in the desert! Dinah's baby had been born shortly after Rachel's death, and Jacob had been so immersed in his grief that he had neither the time nor the willingness to consider his daughter's daughter. Zilpah, Rachel's maid, had been preoccupied with the care of newborn Benjamin, and Leah could not look at Dinah or her child without crying.

So Simeon did what countless others had done throughout history. While Dinah slept, he took the infant from her side, mounted a donkey, and rode away from the camp. When he was quite certain that no one had followed him, he turned toward the family burial grounds—the cave in the field of Machpelah, before the city of Mamre. Once he reached the cave Abraham had purchased from Ephron the Hittite, he dismounted and placed the baby under the shade of a sprawling terebinth tree. There, he thought, at least the child would have some shade and would experience a more merciful death than if he had exposed it on the rocks.

"Dinah, listen to me," he begged her now, a raw and primitive grief erupting in his soul. "You never had a child!"

"As God lives, I did!"

"But it never should have been born! You must forget it, Dinah. You have dwelt on the past for too long! All day you sit here in this tent, never venturing forth unless the women insist that you come out. You do nothing but make clothing for others' little ones; but you should have married and had your own family by now!"

"I had a family, Simeon." Lowering her hands to her lap, she flashed him a sharp look of sorrow. "I had a husband. I belonged to a city. And then you and Levi came through with your bloody blades and put an end to my life. When I felt the movement of the baby within me, I thought I still had a chance at happiness, but you stole that, too. Now I have nothing. My dreams are buried in the earth with Shechem."

Her stare drilled into him. Simeon released her shoulders and clenched his fists, furious at his vulnerability wherever she was concerned. "And you blame me for this?" he asked in a broken whisper. He shouldn't care what she thought, for she was a woman and a slightly mad one at that, but he couldn't shake her words from his mind. "If you must blame someone, Dinah, blame our father! He was the one who cared nothing for you! I am guilty of many things, but the crime of not loving is his alone!"

"Really? Tell me, Simeon, who have *you* loved?"

Leaping to his feet, he ignored her challenge and paced in reckless anger. "Our father didn't defend you when Shechem and Hamor came calling! He didn't care a whit for the babe when she was born! He has never cared about you, or me, or any of us, because we did not spring from Rachel, the true and beloved wife!"

He turned, daring her to refute him, and tensed in surprise when she did. "Our father may not have been perfect, Simeon, but he never killed another man," Dinah answered with easy defiance. "He may not have shown you the love you deserve, but he did not hate you. He grieved over your wrongs. He mourned when you chose to pursue the lusts of your own heart instead of following El Shaddai."

"Can you forget," Simeon muttered, boldly meeting her eyes, "how our mother wept into her pillow each night our father stayed in Rachel's tent?"

"No," Dinah admitted, raising her eyes to his face in an oddly keen swift look. "But can you not see what has happened since Rachel's death?"

"See what?" he yelled, choking on his own words. "I see an old man who adored Joseph and tethered Benjamin to his side like a dog on a leash."

"No, Simeon," Dinah whispered, an almost imperceptible note of pleading in her face. She leaned forward, her steady gaze boring into him. "Open your eyes, Simeon the Destroyer. Open your heart."

Simeon found himself shrinking from the brightness of her watchful smile. Somehow she had gained the upper hand, and that realization sent prickles of cold dread crawling along his back.

"Our mother named her firstborn Reuben, 'God has seen my misery,' " Dinah went on, her face full of strength and confidence. "You she called Simeon, 'the Lord hears that I am not loved.' "

"What are you prattling about?" Simeon growled, spitting the words between his teeth. "I know what my name means."

"Our mother called her third son Levi, 'my husband will now be attached to me,'" Dinah continued, lifting a warning finger. "And Judah means, 'I will praise the Lord.'"

"So?"

"Don't you see, Simeon?" Dinah tipped her head back and offered him a sudden arresting smile. "Our mother came to accept who and what she was. When she stopped striving against our father and God, her grief and jealousy ceased. But by that time, you and the others had grown up and moved out to the fields. And when Rachel died, our father came to depend upon Leah. He loved her, too, not as passionately as he adored Rachel, but in a stronger, more practical way."

Dinah's solid features softened to a sudden delicate dimension of sensitivity. "When Mother died," she went on, after a moment, "Father mourned for her in private, then commanded that she be buried in the Cave of Machpelah with Abraham and Sarah, Isaac and Rebekah. In the tomb of our forefathers, she waits now for the husband who came to love her long after you left her tent. Our mother was honored, Simeon. She was loved."

Simeon looked away, his mind reeling with perplexing emotions. Had he spent a lifetime hating Jacob for his mother's sake, when Jacob had come to love Leah after all? The loneliness and confusion of over forty years melded in one upsurge of devouring yearning—for what? For his mother? Or for the safety of his familiar bitterness and anger? Out of regret, fear, and shame he had built a fortress to defend himself against his father, but now, in one moment, Dinah had breached the wall.

"This is nothing but foolishness," Simeon replied in a sharp voice, more shaken than he wanted to admit. "Your good sense has left you, Dinah, if you ever had any at all."

"I did not think you would understand, but I prayed that you would," Dinah whispered, shaking her head in dismay. "Don't you see? I don't hate you for what you did to my baby. I don't even hate you for killing Shechem. God Shaddai, the Eternal One, has given me peace in knowing that He controls my ways."

"What kind of God would tell you to sit in your room and pout all day?"

She met his accusing eyes without flinching. "I am not pouting. I am praying. But until your stony heart changes, Simeon, you will not understand the difference."

Restless and irritable, Simeon stormed out of Dinah's tent and walked briskly toward the shed where his brothers had penned the donkeys. After fitting one of the creatures with a bridle, he mounted and kicked the miserable animal's bony sides, hurrying it toward the east, toward the Cave of Machpelah and the terebinth tree.

Above him a vulture scrolled the hot updrafts, searching for yet another victim of the famine. The gray bones of desiccated trees had begun to show. The dry and dusty world around him was as stark and bleak as a battlefield. Billows of brown powder drifted from what should have been oases, and shadows of whisper-thin clouds moved like stalking gray cats over the lifeless countryside.

Above the horizon the blurred and blood-red sun baked the earth and everything on it with merciless heat. How could a baby survive in the wilderness? Dinah had always been a dreamer. She was like Joseph in that respect. Her conviction that Joseph still lived—if she had honestly held one—had been based on nothing more than wishful thinking. But her child could not have survived the desert's heat, the threat of jackals, or the nighttime cold.

Sweating and cursing the sun, Simeon rode for a short time, then glanced around for a familiar landmark. The land to the north was as flat as stretched cloth, marred only by the hot sun and whining wind. There were no terebinth trees in sight, no recognizable trails, no wadis to mark

Simeon's progress into the countryside.

But at his right hand the land gathered itself into deep folds. Rocky cliffs rose above the barren landscape, and in the mountainous formation Simeon thought he could see the vague outline of a cave.

He dismounted and pulled the brawling donkey with him toward the rocks. No trees remained to shade the place. Only a few withered stumps marked the spot. Simeon knelt at the base of the cutoff trunk nearest to the entrance of the cave. If the baby had died, wouldn't its bones be buried here beneath the sand? Or had the vultures and jackals scattered them?

He poked a finger into the dry sand and moved aside a handful of dirt.

Nothing.

Using both hands, he scooped out a sizable hole and let the coarse powder trickle through his fingers.

Again nothing.

Crying aloud in frustration, he pushed his hands through the sand to his elbows, struggling against the weight of the earth as he thrust it upward. He pawed frantically, searching for even a tiny bone, some fragment he could show Dinah to prove that her talk of dreams was nonsense, as senseless as describing color to a blind man.

The claws of the wind raked at him, but still he dug, desperate for some shred of evidence. Dirt blew into his eyes and hair and between his teeth. He spat and cursed and continued flinging sand over his shoulders, scraping and burrowing around the base of the dead and withered tree. The heat, radiating from the sand, came at him like a mortal enemy, invading his mouth and nostrils as he gasped for breath. The hot sand beneath his hands and knees scalded and blistered his skin even through the fabric of his robe, but Simeon did not care.

If he could find something here, even a shred of rotted fabric, he could assure Dinah that this chapter of her life was done, forever finished. She had accused him of living in a past where Jacob did not love Leah, but did she not live within a fantasy world of her own making? If she would accept that her child was dead, she could open her eyes to the real world. But she would have to see that God Shaddai did not work miracles, that the past could not be changed, that Simeon was the monster who had murdered her child, that he *deserved* the burden of scorn he carried. . . .

He clutched at a white shard in the sand and pulled it out, but it was the broken bone of an animal, probably a lion. Such a large bone would not fool Dinah. She would insist upon believing in hope, forgiveness, even resurrection.

"God Shaddai!" he screamed, lowering his elbows to the ground. He pressed his sandy, sweaty palms to his wet forehead. "If you are Almighty, why have you never helped me? My father says you guided him. Dinah says you preserved Joseph, and yet you thwart me at every turn!"

The blindingly bright sand beneath him suddenly went dark, and Simeon looked up. The sky above him churned as a mass of dark boiling clouds blew in from behind the horizon. As the atmosphere congealed around him, the donkey brayed and rolled its eyes toward the back of its head. A sudden inexplicable burst of thunder sent the animal cantering over the trail of its own hoofprints.

"Stop!" Simeon cried, rising to run after the animal. The bawling winds snatched his voice away. No match for the terrified beast, after a moment he stopped running. Above him lightning cracked the skies apart, and yet Simeon knew the storm would not bring rain. Jacob's almighty, illogical God had forsaken this land. He now loved Egypt, not Canaan. Just as Jacob had loved Rachel, not Leah, and Rachel's sons, not Leah's. Jacob had even allowed his second son to be named *Simeon*, "The Lord knows I-am-not-loved."

The brooding misery Simeon carried seemed to spawn and spread until it mingled with the innumerable other sorrows borne by Leah, Reuben, Levi, Judah, Issachar,

Zebulun, Gad, Asher, Dan, Naphtali, and Dinah.

"Why, Father?" Simeon cried, floundering in an agonizing maelstrom of emotion. He sank to the sand and pressed his hands over his face, assailed by an overwhelming sense of bitterness and regret. "Why couldn't you love us?"

The wild wind hooted as if to mock him, but through the moving air a shaft of dull gray light broke from the dark clouds and began to inch across the plain. Peering through his fingers, Simeon watched it, tired and uncomprehending, until the searching light shone upon him.

A devouring heat suddenly singed his scalp and shoulders. He gasped, panting in terror, and looked up. A whirling ball of fire hovered in the sky above him, bright as a thousand suns. Simeon felt sweat run from his forehead and under his arms. Then a voice shattered the last vestige of his composure.

I love you.

Beneath the damp hair of his head, his scalp tingled. Panic welled in his throat. Was he losing his mind? He choked back a cry, more frightened than he had ever imagined he could be, and the gale around him increased from its first warning blasts to a great current of roaring air.

Curling to the ground, he closed his eyes and bowed his head, trying to maintain his fragile control. The sun had burned his eyes. The sandstorm had addled his wits. Men often lost their reason in gales like this one. . . .

His muscles turned to water when the Voice spoke again.

I am El Shaddai. I love all them who love me. The God of your fathers is a righteous God, a flame that will not be touched and must be approached with care. Bow your heart, Simeon, son of Israel, and know that you are kneeling upon holy ground.

Awe smote and held him, and he *knew*. No man could hear the voice of God unless he sought it, and Simeon had been more willing in the last hour to hear from God than he had been in his entire forty-six years. He wasn't losing his mind. He had sought God and encountered His majestic presence, and now he could not turn his back on God Shaddai, the Invisible and Almighty One.

He squinted up toward the burning heavens, his knees rooted to the ground. "El Shaddai?" he whispered, closing his eyes against the fierce brightness of the flames. Never had Mandisa or his father prepared him for the dominant and imperious summons of a truly almighty being.

Be still and know that I am God.

The Voice was unmistakable. Simeon's heart turned to stone within his chest, weighting his body so that he could not move.

Do not be afraid to go down to Egypt, for I will make your people a great nation there. But do not serve gods of wood and stone, the work of man's hands, which neither see nor hear nor eat nor smell. Seek the Lord your God. You will find Him if you search for Him with all your heart and all your soul. When you are in distress, return to the Lord your God and listen to His voice. For the Lord your God is a compassionate God. He will not fail you nor destroy you nor forget the covenant that he swore to your fathers.

The Voice swallowed up the wind. When it grew silent, Simeon lifted his eyes. The flaming sphere had disappeared. The earth was suddenly soft and still, the air sweet with the scent of impending rain. Rocks danced in the steaming heat, and from some distance away Simeon thought he heard a bird singing.

Then, like tears from heaven, luscious, blessedly cool rain fell from a widening blue sky, mingling with Simeon's tears and washing the dust of defeat from his face.

～ Thirty-seven ～

TO ANI AND A FEW OTHERS WHO DEVOUTLY followed the gods of Egypt, Zaphenath-paneah showed an appalling lack of concern for his dead wife's eternal welfare.

"I cared for her while she lived and know I will see her in the otherworld," the vizier told Ani one afternoon. "But I do not believe physical objects will be of any use in the spirit world."

Horrified by the master's attitude and the prospect of what others would say, Ani finally convinced Zaphenath-paneah to allow him to fully prepare Asenath's tomb in accordance with Egyptian rites and traditions. Though Ani knew Asenath had placed her soul into the hands of her husband's invisible God, the citizens of Thebes would question both the vizier's love for his wife and his devotion to his God if he did not honor her with a proper burial. They were a practical and sensible people. They believed in corporeal physical preparation and tangible gods.

And so to Ani fell the complete responsibility of preparing his mistress for the tomb. The lady's tomb lay on the west side of the Nile, past the dried-up barren fields that should have been emerald with new crops, past the row of temples lining the Valley of the Dead. Like other members of the nobility, a mastaba had been ordered for Asenath upon the date of her marriage, and the rectangular flat-topped masonry building lay in a neat row with several others, just one street in the necropolis, a city designed for the dead.

The people of Thebes believed that at sunset every night

the spirits of the dead rose from their vaults to linger in the doorways of their tomb chapels. Aided by magic formulas and amulets, they looked over the river to the living city, glowing like a lamp in the gentle dusk. They felt the breath of wind that moved over the river of life, smelled the sweetly damp scent of flowering crops and the aromas of the evening meal.

Burial was not an event to be taken lightly. It was Ani's duty to make certain that Asenath's chamber was adequately supplied with food, furniture, and the lotus blossoms she dearly loved. The temple of her tomb faced the river, and narrow passageways connected the temple with her burial chamber and a storeroom.

Asenath's tomb also would be populated with servants. Because the Egyptians believed her soul would live and work in the otherworld, just as she lived and worked in her mortal life, servants were extremely necessary. No civilized eighteenth-dynasty Egyptian would consider burying human servants with a master or mistress, so specially engraved statues, known as *ushabti figures*, were placed in the tomb. They believed that these figures would be magically animated to rise and perform their mistress's bidding in the otherworld.

Since a host of slaves and servants had cared for Lady Asenath's mortal needs, Ani hired ten sculptors to create her ushabti figures: miniature cooks, litter-bearers, guards, corn grinders, herdsmen, dancing girls, and maids.

The actual burial chamber lay beneath the surface of the ground, and a score of workers descended into its depths every morning to prepare the subterranean house for its eternal occupant. A team of skilled painters adorned the walls with hieroglyphic texts and pictures that described Asenath and depicted her most noteworthy worldly accomplishments. One set of pictures showed her sailing beside her husband, Zaphenath-paneah; another showed her with Ephraim and Manasseh at her knee. The picture of water was essential, for her soul would need water to drink, and the sail would encourage the breath of her *ka* to return.

Tomb paintings customarily showed the deceased standing with the god or goddess she had worshiped in life. When the artist came to Ani for instruction, he scratched his bald head. "The god of my lady?" he murmured, thinking. He knew the lady had worshiped at the temple of Min, the goddess of fertility, in months past, but some inner voice warned him that she would not want that goddess staring at her throughout all eternity.

"Paint the sign for Neter, the invisible God," Ani finally told the artist.

The wall that would stand at the sarcophagus's feet was reserved for an elaborate inscription that would eternally remind Lady Asenath of her glorious funereal procession. Spelled out in careful hieroglyphics, the message foretold what would happen within a few days:

> *A goodly burial arrives in peace, your seventy days having been completed in your place of embalming. Your mortal shell being placed upon the bier and sledge-dragged by young bulls, the road opened with milk until you reach the door of your tomb. Your husband and children, united with one accord, weep with loving hearts. Your mouth is opened by the lector priest and your purification is performed by the Sem-priest. Neter adjusts for you your mouth and opens for you your eyes and ears, your flesh and your bones being complete in all that appertains to you. Spells and glorifications are recited for you. There is made for you an Offering-which-the-King-gives, your own heart being truly with you, your heart of your earthly existence, you having arrived in your former state, as on the day on which you were born. There is brought to you the Son-whom-you-love, the courtiers making obeisance. You enter into a land given by the king, into the sepulcher of the west.*[1]

---

[1]Adapted from a tomb inscription found in A.J. Spencer's *Death in Ancient Egypt* (New York: Penguin Books, 1982), p. 52.

Despite his hard work and the success of his efforts, Ani grew more and more nervous with every day that passed. The master's brothers might return at any time, and the seventy days of mourning for Lady Asenath had not yet been completed. What if the master's family came during the funereal observances? Would the Egyptian rites offend the Canaanites?

Just thinking of the possibilities for disaster shattered his composure. Enough troubles rose to vex him each morning; he did not need to invent new ones. Just that morning, as Ani stood on the deck of the felucca that daily carried him across the Nile, one of the hired stone masons had approached with a basket.

"I have a question about this statue," he said, grimacing as he lowered the heavy basket to the deck.

"No," Ani groaned, peering into the basket. Inside was an ushabti figure, a lovely statue of a kneeling woman. The base of the statue had been inscribed with Asenath's name and a magic formula through which the statue would be brought to life in the otherworld.

Ani's dread altered instantly into relief. "Why, it's perfect. What is the problem?"

"Who is it?" the man asked.

For the first time, Ani looked up into the man's face. With the craggy look of an unfinished sculpture, the man did not look capable of any pleasant emotion. He had a wide-shouldered broad body and wore a working-man's plain linen kilt. His hands, which rested almost protectively upon the statue's head, were callused and stained with dirt.

"It is a maidservant," Ani said, speaking as if to a very slow child.

"I know it's a servant," the man answered, staring back with haughty rebuke in his eyes. "But who is this?"

"Lady Asenath's handmaid."

Unnerved by the big man's power, Ani turned away, but the man grabbed his arm. "The statue looks like someone I know. Does this handmaid have a name?''

Ani turned again. "My lady's handmaid is called Mandisa," he said, an undertone of cold contempt in his voice. "Not that it should matter to a common laborer like you. Mandisa is a lady."

"A lady?" A flash of cynical humor crossed the man's granitelike face. "Yes, I am sure she is. She and her daughter, too."

"Her daughter?" Ani shook his head and gave the man a triumphant smile. "You are mistaken. Mandisa has no daughter. She has only a son, Adom."

The amused look suddenly left the man's eyes. He stiffened, his square jaw tensing visibly.

The felucca had reached the opposite shore, and Ani stepped back from the railing, eager to be away from the man. "Good day," he said simply, transferring his eyes to the wavelets that flecked the surface of the river.

The sooner Asenath is buried, he thought, the sooner life can return to normal.

———

Standing at attention in the vizier's courtyard, Tarik dismissed his guards with a curt command and turned his attention to the list of concerns Ani had dictated for him. A season of adjustment had come to Zaphenath-paneah's household, and Tarik wondered if these changes were truly for the best. Since Lady Asenath's death, Tizara had taken complete and confident charge of the vizier's sons, and Mandisa and Adom had quietly said their farewells and left the house. The steward, whom Tarik had always thought unflappable, seemed irritable and distracted without a mistress to consult for the daily running of the estate. And Zaphenath-paneah, his mind occupied with altogether too many things, spent much of his time in Goshen or at Pharaoh's palace. When he was home, the vizier walked around the villa with a distracted expression on his face. He was preoccupied with his wife's funeral and the soon arrival of his Canaanite family, but Tarik wondered how much of his master's silence was due to concentration and how much was a result of grief.

One of the slave boys from the gatekeeper's lodge skipped across the courtyard, a flushed smile on his face. "Hail, Tarik, captain of the guard! Anhur of the gatehouse salutes you!"

"What is it, boy?" Tarik answered, in no mood for diplomatic pleasantries.

"A stranger stands at the gate, seeking word of Mandisa."

"That lady no longer resides here. Send the man on his way."

"My master Anhur has said as much to the man, but he will not leave. He demands an audience with the vizier."

"The vizier cannot be bothered with petty trifles," Tarik answered, making a shooing gesture as he climbed the steps to the portico. "Mandisa no longer lives here, and we do not know where she has gone."

The boy bobbed his head and followed. "My master Anhur has said as much to the man, but he says he will remain until the vizier hears him. His name is Idogbe, and he says he will not leave until the vizier gives him his wife!"

Tarik halted, shocked. "His wife? But Mandisa is a widow."

The boy's shaved head bobbed again. "My master Anhur has said as much to the man, but the stranger is no spirit, Captain. He is real and has eaten nearly half the figs in my master's breakfast bowl."

Exasperated, Tarik leaned forward. "What has your master Anhur *not* said to the man?"

The boy blanched and took a step backward. "Why nothing, Captain."

"I thought as much," Tarik said, sighing. "All right. Tell your master to hold the man at the gate until I speak with Ani. Then we shall tell Anhur what to do."

———

"He says Mandisa is his wife?" Ani's luminous eyes widened in astonishment. "But she told us—"

"She thought he was dead," Tarik interrupted. He had found Ani with the master in Zaphenath-paneah's chamber, finalizing arrangements for Asenath's internment. "But the man is alive, and he is here, and he demands to see you, my lord."

He had expected the vizier to turn the man away with a polite word of regret, but Zaphenath-paneah looked up from his papyri with an undeniable gleam of interest in his eye.

"By all means, send him in," Zaphenath-paneah answered, a look of implacable determination settling onto his face. "I would like to talk to a man who buys a wife and abandons her when she finds herself with child."

———

Idogbe shuffled behind the guards, trying not to gape at the luxurious surroundings of the grand vizier's house. Mandisa had lived *here*? Unthinkable that such a slip of a girl should rise to such an exalted position. So why on earth had she left this place?

The guards suddenly turned to face him, exposing the reception hall where a stately figure sat upon an elevated dais. Remembering his manners, Idogbe walked forward, then slapped himself onto the polished floor like a swimmer diving into the Nile.

"Life, prosperity, and health to you, exalted Zaphenath-paneah!" he called, trying to inject a brisk formal tone into his voice. For Sebek's glory, he must not fail in this.

"Who are you, and what is it you want?" The vizier was distant, his tone coolly disapproving.

Not deterred, Idogbe lifted his eyes to the solitary majestic figure in the gilded chair. "A woman, O glorious one. I have sought the Canaanite woman called Mandisa for many days, and Sebek, God of my strength, has led me to your noble house. If I had known she was serving you, I might have come sooner to offer myself. But not until I saw her figure among those destined for your wife's eternal resting place did I know that Mandisa resided here."

"You have not sought her in nine years," the vizier answered. The muscles in his back and shoulders rippled in a fluid motion as he leaned forward. "Mandisa told me her story before she entered my household. You abandoned her when she told you she would bear a child."

"How was I to know she would bear a son?" Idogbe asked, smiling with complete candor. He spread his hands in a helpless gesture. "A seer from the temple of Sebek assured me that she would bear a girl."

"And so you left her?" The vizier's left eyebrow rose a fraction. "You took a woman away from her people and homeland, you planted a child within her, and then you departed." His handsome features sharpened into a glowering mask of rage. "I would not treat a dog as roughly as you have treated the woman you called your wife. The law says that if you abandon her, you divorce her. One-third of anything you own is now hers."

"But, O glorious one, I did not make her my wife," Idogbe said, turning his smile up a notch. He lowered his voice and stepped forward, as though being closer would help the vizier understand. After all, Zaphenath-paneah was a man of the world, and a man of his position would have as many concubines and wives as Pharaoh, probably more, since Amenhotep was still but a child.

"Mandisa's true role was more like a concubine's," he said, hoping to disarm the solemn vizier with a confiding smile. "She was a pretty thing I bought for my pleasure. I never promised to love the girl. The silver I gave her father was not a bride-price. After all, she was a Canaanite"—he wrinkled his nose—"fresh from the fields."

"You didn't deserve her," the vizier snapped, bringing his hand to his knee in an explosive gesture. "And you have no right to know where she is." He nodded curtly at the guard who stood at his side. "This man is dismissed."

"But surely a man has a right to his son," Idogbe protested, stepping forward. "Even the son of a concubine belongs to the man who fathered the child."

Two impassive guards grabbed Idogbe's arms. "Stop, I haven't finished," he cried, pushing them aside in protest. "By Sebek's destructive strength and in his name, the boy is mine. I have a legal right to him! By the life of Pharaoh, you should listen to me!"

But the vizier's attention was directed elsewhere, and other guards swarmed forward, ready to forcibly eject Idogbe from the villa. A multitude of hands fell upon him, and though he could have beaten any single one of them easily, Idogbe allowed the guards to drag him from the hall.

"You don't have to knock me about," he said, once they had deposited him on the sands of the courtyard. He stood, brushed a layer of grit from his knees, then fixed a steely eye on the bantam captain who had escorted him to the vizier. "The woman may not be my wife," he said, forcing his lips to part in a curved stiff smile, "but the boy is my son. And as certainly as Sebek is lord of the river, I will find him."

———

Lost in the heart of Thebes, Idogbe moved slowly down a dark street, searching for a market where he could buy a hin of beer or even stronger drink. The confrontation at the vizier's house had lit a hot clenched ball of anger at his center. Passersby scurried out of his way. He knew he made a frightening picture. Frustration always brought a hard frown and a glint of temper to his face.

He would not let himself be stopped by this powerful puppet of Pharaoh's. A man could own but a few eternal things in life: his name, his soul, and his sons. Neither the vizier nor Pharaoh himself had a right or a reason to keep Idogbe from his boy.

Turning toward the west, he moved with an unhurried purpose toward the riverfront. From the birdlike steward he had learned that his wife had been Lady Asenath's handmaid, and he also knew *that* noble lady lay quiet in her chambers, still awaiting her tomb. So if Mandisa had truly left the vizier's house, she had not had time to go far.

And all things moved along the river. Even in its sadly depleted state, the Nile was still the lifeblood of Egypt, carrying its people upon its verdigris back, watering the earth, bringing life and nourishment to an otherwise parched land. No one traveled without stopping for food in its merchant stalls. Wherever Mandisa had gone, she had followed the Nile. And since she would not go toward Canaan in the north, she had assuredly ventured south.

Humming a confident tune, Idogbe advanced toward the river.

~ Thirty-eight ~

THE LONG TRAIN OF OX-DRAWN WAGONS SNAKED from one horizon to the other as Jacob, his sons, their wives, children, and flocks moved from Hebron toward Mizraim. Behind them lay a trampled bit of dry earth with empty pens for sheep and goats, a desolate land that no longer held a chance for life or happiness.

With so many in their caravan, Simeon knew the seventeen-day journey was certain to take twice its normal time. The women did not like to move quickly, and the younger children complained about the heat and the unusual routine. Many of the animals were weak from starvation and thirst, and more than a few collapsed and died as the family moved forward. Reuben commanded that the dead animals should be left where they lay and not skinned, an extravagant waste if Joseph had not promised to provide for all of them.

Simeon made certain that his sons handled his share of the family herds, then he fell into step beside his father's wagon. Dinah rode in the back under a shading canopy, her face hidden by a thick veil intended to keep out dust. Simeon wondered if she wore it to keep out the world.

"Dinah?"

"Yes, Simeon?" she answered with staid calmness.

He squinted toward the horizon, then shifted his gaze to the back of his father's head. Jacob had not turned around. He probably dozed in the heat.

"Before we left I went to our family's burial cave."

She did not lift her veil, and for a moment he wondered if she had even heard him. He could not see her eyes, only a slight movement of the veil as it stirred with her breathing.

"What did you expect to find there?"

He let out a short laugh, touched with embarrassment. He had hoped to find proof that her faith in God was useless. Instead, he had come home convinced that she spoke the truth.

"I didn't find what I expected," he answered, wiping sweat from his brow. "But I did find . . . something."

She shifted slightly under the veil as the wagon creaked and jounced over the trail. "Will you tell me?" she finally asked, her voice echoing with entreaty.

"I felt," he murmured, his pulse beginning to beat erratically at the memory of his encounter, "like a man who has spent his entire life gazing out upon the world and thinks that he sees with the strongest and keenest sight a creature can possess. But then a Voice summoned me, and just as a man's power of sight is dimmed and confused when he gazes at the sun's brilliance, I was compelled to admit that my sight is nothing. And every idea, every belief I have ever held must be reevaluated in the light of this new brightness, in the knowledge that God Shaddai cares . . . about me."

Dinah did not answer, but Simeon had not expected her to. He walked on in silence for several moments, knowing that she understood. Despair and grief had driven her to God Shaddai years ago.

"Were you frightened?" she asked, after a long silence.

"Yes, unreasonably frightened," he answered. "But yet not afraid. He told me . . . that I was loved."

He saw the gleam of a smile beneath her veil.

"Yes, that is how He is," she whispered, folding her hands at her waist. "To embrace Him is to know power, glory, agony, bewilderment, and fear—but never to be afraid. He is unutterable love, Simeon. Though the world burns around you, He is love."

A tumble of confused thoughts and feelings assailed

him. He did not understand everything she meant, but he nodded and slowed his pace until the wagon pulled ahead.

Of all his siblings only Dinah seemed to understand why his visit to the burial cave had left him shaken and unsteady. He had heard countless stories about how God spoke to Abraham and Isaac. Jacob had often told the story of the night when he wrestled the angel of the Lord and earned the name Israel, or "he who strives with God." But until the Cave of Machpelah, Simeon had never heard the voice of God, had never imagined that he might personally strive in a completely different way with such an exalted being.

The experience had humbled him, had broken his furious spirit. After encountering the mind of God, he had seen his anger as a madness that would bring nothing but shame. Unchecked, it would bring death. But God was merciful, He would forgive.

On the long walk from the cave back to the camp, Simeon had realized what Mandisa meant when she told him he was not a man who could love. But if God Shaddai was faithful, Simeon would prove to her that he had changed. But first, there were wrongs to right.

Simeon quickened his pace until he again walked abreast of his father's wagon. Jacob sat at the front, his lined face turned toward the sun, his eyes closed.

"Father?" Simeon walked closer, matching the oxen's plodding gait.

"Yes, my son?" Jacob's eyes did not open, and for a moment Simeon wondered if the old man even cared which son of Leah addressed him. For Benjamin those faded eyes would open, for Joseph they would even weep.

Enough. He had come to make peace, not to stir up old jealousies.

"Father, I have heard the voice of El Shaddai."

Jacob's eyes did open then, and Jacob turned toward him, intense astonishment etched into his face. "*You*, Simeon?"

"Yes." Simeon ignored the insult in the question.

"And what," his father asked, his tone filled with awe, "did God Almighty say to you?"

"The God of your fathers," Simeon answered, staring at the dusty path beneath his feet, "told me that we should not fear to go into Egypt. He warned that we should not worship gods made of stone or wood."

Jacob turned his face back to the sun, his profile strong and rigid. "Anything else?"

Simeon fingered his beard for a moment and stared forward. "The Voice told me that El Shaddai would be found if I seek Him with all my heart and soul. 'When you are in distress,' He said, 'return to the Lord your God and listen to His voice. For the Lord your God is a compassionate God; He will not fail you nor destroy you.'"

Jacob seemed preoccupied for a moment, as if a memory had suddenly surfaced, then he rested his hands on his knees and gave Simeon a rare smile. "El Shaddai spoke to me, too, last night at Beersheba," he said, his voice low. "He told me that He would not forsake us in Egypt. We will go down to Mizraim, but in time God will bring us up to Canaan again. And then," his voice echoed with wonder, "El Shaddai promised that Joseph will close my eyes in death."

Sunshine broke across the old man's face at this last remark, and for a moment the twin adders of hate and jealousy rose in Simeon's breast. In an effort to beat down the emotions that threatened to choke his voice, he punched the sand with his staff. He had come to this wagon to make peace.

"Father, you must forgive me," he said simply.

"Forgive you, Simeon?"

"For hating you." Simeon heard a trace of venom in his voice, but he could not erase it. "I hated you for not loving my mother. I hated you for favoring Joseph, then Benjamin. I hated you for placing my mother and my brothers before Rachel when we advanced to meet Esau. I hated you for not rising to defend Dinah when Shechem accosted her." The bitterness and regret of a lifetime rose in his throat, shredding his voice. "And I hated you especially for not stopping me when I took Dinah's child into the wilderness."

Simeon waited for a response, and when none came, he dared to look up at his father. Jacob sat motionless in the wagon, his chin set in a stubborn line, his expression pained, as though he had been wounded.

"Father, will you forgive me?"

There was a long brittle silence. "I am weary, Simeon," Jacob finally said, his eyes fixed upon the southern horizon.

Had he not heard a word? Or was he choosing to ignore Simeon's deepest feelings?

At that moment Simeon understood both the release that comes from asking forgiveness and the sting of having forgiveness withheld.

Is this how Mandisa felt when I turned away from her at the vizier's house? he wondered. Even though in his heart Simeon knew she had not meant to insult his strength or loyalty, he had enjoyed denying her the freedom of forgiveness. And so he had wounded her again. Just as Jacob's silence hurt Simeon now.

For a long interval Jacob did not speak but sat silently in the cart, staring mindlessly over the heads of the oxen. Finally he drew a deep breath and leaned forward, supporting himself on his hands.

"I have lived a long life," he said in a dull and troubled voice. "I have done a few things to honor God, but many times, in my weakness and deception, I have dishonored His name. In a bit of trickery, I pretended to be my brother to steal his birthright. In a similar bit of trickery, Leah pretended to be Rachel to steal my love. God has not let me escape unscathed from my wanton deeds, and I fear I have paid the price for my mistakes with you, Simeon."

"Father, I—"

Jacob cut him off with a gesture. "I fell short as a son,

and I have fallen short as a father. I am not a perfect man, but neither are you."

He turned, eyeing Simeon with a calculating expression. "I had to keep peace between two wives, Simeon, and you have none. I had to keep peace between twelve sons, and you have only six. Can you be a better father and husband than I with no wives and half as many sons?"

A muscle clenched along his jaw as he turned again to the horizon. "Judge your own house before you judge mine, Simeon. Set your affairs in order. When you are a perfect man, come to me again."

～ Thirty-nine ～

MANDISA SWALLOWED HARD AND SQUARED HER shoulders, willing herself to walk yet another fifty paces. At her right hand the river gleamed coldly pale and gray. The stars of early evening cast a silvery path of light across the narrow waters. "Only a little farther, Adom," Mandisa said, her voice worn, thin, and hollow. Adom did not complain, even though they had been walking all day. She felt as though she had been walking her entire life.

Two full weeks had passed since they left the vizier's house, and in the past twenty days they had wandered through Hierakonpolis, a city nearly as bustling and prosperous as Thebes, and half a dozen smaller villages. Any one of the towns would have been a good place to settle, but she had decided to take Adom to Elephantine, an island city near the river's first cataract. When El Shaddai again blessed the earth with floodwaters, Elephantine would be the first community to receive the benefits and blessings of the Nile's annual inundation.

Though an emerald strip of river grass still bordered the Nile, Mandisa yearned to see green again when she lifted her eyes to the east and west. The emmer fields, from which the sun used to drink steam, now lay empty and barren. Even the skies had changed in the years of famine. The flocks of wild geese, pintail ducks, and widgeons that used to swarm over Egypt had vanished as if they knew they could no longer nest in the bosom of the land.

Beside her Adom yawned, and Mandisa felt a flash of sympathy for her son. The poor boy would have to adapt to life outside a luxurious palace, for there would be no garden or servants or maids in whatever household Mandisa could afford to furnish for him. Yet she was glad that she had left the vizier's house while Adom was young. He was nearly old enough to choose a trade for himself, and a practical, ordinary outlook would be good for him. She would have to learn to make her own way in the world, and Adom would, too.

As the sun sank toward the west and lengthened the shadows along the riverbank, Mandisa pointed toward a small huddle of trees. "There, Adom, is a sheltering place," she said, studying the riverbank to make certain no hippos or crocodiles had decided to beach themselves at the same spot. Since the drought had lowered the river's water level, the fierce water creatures had become hungry and restive in their confinement. Mandisa had been warned more than once that dangerous animals lurked in the river grasses, waiting for a passerby to stumble and fall in the dark.

But the sparse stand of trees lay thirty paces from the river's edge on a high and dry mound of gray earth. "Here, Adom." Exhausted, she found a sheltered spot under the branches of a still green acacia. She cleared the ground with her sandal, checking to be sure no spiders or scorpions hid among the dry brush at her feet, then sat down with her back against the spindly tree trunk. Adom sat next to her, hugging his knees. She knew that within a few moments the boy in him would overpower the emerging man, and his head would fall onto her shoulder or into her lap. Strange how worry and weariness made children of men. Simeon had behaved much the same way.

Adom's breathing slowed and deepened. His head fell upon her shoulder. Relieved that he slept so soon, she sighed and looked up at the sky above. Silver moonbeams laced the branches of the acacias. A quarter moon, the color of dappled bone, hung in the eastern sky. The dense papyrus beds along the edge of the river vibrated softly with insect life. Beyond them the silver water of the Nile shimmered against an endless cobalt sky. Mandisa closed her eyes and thanked God Almighty for another day of survival.

For it was El Shaddai who had brought her safely through the land, and no other god. None of Egypt's divinities had the power to predict the famine or provide the food she and Adom had eaten. They had found dates overlooked by harvesters and grapes growing wild on vines by the riverside. One merchant, about to toss his leftover shat cakes to the crocodiles, had changed his mind and given them to Mandisa and Adom instead.

No, none of Egypt's gods could provide like El Shaddai, yet they were as plentiful as fleas on a dog. As she and Adom had traveled down the riverfront, Mandisa marveled at the many temples, statues, and shrines along the riverbank. Some of the elaborate shrines were made of stone and decorated with festive paintings, while others were as simple as a small statue concealed within a hut of sticks and twigs.

She supposed her years in the vizier's house had dulled her memory of Egypt's pantheon of gods. Though Ani and a few of the household servants held special reverence for certain gods, Zaphenath-paneah had not allowed graven images in his private quarters or his temple.

Apparently the famine had invoked a national resurgence in personal piety. Every city, town, and village had erected a statue of its patron god or goddess at its gate in order to keep harm and want outside the city limits. In addition, each house had at least one replica of a favorite deity standing guard at the doorpost.

A sudden splash cut into the silence, and Mandisa flinched. She scanned the river, her body rigid, until she spied the commotion in the water. Massive jaws churned the surface as a monster chewed its catch, and Mandisa slowly released her breath. The beast floated by her, a dark shadow with bright golden eyes, a stonelike snout, and a wide body. His massive tail, as long as Mandisa was tall, whipped slowly back and forth through the quicksilver river, propelling the creature away.

Sebek, the crocodile god. Idogbe, she recalled, closing her eyes, had been a devout follower of Sebek. A crocodile statue stood outside the door of their small house, and once a year he had journeyed to Crocodilopolis, one of Sebek's sacred abodes, to worship the crocodile that supposedly emerged from the watery chaos at the moment the world began.

But Idogbe was no longer a part of her life, and Sebek was no god. Why couldn't anyone else see the futility of worshiping stone and carved wood?

Despite Zaphenath-paneah's allegiance to El Shaddai and his forthright insistence that the Almighty God and no other had preserved Egypt from ruin, the Egyptians had not hearkened to the voice of their vizier. Mandisa knew that Tuthmosis IV, the present Pharaoh's father, had listened to and respected Zaphenath-paneah's words. But though the new king honored his tutor-vizier, he did not possess the courage to shelve the ancient cults and the priests who also advised him. The great majority of Egypt's people clung with deep veneration to the old gods of their homes and cities. Anyway, Mandisa mused, Pharaoh probably preferred to maintain the old religions because doing so ensured that he would remain at the head of Egypt's pantheon of gods. According to the old beliefs, the king reigned over his people as the incarnation of the god Horus. As such, he was divinity himself, and only he had the right to petition the gods in prayer.

"Not so," Mandisa whispered, her eyes growing heavy. "For I have seen the provision of the Almighty One. He has heard Zaphenath-paneah's voice, and He will hear mine."

Mandisa took a long deep breath, enjoying the cool evening air. It was good to have one God, and logical that only one could be supreme. She had seen the working of El Shaddai in the reunion of Zaphenath-paneah and his brothers after so many years, and He had bountifully provided for her and Adom in the past few days. So why couldn't she understand His will regarding her and Simeon?

Surely she had been right to leave Thebes, for how could she face Simeon when he returned? He refused to love her. He looked for every reason to avoid caring for her. And she could not love a man whose heart had been hardened and carved of hatred and jealousy.

"Almighty God, wherever you are," she whispered, opening her eyes to the darkening sky above, "keep your hand on us as we journey to our new home. Comfort Zaphenath-paneah in his sorrow, and Ephraim and Manasseh. But especially Simeon, O God . . . heal the hurts of his heart."

Under the vast and endless plain of evening, Mandisa slept.

Watching from a small boat floating in the lazy river current, Idogbe recognized the woman who had been his wife. He had been haunting the river for days, moving quietly from village to village, counting on Mandisa's instinct to flee in the opposite direction of Canaan. The wilderness was no place for a single woman and a young boy alone, and he knew she would not want to face her people with a son and no husband. With nothing but desert to the east and west, she could only have gone southward.

Paddling silently, without even a ripple in the windless calm, Idogbe urged his papyrus skiff closer to shore. The boy lay on the ground next to her, one arm resting idly in her lap. Idogbe's mouth puckered with annoyance. She ought to take better care of his son, especially a boy who had spent nine years in the house of a vizier! Undoubtedly the lad was bright. Perhaps he had already picked up a rudimentary knowledge of writing. At scribe school the boy could learn more, and within a few years he would prove himself able enough to serve in the temple of Sebek at Crocodilopolis.

A man needed a son to provide for him, to see that he was properly supplied for the afterlife. Until the day he'd learned that the boy existed, Idogbe had quietly worried that he might die unknown and unmourned, that his immortal soul would vanish like a puff of steam. But he had a son, a bright boy who might be offered in service to the fierce and strong Sebek to ensure bountiful rewards in this life and in the world to come.

His eyes drifted from the sleeping boy to the mother, and Idogbe smiled, thinking about the first time he had seen her. Always restless for fresh horizons, he had been a wanderer even then, one of many merchants on an expedition to the lands of Shinar. The caravan had stopped outside a compound of tent dwellers, and there he saw her standing by the well. She wore an Assyrian garment, brightly patterned and colorful, a stark contrast to the bleached linen garments of Egyptian women. Her dark hair, so different from the neat tidy Egyptian wigs, had tumbled carelessly down her back. One escaping curl fell over her forehead, mesmerizing him.

He had never considered taking a woman for his own, but in that moment he knew he would have her.

He scarcely knew how he found the words, but an interpreter led him to her father's tent. Within the hour he had offered the herdsman ten deben weight of silver, and before sunset that afternoon, he had set the girl with his other possessions onto a pack animal and turned toward Egypt.

She was majestic and beautiful, yet somehow seemed shadowed even with an aura of sunlight around her. She wept frequently, but did not openly protest her father's decision to send her away, and her lustrous eyes widened with some secret alarm every time Idogbe approached her. Her tongue proved quick, and she learned the Egyptian language rapidly. Within six months after Idogbe installed her in his house, Mandisa had become like other Egyptian women, murmuring that he spent too much time away from home and frequently reminding him that he had forgotten some important detail. So when she told him she expected a child, he paid a priest of Sebek a handsome amount to look into a divining bowl and predict the child's sex.

The priest had lied. Perhaps Mandisa had bribed him, or perhaps the man had his own reasons for misleading Idogbe. But rather than father a girl and be responsible for two demanding women, he had gathered his silver and left Thebes, preferring to let Mandisa think him dead than to return and let himself be nagged into an early grave.

She was not often unpleasant, he thought, studying her in the moonlight. Her soft ivory shoulders, barely visible through the linen gown she wore, evoked memories he had long since buried. Her hair, shorter now but still curly, was still as black as a starless night. Even from this distance he could see the hollow of her neck, filled with moonlit shadows. How rewarding it would be to kiss them away . . . but he had not come this far for *her*. And if he were to succeed in his intention to take the boy, Mandisa could not know that Idogbe still lived. She must think that her son had vanished like her husband, without a trace, without a reason.

He would have to plan carefully. Still paddling silently, Idogbe looked up. A small lagoon, used in more plentiful days to irrigate the fields of an entire village, lay off to the west. Pursing his lips, he rowed the skiff forward until it lanced its way out of the flow of the river and into the still waters of the waiting lagoon beyond.

~⊃ Forty ⊂~

"LOOK THERE, FATHER!" ZEBULUN, WHO DROVE the oxen pulling Jacob's wagon, pointed toward the south. "Mizraim! The Black Land!"

Straining against the beating of his own heart, Jacob pushed himself up from the pile of furs where he had been reclining. For several days they had been traveling through desert as gray and lifeless as a tomb, but now green land appeared in the distance. A blush of pleasure burned his cheeks. How good of God to provide fertile fields and Joseph, too!

Reuben, who rode beside the oxcart on a donkey, lifted his head. "What's that?" he asked, pointing in the same direction. A line of Egyptian war chariots bordered the wide green plain, then one chariot pulled away from the others and came forward, churning up the dust of the desert as it raced toward Israel's caravan.

"Who rides at the front of our train?" Jacob demanded, his stomach tightening. "Is it Benjamin?"

"No," Reuben answered, straining to look ahead toward the beginning of the caravan. "Judah rides there. Have no fear, Father. I'll see that all is well."

With his legs pumping wildly against the sides of his donkey, Reuben set out. Jacob sat up and folded his hands, his stomach churning with anxiety and frustration. Though El Shaddai had told him not to fear Egypt, the thought of entering a pagan land aroused old apprehensions and uncertainties. Abraham had nearly lost Sarah here, and Joseph had disappeared into the bowels of this dark place for over twenty years. What if Jacob and his people were totally absorbed, eaten alive? They might never emerge as a distinct and separate race again.

But God had told him not to fear. The Almighty had spoken even through Rachel, who had thought she was only being witty when she named her firstborn *Yosef*, the word for "add," which sounded remarkably like the word for "remove."

"God has removed, *asaf*, my reproach," she had said as the midwife lifted the squalling child from her womb. "May Shaddai add, *yosef*, another son to me!"

"Ah, Rachel," Jacob murmured, his eyes stinging at the memory of her life and her love. "God removed our Joseph and then added him again. As He will remove our people from Canaan, then bring us back. I will not fear. I will trust in God Shaddai."

"Father!" Reuben called, riding back from the front of the caravan. "These chariots are warriors from Joseph himself. He has sent them to intercept us. They will lead us to Goshen, where he waits to welcome you."

Jacob held up a hand in reply, not trusting his voice to answer. Then, as the oxen started forward again, he settled back into his furs, wrapped in a silken cocoon of euphoria.

———

Four hours later, a different company of Egyptian charioteers darted toward them, the horses' hooves drumming the dry desert like a herd of thundering elephants. Onward the Egyptians came, dizzyingly swift, resplendent in white kilts and gleaming chariots pulled by elaborately harnessed stallions.

Jacob stirred uneasily in his wagon. What would he see in Joseph's face? An idolatrous Egyptian or the son he had taught and loved? For so many years he had struggled to accept the fact that his beloved Joseph was dead. Now he struggled to imagine Joseph alive, nearly forty years old, and an Egyptian ruler! Would this Zaphenath-paneah still possess the dear qualities that had made Joseph so special, so extraordinary? Jacob was not certain he could handle the disappointment if the mature man did not resemble the beautiful, valiant youth he held in his memory.

Three chariots pulled away from the oncoming company. They turned sharply in a V formation, then two followed as the leader moved slowly and steadily down the line of Israel's caravan. Jacob frowned, squinting into the bright glare of the sun. Two men rode in the first chariot. One held the reins while the other stood tall and straight, his hands upon the rim of the conveyance, his eyes intently studying the wagons in the procession. The tall olive-skinned man wore a wig in the style of the Egyptians, a flowing crimson cloak, and a spotless white robe.

Abreast of Jacob's wagon, the first chariot suddenly halted. As the tall Egyptian fairly leapt out of his conveyance, Jacob stared wordlessly across at him, his heart pounding.

The Egyptian leaned into the wagon, then his warm hands reached out and clasped Jacob's. "Father," the man said, his voice husky with maturity and deep emotion. Before Jacob could respond, the Egyptian fell on his neck and kissed him, weeping.

Jacob hesitated, blinking with bafflement. "Joseph?" he asked, his voice thick. He pressed his hands to the Egyptian's shoulders and pushed gently. When the vizier of all Egypt lifted his face to within inches of Jacob's, the father searched for signs of his missing son.

The paint-lengthened eyes, the wig, the oiled skin— none of these meshed with the Joseph of Jacob's memory. The man's handsome face was kindled with a sort of passionate beauty far beyond the reach of a seventeen-year-old boy. But there was something in his eyes. . . .

A hot exultant tear trickled down Jacob's cheek as he pressed his trembling hand to the Egyptian's face. He felt his heart turn over the way it always did when Rachel had looked at him with that same pleading, loving expression. "Rachel's eyes," he murmured, feeling the vizier's tears on his fingertips. "You have Rachel's eyes." *If a man dies, will he live again?* Yes! Praise be to God Shaddai!

"Father," the Egyptian exclaimed again, and this time Jacob threw his arms around the son he had long thought dead.

"Now let me die, since I have seen your face," he whispered, relishing the feel of Joseph in his arms. "I can die, knowing you are alive."

———

Joseph's trembling limbs clung to his father. He had no desire to ever back out of that longed-for embrace. God was so good! His father still lived—a miracle in itself—and Jacob's eyes had *known* him, had welcomed him home as if they had been parted only a few hours instead of more than twenty years.

"You shall not die, Father," Joseph said, still holding tight. His tone was playful, but his meaning was not. "You shall live with me in Egypt. And God will give you many years here, so that we may fellowship with each other. And you shall know my children and understand why God Shaddai wrought all these things."

At last, reluctantly, they parted a few inches. Without shame Joseph brushed tears from his cheek, but his eyes never left Jacob's for an instant. "You were always in my heart," he told his father, so choked by emotion that he could hardly lift his voice above a whisper. "And I never forgot the things you taught me about God Shaddai."

"Praised be His name!" Jacob cried, his arms closing around Joseph again.

Tears of joy came in a rush so strong that Joseph sobbed in his father's arms, but Jacob held him close, murmuring the soft words that a father gives to a wounded and much-loved son.

———

Jacob met Ephraim and Manasseh that same day, then

Joseph himself led the children of Israel into the land of Goshen, the place prepared for them. "I will go up and tell Pharaoh that you have come to me," Joseph told his family. "He knows you are shepherds."

"Will he expect us to mingle with his people?" Jacob asked, still uneasy about living in a land of idol worshipers.

"No," Joseph answered, a smile nudging itself into a corner of his mouth. "The Egyptians detest herdsmen. Those who keep livestock are an abomination to them."

"As they are to us!" Levi laughed. "Let them stay away. I have no urge to visit their sinful cities."

"We will remain here in this well-watered land of Goshen," Jacob answered, silencing his headstrong offspring with a stern look. He turned back to the magnificent man who was his son. "And as for you, my Joseph, am I to meet the mother of your two handsome boys?"

A look of tired sadness came over the vizier's face. He sighed heavily, and his voice filled with anguish. "My lovely Asenath was laid in her tomb a few days ago, Father. You will have to wait and meet her in the otherworld."

Jacob nodded silently, appraising his son's silent pain. Joseph's despair seemed genuine. It appeared that he had truly loved the Egyptian woman he mourned. Just as Jacob had loved Rachel—and Leah.

"It is enough, *Yosef*," he whispered. His tongue felt like old paper, dry and dusty with aged memories.

Joseph gave his father a rare intimate smile and placed his hand on Jacob's shoulder. "It may be that Pharaoh will come to visit you, out of respect," he said, the warmth of his smile echoing in his voice. "If he comes and asks your occupation, tell him again that you are herdsmen. Thus he will leave you alone here, and you and your people will not be molested in any way. You will be free to live, work, and worship as you please."

"What of you, Joseph?" Jacob asked, reaching out for his son's hand. "Must you continue living in Thebes?"

The vizier's large black eyes, so like Rachel's, seemed to

fill with shifting stars. "God has set me in another place," he said, his voice gentle but firm. "Though my heart is always with you, I must do the work Almighty God has called me to do."

His heart sank with swift disappointment, but Jacob gave his beloved son a smile and an encouraging nod. "Then go with God," he said simply, holding tight to Joseph's hand until the last possible moment.

~ Forty-one ~

SIMEON WAS PLEASED TO DISCOVER THAT Goshen suited his family well. Bordered by the Mediterranean Sea, called the Wadj-ur or "the Great Green" by the Egyptians, the delta that supported the region of Goshen was part of Lower Egypt. The fertile land, well-watered by seven river branches of the Nile, was heavy with layers of effluvium and silt, perfect soil for fields, flocks, and herds. The vast area, inhabited by few Egyptians, was blessed by continued moisture, gentle winds, and solitude.

Joseph was generous beyond all imagining. He provided the children of Israel with food, the tools with which to construct shelters like those they had known in Canaan, and additional livestock to replace the animals that had died on the journey. The vizier of all Egypt lived with them in a tent for the first week after their arrival, eager to make certain that his father and family were content and settled in their new home. And though Joseph was welcomed with open arms, Simeon sensed that he would always remain apart from them. In a way, he was still Joseph, Jacob and Rachel's son, but the bright aura of his glory kept them at arm's length. Even Israel, who had once scoffed at young Joseph's dream that his parents and brothers would bow before him, prostrated himself at Zaphenath-paneah's feet and called him, "My lord."

Perhaps because he had been imprisoned so long in the vizier's house, Simeon was the least awed of all his brothers. Two weeks after settling his sons into their new home, Simeon said farewell to his family, mounted a donkey, and rode upriver toward Thebes. Ostensibly he had undertaken the journey to bring a report from Jacob to Joseph, but privately he yearned to know if Mandisa would grant him an opportunity to speak with her.

So much had happened since he had last seen her. He had heard the voice of El Shaddai, and the angry fires in his soul had at last been quenched by his confession to Jacob. If only Mandisa would listen to him long enough to hear his heart. . . .

At the vizier's house, Ani greeted him like an old friend, and even Tarik had a smile for his troublesome former captive. "So, Simeon the mighty Destroyer of Furniture has returned," Ani said, still stumbling over the unfamiliar Canaanite words. "What do you intend to break on this visit?"

"Nothing," Simeon answered, happy to meet the smile and the welcoming hand that Ani offered him. "And you can speak Egyptian to me now, Ani. I have learned enough to manage in this country."

"After a year in this house, you should speak it as well as the master," Tarik joked, slapping him on the back. "But if you've come to see the vizier, you'll have to wait. He is with Pharaoh at the king's house, interviewing emissaries from Babylon. A king of that city wishes to marry his daughter to our divine Amenhotep."

"Ah-hah!" Simeon answered, following Tarik toward the kitchens. "Another royal queen!"

Ani turned a suddenly somber face toward Simeon. "I suppose you heard about Lady Asenath."

Simeon nodded. "Yes. The vizier told us when he introduced his boys to my father. I was very sorry to hear the news."

The steward's mouth curved in a mirthless smile. "Things are much changed now, of course. Tizara tends to the young masters when they are not with their father."

"I thought Mandisa would care for the boys," Simeon remarked, looking around. "She has a fondness for the children."

"You haven't heard?" Tarik stopped abruptly on the pathway.

Simeon's stomach dropped like a hanged man. "Has something happened to Mandisa?"

"We hope not," Tarik said, his eyes narrowing. The captain folded his arms. "She left about three weeks after the mistress died. And a short time after that, an Egyptian called Idogbe came searching for her."

"The master dismissed him at once," Ani added, an edge to his voice. "And he left the house. But he seemed quite intent on finding Mandisa."

"Not that he wanted her, for the master ruled that she was not his legal wife," Tarik went on. "The man wanted Adom. He said he left her because he thought Mandisa would bear a girl, but when he came back and discovered that she'd borne a son . . ."

Tarik's voice trailed away, but there was no need to explain. Simeon knew all too well that sons were valued far above daughters. Part of Jacob's prestige in Canaan lay in the simple fact that he had produced twelve sons, and his sons begat sons.

Simeon took a deep breath and prayed that he would not reveal his inner turmoil. "Where did she go?"

"No one knows," Tarik answered. "But I don't think she wanted to remain in Thebes. She has no family here."

"For some reason I think she was especially afraid of meeting you again," Ani said. His bright eyes narrowed into speculative slits. "Why would she fear you, Simeon, son of Jacob?"

Simeon felt suddenly limp with weariness. "I was the Destroyer," he murmured.

Zaphenath-paneah invited Simeon to dinner that evening, and the former prisoner was pleased to discover that the meal would be served in the vizier's chamber without formality of any sort. He was momentarily speechless with surprise, however, when he heard Joseph tell Tarik to place a chair for Tizara between himself and Simeon.

"You expect me to share my meat with a harlot?" Simeon asked in a low voice when Tarik had left the room. "Really, Joseph, has the girl's beauty addled your brain?"

"You once attempted to run away with Tizara," Joseph answered, not blinking as he regarded his older brother. "Why won't you eat with her? What has changed?"

"Things were different then," Simeon explained, shrugging. "I was a captive, and she a slave. And we were both allied against *you*."

Joseph smiled, but his expression held only a ghost of its former warmth. "But now you are brother to the vizier of all Egypt," he said, sinking into his chair. "Are you now too important to eat beside a woman with a troubled past?"

"I'm not speaking of her past deeds. I'm speaking of *what* she is! Haven't you looked at her? You can't be blind, Joseph, for all that you pretend to be."

"I'm not blind," Joseph answered in a soft, mocking tone. "I see far more than you think I do, Simeon. And in Tizara I see a young woman with no one to care for her, a woman in need of friends and family."

"Can you deny her past? She has played the harlot and probably would not hesitate to do so again if given the chance."

"Is your own past so pure?"

Simeon winced, surprised that the words stung. Sometimes he forgot that Joseph knew everything about Shechem, about Dinah's baby, and of course, about Dothan.

"Tizara will sit between us tonight, and you will not be unkind," the vizier went on, his voice regal and commanding. "You will be on your best behavior, whatever that may be. Do not forget that you are in my house, Simeon. Though I am your brother, by the hand of God Almighty I am also lord of Egypt. I love you, but I will discipline you if you insult the others of my household."

Irked by Joseph's words and his cool, aloof manner,

Simeon settled back in his chair, determined to endure the evening and make his way home as soon as possible. Joseph would always be a mystery, an enigma. Sometimes he made no more sense than the incomprehensible images of dreams. Why was he so intent upon cultivating a relationship with the woman of shame? For a moment Simeon considered the ludicrous possibility that Joseph thought to marry the girl, but surely the noble Zaphenath-paneah would never take a tainted woman for his bride!

The doors swung open. Two guards escorted Tizara and the boys into the room. Ephraim and Manasseh fell on their faces before the vizier, then, at a word from their father, they leapt up and scampered to his side. After greeting each of his sons with an embrace and a quick kiss, Joseph looked up and welcomed their nursemaid.

Simeon found himself staring as if he'd never seen a woman before. If such a thing were possible, he would have sworn that some other soul had come to inhabit Tizara's body as she slept. For though the willowy form every man in the villa desired had not altered, the spirit within the woman had completely changed.

Keeping her eyes demurely downcast, Tizara crossed to the empty chair between the two men and gracefully seated herself. The beauty that had once tempted Simeon now fascinated him. An aura of untouchable glory surrounded her and drew him like honey draws a fly.

"Tizara?" he asked, scarcely able to believe *this* creature would know him.

"Simeon!" Her eyes lit with the excitement of recognition when she looked up. Her smile was sweet and serene. "It is good to see you again. Haven't the boys grown?"

"Yes, they have," he murmured, distracted by her nearness. He broke into a wide open grin. "Many things have changed within this house."

"Yes," she murmured, offering him another shy, slightly sad smile. "They have."

By the time the last dish had been cleared, Simeon had convinced himself that Joseph intended for *him* to marry Tizara. He waited until the former slave girl had taken the boys to bed, then he turned on his brother in wrathful indignation.

"I know what you are planning," he said, ripping out the words impatiently. "Tizara is not good enough for *you*, but you would have no problem marrying her to me. She is from Shechem, too, which makes things nice, doesn't it? Do you think you can relieve my guilt by bringing me a bride from that cursed place? You can fix some things, Joseph, but only God can forgive. A Canaanite bride will not correct the wrongs of my past!"

"Marry you to Tizara?" Joseph's mouth quirked with humor. "Why would I want to do that? Good nursemaids are difficult to find."

"Then why did you bring her in to eat with us? Women do not eat with men, especially in Egyptian households."

"Who says families may not eat together?"

"Servants are not family members. You did not invite Tarik to eat with us, or Ani, and they are closer servants than your children's maid."

"Tizara is family."

Simeon looked up, confused. What did he mean? Had he adopted the girl? Betrothed her to one of his sons? The Egyptians were odd people. He should not be surprised by anything Joseph might do as the Egyptian Zaphenath-paneah.

"Come with me, Simeon." Joseph stood and moved toward the balcony stairs. Simeon followed, his brain whirling.

"Do you believe El Shaddai keeps His hand on us always?" Joseph asked, thrusting his hands behind his back as he led Simeon toward the section of balcony that overlooked the garden.

Simeon hesitated. Only a few weeks ago he would have answered no. But since that time, the hand of God had moved through his life like a whirlwind, uprooting old hates and sorrows.

"Yes," he answered, standing beside Joseph at the railing. "I do."

"Then look there," Joseph said, staring into the garden below. "And tell me what you see."

For a moment Simeon could see nothing in the area where Joseph pointed, then Tizara moved into a glow of torchlight at the edge of the reflecting pool. Slender, supple, and lissome, she swayed to the music of the night, dancing with shadows thrown by the moon. The hard and brittle brightness of her manner had completely fallen away. She looked like a playful young girl.

"I see," Simeon muttered, a note of impatience in his voice, "a harlot who has been spoiled by her master."

"Admit the truth, Simeon. You see a different woman," Joseph replied, leaning forward on the railing. He gave Simeon an enigmatic smile. "Forgiveness and mercy change lives, brother. A harlot entices men away from the love of God, and Tizara has enticed no one in this house. But we have other harlots in our lives, other gods we choose to serve."

Simeon felt everything go silent within him.

"Your anger, Simeon, is a harlot," Joseph went on, looking down into the garden, watching the girl. "And your guilt and your rage. And though I can tell that you have changed since you were held here—"

"I have," Simeon interrupted, tightening his grip on the stone railing.

"Even still, anger and guilt have risen within you because Mandisa is gone."

Simeon flinched, resenting Joseph's discernment. How could a man know so much without being told?

Joseph read the question in Simeon's eyes. "I can see, Simeon," he said, without even a hint of boastfulness. "I know that you love Mandisa. And she loved you so much that she left this place rather than face you again."

Simeon caught his breath as a deep unexpected pain smote his breast.

"Go after her," Joseph urged, his dark eyes piercing the distance between them. "Go quickly, before it is too late."

Something—humility?—kept him from arguing. "I'll go now," Simeon said, turning from the rail. He had only taken two steps toward the stairs when Joseph stopped him.

"Wait. There is one more thing. Do you remember what Dinah looked like when we were younger?"

Perplexed, Simeon turned and slowly nodded, his throat too clotted with emotion to risk speaking. He did not want to think about Dinah now. Though she said she had forgiven him, thinking of what he'd done to her still filled him with a deep sense of shame.

But at the mention of her name, memories ruffled through his mind like wind on water: Dinah dancing by the oasis at Hebron, Dinah giggling in the moonlight as he chased her through the camp, just as Tizara laughed in the sheer beauty of a warm and lovely night. . . .

His heart went into sudden shock. The dancing girl in the garden *was* Dinah, not as she looked now, but as she had been twenty years ago—strong, lovely, energetic. Tizara's features were more refined, as if a loving artist's hand had smoothed out imperfections, but there was no denying the resemblance.

He heard his voice, stifled and unnatural. "It is . . . remarkable. Tizara looks very much like Dinah."

There was a short silence, and his words seemed to hang in the air as if for inspection. Joseph turned toward him, smiling as if Simeon were a small child.

"Yes, brother," Joseph answered, speaking in an odd, yet gentle tone. "Tizara ought to look like our sister." Liquid shadows shifted in his eyes as his gaze met Simeon's. "She is Dinah's daughter."

Impossible! Staggering toward the balustrade in hypnotized horror, Simeon trembled at Joseph's words. "It cannot be true!" He stared at the girl, his heart racing and his fingers fluttering with fear. "No. The baby died. I left it alone. No one lived within miles of that burial cave."

"God sent someone," Joseph answered, "just as He sent someone to sustain Hagar in the wilderness. Who are we to question His ways?"

The girl continued to dance beneath the moon, completely unaware of the two men watching from above.

"How do you know this?" Simeon whispered, still reeling in disbelief.

"I suspected something when the Spirit of God spoke to my heart and urged me to buy her," Joseph said, his eyes fastened to Simeon's face. "And she looked so much like the young Dinah I remembered. Even so, I would never have been sure, but I heard Mandisa tell Halima that Tizara had an unusual birthmark on her scalp. Apparently she discovered it while washing Tizara's hair."

Simeon shook his head. "The baby had no birthmark."

"Yes," Joseph whispered. "It did. But you never looked at the child, Simeon. I was playing in Dinah's tent the day you took her baby away. I saw you leave with the infant held close to your breast." His voice trembled slightly in the darkness. "I don't think you were able to look."

"I wasn't." Simeon tore his eyes from the girl and turned to hide the tight place of anxiety in his heart. "Why did you not tell me sooner?"

A faint note of sadness tinged Joseph's voice. "I wasn't certain you—and the others—were ready to hear."

We weren't. Like a drowning man, Simeon held tight to the balustrade as a tumble of confused thoughts and feelings assaulted his spirit. Behind him he heard the soft sounds of Joseph's footsteps on the stairs. Below him Tizara's graceful form melted into the veiling darkness. He wasn't sure how long he stood there clinging to the balcony railing like a frightened cat, but his feet could not move until his heart had made sense of Joseph's revelation.

The child had not died!

He stared silently into the moonlit garden, his heart pounding as the memory of his own words mocked him: *A Canaanite woman will not erase the wrongs of my past!*

But a Canaanite woman had. The baby lived, and by the grace of God, his sin had been obliterated.

His skin burned with memory of the hot sand on his hands at the family tomb, the emptiness of the awful moments when he had frantically searched for proof of his unspeakable crime. His frenetic digging had produced no bones, no trace of a human body, because the baby who had seared his soul with guilt and remorse lived and breathed and danced. . . .

Alive! Simeon thumbed an unmanly tear from his eye. Dinah had believed. She had known that Joseph and Tizara still lived. Though she couldn't touch the objects of her faith, she *knew*. Unsociable, odd Dinah had seen and understood so many things that slipped by him.

With a shiver of vivid recollection he recalled the afternoon he'd spent in her tent.

"Our father loved Leah, too," she had said. "Not as passionately as he adored Rachel, but in a stronger, more practical way."

She'd been right about Jacob, too, of course. Simeon had wasted years despising his father, serving the harsh harlot of hatred who pulled him away from God, who hardened his heart against all that was good and true and worthy. "Forgive me, God Shaddai," he whispered, lowering his head in humility. "Take a chisel to my heart and remove anything there that does not please you."

In that instant, powerful relief flooded his soul. Buoyed by euphoria, he lifted his eyes to the night where stars blazed like gems upon a velvet sky.

You can restore that which was lost. The intensity of the Voice lifted the hairs on Simeon's arms.

Restore what? Joseph had been restored to Jacob. And Leah was dead. It was too late—

You took the child away. You can take her back to her mother.

A cry of mingled relief and surprise broke from his lips as the joy of resurrection enfolded him. Just as Joseph had been restored to Jacob, Tizara would be returned to Dinah. How gracious, how good, was God Shaddai!

As soon as he had found Mandisa and Adom, he would take Tizara home.

~ Forty-two ~

SIMEON SCARCELY KNEW WHAT DROVE HIM, BUT Joseph's revelation lit a fire in his soul, a fevered energy that would not be quenched until he had found Mandisa and pressed his suit with her one final time. He hurried from the balcony and stalked purposefully toward the stable yard. Tarik would give him a horse, perhaps even a chariot.

"Tarik!" Simeon pounded on the door of the captain's quarters. In an instant the door swung open, and Tarik spilled out of the chamber.

"What is it?" he barked, his hands busy tying his sword belt at his waist.

Apparently Simeon had roused him from slumber, for the guard's eyes were heavy, and he had not taken the time to don his wig. "Be at peace, Tarik," Simeon said, trying to keep the impatience from his voice. "But I need a horse. Your master will give permission. You have but to ask him."

"A horse?" Tarik frowned. "By the crud in Sebek's teeth, Simeon, whatever do you want with a horse?"

"I'm going to find Mandisa."

"Tonight?"

"Yes. So please allow one of the stableboys to saddle a horse for me."

Tarik rolled his eyes but moved toward the stable. "You'll need a chariot. No self-respecting Egyptian rides astride. And my best chariot drivers have all been dismissed for the day, but perhaps I can find someone willing to go with you."

"No, I'll go alone."

The captain gave Simeon a look of frustrated disbelief. "You are a madman, and you're not accustomed to handling a chariot. You'll overturn it on the first corner."

"Then forget the cursed chariot and give me a horse! I'm not an Egyptian, and I don't care what people will say when they see me astride one of the beasts!"

"Well." Tarik's face closed in a prim and forbidding expression as he crossed his arms. "I suppose the vizier's brother must know best. Tell Chuma the stableboy to put a bridle on the black stallion."

"Good." Simeon took two steps before a second thought restrained him. "Thank you, Tarik," he said, turning and continuing to walk backward. "And may I give you one bit of advice, my friend?"

Tarik leaned against the wall. "I suppose you will whether or not I want to hear it."

"You're right." Simeon lifted a warning finger. "The kitchen slave Halima loves you, and everyone but you can see it. Marry her, my friend, before her hope is gone. Or you will wake up one day a lonelier man than I."

As Tarik sputtered in confusion, Simeon grinned and turned toward the stable.

———

Idogbe slept fitfully, unwilling to lose himself in deep sleep lest he miss the opportunity to intercept Mandisa and his son. A half hour before sunrise, just as the eastern sky began to glow, he crept from his hiding place and peered through the brush. The woman and the boy still slept, curled together like a mother lion and her cub.

Idogbe looked closely at his son's face and felt pleasant surprise. The boy's single lock of hair emphasized the pale beauty of his complexion, and in his clear-cut features, Idogbe could see the beginnings of genuine masculine beauty. Undoubtedly the lad would prove to be a cut above the ordinary runny-nosed children who dwelt like river rats along the Nile. Yes, this child would be a fine oblation to Sebek. The Prince of Destroyer Gods, the One-Who-Conquers-Life-and-Death would bestow many favors upon Idogbe for surrendering his son to the priests.

"O Sebek, the Crocodile, hail to thee, thou Crocodile of the Land of the West and the sweet river!" Idogbe chanted under his breath, his eyes fastened on the boy. "I am thy kinsman, Sebek! As the sun shall rise, as the disk shall shine, as the services shall be performed in thy temple, so shall this child be better than he was, born of the woman Mandisa, born of Idogbe, the Egyptian! Aid my cause, Sebek, for if thou will not hear my words, I will crush a nest full of thy eggs in the forecourt of Crocodilopolis! Then indeed shall thou come forth from the temple to aid me, to gather thy son, born of the woman Mandisa, born to thee, O mighty Sebek, god of my strength!"

As if he had sensed Idogbe's prayer, the child stirred and lifted his head. Idogbe ducked behind a stand of papyrus, his heart beating thickly. The time was near. When the child left his mother's side, Idogbe would approach and ask for directions to the nearest temple, a friendly question that would not arouse suspicion. Perhaps he would ask the boy to lead him for a short distance, and as soon as they were beyond the range of Mandisa's hearing, Idogbe would restrain the boy's arms and force him into the waiting skiff. Once the child understood the great honor Idogbe intended for him, he would happily accept it.

Dawn lifted the horizon at that moment, sending light up and over the earth. Mandisa stirred, brushing sand and dirt from her hair and shoulders. Her mouth curved with tenderness as she spoke to the boy, then he helped his mother to her feet, and they walked together to the riverfront.

From his hiding place, Idogbe cursed his ill luck. Mandisa was an attentive and devoted mother, but she could not stay beside the boy forever. Like the hovering spirit of Horus the Falcon, Idogbe would remain near. And the moment the mother and son parted, he would make his move.

————

The sun, a dazzling white blur, stood fixed in the wide sky above the travelers. Aching and exhausted, Mandisa forced herself to continue moving one foot in front of the other and wondered if she would faint from the heat. She had never realized how cool and sheltered the vizier's house had been. She had taken the fans, the cool tile, and the high breeze-catching windows for granted. Here the proud sun reigned as master of all in the white-blue sky, and only the faintest scribbles of clouds deigned to shelter mortals on the land beneath.

As they walked, she considered the jobs she might have to undertake to support herself and Adom. Women in Egypt generally chose one of four professions: they entered the priesthood, trained as midwives, or studied to become either professional mourners or professional dancers. Mandisa knew she was long past the agile age of professional dancers. The priesthood was not a suitable profession for a woman with a child, for she would have to leave Adom for extended periods of time. *Why would I do that for a god I do not serve?* she asked herself, reaching out to run her hand over the dark fuzz that had begun to cover Adom's shaved head. She might have considered joining a priestly order to serve El Shaddai, but He had no temples and no cults in Egypt.

Before Asenath's death she might have considered midwifery, for she had delighted in assisting at Ephraim's and Manasseh's births. But with her mind still heavy with the memory of Asenath's travail, Mandisa did not think she could bear to watch another pregnant woman endure labor. The grievous memories of her beloved mistress were still too fresh.

There remained the profession of mourning. Professional mourners were paid well for their roles in the burials of esteemed men and women, and the work was simple enough—one had merely to weep, wail, and tear one's robe at the appropriate moments. And, Mandisa thought, a wry frown twisting her face, of late she had experienced enough grief to give a very convincing performance. Perhaps God Shaddai had allowed her heart to break so she might be of comfort and service to others in grief.

She lifted her head, relieved that she had found a workable and noble solution for her situation. Twining tendrils of hope broke through the surface of her despair, and she knew El Shaddai would provide. Even if she had to beg for a position to grind corn like the lowliest slave women, she would. But no matter what happened, she would remain free. She would not consider selling herself into slavery, nor would she marry because she had no other options. She would never again allow herself to become a man's possession.

———————

Mandisa let out a long exhalation of relief when she and Adom reached Elephantine shortly after midday. After begging a bit of bread from a compassionate merchant, they slipped aboard a ferry boat, which took them over to the island city. Adom was wide-eyed with wonder as they walked around the bustling settlement, but Mandisa quickly realized that she would not find a place to live within the walled city itself. The common people lived on the river's eastern shore and rowed themselves to work for the noble island families. Shortly after dark each night, they returned to their hovels at the river's edge.

A weary fisherman gave them a ride back from the island. When Mandisa and Adom stepped out into the ankle-deep mud, the kindly man gave Mandisa a valuable bit of information. "My sister had a hut about a hundred paces from here," he said, pointing up the riverbank. "But last month she died of the fever. You and your boy should take the place. No one will bother you."

"Truly?" Mandisa felt a warm glow flow through her. El Shaddai had provided again!

"You'll find the house right on the river," the old man said, his round face melting into a smile. "There's a statue of Sebek by the door. My sister believed that the strength of the crocodile god would guard the house."

"Apparently he was not strong enough to guard your sister," Mandisa answered soberly. She thanked the man again and took Adom's arm as they trudged through the mud toward the shoreline.

She found the hut exactly where the man had said it would be, one hundred paces from the boat landing and only ten paces from the dike that would hold back the river during the inundation. The small house was made of gray sun-baked bricks. The door hung askew on its supports, but Mandisa pulled it open and found a quiet corner in which she and Adom could lie down.

As she watched her weary son sleep in the moonlight, Mandisa lifted her eyes to the sky beyond the window and thanked El Shaddai for his provision. In a pouch around her neck she still had a few pieces of fine jewelry, gifts from Lady Asenath. Some noble woman of Elephantine would pay dearly to wear earrings or a bracelet once worn by the vizier's wife.

"We will live and prosper," she whispered, tenderly stroking her son's bare back. "We will make this house a home, and I will find work in the city beyond. And you will grow strong, Adom. We will be free of the past. There will be nothing here to remind us of hard times, no one to remind us of Canaan."

Tears sprang to her eyes, but she rigidly held them in check, determined not to mourn for what could not be helped. El Shaddai had led her to this place. She would not look back.

After a long while, Mandisa drifted into a dreamless sleep.

Outside the house, Idogbe chewed the loaf of bread he'd bought from the Elephantine merchant and grunted, watching the scene before him with ever increasing delight. Though Mandisa had led him on an irritating journey out to Elephantine and back again, she had made his task easy by taking the empty hut. She would grow confident here. She would send Adom outside to fetch something . . . and Idogbe would claim his son.

He took another bite, pleased with himself and the world.

———

"Mother, do I have to stay inside and work? There are boys my age by the river."

Sighing, Mandisa put down her borrowed broom and walked to the window. Despite the many warnings she'd heard about hungry and restless animals in the river, a veritable army of boys prowled the dike and the riverbanks beyond. They laughed, scampered over the sand, and occasionally dipped into the river to splash the heat from their bronzed backs. Her poor son, who'd had only little boys and older men for playmates, desperately wanted to join them.

"All right," she said, capitulating. "But you must not turn your back on the water. Stay with the other boys, find a friend, and do not wander far from this hut."

"I will, Mother!"

Adom raced through the doorway, and she bit down hard on her lower lip. He had lived his entire life in the safe shelter of the vizier's villa. He did not know about rivers, crocodiles, or village boys like these. But, she supposed, watching him launch himself toward the other boys, if they were going to live on the Nile, he had to learn.

"Be careful," she called again.

She stood at the window, watching as he boldly walked

up to a circle of boys. As curious and natural as the fish of the Nile, they circled around Adom, sizing him up. Mandisa held her breath, fighting a momentary panic, but then Adom said something, and within a moment they were all chattering like magpies. She smiled, dismissing her worries, and returned to the business of cleaning the house.

———

Idogbe's heart lurched within him when he saw the boy run out of the house . . . alone. The lad ran straight to a cluster of river urchins and began talking, a sure sign of a born leader. Grinning to himself, Idogbe settled down by a tree in plain view of the boys but behind the house. He didn't care if the children saw him. If his son felt at ease, the snatching would be easier . . . when the time was right.

———

Mandisa worked hard, humming contentedly to herself. Occasionally she walked over to the neighboring houses to borrow tools and supplies, always promising to repay. Her neighbors, all of whom were farming families hard hit by the famine, were cheerful and polite, but expressed no interest in where she had come from or what she intended to do.

Mandisa surmised that many people had been uprooted by the famine. They probably assumed that she would come, remain awhile, and leave like so many others.

The modest house was quite comfortable. Poor families did not have furniture, for wood was scarce and valuable, but two low mud-brick platforms had been built next to the walls to serve as beds. A few dusty baskets had been left in the house for storage, and in one of them Mandisa found a fire drill and a few pieces of tinder that she could use to light a lamp. A small brick dome, open at the top, had been built into the front of the house to serve as an oven. Mandisa smiled when she looked at it. She had not cooked a single dish in over five years. Adom might have to suffer through a few experiments before she produced something edible. But for tonight, this first evening in their new home, she had reserved a loaf of lotus bread, provided by Halima's generous hand.

"Adom?" She looked out the window. He stood outside, waving to one lone playmate who was heading home. "Adom, wash your hands in the bucket by the side of the house. It is time to eat."

"Yes, Mother," he called, reluctantly dragging his feet through the sand.

Mandisa's smile broadened in approval. A boy ought to play so hard that he resisted coming in.

One of the neighbors had lent Mandisa a lamp, a sloping oil-filled bowl filled with twisted rags soaked in tallow. Mandisa lit the rags with a spark from the twirling fire drill, then lifted the bowl to the windowsill. Kneeling on the hard floor of packed earth, she unwrapped the lotus loaf and broke the bread into two generous hunks. Her stomach tightened at the sight and scent of such delicious food, and she mentally thanked Halima and God Shaddai for providing it.

She paused, her hands in her lap, waiting for Adom to open the door. When he did not come, she stood and moved to the window, searching the gathering gloom for a sign of her son. There was nothing.

Lifting the lamp, she moved to the doorway and peered out at the landscape. The children had all gone home for dinner. The aroma of baking bread and boiling stews filled the air. "Adom!" she called, standing on tiptoe as if that would help her voice reach further. "Adom! Come home!"

No one answered. Holding the lamp in an unsteady hand, she stepped out into the night, trying not to tremble as fearful images rose in her mind.

––––––––––

An hour later she sat alone by a bonfire on the riverbank, still clutching the glowing lamp. Her frantic screams had brought a score of people from their homes. After hearing her few words of explanation, the men lifted their lamps and moved away, the night filling with the soft sound of bare feet moving toward the Nile.

"Crocodile," one woman said.

"Drowned," said another.

Closing her eyes, Mandisa shivered with chill and fatigue. *El Shaddai, where are you now?*

The night became a world unto itself. The moments passed in blackness, one after the other, indistinguishable. Someone built a fire of dry rushes on the riverbank in hope that Adom would see the blaze and find his way home. The flames leapt up and threw the darkness back, but still Adom did not appear. Mandisa stalked around the fire in an endless circle until someone forced her to stop.

Now she sat still in the fire-tinted darkness, her back to the flames, her face to the river. Regrets and questions buzzed in her brain. Why had she let Adom go outside? Why hadn't she checked on him five minutes earlier? What devilish spirit had possessed her when she decided to leave the safety of Zaphenath-paneah's house? And where was the vizier's Almighty God when she needed him most?

Behind her someone threw a pile of dung fuel into the fire pit, and she cringed as a volcano of sparks erupted into the night sky. Fire shadows danced on the silvery waters of the treacherous river. She clenched her fist, hardening her frightened heart behind a barrier of anger. *Why, cursed river, why?* she asked, staring at the moving water. *By refusing to flood our valley, you have attempted to kill our people. Since we are still alive, have you settled instead for killing one boy? Why did you choose my innocent son?* Her nails cut into her palm. *After this cruelty, I could almost believe in the vengeful spirits of the river, the crocodile, and the sun. But what would they have against me?*

Something stirred in the darkness at her right hand. Even through the fog of apprehension, she heard the steady tramp of a horse's hooves, a muffled greeting, belligerent voices. But Mandisa did not turn until a dark powerful figure cast a bold shadow into the circle of firelight and called her name with Simeon's voice.

She felt a sudden darkness behind her eyes and a chilly dew on her skin. She had to be dreaming, for Simeon could not be near her any more than Adom could be gone forever.

She lowered her head, confused.

"Mandisa, I've just heard," Simeon said, kneeling beside her. He was real! His flesh-and-blood hand reached for hers and his eyes, when she looked into them, were gentle and filled with compassion. "How long has Adom been gone?"

Mandisa lifted her hand and tried to find the words. "I . . . I looked outside, and he was there. I turned, and a moment later I lit the lamp and called again—"

"At sunset, then." The line of his mouth tightened a fraction more. "Three hours ago. He can't have gone far, Mandisa. We'll find him."

"He's gone to the otherworld," she whispered. She pulled her head to her knees and fought against despair. "Adom is dead."

"No," Simeon answered, his voice breaking with huskiness. "I've been riding for two days to find and warn you. Idogbe, your husband, knows about the boy and wants him. Tarik himself told me that the man appeared in Thebes, at the vizier's villa. Zaphenath-paneah decreed that your marriage was not valid, but Idogbe the Egyptian left swearing that he would find and take his son."

His words didn't register in her confused mind. "Idogbe?"

"He has been following you, Mandisa," Simeon replied, grasping her arms. "At every village where I inquired about you and the boy, those who had seen you repeated that another man sought you, too. Don't you understand? Adom is not dead. Idogbe has certainly taken him."

She pressed her hand to her mouth, absorbing his words and their meaning. Idogbe—*alive?* And wanting her son?

Rage swooped in to replace her desperation. "I will find him," she said, anger and alarm rippling along her spine as she grasped Simeon's hand and pulled herself to her feet. Her breath came raggedly as she struggled to curb her wrath. "How dare he take my son! Adom is mine, Simeon. Idogbe never cared for the boy."

"I know." He released her and stepped back, studying her thoughtfully for a moment. "I am here to help, and I have a horse. I can search faster than you."

"I'm going with you." She began moving toward the animal before Simeon could protest.

"Wait." Catching up, he caught her arm and whirled her around. "I didn't come here only to warn you, Mandisa. I came for another reason as well."

"Whatever it is, it can wait," she answered, wrenching free of him. She hurried toward the horse, knowing he would have no choice but to follow.

‿‿⌐ Forty-three ⌐‿‿

THEY RODE QUIETLY THROUGH THE NIGHT, trying not to make undue noise lest they disturb Idogbe sleeping somewhere along the river. The lush grass at the riverfront made a wet slicking sound against the stallion's legs. The night shadows along the water vibrated with the insect hum of the woods. Mandisa strained to sort through the river sounds for any noise that might belong to a struggling twelve-year-old boy.

Simeon had given her his full-cut cloak to cover herself, for the narrow Egyptian shift she wore was not suitable for riding astride a horse. Without arguing, she donned the cloak, then ripped out the side seams of her tunic. She had never ridden anything but a Canaanite donkey and felt uncomfortable and insecure atop the great moving mountain of horseflesh. But her arms were about Simeon's waist, and he seemed as strong and immovable as the pyramids. Mandisa was unspeakably grateful to have him with her.

Occasionally they stopped during the night to let the horse drink from the moonlit river. "Do you think Idogbe travels on foot or by boat?" Mandisa asked during one stop, noticing with concern the great number of small skiffs moored up and down the shoreline.

"He followed you by boat," Simeon answered. "But now that he has the boy, I think he will travel by foot. It would not be wise to take a twelve-year-old, particularly an unhappy one, in a narrow skiff. Boats are too easily upset, and too many dangers lurk in the water. He would not want to risk overturning."

Mandisa nodded, grateful that at least one of them was

able to think clearly. She was not sure how or why Simeon had come, but she knew with pulse-pounding certainty that El Shaddai had sent him. Clinging to his waist, she felt a strange numbed comfort, almost as if she were clinging to the Almighty God himself.

As the night passed into day, they cut a wide zigzag swath along the riverfront, venturing inland and then returning to the water's edge. Simeon stopped every man with a child and paused to gaze curiously at more than a few women. At first Mandisa didn't understand, then she ruefully shook her head.

"Idogbe would never disguise himself in a woman's cloak and garment," she said. "Never. I am sure he is not disguised at all, Simeon, for he must think I have assumed Adom is dead."

"You're probably right," Simeon admitted, urging the horse forward with a gentle kick in the ribs. "But we must be certain. I would never forgive myself if we let this beast of a man slip by us."

She clung more tightly to him, closing her eyes against the emotion that swelled hot and heavy in her chest.

For three days they slowly made their way downriver, stopping only to eat, feed and water the horse, and steal quick naps in the shade of the trees. Simeon insisted that they travel through the night, for Idogbe was likely to stop at sunset and rest in the darkness. But in village after village, city after city, Simeon and Mandisa found no sign of him or Adom.

While they rode, Mandisa pondered long and hard, trying to guess why Idogbe would take the child. "He wanted a boy. I am certain of that," she explained, her words falling into the rhythm of the horse's brisk steps. "He often spoke of the value of sons as a key to immortality. All Egyptian husbands want a household full of sons."

"But why would he want the boy now?" Simeon asked, tossing the question over his shoulder. "He is a wanderer. He does not seem the type to prepare a home for children.

When you knew him, how did he make his living?"

"Any way he could," she answered. "When I met him, he had just returned from the East with a group of traders. When we lived in Thebes, he would buy grain and lentils from our neighbors and travel upriver to try to sell them at an inflated price." She sighed, remembering. "He was not very successful."

"Did he ever speak of other aspirations? Some occupation he might like to have tried? Something he might want a son to do?"

She frowned, unwilling to open the door to a host of memories she had tried to lock away. "I don't know . . . perhaps. For a time he wanted to work with the masons who make statuary. Once he tried to be a lay priest, but his ideas were too bizarre and antiquated even for the priests of Sebek. He always admired the scribes. He said they held the power of the law in their hands."

"Could he write?"

She shook her head. "No. He had a keen mind for numbers, but he had never been taught the hieroglyphics." Suddenly her mind blew open. "The temple schools!" she said, her hands tightening around his waist. "The perfect answer! He could leave Adom with the priests so he wouldn't have to worry about caring for him. Then, when Adom is of age, a portion of everything he earned as a scribe would go to Idogbe!"

Simeon pulled back on the reins, stopping the stallion. While the horse bent to browse the new grass at the water's edge, Simeon turned in the saddle to look at her. "Which temple school?" he asked, his voice gentle. "Mandisa, there are scores of schools, for Egypt has more temples than—"

"Not for Idogbe," she answered, her eyes watering in the wind. "Idogbe worshiped Sebek. Idogbe would take Adom to the Temple of Sebek at Crocodilopolis."

"And where is this city?"

She closed her eyes tightly, thinking. "It is in the region called Land of the Lakes," she whispered, trying to recall what Idogbe had once told her of his visit there. "A three-day journey north of Thebes."

"Almost to Goshen, then," Simeon said, featherlike laugh lines crinkling around his eyes. "I know the place. I rode through it on my journey from Goshen to Thebes."

She thought he would look away, but he kept his eyes on her. "Well?" she asked, feeling her flesh color. "Are we going or not?"

"Yes, my lady," he said, finally turning. Tightening the reins, he urged the stallion forward. As she slipped her arms about his waist, Mandisa wondered just what she wanted of him.

Since nearly all of Egypt's citizens had moved toward the life-giving river in the time of drought, Simeon planned to follow the winding course as far as Herakleopolis. If he hadn't found Idogbe by then, he assured Mandisa, they would follow the tributary that broke off to the west and fed the area known as *Ta-she*, or Land of the Lakes. If they hadn't found Adom by the time they reached Crocodilo-polis, they would go straightway to the Temple of Sebek and inquire after him. If the boy happened to be there, Mandisa could take her case to the vizier, who would certainly command the priests to release her son.

"I don't care what happens to Idogbe," Mandisa said, agreeing with Simeon's plan. "He never loved me or his son, or he would have made me his wife. And he has been gone from my life for such a long time that it does not matter if he is absent once again. I am content to leave his fate to the vizier. But I cannot rest until I find Adom."

Fed by a tributary of the Nile, the Land of the Lakes was the most bountiful region of all Egypt. Past pharaohs had begun a series of hydraulic systems to evenly distribute the flow of water throughout the land. Though drought had reduced all but the narrowest sliver of land along the Nile to barren desert, here Simeon and Mandisa saw papyrus plants, palms, and olives growing in great abundance. A series of dikes, retaining walls, sluices, and canals regulated the flow of the tributary and the lakes into which the water ran.

A few hours south of Crocodilopolis, Simeon stopped just after sunset. "I will leave you for a little while," he said, offering her his hands as she dismounted. "There's a small settlement over there that might have oats for the horse. I'd hate to return the vizier an unfit and undernourished beast."

Mandisa slipped gratefully from the stallion and walked to the river's edge. As Simeon hobbled the horse and led him to water, she wrapped herself securely in his cloak and knelt to splash her dusty face. As the tepid water washed away her weariness, she dried her skin with the edge of the cloak and smiled. The garment smelled like Simeon—robust, earthy, full of life and temper.

The beauty of the crushed diamond water soothed her anxious spirit. The moon shone full almost directly in front of her, backlighting a few far-flung clouds floating on the eastern horizon. A dozen campfires dotted the darkness of the riverbank. Mandisa knew most of them belonged to families in search of food and trade, trying to survive in the time of famine.

Someone moved farther down the riverbank, and Mandisa's eyes focused there. A young woman held her young daughter by the hand, attempting to bathe the child. Mandisa heard the little naked girl gasp at the first shock of coolness upon her legs. The mother laughed, a tender lilting sound, and the child squealed in glee, trying to scramble into her mother's arms.

Mandisa closed her eyes and turned away from the sight. As long as her arms were empty, she would never be able to look at another mother and child without weeping.

From somewhere in the distance another child cried, a man screamed, someone else yelled. Mandisa pulled the hood of Simeon's cloak over her head, distressed by the sounds.

"Mandisa! Stop him!"

The cry came from nowhere, borne on a gust of river wind. The voice was Simeon's, but who was she supposed to stop? The horse? A thief?

"Mother!"

She froze, a spasm of panic trilling across her body. "Adom!" Frantically she scrambled toward the sound up a mounded dike, and then she saw him. Adom was fifty paces away, running in her direction on the opposite bank of a wide irrigation ditch. Behind the boy came a pursuer, a huge hulking brute who raced in a crouch, his arms pumping.

Her breath caught in her throat as she recognized him. Idogbe.

"Adom!" Mandisa cried, waving her hands above her head. "This way! I'm here!"

A mud levee bordered the canal, and Mandisa plunged over it, struggling as the wet mud sucked at her sandals, her feet, her legs. The silt was thick and heavy, and each step felt like someone beneath the earth attempted to wrench her ankles from their sockets. She felt the thin straps of her sandals give way, then the mud pulled her down, covering her shins, her knees.

Adom stood now at the water's edge, his eyes wide with fear. "Mother!" he screamed again, pausing as he eyed the moving water.

Where is Simeon?

"Adom!" she cried, fighting for the energy to keep moving toward him. She pulled one leg free and staggered forward, then stopped to wrest her other foot free of the greedy muck. "Wait!"

Behind Adom, Idogbe raced forward, as sure-footed as a goat and as strong as the wind. Adom glanced back at the shrinking distance between them, then plunged into the canal.

"No, Adom!" Mandisa cried. There was no way to judge the depth of the water. Though he had often splashed in the garden pool of the vizier's house, she did not think he could swim. She thrust her arms toward him, knowing he remained out of reach, and slipped, falling upon her hands. The mire pulled her downward, muck squirted between her fingers, ooze slapped the side of her face.

"Mother!" The scream was louder now, shriller. With an effort, Mandisa lifted her head. Adom stood in waist-deep water, his eyes wide in a paroxysm of fear, his gaze fastened to something that moved in the canal. A rise of panic threatened to choke her as Mandisa followed his gaze.

Slowly, steadily, a crocodile was thrusting his way up from the river, his powerful tail sweeping in wide arcs as he moved toward the shrieking boy. Her throat worked, she struggled to scream Simeon's name, but no sound would come forth.

Simeon pressed his hands to his forehead, struggling to clear his brain. He had seen Adom and called to Mandisa, then an unexpected blow had come from behind, knocking him senseless. He could feel a sticky wetness on his forehead and warmth on his face, but the fiend who had struck him disappeared. Had he gone after the boy?

Simeon pushed himself up from the ground, consciously commanding his legs to bear his weight. Colors exploded in his brain as he stood, and his chest tightened as a sense of inadequacy swept over him. What if he couldn't reach Adom in time? If Mandisa put herself between the boy and this madman . . .

He bit his lip to stifle the pain and staggered toward the canal he had crossed earlier. Through a burst of blinding white agony, he saw a powerful, well-muscled man in the distance. Then the man disappeared, and Simeon blinked, afraid his eyes had betrayed him.

No. His ears rang with Mandisa's screams. The man had

gone down into the ditch, probably still chasing the boy.

Simeon pushed himself, urging his body forward through pain and blood and darkness. His sandals kicked up dirt as he ran blindly toward the sound of Mandisa's cries, then he stood at the edge of the irrigation canal and took in the scene in one glance.

Mandisa scrambled helplessly on the opposite shore, impeded by the thick mud, her hands outstretched for her son. Idogbe stood on the downward slope of the dike, a bloody battle-ax in his hand, a look of awe and reverence upon his face. And in the water, Adom floundered in terror as the golden eyes of a crocodile advanced from the river.

"Leave the boy where he is!" Idogbe called, his voice like an echo from an empty tomb. "See there! My lord Sebek comes to take his sacrifice. He has rewarded my faithfulness! He will increase my strength a hundred times and grant me authority in the life to come!"

"Adom!" Mandisa threw her head back and screamed a guttural cry of terror.

"Mother!" The boy's shriek chilled Simeon to the marrow.

"Behold the god of my strength, the Destroyer!" Idogbe chanted, hopping like some deranged monster on the muddy bank. "Behold Sebek, great of slaughter, great of fear! He washes in your blood. He bathes in the gore of sacrifice!"

Simeon's blood slid through his veins like cold needles as he considered the barbaric scene before him. The crocodile was advancing steadily. If Simeon attacked the madman, the boy would not have a chance. But if Simeon strode first into the water, the demented Idogbe would find Simeon's head and shoulders an easy target for his battle-ax.

El Shaddai, give me strength.

Simeon stepped down, carefully negotiating the slick mud of the dike, his heart intent upon its purpose. With every step, his jaw became firmer, his muscles tighter, his heart more eager. If he had been born only for this moment, his soul would still praise the Almighty God. For Simeon the Destroyer was ready to surrender his life. Better that innocent Adom should live than one who had killed so many.

His feet found firm footing on level ground near the water, and Simeon plunged past Idogbe into the stream, scooping Adom up with one arm. His ears rang with Idogbe's frustrated scream, and he knew the madman had charged with battle-ax swinging. A blow nearly knocked Simeon from his feet, but he managed to remain standing long enough to thrust the boy to the safety of the opposite shore. Then he turned in the water to face the mad Egyptian.

The bald ex-priest seemed to swell, sizing Simeon up as if in some primal territorial dispute.

"What interest have you in this, Canaanite?" he called, crouching in the water, the ax moving horizontally back in forth in front of him. He circled slowly, keeping his eyes fixed upon Simeon's. "Why have you interfered with my son's appointment with my god? Sebek chose this time and place. He-Who-Destroys was ready to accept my sacrifice."

"A man should sacrifice only what belongs to *him*, not what belongs to another," Simeon answered, circling step for step with his adversary. "And your son will choose his own god. Let him live his life, Idogbe."

The Egyptian threw back his head and laughed. "You know my name! That is good, for a man should know the name of the one who is about to kill him."

"Then you should know that I am Simeon, Son of Israel," Simeon answered, moving carefully through the waist-deep water. He stole a quick look at the glassy surface around him. The crocodile had disappeared.

The ax whistled through the air. Simeon thrust up a hand to block it and succeeded, though the wooden handle cracked against his arm with such force that the bone went numb.

Idogbe screamed in frustration as the ax slipped from his grasp and dropped beneath the muddy water.

Simeon stepped toward the spot where it had disappeared, blocking Idogbe from the weapon.

Suddenly the Egyptian was upon him, his fists striking invisibly, like the mouths of snakes. In a dance of death the two men whirled, splashing in the water, smashing onto the bank of the levee. Simeon spread his feet wide for balance and struck out with his good hand as often as he could, but then a sharp blade cut through the leather of his sandal and into his foot, startling him.

The ax.

Blood and a crocodile in the water.

And then Idogbe's hands were about Simeon's throat. As the night filled with a ripping mayhem of screams that made the very stars above seem to vibrate, Simeon felt himself being pushed downward toward the water. He struggled to breathe, to resist, to fight, but then his eyes saw nothing but murky grayness as the waters swept over his head and filled his nose, ears, mouth . . .

Almighty God, forgive me. Though I showed no mercy and deserve none, if you would look upon me now . . .

The anger that had been welling in Simeon's soul vanished like a swift invisible shadow. Hot emotions never resulted in cool judgment, and Simeon needed wisdom now, for the man who faced him was his superior in height, weight, and strength.

With every ounce of energy he possessed, Simeon kicked upward. His foot found a vulnerable spot. Idogbe groaned and weakened his grasp long enough for Simeon to launch himself toward the sky and fill his lungs in a burst of air.

The muscled Egyptian came at him again, as relentless as guilt.

So be it.

Simeon stopped resisting and went limp in surrender, pulling Idogbe under, too.

All earthly noises but the pounding of Simeon's heart disappeared in the dark, bubbling sounds of the river world. He shifted in the water, bringing the Egyptian to his side, and with a powerful effort Simeon turned, pinning his enemy beneath him.

Keeping his hands on the man's throat, Simeon thrust himself up, gulping for air, then held Idogbe under just until the man's frantic scrambling stilled.

Praise be your name, God Shaddai! For Simeon the Destroyer is no more. I could not have accomplished this but by your hand.

When he was certain the fight had gone out of the aggressor, he pulled the Egyptian to the opposite bank, checked to be sure the man still breathed, then stumbled back through the water to Mandisa.

"Simeon!" Her hands reached out to him, and he collapsed on the bank beside Adom, shivering as the fire of battle left his veins. A strange measure of peace filled his heart when Mandisa's cool hand fell upon his cheek. "Are you all right?" she asked, her lovely face hovering over him like a concerned angel's. "You're bleeding, Simeon."

"It matters not," he said, attempting to smile at her. But he scarcely had the energy, and he settled for reaching out to grasp Adom's hand.

"What shall we do about him?" Adom asked, his teeth chattering as he knelt in the mud. With a trembling hand he pointed toward Idogbe, who still lay unconscious on the far shore.

"We will leave him to his god," Mandisa answered, patting her son to be certain he was unharmed. Watching her gentle ministration, Simeon thought he had never seen a more beautiful woman.

"I thought I'd never see you again," Adom said, turning in the mud to face Simeon. "I didn't like that man, but he said he was my father."

"A father is someone who loves you," Mandisa whispered, slipping out of Simeon's cloak. She draped it across her son's shoulders and Simeon's chest, warming them together.

"Then Simeon can be my father!" Adom whispered, resting his head on Simeon's wet skin.

Simeon lifted his hand to Adom's head. "If your mother approves," he said, his voice tentative as his eyes searched her face.

She didn't answer, but her eyes blazed with an inner fire brighter than the light from the torches that had begun to appear on the banks around them. He felt a lazy, inscrutable smile sweep over his own face, and a delicious shudder heated his body when she pressed her hand to his forehead. "You are hurt," she whispered, loving concern in her voice as she examined the wound. "We should find a physician for that cut on your head. It is deep. I don't know how you were able to stand and fight."

"It is nothing," he said, his heart pounding in an erratic rhythm. He couldn't tear his gaze from her lovely, mud-stained profile.

She lowered her eyes to his, and he saw a depth in her smile that had been missing far too long. "Simeon, son of Jacob," she murmured, her delicate hand holding his face with a tender touch, "I owe you everything."

"It is nothing," he repeated again, his common sense skittering into the shadows of the night.

"It is everything. *You* are everything," she answered, her breath softly fanning his face as she drew nearer. "The first day I saw you, I knew that you were capable of mighty deeds, that you possessed courage, loyalty, and strength of heart. Simeon, son of Jacob, once called 'I-am-not-loved,' " she whispered, winding her hand into his wet hair, "I knew your true heart. You had only to discover it for yourself."

He felt her lips touch his like a whisper, and then in her black eyes he suddenly found all he'd been searching for.

Idogbe staggered away from the muddy bank, shoving away the concerned hands that reached out to give him aid. One glance at the far side of the canal assured him that he had failed, for a knot of people surrounded the man, woman, and child who had destroyed his plans for greatness and immortality.

He left the canal and moved toward the river itself, determined to confront the god who had failed him. "Come out, Sebek!" he cried, lifting his hands as he neared the rushes at the edge of the river. "Come out and face your chosen one! You could have taken them both—the boy and the man—and yet you left me to face humiliation!"

There was no answer from the river, nothing moved in the silvery water beyond. A pair of men who had bedded down on the rise of the bank stood as Idogbe approached, then retreated as if frightened by his bold intensity.

Let them be frightened. No one should interfere with a man who plans to challenge his god.

"Are you there, Sebek?" Idogbe cried, stepping into the water. He shouldered his way through the tall reeds and felt the sharp-edged stems bite into the flesh of his shoulders. "I am here for you! Take my miserable life, since you have no other use for it!"

The water inched up his legs, covering his shins, his thighs, his waist. Still he continued to roar and shout, thrashing as the water crept closer to his chin. Suddenly the muddy river bottom beneath his feet fell away, and the waters closed over his head. Idogbe tried to scramble back to the firm footing he had known a moment earlier, but in all his travels, he had neglected to learn how to swim. He bobbed up and down, once, twice, but could not move toward either shore.

His last thought was that somewhere Sebek was watching and waiting.

⟶ Forty-four ⟵

SIMEON SLEPT FOR HOURS, PERHAPS DAYS. A fever burned through his body. Soft whispers and gentle caresses surrounded him as someone poured cooling water over his head, neck, and shoulders. He was aware that he was being moved, then he lay still for a long time, lost in the twilight world between wakefulness and sleep, between life and death.

He awoke in his prison chamber within Zaphenath-paneah's house. A tray sat by the door, the food untouched. The same chair filled the corner. He lay on the same uncomfortable too-short bed. He even wore a linen kilt like the one Tarik had given him.

He stretched, feeling stiffness in his arms, and his head pounded when he tried to sit up. His mind spun with fuzzy bewilderment. Had he managed to escape his confinement only through starkly realistic dreams? No, everything had changed. Though his surroundings belonged to his old life, he saw them through new eyes.

"I've been sick," he muttered, annoyed with his weakness. "A fever has played tricks upon my mind."

The usual sounds of activity flitted in from the windows. He heard the laughter of little boys, the quiet whisper of slaves about their duties. From far away he heard the excited whinny of a horse and the lowing of cattle. And then, with startling clarity, Mandisa's familiar knock sounded upon the door.

"Come in," he grumbled, sourness filling the pit of his stomach.

The latch clicked and she entered, her glowing face

wreathed in a smile. "I thought you would be better today," she said, hurrying to his side. "Your fever broke last night."

"I feel like I've slept a year," he answered, slowly lowering his legs to the floor. "I'm as weak as a kitten. Look at that!" He lifted his arm, which trembled visibly as he struggled to hold it straight. He lowered it, braced himself against the bed frame, and was about to stand when he caught sight of her face.

There was something pleased, proud, and vaguely possessive in the way she looked at him. Simeon paused, trying to force his confused memories into order.

"Mandisa," he began, closing his eyes to think more clearly, "I have been sick, and my thoughts are not as definite as I would like them to be."

"Perhaps I can help." Laughter echoed in her voice.

"I have dreamed—no, it was real. Tell me. Zaphenath-paneah is my brother, is he not?" When he opened his eyes, he found her studying him with a gaze as soft as a caress.

"Whatever gave you that idea?" she whispered, her tone light and mocking. But her right hand fell upon his shoulder, and he wondered if she could feel the quickening pulse of his blood.

"And Idogbe took Adom, yet you and I found the boy."

"Adom is safe here in Zaphenath-paneah's house, where he belongs," she answered, her hand moving from Simeon's shoulder to his jawline.

"And I fought with Idogbe, and afterward you said—"

"I told you that I loved you, but you weren't awake to hear it," she whispered, her fingers teasing his hair. "You fainted, for you were bleeding badly. Some men on the riverbank tended to your wounds, but then you took a fever. When Zaphenath-paneah heard of it, he sent a litter and brought you here."

Sighing in relief, Simeon caught her hands. "So we are back where we began."

"Yes." A dancing light twinkled in the depths of her black eyes.

"No." He breathed the word and pulled her into his arms. "We are miles away from that day. Simeon the Destroyer is no more. He is gone for good. Simeon the father, the husband, is now your captive."

"And what shall I do with this prisoner?" she asked, looking down, fully, into his eyes. A thread of uncertainty ran through her voice. "Shall I release him so he can join his people in Goshen?"

"Never release him," he answered, his heart aching within his chest. He stood and pressed her to him, bolstering his weakness with her strength. "You were right to refuse him before, but now he has broken his bonds. He is finally free to love you as you deserve to be loved. Let him remain by your side always. Let his people be your people."

"As his God has become my God," she answered, her hand sweeping to the back of his neck. "For none of the gods of Egypt could have broken through the stony stronghold of your heart." She tilted her head back to look into his eyes. "You did not tell me, Simeon, what happened in Canaan to change you."

Simeon looked away, trying to gather his thoughts. He had been broken, bruised, exposed, humbled, uplifted, forgiven, scorned, and loved, all at the behest of the Almighty, and all within a very short time. Only one force on earth could both destroy and comfort, simultaneously give light and pain.

"I saw God as a fire," he said simply, looking her straight in the eye. "A holy fire that cannot be contained or tamed. And yet in Him we can find safety, love, and life."

"How unlike the gods of Egypt," Mandisa whispered, slipping under his arm. "Though the people threaten and intimidate them, they remain silent. People believe their false gods provide what they want, but idols cannot deliver what people need."

"I need you, Mandisa, as I have needed you since the day I first came here," Simeon answered, a new and delightful shiver running through him. "I will always thank God Shaddai for a mercy severe and loving enough to send you into my prison chamber."

"Even with my acid tongue?" she asked, nestling against him. "You were not fond of it in the early days."

"I did not know what was good for me," he answered, locking his arms behind her back. "It took an acid tongue to cut through the hardness of my anger."

Smiling, she lifted her face, and when Simeon bent to kiss her, he felt the reassuring slow and steady beat of his heart . . . no longer a stone, but a new and living creation.

As Joseph watched in approval, Simeon took Mandisa for his wife and Adom for his son. Tizara wept freely at the wedding, knowing that Simeon would soon take her to meet her mother and a host of relatives to which she had never dreamed of belonging. "There is such a wonderful feeling of happiness inside me," she said, looking at Joseph with bright tears in her eyes. "Only your Almighty God, my lord, could show such mercy and love to one like me."

After many warm farewells and heartfelt embraces, the quartet prepared to move northward to the well-watered plains of Goshen. Zaphenath-paneah's entire household—slaves, servants, guards, and stockmen—gathered at the gate of the villa to watch them go. Tarik and Halima, their hands gently intertwined, watched from the shadow of one of the portico's pillars, away from prying eyes.

As Joseph stood on his balcony, his hand shading his eyes from the sun, he looked down upon his household and felt his heart stir with compassion. His people were so dear to him! He led them as wisely as he could, and yet many of them continued to persist in blindness. Though God Shaddai had demonstrated His foreknowledge and power to save, Ani still worshiped the knowledge of Thoth. Though God had bountifully provided for them in times of direst want, Halima still ran to the kitchen and knelt before the food bins, desperately trying to eat her way out of anxiety. And though God Shaddai had demonstrated the most tender, protective love imaginable, Asenath had refused His guardianship, choosing instead to follow a destructive adulterous path.

But Asenath had returned to God Shaddai at the end. Simeon had shattered his heart's temple of hate and anger, and Mandisa had learned that El Shaddai was more than just another god. Those three had left the ranks of deceived thousands who preferred the illusion of a safe and manageable deity, a god fashioned into a congenial, serviceable likeness.

"The others do not know, nor do they yet understand," Joseph murmured to himself, his heart aching as he watched the scene in the courtyard below. "They feed on ashes, their deceived hearts have turned them aside. And they cannot deliver themselves, nor realize that the gods they hold in their hands are a lie."

Oh, what he would give if only they would seek the truth! He had seen too much in his life, witnessed too much pain. God had called him to lead, but there were days when he would willingly cast the mantle of leadership aside to relive even a single hour of service in Potiphar's house. In those days his only concerns had been of pleasing his easygoing master and capturing a sweet smile from Tuya, the love of his youth.

Memories closed around him and filled him with a longing to turn back, but a gentle Voice, hauntingly familiar, nudged him out of his musings. *Why are you in despair? And why have you become disturbed? Hope in God, for you shall yet praise me.*

A sense of strength came to him, and Joseph lifted his head. The four travelers passed through the gates, the assembled company began to break up, and the men and women went back to their duties. Joseph turned and stepped back into the coolness of his chamber, grateful for a moment of reflection. The villa felt strangely quiet without Simeon, Mandisa, Adom, Tizara, and Asenath. He knew that in the days ahead he would find himself often distracted by the harsh realities of loneliness.

But Pharaoh was a young man, just beginning to show real potential. The king's first wife, Queen Tiy, was a commoner and in dire need of a proper education. And there remained Egypt, the bold, brazen Black Land to which God had called Joseph years ago.

Hope in God, for you shall yet praise me.

He would not allow himself to be distracted. His work was not finished.

Epilogue

Jacob was one hundred thirty years old when the children of Israel came into Egypt. There they prospered during the remaining five years of famine and continued to live in Goshen under Pharaoh's benevolence.

After seventeen years in Egypt, at the age of one hundred forty-seven, Jacob called his sons together. From Joseph he extracted a promise that he would not be buried in Egypt, but that his sons would carry his remains back to the Cave of Machpelah, the burial site of Abraham and Sarah, Isaac and Rebekah . . . and Leah.

Jacob called for his sons and blessed them, including the two sons of Joseph—Ephraim and Manasseh. And because he understood that God had willed that Joseph be sold into slavery, he did not fault the sons of Leah for that betrayal. But in his final blessing he did not forget other sins of his sons' younger days:

Reuben lost the inheritance of the firstborn because he once slept with his father's concubine.

Simeon and Levi were passed over because they had killed men and cruelly maimed bulls.

A special blessing went to Judah, and from his descendants arose King David, and from David, a savior, Jesus the Christ.

The firstborn's double inheritance went to Joseph's sons, Ephraim and Manasseh.

Mandisa stood silently with the other women as Jacob

pronounced his final blessing. For an instant, as Jacob harshly decried the past sins of Simeon and Levi, the old unloved look shadowed her husband's countenance.

But then Jacob motioned toward his sons and passed his hands of blessing over each of their heads, bestowing favor and forgiveness in one gesture. As Simeon stood to his feet, his eye caught Mandisa's, and his face lifted in a weary smile. The anger had disappeared from his eyes. Forgiveness from a holy fountain had washed it away.

After Jacob's death, Joseph instructed the physicians of Egypt to embalm his father, and the people of the Black Land mourned seventy days for Israel. When the days of mourning were past, Joseph, his brothers and their children, along with the servants of Pharaoh, prepared to undertake Jacob's final journey.